T0131775

Witty and well-read, best friends Henrietta, Harriet, and Hero know that real love is rarely as simple as a fairy tale. But with the right partner, it can be sweeter—and even more satisfying. . .

A single woman of means generally does not choose the company of seven rambunctious children over the haut ton. Yet since the tragic loss of her sister and brother-in-law, the Honorable Harriet Mayfield has found purpose and pleasure in caring for her orphaned nieces and nephews. If her unorthodox views about how to raise the newly minted Earl of Sedwick and his siblings put her at odds with their strict grandmother, well, so be it. The children's uncle, Colonel Lord Quinton Burnes, however, is a far more complicated—and charismatic—problem . . .

Accustomed to having his slightest word obeyed, Quint hardly knows what to make of the bewitching bluestocking who has taken on the role of guardian in his absence. Quint's mother wants Harriet gone, the sooner the better. She has the perfect bride in mind for him—someone not at all like kindhearted, loyal Harriet. But if he and Harriet can only withstand meddling and misunderstandings, their unconventional attraction might yet come to a delightfully happy ending . . .

Visit us at www.kensingtonbooks.com

Books by Wilma Counts

AN EARL LIKE NO OTHER
THE MEMORY OF YOUR KISS
MY FAIR LORD
IT ONLY TAKES A KISS
RULES FOR AN UNMARRIED LADY

Published by Kensington Publishing Corporation

Rules for an Unmarried Lady

Wilma Counts

LYRICAL PRESS
Kensington Publishing Corp.
www.kensingtonbooks.com

To the extent that the image or images on the cover of this book depict a person or persons, such person or persons are merely models, and are not intended to portray any character or characters featured in the book.

This book is a work of fiction. Names, characters, places, and incidents either are products of the author's imagination or are used fictitiously. Any resemblance to actual events or locales or persons living or dead is entirely coincidental.

LYRICAL PRESS BOOKS are published by
Kensington Publishing Corp.
119 West 40th Street
New York, NY 10018

Copyright © 2020 by J. Wilma Counts

All rights reserved. No part of this book may be reproduced in any form or by any means without the prior written consent of the Publisher, excepting brief quotes used in reviews.

All Kensington titles, imprints, and distributed lines are available at special quantity discounts for bulk purchases for sales promotion, premiums, fund-raising, educational, or institutional use.

Special book excerpts or customized printings can also be created to fit specific needs. For details, write or phone the office of the Kensington Sales Manager: Kensington Publishing Corp., 119 West 40th Street, New York, NY 10018. Attn. Sales Department. Phone: 1-800-221-2647.

Lyrical Press and Lyrical Press logo Reg. U.S. Pat. & TM Off.

First Electronic Edition: December 2020
ISBN-13: 978-1-60183-911-4 (ebook)
ISBN-10: 1-60183-911-1 (ebook)

First Print Edition: December 2020
ISBN-13: 978-1-60183-912-1
ISBN-10: 1-60183-912-X

Printed in the United States of America

For
Dorothy Frances Behm
OK—db. This one is for you alone.
A sort of thank you, if you will, for
seeing me through not one, but two knee
surgeries—for being nurse, chauffeur, cook,
general secretary, the best of hostesses—and
most of all, for just being there as a friend!

Prologue

Late April, 1814
Toulouse, France

Colonel Lord Quinton Frederick Burnes—Quint to his friends and to his family, except for his mother who used the more formal version of his name—rolled back from his half-raised position, resting on the elbow of his good arm. The other arm, still in a splint but out of the sling for the moment, rested across his middle. He had stubbornly held that position longer than he should have, and he could not stifle the groan that slipped out as he moved.

"All right, sir?" His aide, Lieutenant Chester Gibbons, sat on a chair beside the bed, balancing the colonel's travel desk on his knees. Gibbons and the colonel were of an age—early thirties—and they had been together long enough to know each other's quirks, likes and dislikes, when to talk and when not to. At nearly six feet, the two were similar in height too, but there the physical resemblance ended. Gibbons, with red hair and a profusion of freckles, was a slim, gangly man who looked deceptively awkward. His colonel was a sturdy athletic sort with dark hazel eyes and light brown hair with lighter streaks in it from years under a relentless sun, first in India, then in Spain.

"I'll live, Chet. I'll live." *Unlike those poor bastards we lost in battle two weeks ago,* he thought bitterly. The Battle of Toulouse had occurred roughly a week *after* the abdication of the once insanely ambitious Napoleon

Bonaparte—"Boney," "the Corsican Monster," the self-proclaimed Emperor of France, or "that upstart corporal with delusions of grandeur," depending on one's point of view.

Quint's point of view at the moment was decidedly sour. He lay staring blankly at cracking plaster on the ceiling of a house in southern France. The house, one of the finest in the town, belonged to the mayor who—as a Royalist rather than a follower of the deposed emperor—had willingly, if not enthusiastically, allowed the British Army to commandeer it for wounded officers. Ordinary soldiers, Quint knew, were treated in the local cathedral. This information had come to him rather belatedly, for Quint had been barely aware of his surroundings for several days.

He had survived nearly six years on the Iberian Peninsula—not to mention three in India prior to that—following in the wake of the intrepid Wellesley, now Duke of Wellington, and he had done so having suffered little more than what Quint dismissed as "scratches." Now, here he was at the end of that long, long campaign confined to a damned bed for who knew how long! He considered the broken arm, despite its being his right arm, in line with those previous "scratches." After all, he still had the left one, did he not?

"You are one lucky devil," the doctor, who had visited again only this morning, had told him. "That bullet in your belly ripped up a bloody mess, but at least vital organs escaped. Your pain is coming from the fact that I had to dig what was left of that bullet out of the home it had found near your spine. You could have ended up totally paralyzed—but you won't."

"Well, there is that, I suppose," Quint muttered. "But, how long, Doc? I need to be in England even as we speak."

"I would guess that you will be the ultimate judge of the time element," the medical man said. "When the pain allows you to walk about and stand for more than a few minutes at a time. I know you don't want to hear this, but I'm afraid you are looking at a matter of some weeks at least."

This announcement had elicited another groan—this time of protest and frustration more than pain. That is, not physical pain, but deep, devastating pain nonetheless.

Colonel Lord Quinton Burnes was the younger son of the Fifth Earl of Sedwick—at one time the "spare" as it were. Only days prior to his managing to get himself sorely wounded in that needless battle, he had received a letter—long delayed in transit—in which his mother reported the sad news of the death of his brother, Winston, the Sixth Earl of Sedwick. Quint's brother and his countess had both died in a carriage accident during an ice storm in the latter weeks of the worst winter England had suffered in decades, a winter so severe that in February, the Thames itself had frozen over and all London turned out for a Frost Fair on the river. Frivolity aside, the weather claimed many victims, among them the Earl of Sedwick and his charming countess.

Quint clenched his jaw and wiped his good hand across his brow.

All his life, Quint had loved his brother dearly. The two were not only very close in age—separated by only a year—but they were also close friends. They had shared a tutor and had gone off to Eton together and then to university, where they had shared quarters and a good many escapades in which it had usually been Quint who managed to save them from the worst consequences of youthful exuberance. No one—least of all Quint—was surprised that the Sixth Earl of Sedwick had named his brother Quinton to be executor of his will, and guardian of all the earldom until such time as the Seventh Earl—now all of twelve years old—should reach his majority. Moreover, there were six siblings—also part of the Sedwick earldom for which Quint was now responsible.

As all this flashed through his mind, Quint did not allow himself to groan again, but he wanted to. "Read it all back to me, Chet," he ordered, laying his head against the pillow and closing his eyes.

"My Dear Mother—" the aide began,

Thank you for keeping me apprised of matters at Sedwick Hall. Your decision to move from the dower house into the Hall in order to supervise matters regarding the children seems perfectly proper to me. I find it gratifying that I may rely upon you not only to keep me informed of day-to-day matters, but also that you will see to it that my wishes are carried out in every detail.

I am at last coming to terms with our loss. Win and I always thought that it was I, not he, who was more in harm's way. Over some matters, of course, mere mortals have no control.

I am grateful that General Browning saw fit to inform you personally of my being wounded, but you must not be overly concerned. My injuries are not life-threatening, [here the aide paused and raised an eyebrow before continuing] *though I am as yet unable to walk more than a few steps. As you must know, the inactivity is driving me crazy, but I am assured that in another two or three weeks, I shall be able to travel to the coast and take a ship home to England. Overland travel at present is simply too dangerous through occupied France. (I must wait to see Paris again!)*

Your admonitions regarding my responsibilities to the new earl and, indeed, to the entirety of Sedwick, are quite unnecessary. Winston and I discussed matters thoroughly during my last leave. I am fully aware of my duties. I shall be back in England and able to assume full control of the properties—and the children (all seven of them)—by mid-June at latest.

I doubt not that Miss Mayfield is quite fond of the nieces and nephews she and I share, but a mere godmother is hardly in a position to make substantive decisions regarding disposition of the children. First off, they must all be properly educated for the roles they will eventually assume in English society. As the heir, Phillip, especially, should have gone off to Eton at least a year ago and the twins are now of an age to accompany him. The girls, too, need more formal training, I think, than they have heretofore had.

Meanwhile, Miss Mayfield's suggestion of taking the children to London seems most unwise to me, but for the nonce, I leave these matters in your capable hands, Mother, until I return—very shortly, I hope.

"Good. Sign it for me, Chet, and see it sent out in the next dispatch."

"Yes, sir."

Chapter 1

Sedwick Hall
Derbyshire

One morning in mid-May, the Honorable Harriet Mayfield was engaged in one of her favorite activities: entertaining and being entertained by her late sister Anne's seven orphaned children. Since the tragic loss of their parents nearly three months earlier, Harriet had consciously put her own life aside in order to fill some of the void in the children's lives. She often felt herself woefully inadequate to the task. Having lost her own parents fully two decades earlier, she remembered well how an orphaned child felt: lost, anchorless. Just as she had had Anne to cling to, Anne's children had one another—and Harriet vowed to fight tooth and nail any attempt to tear them asunder.

The sixth Earl of Sedwick and his countess had not fit the "norm" of *ton* parents: they had actually *enjoyed* their children. Rather than consign the little people to the nursery and the impersonal care of servants, Sedwick and his wife planned family outings and made time for their children as individuals. Harriet had been forcibly reminded of this fact only the day before.

Passing by the music room, she heard desultory plunks of random piano notes. She opened the door to find twelve-year-old Phillip perched on the piano bench staring into space.

"Phillip, dear," she said, noting his attire, "I thought you were out riding."

"Changed my mind," he muttered, not looking at her and hitting a loud note.

"Why? You have always enjoyed riding, have you not?" She gathered her skirt in hand and slid onto the bench beside him.

He moved over slightly and looked up at her, hazel eyes full of anguish. "Used to. It's not the same without Papa."

She put a comforting arm around his narrow shoulders. "I know, darling. Nothing is the same. But we must carry on, regardless."

He shrugged her arm off. "I do not want to 'carry on.'! I do not want to b-be S-Sedwick. Everyone calls me 'Sedwick.' That is Papa—not me! I am Ph-Phillip, Viscount Trailson. I hate being Sedwick!" His outburst ended on a sob.

Hesitating to touch him again, she sat quietly sharing his space, sharing his pain. Then she said softly, "I miss them too. Terribly. But, Phillip, you *are* the Earl of Sedwick now—and I think your papa would be very, very proud to know that you will take his place."

He gazed up at her. "D-do y-you really th-think so, Aunt Harriet?"

"Yes, darling, I truly do. And it would break his heart to see you give up things you love. Things he loved and that you enjoyed with him."

He drew in a deep, shuddering breath.

After a moment, she patted his shoulder. "How about you allow me a few minutes to change into a riding habit and I shall meet you at the stable? You and I will go riding. All right?"

"All right," he agreed reluctantly.

He managed to rally to the point that before their ride was finished, he was regaling her with anecdotes of rides he and his father had enjoyed together.

Nor had that been the only instance of the children's grief manifesting itself. The nursery servants had reported irritability and sleeplessness. Harriet herself had noted a certain clinginess—as though the children feared letting the adults in their lives out of their sight. Lately, though, she welcomed signs of improvement, of matters settling into a new normal.

She absolutely adored these younger members of her family—nor did she resent for a moment helping them cope with the cataclysmic changes in their lives. She remembered adjusting to such loss. She said a prayer of thanksgiving that at least Anne's children had not lost their childhood home as well. For a moment an image flashed into her mind: two young girls, aged twelve and seven, uprooted from a comfortable home in the country and summarily shipped off to live in the largest city in the nation with grandparents they scarcely knew. The new Baron Ralston had been eager to take over the title and such entailed properties as accompanied it. He was quite content that guardianship of his predecessor's daughters lay with their maternal grandparents.

Only as an adult had Harriet learned to appreciate the fact that, aside from the entailed properties, her father had been independently wealthy—and that his legacy, along with her mother's marriage settlements, had made the orphaned Anne and Harriet acknowledged heiresses. That bit of information might well have been a factor in the Sixth Earl of Sedwick's initial pursuit of the lovely Anne when she made her debut, but it quickly became apparent that his lordship was "absolutely besotted," as the saying went.

Anne had been a social success during her coming out—a "diamond of the first water"—but a few years later, when Harriet made her own debut along with her friends Henrietta and Hero, Harriet had found herself decidedly on the sidelines: None of the "Hs" had "taken" that year—not that they had been overly concerned about that turn of affairs. In general, the three of them found the antics of the *ton* a source of amusement; they refused to take seriously a young woman's primary mission in life—the hunt for a husband.

Even now, dangerously near to being "on the shelf," none of the three greeted her unmarried status with more than a bit of a shrug. Lady Henrietta—Retta—devoted much of her time to a London charity for abused women and abandoned children. Hero had for several years been a true assistant in all but name to her respected physician father in Cornwall. And the truth was that Harriet also had a life of her own to which she felt pressed to return.

Taking a cool writer's view of the current matter—for that is what she was: a writer—Harriet poured out her thoughts in letters to her erstwhile school friends Retta and Hero.

Even for adults, she wrote, *mourning takes a deal out of one. Sadness and regret are understandable, but one is hardly prepared for the anger—the resentment—that accompanies grief! Adults manage to cope, but children flounder terribly with these emotions. Sometimes all you can do is hold the little ones close and murmur meaningless words of comfort, and hope that they do indeed offer comfort. On a positive note: children are resilient. And I am hoping a change of scene may hasten their healing...*

So on that May morning, Harriet was once again devoting herself to her sister's children. She sat on the floor of the nursery playing jackstraws with the blond, eight-year-old twins, Richard and Robert—"Ricky" and "Robby" to the nursery set—and their six-year-old sister, Sarah, whose hair was almost as dark as her Aunt Harriet's, her eyes the same blue-gray.

This game, as usual, was marked by an abundance of giggles and merriment. Also as usual thirteen-year-old Maria sat on a couch nearby with her head in a book, one hand toying with a loose strand of light brown hair. Phillip, still seeming too young and too slight to wear the heavy title Earl of Sedwick with which he had been so suddenly burdened, was idly spinning a huge globe that was a permanent fixture in the nursery's schoolroom-playroom. At a table nearby, one of the two servants regularly assigned to the nursery set was trying to feed the youngest, two-year-old Matilda. Tilly, determined to do the deed herself, kept grabbing the spoon, and thus ended up wearing as much of her porridge as she ingested.

As Harriet tried carefully to free one of the sticks of the game from the pile in front of her, she felt a pudgy little hand on her cheek. "It isn't true, is it, Auntie Harry?"

She drew four-year-old Elinor into the circle of her arm and gave up her turn at the game. She nuzzled the little girl's blonde curls. "What, Elly? Isn't what true?"

"What Ricky says."

"What does Ricky say?"

Elly emitted an exasperated sigh. "Ricky says we are goin' to Lunnon."

The room went quiet and Harriet could tell that this topic was not a surprise to the group.

"Ricky, did you say that?" Harriet asked, stalling for time. She was not surprised the cat was out of the bag, but she had thought to have matters more settled before informing the children of the possibility of a trip to London.

Ricky had jumped up from being on his knees on the floor. He looked down at his feet. "Uh—well—I—uh—heard the footman Tom talkin' with Nurse Tavenner an'—"

"Oh, Miss Harriet, I never said—" the nurse called from the table where she was feeding the toddler.

Harriet held up a hand to forestall the maid's explanation and looked at the little boy. "You eavesdropped on a private conversation, did you, Ricky?" She was careful to keep her tone gentle in admonishing him.

"I didn't mean to. Really, I didn't."

"But then you repeated it?"

He nodded sadly. "Uh-huh."

"But is it true?" Elly demanded with an insistent stamp of her foot, small hands on her hips.

Harriet sighed inwardly, but she refused to lie to them. "I—we—do not know yet. We *may* all go for a few weeks. It is not settled yet. Would you like to do that?"

Maria put down her book. "I should like that very much," she said. "Could I go to Hatchard's bookshop?"

"Can I take Muffin?" Elly picked up her kitten and held it close. Harriet smiled sadly at the thought of how very important that little ball of fur had become to Elly since the loss of her parents.

"If Muffin can go, can Sir Gawain go, too?" Ricky asked, brightening. On hearing its name, the mixed breed mutt—mostly black and white collie—thumped its tail against the marble hearth where it lay.

Phillip stopped whirling the globe walked and over nearer the rest of the group. "What about the ponies?"

"Muffin and Sir Gawain can surely accompany us. The ponies, probably not. But," Harriet quickly added, "there are ponies to ride in London, too. But, really, children, you must not get your hearts set on going to London. It is by no means settled. It would be nice to have your grandmother's agreement to such a scheme."

This comment elicited pained expressions from the two oldest children. Maria got up from the couch and put her hand on Ricky's shoulder. "But we may hope, may we not, Aunt Harriet? Going to London now will not be the same as it was with Mama and Papa, but..." Her voice trailed off wistfully.

"Yes. We may hope," Harriet assured her and vowed to herself that she would make this happen, regardless of the objections of the Dowager Countess of Sedwick—or those of the dowager's son, the children's guardian.

* * * *

That afternoon Harriet was alone in the music room idly playing a new piece of music her own grandmother had sent her from London when the dowager swept into the room with what was clearly a letter in her hand.

"Ah, there you are," she said brightly. "I wonder if I might have a word with you, Harriet."

"Of course, my lady." Harriet turned on the piano bench to face the older woman, who took a straight-backed chair nearby.

Lady Margaret was a well-preserved woman in her mid-fifties. Her once blonde hair was now more of a nondescript gray than gold, but it was always carefully coiffed, and her attire, if not in the first stare of fashion, was very close to being so. Of course, the black bombazine of a mourning dress could hardly be labeled ultra-stylish. She was tall; the word that always came to Harriet's mind about her sister's mother-in-law was *stately*.

"I have had a letter from my son Quinton, and I should like to share it with you."

"By all means, my lady."

The older woman read the letter without editing. Harriet winced inwardly at the line about a "mere godmother," but she refused to acknowledge the hit, though she was sure Lady Margaret had relished the line. *The nerve of that man! How dare he try to relegate me to the sidelines. Why, I have loved every one of Anne's children from the moment they were born! Even before they were born.*

"So you see, my dear," the dowager said, "this trip to London that you have the children so churned up about is simply out of the question. Quinton *is* their guardian and he prefers that they remain here at Sedwick Hall. Besides, a pleasure trip such as you propose is not quite the thing, now is it? Even children are expected to mourn properly. Six months is customary for a parent—and these children are mourning *two* parents."

Harriet gripped the piano bench on either side of her and steeled herself to respond. "First of all, it was not *I* who mentioned the possibility of a trip to London in front of servants so it could be repeated in front of the children. Yes, the colonel does have legal guardianship, but perhaps he did not read carefully those paragraphs of Winston's will dealing with the children. My brother-in-law stated quite clearly that in the absence of Colonel Burnes or their mother, *I* should have final say on the children's welfare. Moreover, he granted me full authority and means to carry out my decisions. Winston and Anne were quite, quite clear in that regard."

The dowager emitted an almost unladylike snort. "I doubt my poor besotted son gave any thought to what he was agreeing to."

"Nevertheless, he *did* agree—and he repeated his agreement in a codicil to his will just this last December. I am sure there is a copy among Winton's papers in the library...." Harriet allowed her voice to trail off. When the dowager did not respond, she added, "In any event, I would say that the colonel's being confined to a bed in southern France constitutes an absence. Would you not agree?"

The dowager waved a dismissive hand. "That is beside the point. Perhaps you care so little about propriety that you would make my grandchildren the subject of gossip if they are seen to be so disrespectful of their parents, who loved them dearly, but I am not. And neither is my remaining son."

"Lady Margaret, please try to understand. We—you and I—cannot disappoint the children now. Try to see it is an opportunity for education, not merely pleasure. Or as a chance for them to heal in spirit. It has been ten weeks already. They are children! They cannot go about dressed in black every day, all day with long faces. They are not forgetting their parents. They beg me constantly for stories of their mama and papa. They talk about them and pray for them every day. They miss their parents horribly. Here at Sedwick Hall, every time they turn a corner or see an object outdoors, they are reminded of their loss, of something they may no longer do with Mama or Papa." She paused and then added, "I have not the heart to disappoint them now."

The dowager's lips thinned. "It is not proper. I heartily disapprove and I find it extraordinary that you consider my opinion to be irrelevant in a discussion about my grandchildren. I cannot sit back to see them the subject of gossip."

"I think," Harriet said softly, "that, unless we who are most concerned, make it a topic of general discourse, it will not be so."

Lady Margaret tried a different tactic. "Surely you cannot mean to open Sedwick House in London for your little jaunt to the city. There is only caretaker staff there now, you know."

"I do know. No, I will not open the house in Mayfair. We will stay with my grandparents in Bloomsbury. Their house is large and well-staffed—and they keep the nursery ready for their grandchildren and their great-grandchildren. I will take the Sedwick nursery maids and sufficient footmen for our travel."

"You've thought of everything, haven't you?" the dowager asked coldly.

"Not yet. But I would welcome your suggestions."

Lady Margaret rose and stepped toward the door. "I have told you what I think."

* * * *

For the next three days, Harriet saw little of Lady Margaret. When they chanced to meet at meals, both were too well-bred not to be civil, but there was little warmth in their conversations. Lady Margaret made a point of being away from home much of the time, paying calls in the local neighborhood. Harriet feared her own infractions might well be a central topic of discussion during those calls, but she chose to ignore that possibility.

Her own attention centered on preparing for the trip to London. Having never planned such an elaborate journey on her own before, she sought the advice of the Sedwick steward, Mr. Stevens, as well as the butler, Patterson, and the housekeeper, Mrs. Ames. Within the week, the entourage was on its way. Although it was expensive, travel by post chaise was most expedient. The entire group included the seven children, Harriet, two nursery maids, Harriet's personal maid, and sufficient footmen to provide adequate protection along the way. Three days after departing Sedwick Hall, the party arrived in the early evening at the somewhat dated but elegant townhouse of the Earl of Hawthorne in the Bloomsbury district of London.

Chapter 2

Having seen her charges tucked into their beds in the nursery, a weary Harriet retreated to the drawing room. Simple courtesy required that she spend at least a few minutes in polite conversation with her hosts, two of her favorite people in all the world—her own maternal grandparents, the Earl and Countess of Hawthorne.

The elderly couple had been on hand to greet the arrival of their favorite granddaughter and seven of their numerous great-grandchildren when the group arrived that afternoon. They had received the lot of them in the drawing room, but perceiving the children to be tired and hungry had quickly dispensed with customary greetings and sent them off to the upstairs nursery, always kept in readiness for such welcome invasions. Harriet had been proud of the children, and had expressed to them her pride in their having shown themselves to be polite and well behaved in extending proper greetings to their mother's grandparents.

"We done good, huh?" Ricky asked, preening.

"You did very well, indeed," Harriet said. "Those were most correct bows, Richard and Robert." The boys preened even more.

Harriet had escaped to her own room only long enough to change from her travel dress to a more comfortable day dress and then returned to have supper with the children in the nursery—as she had informed her grandparents she would do in order to help get the youngsters oriented to their new surroundings. Having achieved that order of business, she now welcomed the refuge offered by adult company.

She sank happily onto a gold and maroon striped couch next to her grandmother, a small woman with a determined chin, gray eyes, and iron gray hair that had once been the near-ebony shade of Harriet's hair. "Ah,

Nana! Poppy! I cannot tell you what a feeling came over me as I came through that door earlier!" She gripped her Nana's hand as she pointed at the drawing room door with her other hand. "I remembered how frightened and lonely Anne and I were at being sent here after Papa died—scarcely two years after we lost Mama. I was—what?—seven, I think; Anne, twelve. We'd never been to London before—never been away from Lancashire, to be sure. But you made us feel so welcome!"

Her grandmother returned the pressure of her grip. "That was a very difficult time for all of us. And this is as well. I am glad Anne's children have you to help see them through at least this initial upheaval in their lives."

"I thought a change of scenery would help ease their grief," Harriet said.

"We shall do what we can to help as well," the older woman said. "There are military reviews and what not—you know the Prince Regent is going all out to entertain the German and Russian royalty who are visiting to celebrate the end of Napoleon's reign. The children will surely find all that pomp and finery impressive."

"Probably," Harriet agreed. "The boys, especially, are quite mad about the army, what with their uncle's serving in the Peninsula."

Harriet had scarcely noticed as her grandfather unfolded his lanky form from a maroon winged chair across from the couch she shared with his wife, but she was abruptly aware of his thrusting glasses of sherry at the women with one hand as he balanced a goblet with a splash of cognac in his other hand.

He sat back down, swirled his glass, savored the aroma, issued a satisfied sigh, and finally sipped. He looked up to catch an exchange of amused glances between the women as they observed this ritual. "A man's entitled to enjoy a fine cognac, is he not?" he asked rhetorically.

"Especially now that he may do so legally, eh, my dear?" his wife agreed indulgently.

"Well, there is that," he said, taking another sip. He leaned forward in his chair, his hands clasped loosely around the bottom of the glass on his knees. "We are quite pleased that you chose to visit us, Harriet. Saved us a trip to Derbyshire, don't you know?"

"Is that so?" Harriet asked.

"Oh, yes. You know how I hate traveling out of the city, but there are certain matters you need to know about."

"Laurence," his wife admonished. "The poor girl has scarcely had a moment to relax. Legal matters can certainly wait until morning."

"If you insist, my dear," he said.

But Harriet's interest had been piqued. "Legal matters? That sounds ominous—or at least interesting."

"Not ominous," he assured her. "Concerns your mother's marriage settlements." He drained his glass and set it aside.

"Mama's marriage of—what?—three decades ago?"

"Oh, yes. At least that," he said, with a nod of his snow-topped head. "As is customary, you and Anne received allowances based on not only your mama's dowry, but also your father's will, which made ample provision for his daughters."

"My allowance has always been quite adequate," Harriet said.

Her grandfather coughed politely. "Yes, I should think so. It is all somewhat complicated, and the solicitor will explain it to you fully, but your fortune was separated from Anne's when *her* marriage settlements were negotiated. Sedwick was more interested in cash settlements than in the properties you Mayfield girls inherited from your father, so that was arranged and your interests were severed from Anne's."

"I do not recall any mention of these matters," Harriet said.

"'Tis not something one ordinarily discusses with females, especially as young as you were then," the old man said.

"Yet another example of men underestimating us women," her grandmother interjected.

"Now, Celia," the earl admonished mildly. "Don't you be haranguing me with another litany from that Wollstonecraft woman. I refuse to take responsibility for the way of the world." He shifted in his chair and said to Harriet, "Hinckley, the solicitor, will explain it all to you in great detail later, but the short version is this: as of your twenty-seventh birthday, should you still be an unmarried woman, you will yourself have total access and control of what is, to put it simply, an immense fortune. Property—mostly in Kent—and investments on the 'Change."

"My twenty-seventh—? What a strange number," Harriet murmured, trying to take all this in.

"Your father undoubtedly thought it highly unlikely either of his pretty little girls would be single past her twentieth birthday," the old man said.

"My goodness. Your birthday is only a few weeks away," her grandmother said in some surprise.

"September, Nana," Harriet said. "And, yes, it is that one."

"Well, now that you are independently one of the richest women in England, don't you be thinking of moving away from us—setting up your own establishment like that Holstenmeyer woman," her grandmother said in a worried tone.

Harriet patted her hand. "I wouldn't dream of bringing such scandal down on either your household or Sedwick's. I have quite, quite enjoyed being able to switch from your house here in town to Anne's in the country as the whim suited me. I just hope..." But she refused to finish that thought, at least for the moment.

Harriet stifled a polite yawn and a few minutes later her grandmother declared it time that they all sought their beds.

Still, Harriet lay awake a long while considering her grandfather's announcement. Harriet had never thought much about financial affairs. She had never had to do so. Bills for clothing and other necessities were sent to her grandfather. Her allowance had always been adequate for everything else—and suitably increased as she grew older. In recent years, it had been supplemented modestly by earnings from items she published in newspapers and magazines. She was always very proud of these achievements, though she could never have lived on such pittances.

She deliberately turned her mind to that other matter to which they had barely alluded. Since leaving school, she had lived either in London with her grandparents or in the country with Anne and Sedwick, and felt totally at home, having her own suite of rooms—her own space, her own place—in each household. Would that change now? If so, how? To what extent? *Well, of course it will change, you ninny,* she chastised herself. *It already has. The dowager's moving into the Hall was a start.*

With the marriage of her eldest son, Lady Margaret had—quite reluctantly, Anne had confided later to Harriet—removed with her companion, Mrs. Sylvia Hartley, to the dower house where they were attended by a large staff that was supplemented from time to time by members of the staff from the hall itself. The two ladies had often dined at the Hall and were included in any festivity the earl and his countess hosted. Lady Margaret was very much a fixture at Sedwick Hall. The dowager rarely hesitated to offer her opinion on the shortcomings of her daughter-in-law's management of the household that had, after all, once been her own, and she readily offered her suggestions on how occupants of the Sedwick nursery should be dealt with. Harriet had always admired the forbearance of her sister and brother-in-law in the face of the woman's criticism. *But really, it was none of Harriet's concern was it? Only now, perhaps it was.*

Harriet had not been greatly surprised at Lady Margaret's presuming to move into the Hall almost immediately on their receiving word of the deaths of the earl and his countess. The dowager's directives were often more disruptive than otherwise, and the staff, used to seeing Harriet as a surrogate for their countess, often looked to her to straighten matters out—which she did, but incurred the annoyance of the dowager, even on a matter as trivial as a change on a menu item for the nursery. Harriet had ordered the change because Robert was allergic to strawberries, though the child's grandmother seemed unaware of that fact. Harriet had noted subtle changes in the Hall since the dowager's arrival: furniture that had been repositioned, knickknacks that had been rearranged or removed, but refused to dwell upon such things.

Finally, she allowed her mind to veer to what was likely to pose the most monumental shift in matters at Sedwick Hall: the arrival of Colonel Lord Quinton Burnes. Harriet had never met Colonel Burnes. At the time of his brother's marriage, the colonel, then a lowly lieutenant, had been serving in India. A few years later, he had had leave from service in the Iberian Peninsula, but Harriet had missed meeting him because she had been on an extended visit in Cornwall with her friend Miss Hero Whitby. However, for years she had heard his praises sung—to the point that she was sure such a paragon could not exist. Nevertheless, Anne had found him very personable and had expressed genuine regret that Harriet had not met the man. Two portraits in the Hall provided a glimpse of his character. One hung in the Hall's portrait gallery and depicted the Fifth Earl, his countess, and his two then-teenaged sons: the earl and his wife seated in throne-like chairs, their sons standing rather stiffly at either side of them. The other was on the first landing of the main staircase: a life-size portrait of the then-major in dress uniform. In both instances, Harriet had always thought the boy and then the man in the paintings to be a person of thought and self-confidence—and not at all bad looking, with a steady gaze at the world and a firm jaw. She wondered if that firm jaw signified stubbornness and intolerance. She reached to turn out the lamp and punched her pillow into submission.

* * * *

The next morning as she had promised them, Harriet set out with all seven children and a nursery maid in an open landau for the park. They were crowded, with a footman crouched at the back of the vehicle, Phillip happily riding ahead with the coachman, the maid holding the littlest one, and others loosely squeezed into the two seats. A basket with a blanket, a jug of water, and some biscuits for snacks was tucked under a seat.

Her grandmother had come out to see them off. "Are you sure about this, my dear?"

"Yes. 'Tis only a short distance to the park." Harriet checked to be sure they had umbrellas just in case London's always unpredictable weather turned on them, and that they were well supplied with bread to feed the birds and toys to occupy the children, before signaling the coachman to start. It was early enough that they would have time to frolic in the park before the usual "see and be seen" crowd of the *ton* began to fill up the pathways. When they reached the park, the coachman parked the landau outside one of the gates in a line of similar vehicles. Each child was given something to carry—a toy or a small sack of bread crumbs—and the lot of them set off for the pond amidst a good deal of boisterous skipping, running, and yelling. Harriet made no attempt to quell their exuberance beyond being sure they did not overrun others in the park.

She was amused to see that Maria, at almost fourteen, was too much of a lady to be quite so caught up in the moment as the others were. "You will help me to keep track, to see that I do not lose anyone, will you not, my dear?" Harriet said to her eldest niece.

"Of course, Aunt Harriet. I always did so for Mama."

"Yes, you did. She once told me how much she appreciated that."

"Did she really, Aunt Harriet?" The girl turned anxious blue eyes up to Harriet and Harriet was reminded yet again of how much these children missed their parents and how much they still needed reassurances that they had been and were important—and loved. She put an arm around Maria's shoulders. "She certainly did! Actually, she told me on more than one occasion just how much she relied upon you."

"Oh." Maria looked down, but Harriet could tell that she was pleased.

While the footman Beaton hovered over the three boys and Sarah as they sailed toy boats on the pond, Harriet and the maid accompanied the other girls slightly farther along the bank, where they fed the ducks and geese with much awkward flurrying of arms, flapping of wings, avian quacks and honks, and human giggles and shouts of alarm, real and feigned. Soon enough, the boat people joined the bird feeders. In all, they were having a wonderful time. The children were genuinely enjoying the outing and Harriet was immensely glad to see them simply losing themselves in having fun.

Eventually, she became aware that the park was beginning to fill up—and that the nature of the crowd had changed remarkably. She had quite lost track of time. Many of the people now filling the byways of the park were members of the see and be seen crew. It was time to gather up her little group and set them to collect their belongings strewn about on the grass. Just as this thought flashed into her mind, she heard a loud very young female screech, "Robby, no-o-o."

Harriet whirled around in time to see eight-year-old Robert grab the sack of bread crumbs from which four-year-old Elly had been feeding the ducks at the edge of the pond. Elly reached for the sack, slipped on the muddy bank, and fell into the water. Before Harriet could manage the five or six feet to where Elly had fallen into the pond, Beaton, the footman, plunged into the knee-high muddy water and retrieved the screaming, drenched child.

"Sh-h. Don't cry, my lady," Beaton soothed. "You're safe." But the child, obviously terrified, continued to cry out and reached for the only figure of rescue she readily recognized: her Auntie Harry.

Beaton hesitated to hand over the little girl whose pretty pink outfit was not only soaking wet, but caked with mud. "Never mind," Harriet said and took the child from him, aware only of those little arms around her neck, the terror subsiding in the small body. Then she became aware of another small person at her elbow.

"Is Elly all right?" Robert asked in a worried tone. "I didn't mean for her to fall. Really. I didn't mean it."

Harriet reached her hand down to clasp his shoulder. "I know you did not mean to hurt your sister. It was an accident. But maybe you were not thinking as well as you should have been."

"Maybe. Next time—"

Nurse Tavenner came up with the baby Matilda on one hip and holding a small blanket out to Harriet in the other hand. "Oh, Miss, your dress. That mud will never come out," she said in a mournful tone.

Harriet set Elly on her feet and wrapped the blanket about the little girl's shoulders, then looked down at her own light gray wool walking dress splashed with mud on both the chest and skirt and sighed. "I don't suppose it will."

She suddenly became aware of an open carriage that had come to a stop nearby. A young woman, blonde, in an apple green grown with a frilly matching parasol, was standing in the carriage, holding court, as it were: two gentlemen sat on mounts on the other side of the carriage and three young men stood with doffed hats gazing up at her admiringly from the near side. Harriet's gaze traveled up to meet the woman's belittling glance.

Angelina Grampton, now Lady Bachmann. This I do not need, she thought as she bent her knee in a quick polite curtsy of greeting and turned to call, "Come along, children. Our coachman awaits."

"Oh, la, gentlemen!" the beauty of the moment called in a loud, falsely merry tone. "How lucky are we? We have stumbled into the very midst of a fairy tale. Behold! We have Snow White and her Seven Dwarfs!"

"Snow White indeed! So clever, my lady!" the youngest of the gentlemen echoed with a chuckle. Harriet recognized him as a sycophantic follower of the Bachmann woman.

Lady Bachmann indeed! Harriet thought in a sarcastic play on the young man's fawning tone. Miss Angelina Grampton had been one of that group at Miss Penelope Pringle's School for Young Ladies of Quality who had disparaged and dismissed the "Hs" as mere bluestockings. Later, Angelina and her lot had tried to make the Hs miserable during their shared come-out year. Their catty gossip might have been effective had Harriet, Henrietta, and Hero actually set much store by their talk. Angelina had quickly made what was considered a good marriage—that is, one that came with money and a title. Now, not only having provided her aged spouse his requisite heir, but also having seen him laid to rest in the family vault, she had reemerged on the social scene two seasons ago as one of the so-called "Winsome Widows." This was a sobriquet that some wag had attached to three women who had been widowed while quite young and had rejoined the social whirl of the *ton*. Harriet and many others were convinced that the three worked to live up to that frivolous title.

"Come, Maria." Harriet called, eager to be away. "Take Elly's hand and help me keep the blanket about her lest she take a chill."

"Ew. She's muddy."

"I know. Here. Put this handkerchief between your hands."

"Yes. I think that will work."

"Oh, Miss. Uh, Miss—Uh—Mayfield, is it not?" the beauty in the carriage called down. "Would you like one of my gentlemen here to help you?"

Harriet gritted her teeth. Angelina knew very well who she was. She looked up and smiled despite the streak of mud she knew she had on her cheek. "Thank you for your kind offer, but I have sufficient help."

"Perhaps we shall see you at Lady Carstairs's musicale this evening," Angelina trilled as a parting shot.

"Perhaps," Harriet said, breathing a sigh of relief as she brought up the rear of her little group leaving the park.

Chapter 3

For the next few weeks Harriet happily divided her time between her own pursuits and those that would keep the children suitably entertained or occupied. She shamelessly indulged herself in attending not one, but two meetings of the London Literary League. Besides the Carstairs musicale, she attended other such social functions with her grandmother, and the two of them made and accepted "morning" calls. Almost immediately, Harriet heard whispers of the "Snow White" story, but she shrugged them off, sure that *on dit* was too silly to last.

Then, as happened so often, the Prince Regent managed, with little effort on his part, to divert society's attention to himself, though in this instance Harriet had to admit that he had a sufficient degree of help. Harriet and her grandparents had actually been present on that occasion. Along with most of the rest of the audience in Drury Lane Theatre, the Hawthorne party had already been seated when the Prince Regent entered his royal box, accompanied by his royal guests, the King of Prussia, the Czar of Russia, and the renowned General Blücher—all dressed for show in military finery as befitted the allied conquerors of the villainous Napoleon, who was now consigned to the island of Elba. They bowed and waved to the theatre crowd for some minutes, clearly basking in the adulation. Then Harriet heard her grandmother's sharp intake of breath and her whispered, "Oh, my goodness."

Harriet followed the older woman's gaze. There, directly across from the royal box, the Prince Regent's estranged wife, Princess Caroline, was entering a box of her own. People seated on the floor of the theatre had caught sight of her and jumped to their feet, shouting her praises. There was no doubt where the sympathies of his subjects generally lay in the prince's ongoing dispute with his wife. The princess rather brazenly waved at the royal box and the visiting royals quickly bowed to her, so her husband was forced to follow suit, albeit with little grace. Harriet had no doubt what the main topic of tomorrow's gossip would be in every London drawing room.

* * * *

Harriet did not immediately act on her grandparents' information that she was an immensely wealthy woman. She told herself that she needed time to digest that information, though the truth was it had not come as *such* a great surprise. She had always known there was money in the family: her grandfather's closeness to the crown did not come merely from political considerations, and, though she had been but thirteen at time of Anne's debut, she had been aware of the rumors swirling of the Mayfield heiresses—in the plural. She had simply never paid much attention then, and had had little cause to do so later. Now, perhaps, she had more than enough cause to take notice....

With this in mind, she met with the Earl of Hawthorne's solicitor, one Josiah Hinckley and his son Josiah Junior, who would be taking over for his retiring father. Her grandfather accompanied her, and the four of them sat on cushioned chairs around a polished mahogany table in one corner of the law office, papers spread before them. Both Harriet and Lord Hawthorne had made it abundantly clear that Miss Mayfield fully intended to assume control of her affairs herself from here on.

"Or until such time as she should marry, I assume," the younger Hinckley said with a smile. He was a man of middle years and medium height, with slick black hair and warm, dark brown eyes. His broad forehead and long nose were exact duplicates of his father's, as were the brown eyes, though the father's hair was white and thinning.

Harriet shifted uncomfortably on her chair. "That is not likely, but should such an unforeseen event occur, you will be notified immediately."

"Of course," father and son murmured in unison.

"There is, however, a financial matter I should like to have taken care of as soon as possible, and in as discreet a manner as you can manage."

"As you wish, my lady," the elder Hinckley said and extended a hand. "If it is a matter of gaming debts, just give me the vouchers, and I shall take care of them. I have often performed such services for ladies of the *ton*."

Harriet felt herself coloring. "You misunderstand. I think—that is—they *may* be largely a matter of gaming debts, but not mine. I should like for you to investigate fully the nature and extent of indebtedness and liabilities against the estate of my nephew, Phillip, the Earl of Sedwick."

"My lady?" the two lawyers asked in unison again.

"Harriet, my dear?" her grandfather questioned.

"You all hear me aright, I think. I wish to know the full extent of Sedwick's problems—so far as they are known in the financial community, that is."

The younger Hinckley cleared his throat. "If rumor has any basis in fact, that may be quite a basketful, Miss Mayfield. And—uh—then, what might you have in mind, if I may be so bold as to ask?"

"Hmm. A basketful, you say. I feared as much. *Then,*" she said more decisively, tapping a fingertip on the table, "I should like you to buy up such of the Sedwick debts and mortgages as I can afford without risk to my own properties or holdings. However—I do not want my name involved in these transactions at all. Is that understood? It must be done anonymously."

"I am quite sure we *can* negotiate such a private arrangement, but are you absolutely sure you wish to do this, my lady?" the elder Hinckley asked. "It could be a tremendous amount of money—and on a risky venture."

Harriet looked at the man directly. "Mr. Hinckley, if my grandfather had come to you with such an order about his own funds, would you have asked him that question?"

The man colored slightly. "Uh, perhaps not. My apologies, my lady."

"Suffice it to say then, that I have my reasons and I am willing to take the risks. And you will note that I am not putting at risk the substance of my fortune."

"Yes, miss. We shall do as you have directed. It will take some time to gather the necessary information and then to negotiate the best deals on your behalf. We shall contact you in, say, two weeks?"

"Fine," she said.

Back in their carriage, the Earl of Hawthorne said, "Harriet, are you sure about this?"

They were sitting side by side on the seat facing the horses. She leaned her head on his shoulder. "Not entirely, Poppy. And thank you so much for supporting me. But I have to do what I can to help Phillip."

"His guardian should be the one to take over Phillip's problems, not you."

"I know. Phillip's father was a fine and honorable man, but what if his uncle—his guardian—is as much of a gamester as the fourth and fifth earls were?"

The old man snorted. "If he is, have you not just given him carte blanche to send the earldom up the River Tick again?"

"That is precisely why I shall continue to hold the mortgages on the unentailed properties. With tradesmen's bills paid, things may begin to fall into place. Or not. We shall see."

"I do not see your reason for anonymity, my dear."

She patted his hand on his knee. "Need to know, Poppy. Need to know. Phillip does not need know his Aunt Harriet is trying to come to his rescue. At least not now. Maybe some day. Not now. And Colonel Lord Quinton Burnes has no need to know at this time, either."

"If you say so, my dear.

* * * *

As did many families mourning the loss of loved ones during this time of national euphoria and celebration, Harriet and her grandparents found themselves bending the rules when it came to attending social functions. Harriet accepted invitations to three balls during her sojourn in the city.

"It does seem as though the *ton's* hostesses were trying to outdo each other in entertaining the visiting royalty," Harriet observed, sitting across from her grandparents as the three of them departed early from a grand ball.

"One can hardly blame them," her grandmother commented indulgently. "It has been many a year since our royals have entertained at all, what with the king's bouts of illness and the unrest on the continent." The older woman sighed. "In any event, I am glad your visit has given you a chance to get out some. I enjoyed watching you dance with Lord Beaconfield tonight."

Harriet grimaced. "But it was a waltz. The tabbies are even now hissing about that, I am sure, with our being in half mourning as it were."

"Let them," her grandfather growled. "Our Anne would not have cared a fig for them!"

Harriet smiled. "No, she would not. And she would not have put up with all these drab colors, either."

"But, my dear," her grandmother protested, "you look quite well in mauve and lavender, old lady colors though they be."

"Nevertheless, come the autumn," Harriet said emphatically, "I am going to break out in fiery orange and yellow and bright green!"

"That's my girl!" Her grandfather chortled and his wife giggled beside him.

There was a moment's pause, then the Lord Hawthorne's tone turned deep and serious, belying the distinct twinkle in his eyes that was discernible even in the light of the carriage lantern. "Now. My dear Harriet, what is this that I am hearing about Snow White? Is there a prince to be found in this picture?"

"S-Snow—? Oh, Good heavens," Harriet responded. "That nonsense has now made it to the cardrooms, has it?" She had herself continued to overhear occasional whispers in ladies' retiring rooms and she had been subjected to sly looks during morning visits, particularly when Lady Bachmann was among the guests. Gifted with a good sense of humor—one that extended to self-humor—Harriet had so far been able to dismiss what she saw as Lady Bachmann's attempt to gain attention at someone else's expense—a distinct carryover of habits of the schoolgirl Angelina Grampton.

"You did not answer my question, my girl," the earl responded in a mock growl. "Is Beaconfield the prince in this tale? Should I expect him to come calling in the morning?"

Harriet laughed. "Of course not, Poppy. Lord Beaconfield is simply a dear friend. A fellow writer. You read his book. I know you did."

"Ah, yes. So I did. Too sympathetic by half with that Paine fellow, if you ask me."

"Tut, tut," the countess interjected in a tone of mock umbrage, "do not, I pray, the two of you start that argument again while you have me imprisoned and unable to escape in a closed carriage."

"But, my love," her husband said in an equally mock tone of defense, "'tis your fault. *You* saddled me with these free-thinking females in my family. Wife. Daughters. Granddaughters. And, now, if young Maria is any example, great-granddaughters!"

"And you wouldn't have it any other way, would you?" his wife asked, stretching to give him a quick kiss on his cheek.

"No, I would not." He slipped an arm around his wife's shoulder and gave it a comfortable pat.

Harriet had always loved that her grandparents never hesitated to show their affection for each other in front of family members. They were, of course, all that was correct and proper in company and in public, but it was clear that these two people genuinely cared for and respected each other—even when they vehemently disagreed about something. Not for the first time Harriet found herself thinking *Yes,* that *sort of relationship with a man might very well be worth it*—"*it*," *of course, being some monumental unknown of sacrifice and effort beyond current comprehension. But who had time for it, anyway?*

Well, you might have once, she reminded herself. For a moment, she allowed her mind to drift back—to Anthony, to what might have been— once upon a time. It had, indeed, been an enchanted time: her first season and she felt like a princess; a handsome young guardsman scarcely two years older than she—a fun-loving daredevil—fulfilled the role of prince; those "accidental" touches; a few stolen kisses; whispered secrets. He was a younger son of an Irish nobleman, but "Someday..." he promised—and she believed him. Then, as suddenly as he had entered her life, he was gone from it—shipped off to Portugal to join with the British forces being amassed there. She had railed futilely at king and country when Anthony came to bid farewell—and railed at him for being eager to go. She railed even more and cried bitterly when her grandfather, having seen Anthony's name in the casualties list in the newspaper, gently informed her of his death in one of the first battles of the Peninsular War. Looking back, though, she often wondered how a relationship between a more mature Harriet and Anthony might have progressed.

As for Lord Beaconfield, he was, as she had explained, a friend and a fellow writer. Although his lordship was some seven years older than Harriet, they had first met as new members of the London Literary League to which both had been reluctantly dragged, she by her erstwhile school friend Lady Henrietta Parker, he by his Aunt Gertrude, one of the founders of the League. Both felt instantly at home in the group and gravitated toward each other through their mutual interest in writing about politics. Beaconfield tended to take a philosophical and historical view of current ideas and affairs, while Harriet tended to take a more direct view of the specifics of who and what and why of events as they occurred—so far as she could ferret out such information. Their discussions were often quite lively; both had been embarrassed one day at being asked to be quieter in the library at the British Museum.

* * * *

Besides reaffirming her own place in London's social world during these weeks, Harriet set about seeing that all seven children were diverted as well. There were other trips to the park. She took early rides in the park with Phillip. Both Phillip and Harriet were pleased when Maria occasionally agreed to join them on these outings. Phillip reciprocated by agreeing to spend an afternoon at Hatchard's bookshop with them—especially as he knew that outing would be topped with a visit to Gunther's ice cream shop—and he was allowed to come away from Hatchard's with a book of fine illustrations of military uniforms and equipment that he was eager to share with his Uncle Quint. Harriet smiled as he tried not to be too disparaging of Maria's choices of two new gothic novels. Harriet was sure that Phillip would probably be the second person to read those books. She also took the older children on a shopping expedition to purchase gifts for their Sedwick grandmother and their Uncle Quint.

After much discussion, the adult members of the family agreed to allow Phillip and Maria to attend a showing at Vauxhall Gardens of a popular reenactment of the Battle of Vitoria, deemed to have been a turning point in the Peninsular War. The younger children, especially the twins Richard and Robert, objected vehemently at being excluded, but their outcries were appeased when Harriet promised an outing to the Tower to see the exotic animals there.

In part to even out their numbers, and in part because she simply enjoyed his company, Harriet suggested her grandparents invite Lord Beaconfield to join the excursion to Vauxhall Gardens. When Lord Hawthorne's party arrived at their box in the Gardens, Harriet was delighted to see that her grandparents had also invited their youngest son, Sir Charles Montieth, his wife, Elizabeth, and two of their children to join them. Having already reached his mid-teen years by the time she and Anne had been thrust upon his parents' household, and thus away at school during much of their mutual growing-up years, Harriet's uncle Charles Montieth was nevertheless as close as Harriet had ever come to having an older brother.

"Charles! Elizabeth!" She greeted both with a warm hug and quickly drew Phillip and Maria into the circle to reintroduce them to their cousins, Jeremy and Rebecca.

"Nana, you sly puss, you," Harriet said with a wink.

"Elizabeth and I agreed it is time these youngsters got to know each other. After all, they will all be going away to school soon enough, I imagine," the older woman said.

"Rebecca is already slated for Miss Pringle's school," Elizabeth said, restoring a strand of chestnut colored hair to its place behind her daughter's ear.

"She should enjoy it. I know I did," Harriet said. Glancing to see that the four children and the men were occupied in their own conversations, she leaned closer to Elizabeth and her grandmother to confide, "Neither Phillip nor Maria seems enthusiastic about going away to school. I think they fear being separated from the other children. They even showed some ambivalence about coming out this evening."

"Oh, dear," her grandmother murmured.

"That could pose problems," Elizabeth said softly.

"Oh, yes," Harriet said, thinking of the colonel's letter.

Situated in a central location on the edge of the arena, the Hawthorne box soon became something of a "crush," for all six of these adults were well known and well received in London's social circles. Harriet was well aware that the Montieth men were also very well respected in London's business and financial circles. After all, that earldom had been awarded early on in the previous century and still quietly served as something of a piggy bank to the crown—hence the knighthood accorded Charles only a few years ago. The press of casual visitors diminished as the orchestra began to warm up for a lively concert of military music, followed by the customary supper of melon and thinly sliced Venetian ham for which Vauxhall Gardens was known.

During the intermission—after some covert discussion among themselves—the four youngsters begged permission to stroll about the paths in the gardens, their enthusiasm spiked no doubt, Harriet was sure, by the whispers and rumors of naughty meetings said to transpire in the byways of the trails and pathways of Vauxhall Gardens. In the end, Harriet and Lord Beaconfield, Charles and Elizabeth accompanied them for a short walkabout before the main event of the evening's entertainment. Harriet was sure this entourage was not exactly what the children had had in mind, but, considering the eclectic nature of some of the people hanging about on these dimly lit paths, Harriet was glad for the additional adult company.

The main show of the evening was, of course, the spectacular reenactment of the Battle of Vitoria, which involved much shooting of cannon and exploding bombs in the arena as well as incredible displays of horsemanship, swordsmanship, and other feats of derring-do. The musicians added appropriate touches from time to time. The action was punctuated by loud cheers from the audience for characters costumed as English soldiers and equally loud boos and hisses for those in French uniforms. The exhibition ended with a resounding crescendo of music, booming cannon, and a great swirl of dust in the arena.

"Oh, my goodness!" Rebecca said in something resembling a squeal to match several she and Maria had emitted intermittently during the performance. "That was spectacular!"

"But horrifying all the same," said Maria who was sitting between her great-grandmother and her cousin Rebecca.

Jeremy, sitting with Phillip across from the girls, snorted. "And probably not at all like the real thing.

"My Uncle Quint could have told us what it was really like. He was there," Phillip said. "I remember his writing my father about this particular battle."

"Truly?" young Jeremy asked with interest.

"Uncle Quint said when the English troops discovered the Spanish king—well, he was not Spanish, was he? but French, Boney's brother he put on the Spanish throne. Anyway, at Vitoria, as Joseph, the king, was trying to escape Spain along with his entourage and a tremendous amount of Spanish treasure, our English troops discovered them, and set upon them like bears on a honey pot! Old Nosey—that's what our soldiers called Wellington—had to threaten to hang some of his own troops to restore order!"

"I am sure that cannot be true of English troops," Rebecca declared loyally. "Our English heroes would never behave in such a dishonorable manner."

"I am just telling you what Uncle Quint wrote to my father—and Uncle Quint was there," Phillip said. "You read his letters too, Aunt Harriet."

"Yes, Phillip, I did," she replied. "Many of them. They were quite detailed. I should think that conditions of war bring out many facets of behavior in all people, though we like to focus on the best ones in our own such as heroism."

Charles said, "Reality sometimes needs to be embellished to make good theatre."

"Especially if one wishes to cut down on the amount of bloodshed and brutality, knowing there will be ladies in one's audience," Lord Beaconfield offered.

"Well!" Maria said emphatically, "I think it is just ridiculous to expect men to shed buckets of blood and then to expect women to pretend it did not happen."

"I quite agree, Lady Maria. I quite agree." Lord Beaconfield glanced at Harriet with a slightly lifted eyebrow.

Harriet merely smiled, but was not surprised to hear her grandmother say, without a shred of disapproval directed to Maria, whom she hugged close, "You will find, Lord Beaconfield, that women of this family tend to be dreadfully outspoken."

Beaconfield laughed. "Oh, yes, ma'am. I have, indeed, made that discovery." He winked at Harriet, who found herself blushing, but before she could reply the musicians began to introduce the show's finale, a huge display of fireworks.

Afterward, Lord Hawthorne's party made small talk as they waited for the crowd to thin before joining the exodus from the Gardens. In the process, the young Earl of Sedwick shared with his cousins Jeremy and Rebecca that he and his siblings—that is, the five older of his siblings—would be visiting the Tower of London in the afternoon two days hence.

"Oh, Papa, please say that we may join them," Rebecca begged of Sir Charles.

"Rebecca!" her mother admonished. "You might at least wait until you are invited. Perhaps Cousin Harriet would prefer not to be accompanied by an army."

Harriet quickly responded. "No. No. The more the merrier. Maria and Phillip and I will welcome any help we can get in keeping track of the twins and Sarah and Elly." She laughed. "We are leaving Tilly at home with Nurse, lest we lose her among the Tower's band of monkeys."

"Wise move," Elizabeth said. "As long as my two urchins are keen on going, I will gladly lend a hand." She looped a hand into her husband's arm, glanced up at him flirtatiously, and added, "And perhaps I can persuade Charles to tear himself away from that stuffy office for one afternoon at least."

Charles heaved an exaggerated sigh and murmured, "Yes, dear. Whatever you say, dear." Which earned him a firm shake of the arm she clutched.

"If you are truly serious about 'the more, the merrier,' perhaps you will allow me to invite myself along on this excursion," Lord Beaconfield said, gazing directly at Harriet.

"Why, of course." She was somewhat taken aback. Gavin Castlemere, Viscount Beaconfield, heir to a marquis, was deemed by blushing debutantes and avaricious mamas to be one of the most eligible—and elusive—catches on the marriage mart. His handsome blond good looks coupled with an athletic build never failed to draw attention. Such men did not go about making themselves part of family outings. On the other hand, Gavin had been a particular friend of hers for several years. "You do know what you are in for?" she warned.

"What?" he said defensively, "you think I will not acquit myself well with the younger set?"

In the event, she had to admit—and she did—that he acquitted himself quite well with the younger set. He was on hand to stop Robert's climbing the fence into the enclosure that held a female tiger and her cubs.

"But they was asleep, Auntie Harry."

"Nevertheless, you keep hold of my hand!"

The Tower of London, one of the oldest walled castles in Britain and forever a favorite tourist site in the city, had served as a royal household in ancient times, then as a prison for several famous—even royal—persons. Now serving as more of a museum than anything else, the Tower had, since medieval times, housed various exotic animals. Monkeys, pigeons, and peacocks were allowed to roam at will on the grounds within the walls.

Other animals—a grizzly bear, leopard, hyena, baboon, elephant, and certain exotic birds, as well as the tiger and cubs—were caged or tethered and fenced away from spectators.

Besides the animals, the older children were ghoulishly interested in seeing where the little princes of Tudor times had supposedly been killed and where Anne Boleyn had been beheaded, as well as prison cells that had held such notables as Sir Walter Raleigh and Sir Thomas More. For the younger children, the high point of the visit was seeing what Elly called the "efflemunt." The four-year-old grew tired as the whole group traipsed along the battlement known as "Elizabeth's Walk" and Harriet bent to pick her up and hold her, only to have Lord Beaconfield gently take the child into his own arms. Without protest, Elly accepted this exchange, cuddled close to him, and within minutes she was asleep.

"Told you I could be quite useful," Beaconfield said softly, grinning at Harriet.

"So you did. 'Tis obvious that someone missed her nap. The others will tire soon too, I fear. Perhaps we should go."

"You be the judge," he said, "but Lady Elinor and I are doing well at the moment, so let the others enjoy for a while yet."

"Oh, la, Lord Beaconfield," Harriet teased in the gushing tone of a mincing belle of the *ton*, "if you continue in this most untoward behavior, your reputation in the beau monde will suffer abominably."

His grin broadened. "I won't tell anyone if you don't. Now don't make me laugh and wake this child."

"Yes, sir." Harriet gave him a mock salute as Sarah tugged at her hand to drag her farther along the walkway.

* * * *

Within a week Harriet and her charges were on their way back to Sedwick Hall. On the second day of their journey, the weather turned cloudy in the morning and by midafternoon, the heavens issued a pouring rain that turned the road into a muddy quagmire and forced them to stop earlier than they had planned. The rain followed them north, slowing their progress considerably, and a broken wheel slowed them even more. Having sent a message of their intended arrival, Harriet chose to push on, hoping they would arrive at Sedwick before dark. It did not happen, but they were so close and the local men driving the vehicles assured her that yes, indeed, they could manage through this remaining drizzle what with carriage lanterns and the moon flitting through clouds from time to time. So they pushed through, though not without necessary stops for animals or humans, each stop requiring dashes through the rain.

When they finally did arrive at the Hall tired and wet, Harriet directed the nursery maids simply to take all the children, the dog, and the kitten directly to the nursery rooms. Harriet would see that a kitchen maid sent up some warm food and milk or tea for all of them and they were to prepare immediately for bed. Testimony to their degree of fatigue was the fact that not one of them protested this plan.

Chapter 4

Harriet retreated to her own rooms to remove her wet cloak, her wind-blown bonnet, and mud-begrimed half-boots. Having lost half the pins from her hair in the wind and rain at their various stops, she told her maid Collins to give her hair a hurried brush and then leave it hanging. She washed her face and hands and returned to the nursery to check on the children again. She found Tilly already asleep in her crib, and the others, attired for bed, gathered around the table in the schoolroom-playroom, making short work of the supper that had been sent up.

She squeezed into the chair Phillip had jumped up to hold for her between his own place and Sarah's. Harriet noted that they had made their way through a good deal of the cheese, bread, sliced ham, and ginger biscuits that had been brought up for them, along with milk and weak tea.

As Harriet settled into her seat, Robby leaned around Sarah and asked Phillip in an eager tone, "Did you give it to her yet?"

"'Course not," Sarah said disdainfully. "You be quiet afore you ruin the s'prise."

Robby settled back with a pout.

Phillip had remained standing next to Harriet.

Maria, in charge of the drinks, handed Harriet a cup of tea, which Harriet took with a silent "thank you" and a smile of approval. It dawned on her that there was a sense of anticipation about this little group. The twins and Sarah leaned forward, looking at Phillip; Elly sat on her knees leaning forward on her elbows on the table, though Maria tried to urge her to sit properly.

Phillip cleared his throat and bowed to Harriet. "Aunt Harriet. As the current Earl of Sedwick I speak for all of my immediate family—those presently awake, at least—in expressing to you our sincere thanks to you for taking us to London."

She smiled at the practiced formality of his speech. "It was my pleasure, and something your parents and I often talked of doing."

Phillip reached into the pocket of his robe and extracted a small blue box, which he handed to her. "This is from all of us. To say thank you."

"Oh, my goodness." She stood and hugged him as she accepted it, then quickly sat back down, stunned.

"Open it," Robby demanded.

"Wait," Maria admonished him.

"Oh, my goodness," Harriet said again, recognizing the box from one of London's most exclusive jewelry shops. She lifted the lid with trembling fingers. Nestled in folds of blue velvet was a lovely piece of jewelry shaped like a basket of flowers that might be worn as either a brooch or a pendant. The "basket" of very fine gold filigree work held seven "flowers" fashioned of different-colored semiprecious stones: garnet, lapis lazuli, gold topaz, amethyst, pink crystal, and two of aquamarine. "It's beautiful," she murmured.

"Can I see?" Sarah asked.

"You saw it before—in London," Robby said.

"I want to see it again. I like to look at pretty things," Sarah said.

"As do we all!" Harriet agreed, showing her the object at a better angle. "How did you all manage to keep this a secret from me all this time?"

"It was not easy," Richard said. "Elly nearly spoiled the surprise when she asked at supper yesterday if you liked flowers."

"Do you like it?" Elly asked. "Do you really, really like it?"

"Yes, my darlings, I really, really like it."

"But you're crying!" Elly and Richard said at the same time.

"These are happy tears."

"Oh."

They were all quiet for a moment as Harriet gathered her composure again. She straightened her shoulders and smiled at each of them and looked at the piece of jewelry again. "Seven flowers. One for each of you. Who chose the colors?"

"We mostly picked our own," Maria explained. "Sarah wanted red—so garnets; I wanted the topaz; Phillip chose the blue lapis; Elly liked the sparkle of crystals; and we persuaded the twins that aquamarines matched their eyes, just as amethyst matches Matilda's eyes."

"So it does," Harriet agreed. "I shall never get my flowers mixed up. And I shall treasure this gift forever. Forever." Her voice caught.

"It was Maria's idea," Phillip said in an apparent attempt to lighten the level of emotion in the room.

"But we all agreed," Maria added hastily, "and it was Phillip who actually approached Uncle Charles and Great-grandfather to negotiate the funds and the trips to the jeweler."

"I wanted diamonds and sapphires, but Grandfather said I should wait until I was of a proper age and had full control of my fortune," Phillip said. "So someday—"

"Hmm. Still, that took some strategy," Harriet commented.

Phillip grinned. "Remember all those trips Uncle Charles and Great-grandfather and Jeremy and I took to Tattersalls to inspect horses and go to Gentleman Jackson's Boxing Salon?"

"I may never trust any of you Sedwick or Hawthorne men again," Harriet said fondly and stood. "Now, off to bed with the lot of you. But first, as we did on the journey, let us say the Lord's Prayer together, then you can say your individual prayers as you get into bed."

They said the group prayer and she kissed each of them good night as they went off to their own rooms. She turned Lady Elinor over to the nurse, who would see her to the room she shared with Lady Matilda.

* * * *

Despite her own exhaustion from the day's journey, Harriet was too keyed up to seek her own bed just yet. Given the hour and the general silence of the house, she doubted anyone else was still up, so she ignored the fact that her hair hung in tendrils about her face and that besides a few small spots of mud on the plain gray linen of her dress, the entire hem was decorated with three inches of that still-drying addition to the embroidery there. The dress was ruined, but as she had told her maid earlier, "With luck, once the next few weeks are over, I shall not have to wear such a garment again for a long, long time." Using the servants' stairway, she would just slip down to the kitchen and make herself a cup of tea and raid the pantry for another biscuit.

Expecting the subdued light of the lowered lamp that Mrs. Hodges, the cook, always left at night in the middle of the kitchen work table, Harriet was startled as she pushed open the door from the stairway to see the table brightly lit. And two people were calmly having tea—at this hour! Mrs. Hodges and a man! Before Harriet could just quietly retreat, Mrs. Hodges spotted her.

"Oh, Miss Harriet, do come in. Join us."

The man rose from the opposite side of the table and seemed to just keep rising. He was dressed in buckskins and a woolen shirt such as field workers might wear, the sleeves rolled to the forearms. He was deeply tanned, had light brown hair, and a riveting look about his hazel eyes that seemed to miss absolutely nothing. She had never seen him before, but she knew at once who he was. She came nearer the table, transfixed by his gaze, unable to avert her own gaze.

"Miss Harriet," Mrs. Hodges said, "I don't believe ye've met—"

"Colonel Lord Quinton Burnes," Harriet said, managing to find her voice. Without taking her eyes from his, she accorded him a formal curtsy.

"Miss Harriet Mayfield," he said with a polite bow and gestured to a seat at the table beside Mrs. Hodges. "Do join us. Mrs. Hodges was just telling me of your perilous journey."

"Thank you," she said, pushing an errant strand of her hair behind her ear. *Drat. Why had she not allowed Collins to at least tie it up with a ribbon?* She took the seat on the bench opposite him, scarcely aware that she continued to breathe in and out, scarcely aware that Mrs. Hodges had risen to procure another mug. Somehow her whole being seemed to be in a state of suspension, focused on the expression in a pair of dark hazel eyes across the table from her.

"Not so much perilous as tedious and bothersome. The closer we got to home, the harder the rain fell and the muddier the road, it seemed. And then we were delayed by a broken wheel and had to change our route because a bridge had been washed away."

"The hazards of travel," he said. "Try it across uncharted territory with several hundred troops, along with attendant camp followers, gear, carts, pack animals, and—whatever. At least you had some choice in the matter."

"Here ye go, dearie." Mrs. Hodges placed a ceramic mug of hot tea laced with milk in front of Harriet. "Master Quint—I mean his lordship, the colonel here—he likes his tea on a cold night like this one same as you and I do: with ginger and cinnamon and milk and honey."

"It was a treat I longed for as we were crossing the Pyrenees last winter," he said. "But Hodgie, you must drop that 'lordship' business." Harriet knew that Mrs. Hodges had been working in the kitchen at Sedwick Hall for nearly three decades, and that both the Burnes brothers had regarded her with a great deal of affection as they were growing up.

Mrs. Hodges bristled. She shook a finger at the colonel. "Now don't ye be tellin' me how I'm s'posed to address me betters, Master Quint. I had right proper trainin', I did. Your mama—"

"I don't doubt my mother can quote Debrett's guide to the peerage chapter and verse, but that nonsense has little meaning in real life, and so long as I am in charge at Sedwick Hall, we shall minimize it. And for the record, I *am* in charge—until the current Earl of Sedwick reaches his majority. Would you not agree, Miss Mayfield?"

"With what, my lord? Er, Colonel? Er—?"

He sighed. "Colonel. At least I earned that one. Do you not agree with what I just said? Or would you like me to repeat myself?"

"Oh, there is no need to repeat. Yes, I agree that Lady Margaret is well versed in forms of correct address for various elements of titled personages. And certainly I agree that you are at least nominally in charge of all that is of concern to Sedwick Hall until Phillip reaches his majority."

"*Nominally?*" He raised an eyebrow.

"I doubt you are keeping count of the sheets in the linen closet or the number of deer in the park." She pushed that errant tendril of hair behind her ear again and locked her gaze with his again. "But, no, I do not agree that having people aware of their places in society—and their responsibilities—is mere nonsense."

"Good grief! You are not at all the democrat you pretend to be, are you?" he challenged.

She sat back. "W-why? W-what do you mean?"

"Win told me about your writing. Sent me clippings from the 'Lady Senator' he thought I would find amusing."

She raised her mug to sip her tea to hide her surprise—and the glare she wanted to direct at him. "I'm glad you found my work 'amusing.' My writing is not a secret, though it *is* easier as a woman to publish under a pseudonym."

"I meant no disparagement of your writing, Miss Mayfield."

"Thank you," she said stiffly.

He drank deeply of his tea and stood. "We've all had a long day of it. I shall bid you ladies good night." He looked at Harriet. "We shall continue this conversation tomorrow, Miss Mayfield. We have much to talk about."

"As you wish, my lord—uh—Colonel."

He smiled, nodded, and left.

"That one allus did have the nicest smile," Mrs. Hodges said, and Harriet had to agree: even, white teeth against a rich tan and a smile that showed natural dimples deepened by laugh lines was, indeed, "the nicest smile"—even if the man promised to hold views with which she would have to take issue.

"He was out all evening looking for you and the young ones," Mrs. Hodges went on. "We was so worried when we got word you was at Hendley at noon and then you hadn't arrived here by suppertime. So Lord Quint and his man, Mr. Gibbons, and two grooms set out looking for you, 'spite o' the rain. Course they was looking on the very road you did *not* take—'cause of that washed-out bridge an' all. Wild goose chase. They come in 'bout an hour after you did. What a night!"

The two women bade each other good night and Harriet made her way to her bed, half afraid that a nice smile and a pair of hazel eyes that seemed to see more than they should would keep her awake, not to mention the fact that she thought she sensed a certain animosity in his demeanor. They did keep her awake—though not for long—but they *were* the last things on her mind that night—and the first that popped into her mind when she awoke.

* * * *

Quint cursed himself as he climbed the stairs to his bed chamber. *Didn't handle that well, did you, Burnes? What happened to all those vows of "putting that infernal woman in her place immediately," of "not letting a single moment pass before she understood quite, quite clearly just who it was who was in charge at Sedwick"?*

Instead, he'd been ambushed.

That's what it was: ambushed. Struck dumb by a mass of dark hair, a creamy complexion, and downright mesmerizing smoky blue eyes. He feared he'd made a fool of himself staring into her eyes as he had. Were they blue? Or were they gray? And that hair. Black. Or very dark brown. Hard to tell in lamplight. He grinned at himself. It was a mess, but his fingers had fairly itched to touch it. He quelled a fleeting image of it spread across a pillow. *Jesus, Burnes! It really has been a long time, hasn't it?*

And he ought to be exercising more caution about this woman. Had his mother not warned him of the extraordinary influence she seemed to have on Win and Anne's offspring? Had Miss Mayfield not already deliberately defied him in taking the brood to London, and look how that had turned out!

Quint had arrived at Sedwick Hall ten days ago, fully expecting to find the new earl and his siblings in residence, presumably anticipating his arrival. At first, he merely thought it a bit inconvenient that the family were not present when he arrived, but after all, he'd not given them a specific date, had he? On the other hand, had he not made it quite clear that he expected the children to remain at the Hall? Colonel Lord Quinton

Burnes was accustomed to having his slightest suggestions obeyed as ironclad orders, so their absence did not sit well with him. Never mind the fact that, initially, he was frankly grateful for a day or so of quietude and rest, for the long journey had not been easy on his still mending body. His mother, of course, had been on hand and not only welcomed him warmly, but tried to bring him up to date with family news and with such of the local community as he remembered—which was a surprising number of the inhabitants of several villages.

As he waited none-too-patiently for the return of his charges, Quint found himself filtering out much of his mother's chitchat—just as he had done during most of his youth. Quint and his mother had never been close. As Countess of Sedwick, Lady Margaret had scarcely had time for the heir she had dutifully produced, let alone the mandatory spare. She and her husband had been far more interested in the social and sporting sets than the nursery lot when their children were young. Later, both parents and children had welcomed the separation when the boys went off to boarding school and seemed to spend as many holidays away with school friends as they had at Sedwick Hall.

Quint knew that for a short while after her husband's death, Lady Margaret had reigned supreme as chatelaine and hostess at Sedwick Hall, but then Winston, the sixth earl, had brought home his bride—the beautiful and personable Anne—and the dowager countess had not taken well her banishment to the dower house, elegant and lavishly equipped though it was. Quint remembered those long letters in which Win poured out the sometimes amusing, sometimes frustrating clichés of a husband caught in the throes of not-quite-open conflict between wife and mother. Now his mother seemed to have assumed that, in the absence of a true Countess of Sedwick, it was her prerogative to move back into the Hall and take on the duties and privileges she had once enjoyed in that position. As he reflected on some of the comments his mother had made over the last few days, it occurred to him that she might have transferred her antipathy toward her daughter-in-law to the daughter-in-law's sister, for she had had precious little positive to say of "that willful girl."

He shook his head at his own blind stupidity. He knew exactly how old the Mayfield sisters were. Win had described both young women at the time of his falling for the elder one. Yet Quint had allowed his mother's current portrait to take precedence over what his brother had given him over the years and he had half expected a scatterbrained schoolroom miss instead of the quite lovely woman who had all but stolen his breath away. He'd had to struggle to remember that he was annoyed with her.

Chapter 5

Harriet slept much later than usual.

"Why did you not wake me earlier?" she asked in a bit of a panic when Collins delivered her morning chocolate after nine o'clock.

"I did look in as usual, and again later, but you were sleeping soundly, and as ye'd not given me any order otherwise..." The maid's voice trailed off.

"I'm sorry, Collins. I did not mean to snap at you. His lordship will think me a real slugabed, and I did so want to introduce him to his nieces and nephews this morning."

"Lady Margaret is seeing to that. She sent word up to the nursery earlier and told me special to tell you that you needn't trouble yourself further with the children."

"I'll just bet she did," Harriet muttered under her breath, already annoyed at the way this day was starting—had started.

A short time later, having performed her usual morning ablutions, she sat attired in layers of undergarments and a bright red silk dressing gown as Collins managed at last to confine her hair into two thick coils to form a natural, gleaming dark crown. The side tendrils were curled to form a soft frame for her face.

"Sometimes I feel like just cutting it off—as in those statues of Greek goddesses," Harriet said.

"Oh, no, ma'am," Collins protested. "Your hair is your crowning glory, as they say." Collins—Caroline Collins—had been an ambitious upstairs maid with in Lord Hawthorne's household when Harriet returned from school to make her come out and suddenly needed a lady's maid. Longevity in her position had given her a certain entitlement to opinion, and Harriet felt totally at ease with her.

"They who spout such nonsense do not wash it, wait for it to dry, or deal with the snarls, do they?"

"Well, there is that." Collins chuckled softly. "Which dress, my lady?"

"I'd love to break out in that delicious apple green muslin I had made up in London, or maybe the pink silk, but Lady Margaret would surely have a serious case of the vapors, so I will settle for that gray with the silver embroidery."

Collins bit back her smile. "Yes, ma'am."

Harriet had chosen the gray in part because she wanted to wear something that would display the children's gift to her to advantage. She knew it would please them to see her wear the brooch. The dress was fashioned in simple lines of a soft fabric of a cotton and wool blend that draped nicely. The medium gray dye formed a subtle backdrop for a pattern of silver embroidery that ran halfway up each sleeve and was repeated twice in a larger pattern on front panels of the skirt. The bodice, plain with a square neckline, would show the jewelry nicely.

She took one last look in the cheval glass, drew in a deep breath, and muttered to herself, "Well, into the lion's den."

* * * *

Quint had hardly digested the awful news of Win's death when it hit him that *he* was responsible for those seven young lives his brother had left behind. Having led literally hundreds of men into battle in the last several years, the idea of being in charge did not dismay him. But these were *children* for God's sake! What did he know about children? How on earth did one cope with *little* people? Up close, that is? On a daily basis? He had spent many an hour during his convalescence musing on the dilemma, especially since arriving at the Hall. He had even searched the well-stocked library of Sedwick Hall, but found no tomes of the sort he thought might help him.

It occurred to him that his mother might have been a marvelous source of information, but when he dwelt on his own childhood memories for any length of time, he was reluctant to ask her the sorts of questions to which he wanted answers. Besides that, he hardly knew how to articulate the questions themselves!

Thus it was that on the morning after the return of the London travelers to Sedwick Hall, a rather befuddled Quint—Colonel Lord Quinton Burnes, late of his majesty's Army in the Peninsula—sat on a green couch in the morning room nervously awaiting his charges, pretending to read a newspaper. The butler had supplied him with this reading material, informing him that Miss Mayfield had given it to him last night, thus it was likely to be more up to date than anything that could be obtained locally.

Quint had announced earlier at the breakfast table his intent to drop into the nursery later to make himself known to his young relatives, but his mother protested vigorously. "Oh, no, dear. We shall have them brought down to us in the morning room. The nursery is always somewhat messy and chaotic, particularly in the morning."

"I'm told Miss Mayfield often takes her breakfast in the nursery. Perhaps she has chosen to do so today."

Lady Margaret sniffed. "That one, my son, thrives on chaos, often of her own making. Though she seems to have chosen to sleep in this morning—or so the maids say."

"She did have a rather trying day yesterday," he said.

"As I said—chaos of her own making." She rose to give the bell pull a tug. When a footman answered, she ordered him to "have Nurse Tavenner see that the children are all properly attired and presentable within the hour."

Now Quint stood politely as his mother swept into the morning room and with a long-suffering sigh said, "I have just come from the nursery. I declare those children are more spoiled and fractious than ever. I did tell her it was a terrible mistake to take them to London."

"Have they had their breakfast at least?" he asked as he glanced at the small gold mantel clock on the white marble fireplace. This was one of his favorite rooms since coming home and seeing how Win's wife had redecorated it in white and gold and green. The room faced east and caught the morning sun through long windows that were additions Quint quite liked. He remembered the room as being dark with a great deal of pink and maroon and navy blue.

"Oh, yes, they have eaten," the countess said, taking a seat in a gold upholstered chair. "However, they were not properly dressed. The twins' shirts were not fastened correctly. Elinor was refusing to wear the dress Nurse laid out for her and Sarah had donned a bright blue frock all by herself. I instructed Tavenner to change it and the child objected strenuously. Threw a regular tantrum, she did. She has only six years! And thinks to decide what garment she will wear on any given day? She is supposed to be in mourning! Now I ask you—I should think a day or so on bread and water would cure that sort of behavior!"

Quint ignored this rant, so his mother went on.

"I must say, I think I was blessed in having only boys. Little girls are just very difficult to deal with."

Quint did not dare respond to this. He could not remember a single occasion as a child when his mother had ever noticed what he was wearing. Or when she had noticed much of anything else about him. He doubted if she knew which subjects or sports he excelled in at school, or in which ones he needed help. He could not recall ever talking about such things with her.

A few minutes later a knock at the door signaled the arrival of the Earl of Sedwick and his siblings. Quint called "Come," and stood to receive them.

Phillip entered and held the door for the others, who lined up next to him: the twin boys, the girl Quint assumed to be the six-year-old rebel, then Maria, holding the hands of the two youngest girls. A maid slipped in behind them and set two wrapped packages on the floor behind the children, then left, closing the door quietly as she did so. The children all stood straight and tall, little soldiers standing inspection, and casting apprehensive glances at their grandmother. The boys were all dressed in short gray pants, white shirts, and black jackets; the girls in gray ankle-length dresses with stiff white collars.

Phillip executed a very correct bow to his uncle. "Sir, allow me to present my brothers and sisters."

Quint acknowledged his bow with a nod. "Please do."

As Phillip recited their names, each child stepped forward and bowed or curtsied as protocol dictated. The twins glanced at each other as though sharing a secret and Sarah grinned impishly, revealing missing teeth.

Quint smiled at them, trying—unsuccessfully, he was sure—to put them at ease. "I am pleased to renew my acquaintance with you, Phillip, and with you, Maria, whom I remember well from my last leave, though I must admit you have both grown much since then. Richard and Robert were but toddlers then, and Sarah was just a babe. Elinor and Matilda are entirely new to me, but I look forward to getting to know all of you better."

"Give that a week," one of the twins said, almost under his breath, and the other one jabbed him in the ribs with an elbow, but Quint was already turning back to his seat on the gold couch and chose to ignore that byplay.

His mother, however, did not. "You children behave yourselves," she admonished. "You have been taught proper manners, I know, however much they have been allowed to lapse in recent weeks. Now sit down and try to engage in intelligent conversation. Phillip, you sit on the couch next to your Uncle Quinton; the twins can sit on those chairs nearby. Maria, you and the little girls sit on that gold settee, and Sarah, you sit on this footstool by me so I can keep a close watch on you."

"Yes, Grandmother," several voices repeated at once and Quint noticed with amusement Sarah's grimace, but the child dutifully sat on the stool at her grandmother's knee. A moment of silence followed, during which Quint wondered what the children might think would constitute intelligent conversation. Before he could take pity on them and ask some prosaic adult question, Phillip, who had remained standing, went over to lift the packages the maid had left near the door. He handed one to his grandmother and the other to his uncle.

"Grandmother, Uncle Quint. We have brought gifts for you from London. We hope you like them."

"How very thoughtful," the dowager murmured, accepting the flat rectangular package.

"Aunt Harriet took us shopping. Just like grown-ups do," Sarah announced.

"Goodness. *All* of you?" their grandmother asked.

"Just us older ones," Maria explained. "Elinor and Matilda stayed in the nursery at Hawthorne House."

"Surely you five were not turned loose on the streets of London with no other adult than your Aunt Harriet to accompany you," the dowager said in a shocked tone and with a raised eyebrow directed at her son.

"'Course not," one of the twins answered with a disparaging snort. "Uncle Charles and Aunt 'Lizabeth went with us too. They helped us choose the presents."

"The Montieths," his mother explained to Quint, without lowering her eyebrow in the slightest. "Mayfield relatives."

"Open the presents," the same twin said impatiently.

"You first, Mother," Quint said.

She unwrapped the gift slowly and carefully. Quint could see that the younger children, especially, were eager to see her pleased at their gift, but even he could not read her reaction. When she opened the box, she removed a beautiful paisley shawl in a blend of muted colors of the rainbow with a wide silver fringe. She held it up for all to see, then carefully folded it up and put it back in the box and set the box aside. "I thank you very much, children. It is a lovely gift."

"It would look very well with the black gown you have on, Grandmother," Maria offered tentatively.

"Oh, my darling girl," her grandmother said in a shocked tone. "I am in mourning. As you should be as well. I could not possibly wear something so garish while I am still in mourning. I would not be so disrespectful to my son, your father."

Seeing the stricken look on Maria's face, Quint wanted to slap anyone who would so reject the good will of a child. He wanted to slap his own mother? His *mother*? He was grateful for that same twin's "Open yours, Uncle Quint."

His box was larger than his mother's and more cubical in shape. He made quick work of removing the wrapping and extracting the treasure within. "A hat? Hmm. And something else. Gloves." He withdrew a stylish beaver hat and a pair of white gloves.

"It is what civilian men are wearing these days, Uncle Quint," Phillip assured him, taking a seat on the couch with Quint. "Father and I wore the same size hats and he said you and he did as well, so it should fit, but if it does not, there is tool there that will help to size it properly."

Quint put the hat on, pushing the brim up slightly on the sides. "It feels fine. How do I look?" He preened a bit, trying to take some of the sting out of his mother's rather cold reception of her own gift. "Will I be able to blend in with the rest of England's finest on the streets of London?"

"Oh, yes. You look ever so handsome," Maria said, rallying from the set-down her grandmother had given her.

Just then the door opened and Harriet came in.

"Oh, dear. I missed the fun," she said, seeing Quint in the beaver hat.

He quickly removed it, saying, "It is truly a fine gift, but as gentlemen do not wear headgear indoors, I shall have to manufacture an excuse to wear this very, very soon. And the gloves are quite elegant too."

Harriet laughed and waved the male members of the group back into the seats from which they had risen when she entered the room. She herself sat in an upholstered chair matching the one the dowager occupied. "You would not believe the serious negotiations that went into the selection of that hat and that shawl."

"They are quite lovely gifts," the dowager said, "though somewhat inappropriate in my case."

"I am so sorry you feel that way," Harriet said. "Elizabeth and I both thought it very appropriate for half mourning, and my grandmother, Lady Hawthorne, quite agreed. Surely you cannot be faulted for going into half mourning at this late date."

Aha! Score one for Miss Mayfield, Quint thought, for he remembered very well his brother's telling him that in her day Lady Hawthorne had been known as one of the leading arbiters of London society.

His mother sniffed and shifted the subject slightly. "I cannot condone having the young Earl of Sedwick and his even younger brothers and sisters exposed to riffraff of the streets of London on a shopping expedition."

"Come now, Mother," Quint said. "They seem to have been well supervised. Have to learn the ways of the world sometime."

Suddenly four-year-old Elinor called in a little squeal, "Oh, look! Auntie Harry is wearing our pin. Our flower pin. Look!" She jumped from the settee where she sat next to Maria and dashed over to point at the brooch Harriet had pinned beneath her left shoulder.

All eyes turned to Harriet, who Quint thought looked disturbingly attractive this morning and possibly more formidable as an adversary than he had thought before. Her hair was so tightly confined in some sort of braided style that it was hard to remember the wild freedom it had represented the night before. He had not been wrong about that clear complexion or those eyes, though. They were definitely gray today—possibly reflective of the trim gray dress she wore. He noted the simple lines of the dress with a square neckline that showed the barest hint of cleavage. Somewhat reluctantly he brought his attention back to the scene unfolding before him.

"Do you 'member which flower is which?" Elinor was asking her aunt in a skeptical tone.

"Of course I do, you little imp," Harriet said. She reached down and lifted the little girl onto her lap without regard for wrinkling her dress. Elinor giggled as Harriet removed the brooch and held it in position near her own and the child's waists. "Elly, you point to the flower, and I shall tell you for whom it stands."

"Aw right, but if you get one wrong I get a extra biscuit at tea."

"We shall discuss that later."

As the child pointed to each jeweled flower, Harriet named the stone for the benefit of the grandmother and uncle and the name of the child for which it stood. "The blue lapis is Phillip. The gold topaz is Maria. The amethyst is Matilda. The garnet is Sarah. The aquamarines are Richard and Robert. And the pink crystal is—Oh, dear. I forget who that pink crystal stands for. Cousin Rebecca, maybe?"

Elinor looked up at Harriet, exasperated, her little fist on her waist. "Auntie Harry! You know very well the pink crystal is me! Pink crystal is Elly!"

"Ah, yes. Of course. How could I have forgot that?"

Elly shook her head. "You didn't forget. You was jus' teasin' me."

Harriet hugged her close and kissed her on the cheek. "Yes, I was. Now go and show this lovely brooch to your grandmother and to your uncle so they can know how lucky I am to have such a nice gift."

"Yes, ma'am."

As the pin made its way around the room, Maria related the story of its creation and Quint found himself reflecting on the difference between the ways these two women had made the children feel about their gifts. When the brooch was back in place on Miss Mayfield's gray dress, and Elly had returned to her seat with Maria and Matilda, Quint asked the group, "So—what was the most memorable aspect of your trip? The best thing you did or saw?"

They were all silent for a moment.

"The efflemunt," Elly said.

"The what?" he asked.

"She means the elephant at the Tower," one of the twins said. Quint did not exactly know which twin was which and he was sure they would try to trick him sooner or later, but he would be ready for that event.

"When Robby pushed Elly into the Serpentine," the other twin said, thus informing Quint that this speaker was Richard, whom he looked at more closely now. *Ah, yes. Exactly as the proud father of twins had once written: Richard had darker flecks in his eye color than Robert had. But Lord, they did, indeed, look alike.*

"What?" Lady Margaret all but screeched, aghast. "He did *what*?" She turned accusingly toward Harriet. "And just where were you when this was going on? The Serpentine! In Hyde Park yet! I knew we'd end up the laughingstock of the *ton*."

Harriet sighed. "It was an accident, Lady Margaret. Robby did not mean for her to fall into the pond. She was not hurt. She merely got wet."

"But she could have been injured. And with proper care, such an incident need never have occurred."

Maria said, "I enjoyed visiting Hatchard's bookshop the most." Quint was sure she intended her comment to divert the discussion from her grandmother's criticism.

"The exotic animals aside, I thought the Tower quite interesting," Phillip said, "but I think most intriguing was the reenactment of the Battle of Vitoria we saw at Vauxhall Gardens. I should like to discuss that some time with you, Uncle Quint."

"Of course, Phillip."

"Vauxhall Gardens!" The dowager was not even pretending to curb her disapproval as she glared at Harriet. "You took my grandchildren to Vauxhall Gardens?"

"I'm sorry, Aunt Harriet," Phillip said.

"Phillip and Maria were allowed to go, along with the eldest of Charles and Elizabeth's children—and their parents. Others in the party included Lord and Lady Hawthorne and Lord Beaconfield. We were well chaperoned and well protected. I would challenge even the highest stickler to find fault."

"This is not the first instance in which we have seen that you have a very different set of standards than those of the family of the Earl of Sedwick, is it, my dear?" the dowager said sweetly.

Quint could see that even the younger children were disturbed by the tenor this conversation was taking. "I think we can postpone this discussion for another time, Mother. Did you not tell me you and Mrs. Hartley were engaged to go shopping today?"

The dowager made a point of looking at the clock. "Oh, my goodness. Yes. She will think I have forgot her." She picked up the boxed gift she had laid aside earlier. "Thank you, children, for the lovely gift."

Quint was sure he imagined it, but it did seem that there was a collective sigh of relief as she left the room.

Chapter 6

Harriet's preconceptions of Colonel Burnes had been rather mixed. Older servants at the Hall—the housekeeper, cook, butler, and head groom—had all known him as a child or youth and quite liked him. Win had loved him dearly and Anne had admired him greatly. His mother doted on him. Especially after losing her elder son, she had turned her attentions to the second son and discovered a wealth of memories of him that she felt compelled to share—all of which showed him to be a paragon of English manhood. But Harriet knew very well, even before Lady Margaret announced it so blatantly, that her own standards were likely be very different from the dowager's.

Harriet had also read many of the letters that "Quint"—Lieutenant, then Captain, then Major, and finally Colonel Burnes had written to his brother, for Win had frequently shared those missives with his wife and sister-in-law. Thus Harriet was convinced that she had a somewhat different view of the man than the one his mother presented to the world. However, to say she felt she had a firm understanding of his character would be a gross misstatement. And certainly her own intensely physical reaction to the man the night before had come as a surprise. She watched him carefully now in his initial interaction with his nieces and nephews—*her* nieces and nephews.

As soon as her grandmother left the room, six-year-old Sarah slipped from the footstool to which she had been relegated and marched over to the couch where Quint and Phillip sat.

"May I sit with you?" she asked politely.

"Why, of course," Quint said, scooting over slightly and patting the cushion next to him. "Phillip and I would be delighted to have a lady join us."

Phillip, too, moved slightly as she plopped herself between them. She made a show of sedately smoothing her skirt and looked up at her uncle.

"We saw the Prince Regent in London," she confided.

"Did you now?"

"On a white horse. He was dressed in a fancy red uniform. With lots of gold."

"Lots of gold, eh?" Quint encouraged.

"Yes." Sarah leaned close and lowered her voice. "He is quite fat, you know."

"He is?"

She nodded very seriously, and Harriet saw that Quint's eyes were fairly dancing.

"It was a parade," Richard explained.

"I had gathered as much," Quint said, apparently willingly diverting his attention to that twin. "I understand Prince George likes military parades."

Two-year-old Matilda had apparently had enough of being a good little girl, and Maria had apparently reached her limits in coping with both of the youngest ones.

"I want *dooowwwn!*" Tilly demanded in a loud voice and wriggled to the floor, her dress hiked around her chubby little legs in the process.

"Come here, Tilly." Harriet leaned forward and extended her arms as the child stood up and toddled toward her, casting her eyes at the man who held everyone's interest. Then she seemed to decide she could observe the rest of the proceedings very well from the throne of her aunt's lap.

"She is such a babe," Elly announced in her most grown-up voice—such wisdom coming, of course, from her two years advantage in age over the clan's youngest.

"Did you kill any frogs while you was in the war, Uncle Quint?" Robby asked.

Ricky hit him on the shoulder. "Aunt Harriet told us not to ask 'im that—an' not to call 'em 'frogs.'"

Quint exchanged a look of understanding and pain with Harriet, but said, "It is all right, Robert, though that is not a good word to be using. Yes, I suppose I did. I fought many *French soldiers*. However, killing is not something one likes to talk about."

"Oh." The boy dipped his head self-consciously.

"I have been trying to think of something we might all do together," Quint said, clearly diverting the subject from killing. "Something fun. What if we were all to go on a picnic—say, at the old Abbey Ruins, as long as the weather holds?"

This brought bursts of delight all around, with even Tilly clapping her hands and giggling happily, though Harriet doubted she understood what she was approving.

"Auntie Harry too?" Elly insisted, slightly worried.

"Of course," Quint assured her. "Grandmother too. It might be one of our last chances for a family party before the older ones go off to school."

"School?" The single word was repeated in different tones, none distinctly positive. Harriet observed dread in Maria's expression and downright panic in Phillip's.

"A picnic sounds like a marvelous idea," Harriet said quickly. "Perhaps we can discuss school and other future matters later. Right now, it is such a beautiful day, and even if a bit chilly, it is a shame to waste it indoors. Why do we not all take a turn in the gardens before it is time for the midday meal?"

"That sounds like a splendid idea." Quint stood, thus signaling all to rise. "I shall wear my new hat for the first time."

As they were leaving the morning room in pursuit of sweaters or shawls, Quint touched Harriet's elbow to hold her back for a moment. "What was that about?"

"We need to discuss the subject of school."

"There is nothing to discuss."

* * * *

The gardens at Sedwick Hall had been laid out in the previous century by a very capable horticulturalist of the day, and successive earls had been wise enough to employ others who respected the knowledge and expertise of that original expert. The gardens themselves occupied several acres of land that lay next to a vast acreage of forest, eventually giving way to farmland. Besides many well-planned walking paths, they offered a variety of vistas to please the eye, ranging from carefully pruned topiary and strategically placed stone fountains and benches to an area that was allowed to grow naturally—or at least appear to do so—and included a large pond. There was also a maze that provided endless fun, especially for the twins.

Harriet was glad to see that she had not been wrong about the weather. It was a lovely day. English summers were likely to be uncertain, even in late July, but this day was turning out to be perfect. She had gathered up Nurse Tavenner to accompany them, largely to be prepared to return Matilda or Elinor to the nursery if necessary, so Harriet was free to lag behind and merely observe as the colonel furthered his acquaintance with his young relatives. She was not surprised to see that the entourage had somehow grown to include Muffin and Sir Gawain. The "kitten" was now nearly full grown, though Elly insisted on holding it as much as the feline would allow. The twins never tired of sending the collie chasing after a ball or stick and the dog never tired of the game. When the cat wriggled free to join the melee, children and adults alike laughed hysterically.

Harriet could not have said why she was surprised, but she was, to see the ease with which the colonel seemed to get on with the children. He answered questions patiently, even when he had just answered the same question only a moment before. At one point he had even stooped to hoist a giggling Tilly onto his shoulder. They arrived at an area near the "wilderness" section where a gazebo had been built and swings fashioned on the limbs of two huge oak trees.

"Ah. I'd forgot these were here," Quint said a bit wistfully. "Your father and I used to spend hours out here."

Sarah dashed ahead. "Come on, Pip. Push me," she demanded of Phillip, who readily complied.

"No. Me," Elly said.

"There are two swings, Elinor. You may have your turn," her uncle told her.

"Will *you* push me?"

"If you ask nicely."

"Please?"

"That is the magic word. Of course." As he turned Matilda over to Nurse Tavenner, he caught Harriet staring at him and grinned a bit impishly.

She had to grin back, for it did seem rather ridiculous for a man to wear a top hat to push a child on a swing. The twins soon lost interest in tossing the ball and stick for the dog to chase and joined the group at the swing. Harriet turned around to see where Maria had gone. She spotted the girl sitting on a bench under the branches of a willow overhanging the bank of the pond.

"Aha!" she said in mock challenge as she approached. "Just as I suspected. You managed to sneak a book along on our outing."

"And I thought I hid it so well. But you know I rarely go *anywhere* without a book."

"I know." Harriet sat on the end of the bench and said in pretended shock. "People are beginning to talk about a certain Lady Maria Burnes. They say she is nearly as bad that aunt of hers! Poor young lady. She is in danger of becoming a proper bluestocking!"

Maria closed her book, pursed her lips, and shook her head in a gesture of despair. She heaved a sigh. "Well, I do suppose there are worse fates to befall one. Though perhaps not, to hear Grandmother tell the tale."

"Oh, dear. Has she been haranguing you?"

"She happened to see all those books I bought at Hatchard's."

"Did you not show her your new dresses?"

"Yes. That diverted her attention, but only a bit." Maria grinned, then her expression sobered. "Aunt Harriet—"

"Yes, dear?"

Maria heaved a heavy sigh. "Aunt Harriet, neither Phillip nor I want to go away to school this autumn. We just do not want to leave—not yet. Phillip, especially. Even before we went to London, Grandmother talked about our going and we did not like the idea. Just the thought of not being at home—of not seeing the others—" Her voice trailed off on something like a sob. "Y-you know Papa and Mama were going to examine a school for me when—"

"Maria, you must be properly educated," Harriet said gently, pulling the girl close.

"I know. We both know. It's just that losing Papa and Mama, now the idea of losing everything else—don't you see?"

"Yes, I do understand. Truly I do."

"Going away to school is not the only way to be educated, is it?" Maria asked. "I mean, we are not exactly uneducated for our ages, are we? I felt quite comfortable with Rebecca and Jeremy."

"No, you are not," Harriet said emphatically. "You are both quite advanced for your ages. I am very proud of you. Your parents would be too."

"Thank you." Maria was quiet for a moment, her head on Harriet's shoulder, then she sat up straight and said, "I'm a year older than Phillip, I think I could bear up if Uncle Quint makes us go away, but, Aunt Harriet, you know how Phillip is, how he worries about every little thing—especially now that he is Sedwick and everyone keeps telling him how responsible he has to be for all of us and everything now he is the earl. He—he's just not ready!"

"I think your uncle has his mind made up about the issue of school, but the term does not begin for a few weeks yet. I will talk with him, but do not get your hopes up." She repeated: "Do. Not. Get. Your. Hopes. Up."

A short while later, observing that both Matilda and Elinor had probably had enough of this outing, Harriet suggested that she and Nurse Tavenner would take the females of the party back to the Hall and leave the gentlemen to their pursuits, whereupon Colonel Burnes agreed that, indeed, it had been a splendid outing and as soon as he could get the twins down from the tree they had climbed, the males of the party would follow suit.

* * * *

Although breakfast this morning—the first after their return from London—had been an exception, Phillip and Maria often took their meals with the adults of the household, unless guests were being entertained in the Hall. Harriet remembered with fondness how Win and Anne had made a big ceremony of inviting their two eldest to join them that first time, on the occasion of Phillip's tenth birthday.

"Primitive tribes have their rites of passage. This will suffice for the family Burnes," Win had said with a laugh.

As Anne explained it to Harriet, "Phillip and Maria must be able to comport themselves acceptably—and comfortably—at table. You do remember how Nana introduced us to that strangely formal world of adults?"

Phillip had declared at the time that henceforth he would refer to his parents as "Father" and "Mother," but Harriet had often heard him slip into the comfort of the more familiar "Papa" and "Mama."

Harriet had readily fallen in with the change in dining custom, though the dowager had had reservations. *At least Lady Margaret has not seen fit to consign Phillip and Maria back to the nursery table—yet,* she thought as she prepared to go down for the midday meal. When she arrived in the dining room, she was glad to see that apparently the colonel had no objections to dining with the eldest of his charges. The dowager and her companion being still out, four places had been set at one end of the long table. The colonel and both youngsters had already arrived when Harriet entered the dining room, and the uncle now directed the seating.

"We shall begin as we mean to continue," he said rather formally. "Phillip, as you are Sedwick now, you shall sit at the head of the table. Miss Mayfield, will you sit at his right in the place of an honored guest? Maria will sit on his left, and I shall sit next to her. Since there are only the four of us, we shall dispense with that nonsense about not talking across or down the table, but I assume we all do know the usual rules."

"Phillip and Maria surely do. I may need a gentle reminder now and then," she said with a smile.

She was pleased when, with no prodding and without glancing to see his uncle perform the same service for Maria, Phillip held her chair and waited for her and Maria to be seated before sitting himself. Harriet gave him a secret quick wink and a smile. She thought both children somewhat subdued during the meal, the main course of which was a white fish sautéed in butter and served with a lemon sauce, plus side dishes of new potatoes and fresh peas. Though restrained, the children were more than willing and able to uphold their share of proper table conversation ranging from the weather—of course—to more of their adventures in London, and a series of highway robberies plaguing the area recently, which the Sedwick travelers had happily not encountered.

"The weather undoubtedly discouraged them," Harriet said.

"We were well guarded," Maria said.

"Still, 'tis lucky you avoided them," Quint noted. "These are said to be ex-soldiers, so might be more dangerous than ordinary highwaymen."

Phillip's eyes lit up when a footman set his dessert dish in front of him. "Trifle! Hodgie remembered it's my favorite!"

"Mine, too," his uncle said. "Whose favor do you think she is trying to curry? Yours? Or mine?"

"Maybe she just likes to please?" Harriet suggested on seeing Phillip's expression become more speculative than sparkling.

"Perhaps," the colonel said with a nod of acquiescence. He turned to Phillip, but included Maria in his next comment, "There is a new foal in the stable. You might like to look in on it when you have finished here."

"Sundance had her babe? I knew she would do so while we were gone. Did I not tell you so?" Maria said to her brother.

"'I told you so,'" he said mockingly. "Well, do let us go and see it." He started to rise, then sat back down, turned to Harriet, said in a formal tone, "May we please be excused?"

She looked at the colonel and then nodded, amused at seeing his tolerant consideration of this little sibling byplay.

His tone was rather chilly, however, as he asked, "Miss Mayfield, will you join me in the library, please?"

Oh, dear. Now what? She did not bother to try to make idle conversation as they strolled down the hall to the library. Preceding him through the door he held open for her, she caught a whiff of sandalwood as she brushed past him, and she noted that he had apparently ordered a small fire to be lit to take off any shred of chill in the room and give it a distinct sense of welcome. He gestured her toward the beige wing chairs that flanked the fireplace. She waited expectantly for him to say whatever was on his mind.

When they were both seated, he said in a flat tone, "Are you, by any chance, the one who put a flea in Phillip's ear about his going off to school this autumn?"

"Am I wha-at?" she asked, on the edge of being outraged.

"I think you understood me. Phillip accosted me in the garden this morning. Drew me aside as we waited for Richard and Robert to disentangle themselves from the tree they had climbed. Phillip just stood there, his arms folded in that way that Win always had, and told me quite earnestly that he preferred not to go away to school this autumn."

"And you responded with—?"

"I told him with no equivocation whatsoever that he absolutely would be going to Eton this year, that six generations of Sedwick earls before him—and their brothers too—had been educated there and he was *not* going to be the exception to that rule."

Harriet drew in a deep breath. "Phillip has had a very difficult time adjusting to the death of his parents," she said tentatively. "Perhaps because they are older and so close, he and Maria have felt the loss keenly."

"Yes. Well, we all have. But life does go on, does it not? They cannot go through life as uneducated dolts. That I cannot—I will not—allow."

"Colonel Burnes! Neither Phillip nor Maria is what any right-thinking person might label a 'dolt'! They have attended the vicar's day school, as have the twins and Sarah, and in recent years the vicar has given them extra lessons as well. What is more, their *parents*, as you well know, were well-educated and they saw to additional opportunities for all their children."

"A vicar's day school hardly constitutes a complete educational program," he said dismissively. "Most vicars are barely literate themselves in my experience."

"Sir, have you met Mr. Powers?"

"Haven't had that dubious pleasure yet. But my point stands: my brother's children are not being educated to the positions they may hope to assume in the English world one day."

Harriet sat silent for a moment. *How to get through to this obtuse man?*

"Miss Mayfield?" he prodded.

"Colonel Burnes, I am not sure how much time you actually spent with your brother and his family when you were home on leave a few years ago."

"A fair amount, I would say."

"Then you know that as *ton* parents go, they were quite unusual."

"I know they were not only besotted with each other, but they doted on that lot in the nursery."

"Yes, they did. But not to the point of doing 'that lot' injury. They spent far more time with their children than I gather your parents ever spent with you."

"What is your point, Miss Mayfield?"

She sighed. "These children and their parents were very close, but beyond that, the children themselves are very close—just as I gather you and Win were as children and then when you went away to school—*together.* You are proposing to send Phillip and Maria away from the others *and* from each other."

"Good God, woman! They can hardly go to the same school. Last I heard, Eton was not admitting females."

"I know. But does it have to be now? This year? Did Phillip tell you he *never* wanted to go to Eton? And don't swear at me!"

"I apologize." He glared at her, then ran his hand through his hair. "I don't think he said it exactly like that, but he is already twelve years old. His father and I were ten when we went. That is, Win was ten. I was nine."

"But you went together."

"Perhaps the twins could go too. It is not unknown for students to be that young."

"Oh, my heavens! They are just babes! What about Maria? Are you going to send six-year-old Sarah off to keep Maria company? Or why not Elly? Or Tilly?" Harriet had to pause, for she knew if she went on much longer, she would burst into tears.

"Oh, for—" He ran his hand through his hair again. "Now you are being silly. And you are refusing to acknowledge the basic point that these children need an education commensurate with the positions they will expect to hold in life as adults."

Harriet drew in a deep breath and, resisting the urge to grab a pillow from a nearby couch and throw it at him, she said calmly, "While we were in London, I took the liberty of exercising to the full the authority Winston had given me in his will regarding the children when you were unavailable."

"Why am I wary of whatever you are about to say?"

"I have no idea. But what I did was this: I had Phillip and Maria, the twins, and Sarah all examined rigorously by Sir Charles's son's tutor and my own former governess to try to determine the level at which each of them would be placed in one of London's finest day schools."

"And—?"

"Robert is the only one who functions intellectually at his age level."

"There. You see?"

"The others are above or far above their contemporaries."

"Oh." He looked thoughtful. "Well, then. Phillip and Maria should do very well in their respective schools this year."

"You are adamant about this decision then?" She could not hide her dismay.

"Yes, Miss Mayfield. I am quite determined to do what is right for *my* wards—regardless of whether you or they agree at any given moment."

Thinking that he might be making an effort to control his own anger, she merely rose and said, "So be it, then." However, she could not help muttering under her breath as she left, "But there *are* alternatives!"

"I heard that!" he called as she closed the door.

Chapter 7

Having risen from his seat when Harriet left the room, Quint stood with his hands on his hips, shaking his head in some confusion at the closed door. *Damn!* he thought, *that woman could drive a man crazy if he allowed her to.* It annoyed him that he found himself distracted by her person—by that trim figure, those intriguing eyes, and a smile that flashed unexpectedly and dazzled. He marveled at the easy rapport she had with the children. It also annoyed him that her questioning the matter of schooling for Phillip, especially, was causing him to entertain second thoughts on the issue, even for a moment. *Of course* the boy would go to Eton *and of course* he would do so in the next school term. Adults had to act in the best interests of children for whom they were responsible, even when others, including the children, raised objections. A child whose future held a seat in the House of Lords needed an education equal to that of his peers. And Quint intended to see that one Phillip Burnes, Seventh Earl of Sedwick, was *at least* equal to his peers.

As for Maria's schooling, he was feeling magnanimous enough to leave himself open to the choice of school for his niece. After all, what did he know of schools for females? Perhaps there was mention of specific schools for the girls in his brother's papers. With that thought, he strolled across the room to the huge oak desk, the contents of which he had not yet forced himself to examine. He glanced at the mantel clock. *No time like the present.*

He spent the rest of the afternoon poring over a mass of documents that had been shoved haphazardly into the various drawers of the desk and a glass-doored cabinet behind it. He was amused, but also shocked at the incredible disorder he found there. He chuckled to himself. *Win was never very organized, but good grief, some of these things were signed by our father!* Besides dozens of loose papers, there were several ledgers with entries dating back forty years. When he had been at it for about two hours and arranged the loose papers in several neat stacks, he stood and sent for his man Gibbons.

"Chet, I think I have found something truly worthy of our talents. You have always had a better head for numbers than I have, so perhaps you can help me make some sense of this mess."

"Yes, sir. 'Twill be a welcome change from shining those boots you near ruined the other day."

"I did not drag you into the wilds of Derbyshire to serve as my valet!"

"I know. I know. But I doubt any of these pretty boy footmen can produce a proper shine on these things."

"What would your Scottish laird da say of your doing such work?"

Chet snorted. "Who cares? Did he no like it, he shouldna ha' sent his baby boy off to fight alongside ye Sassenach devils."

Quint laughed. "Good job for me he did! Anyway, you are my *guest* while you are here, so stop lurking around the servants' hall."

"Yes, sir, Colonel, sir," Chet mocked. "I thought to give you some time to get acquainted with your charges."

"Thank you."

"An' I must say getting acquainted with their aunt shouldna be too painful."

Quint merely rolled his eyes and gestured at the paperwork.

Chet pulled up a chair next to Quint's and the two of them worked at sorting tradesmen's bills and invoices for farm equipment and animals, and for machinery and supplies for woolen mills and cottage weavers. Tucked away in a hidden drawer he had found a dismaying number of what could only be vouchers from gaming tables with some intriguing handwriting and dates. Win had often worried in his letters about the state of finances in the earldom, but the situation was far worse than Quint had expected from the cursory inspections he and Chet had made in their first few days. Those little jaunts about the countryside had revealed some obvious repairs needed—a fence here, a roof there, a shed or a barn falling down. Yet, overall, the morale of tenants and cottage workers seemed higher than Quint might have expected. They had not yet visited the mills, however.

Finally, Chet leaned back in his chair. "Kind of like looking at muddled battle plans, ain't it? But this is sort of sad. I feel sorry for that young lad."

"It's a bloody disaster!" Quint said. "The land is entailed, so it is protected, but there is no money for improvements to it or the farms. The mills were not entailed, so they are mortgaged to the hilt—which is the worst of it, for in the last forty years or so, the mills have been the principal source of Sedwick wealth."

"So what happened, do you think? Not that it's any of my business," Chet said apologetically.

Quint snorted. "I don't think. I know. My father and my grandfather could not resist a throw of the dice or the turn of a hand of cards. My brother inherited a mess. He did his best, but it was not good enough. Now Phillip is faced with it."

"Can you save it?"

"I have to try."

* * * *

I have to try. I have to try. The words pounded in his brain like a mantra as he put the papers and ledgers back into the desk and cabinet—in far better order than he had found them—and later as he dressed for supper with the family. It was as he dressed that he pulled from a pocket a paper he had stuffed there earlier. On it was written the name of a school, Miss Penelope Pringle's School for Young Ladies of Quality, and an address in the city of Bath, as well as a date. Quint looked again at the date. *Good God! Win and Anne were on their way to or from checking out this school when they died!* Now he supposed he would have to do so too, but he put that matter out of his mind for the moment.

Instead he allowed his mind to drift to the more diverting image of Miss Mayfield, telling himself that her presence had come as a pleasant surprise. However, he cautioned himself not to let a pretty face distract him, for he suspected this was a woman of very decided opinions, and she could either be a formidable adversary or a welcomed partner. He hoped for the latter.

He chuckled to himself. Had he not already seen her worth as an ally? It had been only a couple of years ago, but he remembered writing Win about the hardships his men were enduring in their fight against the elements during a cold, wet autumn. Officers could usually be billeted in homes or cottages, however rude, in the villages, but the men were left to fend for themselves: dig holes in the ground and pull branches or debris over themselves to provide some protection. It seemed no matter how many times Wellington appealed to Parliament for a simple thing like tents, the men of that august body turned a deaf ear. Then the Lady Senator had blistered those ears in one of her essays and apparently her readers, especially the mothers among them, had taken note. Quint had recognized with both pride and amusement some of his own phrases in her essay. Within weeks, tents were on their way to the Peninsula.

After that incident, Colonel Lord Quinton Burnes had become an avid reader of the Lady Senator's work, which he always found entertaining, though he did not always agree with the positions she took—too reformist by half! Just consider her recent treatise on labor unrest. Did that silly female mind not comprehend the impact that thousands of demobilized soldiers was having on the labor situation? And now she was apparently putting her reformist nose into the matter of educating the aristocracy— beginning with the new Earl of Sedwick. It simply would not do.

Bolstered by this sense of determination, he entered the drawing room to find the others before him, except for Chet, who was still leaving the family to itself. His mother and her companion had returned from their shopping trip; Miss Mayfield had come down with Phillip and Maria. The youngsters were sitting on either end of a horsehair sofa drinking lemonade. Both Maria and Phillip had changed for the evening meal, but both still wore subdued clothing, Maria's dress a dull mauve. With glasses of ratafia on a small table nearby, the older ladies occupied red barrel chairs, the dowager in her black bombazine, and her companion in gray. Miss Mayfield, on a dark gray couch, held a glass of sherry in her hand.

"Sorry if I kept you all waiting," he said, going to the sideboard to pour himself a whiskey, then taking a seat in a chair near the couch. In a quick glance he noted with appreciation that Miss Mayfield's gown this evening was definitely more blue than gray, and that it definitely showed more of that delectable cleavage than her garment of the day had shown. She had again attached the flower brooch to her dress and added some aquamarine earrings that swayed and sparkled as she moved her head.

"Oh, not at all, my son," his mother said. "Sylvia and I scarcely had time to change when we returned from Hendley. Such a pleasant outing we had. I think every time I go into town, there are at least two new shops to explore."

"We had quite a nice outing here too," he said, his smile including his wards and their aunt.

"Ohhh?" His mother drew out the single syllable in almost disbelief.

"Yes, Grandmother," Maria eagerly picked up the conversation. "We reacquainted Uncle Quint with the gardens."

"I hope you noticed that they need some tending to," the dowager said.

Quint nodded. "The gazebo needs some repair, and the boathouse definitely needs to have one wall replaced. I did not check the boats."

"They were mostly all right in May. Before we left for London, the twins and I took one out," Phillip said.

"I do hope you had proper supervision," his grandmother said hastily, with an accusing glance at Harriet.

Phillip heaved what could only be deemed an adolescent sigh. "Yes, Grandmother. Tom, the footman, sat on the bank. Though we *can* all swim, you know. Father saw to that last summer. Even Maria and Sarah can swim."

The older woman pursed her lips. "Shocking. That is what I say. Shocking that a mother would allow her daughters to engage in such unladylike behavior."

Harriet lifted a hand in weak protest. "I believe their father was quite insistent that all the children should learn to swim what with there being such a large pond on the property."

"And you do know how persistent Win could be when he got a bee in his bonnet," Quint said, and finished his drink.

"Hmmphf." The dowager rose. "Shall we all go down then?"

Quint jumped to his feet and gestured at Phillip to offer his grandmother his arm, which the boy dutifully did. He then offered his own to Miss Mayfield, and waited for Maria and the companion, Mrs. Hartley, to precede them down the stairs.

"Thank you," Harriet whispered.

He looked at her questioningly.

"For coming to Phillip's rescue—and possibly mine."

* * * *

The supper finished, Phillip and Maria asked to be excused as the adults again repaired to the drawing room. Quint declared that he had no intention of remaining in the dining room imbibing port or anything else in solitary splendor, and joined the ladies for tea. As Lady Margaret presided over the brewing tea a footman had delivered, Harriet mused silently at how pleased she had been that Phillip and Maria had comported themselves so well this evening. She doubted even the dowager could find anything about which to quibble.

"So," Quint said conversationally as he accepted the cup of tea his mother had prepared for him and took his seat, "we know that Mother and Mrs. Hartley had a successful shopping expedition. How did you spend the rest of the afternoon, Miss Mayfield?"

"Writing, mostly." She lifted her hands for all to see. "'Tis a wonder I was able to remove all the ink stains. I did not want to appear at the dining table with blackened fingertips."

"It would not have been for the first time, though, would it, my dear?" Lady Margaret asked sweetly.

Harriet laughed. "Probably not."

"May we know what it is you are working on?" asked the usually quiet Sylvia Hartley.

"An essay on the lives of working people," Harriet replied. "Actually, it is to be a series of at least three articles—if I can just manage to whip those words into shape."

Lady Margaret gave a tiny, very ladylike shudder, careful not to slosh the tea in her cup. "I simply do not understand why a lady of your position in society should trouble herself about those kinds of people."

"Perhaps because we are the very sorts of persons who *should* be so troubled?" Harriet asked innocently.

"We do what we can," the dowager said. "Why Mrs. Hartley and I dropped off a bundle of clothing and linens at the vicarage just today as we were on our way." She turned to the business of handing around a plate of biscuits to go with the tea.

"And are the words shaping up well?" Quint asked.

Harriet suspected he was deliberately deflecting what might be his mother's next line of discussion. "I misspoke. It is not so much that the *words* are not cooperating as that I simply do not have enough solid information at hand."

"Hmm. I can see where it would be difficult to write about a topic in which one's knowledge is limited," he said with a grin.

Is he belittling me or my work? Harriet wondered, but she replied, "I certainly feel I have knowledge of a general nature—facts and figures from government documents and newspapers and so on—but I need the sorts of details that bring a story to life, that catch the reader's imagination."

"I am not certain I understand what it is you think you need, Miss Mayfield," Mrs. Hartley said. Sylvia Hartley, Harriet often thought, was one of those basically shy women to whom fate had not been at all kind. Rather plain and self-deprecating, she had not only been left a childless widow at a young age, but she had been left without enough fortune to sustain her. She was the perfect foil for the more robust, decisive dowager, but Harriet felt more sympathy than affection for the little companion.

Harriet turned to her. "I need to know how these people actually live. Who they are. Where they come from. What they eat. What religion they practice. What they read, if they can do so. The sorts of information that is usually missing in official papers."

"I should think you'd best leave well enough alone," the dowager said. "We do not need any more needless gossip touching on our family going the rounds. Speaking of which—" She paused dramatically before continuing, "I had a letter recently from my friend Lady Martha Frobisher, and she imparted some rather startling information regarding your sojourn in London."

Harriet closed her eyes momentarily and steeled herself for what might be coming. Lady Martha was one of the *ton's* most infamous tattlemongers— the more salacious the gossip, the better.

"Did she now?" Harriet asked, trying to sound indifferent.

"Yes, she certainly did. You may be interested to know, Quinton, dear, that your wards have been paraded about in a bizarre replay of Snow White and the Seven Dwarfs."

Harriet felt the man's gaze turn to her, but she could not bring herself to look at him directly. *Well, it was only a matter of time until that ridiculous story reached Derbyshire. England's mail is nothing if not efficient.*

"I knew it would come to something like this," the dowager went on. "Now it is just as I predicted: my grandchildren are the laughingstock of the *ton.*"

"Truly, Lady Margaret, your friend rather exaggerates that *on dit,*" Harriet protested. "It was but a casual comment of a young woman seeking attention. A few foolish but forgettable words spoken in haste." She leaned forward to set her cup on a low table before the couch on which she sat. "And, in any event, that snide remark was aimed at me, not my nieces and nephews."

The dowager looked at her with a lifted eyebrow. "Nevertheless, I cannot condone the idea of our name being bandied about in idle gossip. We must protect the children from such. Would you not agree, Quinton dear?"

At last Harriet allowed herself to look at him directly and tried not to be distracted by what an attractive man he was. Even in civilian attire and slouched comfortably in an easy chair, he seemed to exude the same aura of control and confidence that one saw in that portrait of him on the stairway. He smiled at her and shook his head. "Sounds like something less than a tempest in a teapot to me," he said. "In fact, it sounds rather amusing, but one of those things that is probably much funnier in the event than in the retelling."

"Exactly," Harriet said.

The dowager merely sighed and turned her attention to replenishing her tea.

Sylvia Hartley apparently felt compelled to fill the conversational gap. "We have had such a lovely summer. I do hope we may continue to enjoy fine weather into the autumn."

The dowager set aside her teacup and sat even straighter than usual. "That reminds me, Quinton dear. I have not had occasion to bring this matter up with you before, but I am planning to host a house party in late September and October. It will be like old times when your father and I hosted a house party every autumn. Sylvia and I have been busily planning it for the last month or so and making a guest list."

Harriet was sure this came as an unwelcome surprise to the woman's son, for he put aside his own cup and sat up straight to stare at his mother. "You have done what?"

"I am planning a house party. We shall no longer be officially in mourning, and besides renewing a Sedwick tradition that was unfortunately ignored in recent years, the party will present a splendid opportunity to announce our return to society—*and* reintroduce my beloved son to the society he has missed all these years in serving his country."

"Have you already sent out invitations?" he asked.

"Not formally. But I have mentioned it in correspondence with a few of my friends to be sure they will not accept invitations from others, you see."

Quint sat in rigid silence for several moments, then rubbed his knuckles along his jaw. "I do wish you had mentioned this earlier. Had written me before I came home. I would have tried to discourage you."

"Why ever would you do that?" she demanded in a hurt tone. "I have not had a chance to host such a party in years and years and I used to do so frequently. The late countess was not so inclined, but I was known as a splendid hostess, if I do say it myself."

"To put it bluntly, Mother, it is an expense Sedwick can ill afford right now. I remember very well some of those parties you and Father hosted. Twenty or thirty or more people. They went on for weeks. Food and drink alone must have cost a small fortune—not to mention entertainment."

"But a house party is such fun," his mother protested. "Winston did not bring up finances when I mentioned it to him last year."

"Win approved this affair?" he asked.

"Um—not precisely, but he did not object to it."

"He probably did not really consider it at the time and then forgot about it," Quint said. "Lord knows he had plenty on his mind in the last year or so."

"Well, they certainly were not things he shared with his mother," the dowager said.

"They would not be, would they? But under the circumstances, I seriously doubt my brother would have given approval for this sort of thing."

"Are you forbidding me to do this? When I have already told a few of my friends..." She sounded as though she might dissolve into tears—a phenomenon Harriet had not witnessed in Lady Margaret before.

Quint sighed. "No, Mother. I am not forbidding you your house party. I know as well as anyone that 'a few of your friends' constitutes half the *ton*. In effect, you have handed me a *fait accompli*. You will kindly not do that again, for there will have to be some serious economizing measures taken if Sedwick is to survive as even a shadow of itself."

"Surely you exaggerate, my son."

Harriet wondered how the woman could sound both triumphant and condescending, but her son was clearly having no more of it. He stood and stared at the older woman directly. "No, Mother, I do not. I do not know the full extent of what we shall have to do—I must meet with the bankers and other creditors first—but at the very least, I fear we will have to lease out the London townhouse for a few years. Now, if you will excuse me—" He reached for the door.

"No-o-o," she whimpered as he closed the door behind him. "He cannot mean it. Give up the house in Mayfair? Not go to London for the season?"

"Perhaps it will not require such drastic measures, my lady," the companion said soothingly.

"There is nothing else for it," the dowager said, almost as though she were talking to herself. "I shall have to see Quinton suitably married and, when the time comes, that Phillip, too, chooses the right sort of bride. No more of these imprudent love matches." Brightening, she turned to her companion and said in a more cheerful tone, "Tomorrow morning, Sylvia, we shall go over our guest list again."

"Yes, ma'am."

"I shall, of course, invite the Hawthorne and Montieth family connections," Lady Margaret said to Harriet. "Do you think they might come?"

"Grandfather dislikes traveling, but he dearly loves company and he adores his great-grandchildren," Harriet said. "I think it highly likely that Charles and Elizabeth would agree to accompany him and Nana."

"Good." The older woman sat in silence for some moments, but Harriet could tell that she had something else on her mind. Finally, she said, "I wonder, my dear Harriet, if you have given any thought to the fact that if I were to return to the dower house, that Sedwick Hall would, in effect, be a bachelor residence?"

"What? What are you suggesting?"

"I am suggesting nothing. Merely pointing out that my son is an unmarried man and you are an unmarried woman. Were I not available as chaperone, your presence here would be most improper."

"Never mind the fact that there are seven children and perhaps as many as fifty servants on the premises," Harriet said. *What on earth is behind this? Does she think to get rid of me?* She sat still, her hands in her lap, her fingers entwined, trying to look relaxed.

"Children and servants are not considered proper chaperones," the dowager said.

"And *are* you planning to move back to the dower house?" Harriet asked. "I thought you had settled in here quite firmly."

"Well, I always have that option, do I not?"

"Perhaps we can deal with this problem when it becomes one," Harriet said. "I have always felt welcome here."

"Oh, I did mean to suggest that you are not welcome."

Did you not? Harriet thought bitterly.

"But you must consider also that Quinton may marry and I am sure a new wife would not want either of us underfoot, now would she?"

"Is he planning to marry?" Harriet asked, wondering why that idea should be repugnant to her.

"Well, not immediately," Lady Margaret said with a laugh, "but surely one day—"

"Another issue that can be dealt with later, I think." Harriet stood. "For now, I am rather tired, so I bid you a good night."

She was more annoyed than furious at Lady Margaret's not-so-subtle hint that she should remove herself from Sedwick Hall. Were it not for the children, of course, she would do so in a heartbeat. But she could not bring herself to desert them. Not yet. Not while there was so much need still unfulfilled.

Her mind turned to the topic that had obviously been uppermost in the colonel's mind this evening. Harriet was sure she had always had a better understanding of the earldom's financial affairs than the dowager had, for Win had always been quite frank in discussing things with his wife and her sister. The Sixth Earl of Sedwick had not been one of those men who undervalued the brains of women. In fact, Harriet had often thought her sister had been attracted to Lord Winston Burnes in part because he resembled Lord Hawthorne in some respects. However, finance was not a topic the dowager had ever been comfortable discussing. So long as her pin money was available, it had never seemed to occur to her to ask where it came from.

And just who are you even to think of criticizing? Harriet chastised herself as she sat her desk dawdling over the diary she kept faithfully every night. Had she not only half listened to Win's laments? After all, the running of the Sedwick earldom had never been any of her business, had it? Actually, had she not more or less blindly gone about her own affairs all her adult life, paying but little heed to matters like the wherewithal to make those affairs transpire satisfactorily? That visit with the Hawthorne solicitor had torn the blinders away and brought her face to face with the realities of responsibility as well as privilege of great wealth. She was aware that she could probably ease many of the problems at Sedwick, if not erase them. But how far dare she go? She was reluctant to interfere beyond what she had already done. To do so would be presumptuous and the colonel would likely see her concern as just meddling. And besides, *I still do not know this man. How could I even think of betraying Phillip by giving so much power to someone who had yet to prove his worth?*

She rang the bell pull for her maid. She and Phillip were to go riding early the following morning.

Chapter 8

When Harriet arrived at the stables the next morning, she found Phillip there before her. He and Dolan, the head groom, were just outside the door of the stables, putting the finishing touches on saddling Phillip's pony and Harriet's mare. The sun, already promising a warm day, had dried away much of night's moisture, and birds were offering a pleasant if somewhat discordant greeting to the coming day.

"Good morning," she called, tossing Phillip an apple for his pony as she snuggled up to her mare with another for it and murmured, "Did you miss me, Miss Priss?" as she stroked the animal's muzzle.

"I'm sure she did, Miss Harriet," Dolan said, "though we exercised 'em all real good while ye was all gone—'specially after the colonel an' his friend arrived 'bout two weeks ago. Good to have ye back now."

"It is good to be back." She looked at Phillip. "Shall we be off, then?"

He glanced toward the door of the stable, nodded, and came around to help her mount.

"Here. I'll do that, Phillip."

Harriet whirled around, surprised to see Colonel Burnes hand the reins of a majestic black stallion to another rider beside him and come to stand before her. "Good morning, Miss Mayfield. Fine day for a ride, is it not?" he asked with exaggerated cheerfulness. He knew he had caught her off guard, *drat the man.*

"Why—uh—yes. Yes. Yes it is. A very nice day for a ride. How nice that you could join us."

"Or vice-versa," he said, offering his gloved hand to help her step onto the mounting block. "I have been taking this brute out daily since I arrived."

She braced her gloved hand against his shoulder as she stepped up and swung her leg and voluminous skirt over the tree of her side saddle. She was acutely aware of the scent of his shaving soap and of the sheer masculine power and flow of muscle as he saw to the simple task of adjusting her stirrup. She wondered fleetingly why she had never noticed such sensations before when Dolan or any other groom had routinely performed this duty for her. The moment left her slightly out of breath, him not at all.

To cover her momentary lapse, she said in some surprise, "You have been riding Lucifer? Win was the only one who could really handle that great beast. Far too temperamental."

Quint stepped away from her mount and took the reins of his own from his fellow rider. He patted the stallion's nose. "Ah, Luce," he crooned, "she does malign you, does she not? Perhaps Miss Mayfield is not aware that your manners have improved remarkably, especially when you are allowed around such beauties as her Miss Priss." Then to Harriet he said, with a gesture at his fellow rider, "Miss Mayfield, allow me to introduce my friend Chester Gibbons, who agreed to a sojourn here at Sedwick until I get my bearings with this new lot in my life."

"Couldn't turn him loose in the wilds of England all by himself now, could I?" Gibbons asked with a grin and Harriet immediately liked the man for his warm friendliness. She also noted reddish brown hair, a profusion of freckles, and blue eyes that bespoke intelligence.

She laughed and said, "I suppose not, though I doubt many of us will be shooting at either of you." She turned back to Quint. "So—am I to understand that you have been taking the devil's own out on a regular basis?"

"Since I was one who talked Win into buying this fine piece of horseflesh, I thought I had at least best help keep him exercised."

"Is that a way of saying we all end up paying for our sins somehow?" she asked with a smile.

"Perhaps. But Win and I thought Luce might also be the start of a great line too. Have you seen the new foal yet?"

"No, I have not."

"He's a beaut, Aunt Harriet," Phillip said. "Father would have been so proud."

"I think Win meant to breed Luce to that mare you are riding too, Miss Mayfield," Quint said.

"Really? He actually said that?"

"I think so. He spoke of 'a solid little bay mare that Anne's sister always rides'—that's the way he put it to me. Why? You sound surprised."

"I am. Miss Priss is *my* horse. I own her. She does not belong to the Sedwick stable. Win never mentioned such a plan to me."

"Surely he would have done so in due time." When she nodded polite agreement, he added, "Do you mind if Gibbons and I join your ride this morning?"

"Not at all, though I doubt that horrid beast will agree to keep to even our most challenging pace. I have seen him in action. He is difficult to control."

Quint leaned forward and patted the stallion's neck. "Don't listen to her, Luce. She cannot mean to speak so meanly of such a fine fellow as you." The horse lifted his head arrogantly and pranced impatiently.

Harriet shared a knowing glance with Phillip and the other two riders. The five of them set off at a fairly sedate pace, the groom Dolan on a gelding whose name, Etna, had once fit him, but those days were long gone when he had had a tendency to "explode" unpredictably. These days Etna was considered one of the most dependable riding horses in the Sedwick stables. Gibbons was mounted on an equally fine example of the previous earl's eye for a fine horse.

"Me an' Etna been goin' out regular with the colonel an' Mr. Gibbons," Dolan informed Harriet and Phillip as Quint and his friend quickly pulled ahead of the others.

"I am glad the colonel is willing to take on that animal," Harriet said. "He is dangerous—but oh so magnificent—and your father loved him dearly, Phillip."

"I know. Aunt Harriet, I've been thinking—and I talked about it with Dolan here—it's time I moved up from this pony to maybe Etna there. What do you think? Maybe let Sarah have Toby for hers now?"

"I told his lordship he should ask you," Dolan put in quickly.

Harriet glanced over at her nephew. Every once in a while, there would come a moment when she was forced to recognize the inevitable march of time. All too soon this boy would be an adolescent, then a man. "I think," she said slowly, "that would be fine if your uncle approves. As your guardian, he has the last word on such things. Ask him. But if you feel comfortable doing that, he should have no objection."

She considered the boy's slight figure. Phillip had been a rather sturdy toddler, but had suffered a bout of fever when he was three that had set him back—and worried his parents prodigiously—but he had recovered fully and nothing ever seemed to hold him back in terms of activity or stamina since. Still, his build was more lithe than husky, though Harriet supposed that soon enough Phillip would develop that adolescent growth spurt with which young men seemed always to surprise their friends and families overnight. How sad that Anne and Win would miss witnessing that in their son. And such changes in the others as well.

"Look at them go!"

Phillip's cry interrupted her musing. She looked up to see Quint and the black stallion take off at a hard run, the rider bent low over the horse's neck, apparently urging the animal on. Low rock fences separating fields of grazing sheep offered no obstacles as the stallion sailed smoothly over them. *Perhaps it is not just Lucifer who needed the utter freedom of this run,* she thought. The rest of them followed at a more leisurely pace, often going around, not through a field, but finally they caught up with the stallion and its rider, who had stopped at the edge of a cliff overlooking the river that ran through one section of the Sedwick property.

"That was great, Uncle Quint!" Phillip said.

"You make an admirable team." Harriet gestured at man and horse.

"He is a handful," Quint said, "but I think he's worked out the kinks for a bit at least. He should be an amiable companion for your pony on the return ride, Phillip."

"Oh, very good, sir."

Harriet caught Quint's gaze. Knowing that Phillip was torn between developing a full-blown case of hero-worship for his uncle and feeling apprehensive about the question of school, she wanted to scream at him, "Don't you dare hurt this boy!" However, she merely smiled and not only pulled her mount back to ride beside Dolan and Gibbons, but deliberately set a slower pace to put more distance between them and thus allow the colonel more privacy with his ward if he wished it.

"Captain Gibbons," she said, making conversation, "did I or did I not detect a slight bit of the Scot in your speech, sir?"

"Ah, aye, lassie, ye did, ye hae caught me oot, ye hae," he said with a laugh.

She laughed with him and went on, "And is not Gibbons the family name of the Laird of Aberdeen?"

"Why, bless my soul," he said in exaggerated surprise, his hand over his heart, "I do believe it is."

"Doing it too brown, Captain," she said. "I assume that means you are of *that* Gibbons lot?"

"Yes, Miss, I am, but I do not trade on the family name—nor do I wear the military title any longer since I've given up the uniform. Plain mister will do for me."

She gazed at him, sure there was good deal of pain behind the warm sincerity in his tone. She nodded her understanding. "It shall be as you wish, Mr. Gibbons."

When the entire group arrived back at the stables, Harriet thought that both Phillip and his uncle seemed rather subdued, but neither said anything to her or to each other that seemed out of the ordinary. At breakfast Quint announced that, weather permitting, their picnic would take place during the next week.

"Picnic?" His mother was confused. "I know nothing of a picnic."

"Next week?" Maria and Phillip uttered in unison, turning crestfallen expressions toward him.

"Yes, Mother," Quint explained. "A family picnic at the Abbey ruins— like we used to have. The subject came up yesterday."

"A family picnic," she repeated, "and you were indeed thinking of inviting me?"

"Of course." He paid little heed to her exaggerated tone. "You and Mrs. Hartley." He gestured at Maria and Phillip. "What's with the long faces on you two? I thought you welcomed the idea of a picnic."

The two youngsters looked at each other and Maria said hesitantly, "We did—we do—we all did—do. It's just that we—uh—we thought it would take place today or tomorrow—"

"We never set a time, did we?"

"Well, no, but—"

"It cannot be this week," Quint said, rather tersely, Harriet thought. "Today is your grandmother's tea; tomorrow, Phillip is visiting tenant farmers and cottagers; the next day, he is touring the mills; the following day is market day; and the one following that is Sunday and church—so, you see, it must be next week."

"Well, yes, one can certainly see that *now*," Maria said, sounding as imperious as the dowager herself. Harriet smiled inwardly and kept her eyes on her plate, knowing the colonel was not used to answering to children.

"It sounds like a pleasant outing," the dowager said. "And it gives me an idea for an entertainment for my house party some weeks later, if the weather remains fair. I will speak with Mrs. Hodges later."

* * * *

Quint retreated to the library after breakfast. He wanted to go over those figures yet again before trying to share any of that information with Phillip. *No sense worrying a twelve-year-old overmuch, but the boy needed to have some inkling of what he would one day be taking on.* A tap at the door interrupted him.

"Colonel Burnes, may I have a moment of your time?"

"Of course, Miss Mayfield." He rose behind the desk and gestured at a chair in front of it, which she took.

She wore a blue-gray dress trimmed with wide satin ribbons of the same color that not only caught and reflected the light as she moved, but also enhanced the color of her eyes. *She has to know the effect those eyes have on a man!* He still could not decide whether he thought they were more blue or gray.

"What may I do for you?" he asked, sitting back down.

"It's about your taking Phillip to see the cottagers and the mills."

"You do not approve?"

"Oh, no. It is not that I do not approve. I think Phillip should know the people for whom he will be—is—responsible. Win and Anne often took the children—especially Phillip and Maria—with them when they visited tenants." She paused and held his gaze directly. "I—uh—I should like to come along. That is, with your permission, of course," she finished hurriedly.

"What?" He was caught off balance. He leaned forward in his chair and stared at her. "Cottagers? Woolen mills? Those are not exactly places for ladies of your sort, you know."

She continued to hold his gaze. "As I am sure you must know by now, sir, I am not one to remain fixed on what those of 'my sort'—whatever that may be—should and should not do. However, it strikes me that you are proposing to introduce Phillip to precisely the folks I need to meet to give my series of essays the vitality and energy I want it to have. I promise that I will not embarrass you or Phillip or in any way tarnish the Sedwick name."

"Hmm." He tore his gaze from hers, only to have it directed at a corner of the ceiling painting that depicted the judgment of Paris. He ran a knuckle along his jaw. "As to that, enough of the Sedwick line have achieved that end already. You do know that my mother and her lot would be apoplectic at the very idea of what you are suggesting?" He raised a questioning eyebrow at her.

"Perhaps they will be—*after* the fact."

"Ah, Miss Mayfield, you may steal my heart yet," he said lightly, stalling for time, trying to foresee any consequences. Then he sighed. "All right. It is against my better judgment, but all right. Dig out the plainest, most nondescript garment you own—best we not make a show of too much finery in these places."

Her smile literally took his breath away.

"Thank you, sir. Thank you. Thank you."

Even as she closed the door behind her, he wondered how wise that decision had been. When Chet joined him for another round with the books, Quint informed him of the next day's outing and added, "You'd better come along too, Chet."

"What? You suggesting one of Wellington's finest ain't up to protecting a woman and a boy on the boy's own property?"

Quint rolled his eyes. "We have footmen for that task. But I might *suggest* that cheeky employees tread on thin ice."

Chet pulled at an imaginary forelock. "Yes, sir. I shall keep that in mind, sir. What can I do for you, sir?"

"You can *help* look out for Miss Mayfield—see that nothing untoward happens to her or some unsavory type does not accost her. I shall have my hands full with Sedwick, I am sure. But mostly, I'd like you to have that trusty little notebook of yours handy. You know the sorts of things we are looking for—know them better than I do, as a matter of fact."

"Helps when one's daddy owns a mill or two," Chet muttered.

"I'm sure," Quint said absently. "By the by—how long do you intend to hide away down here, my friend?

Chet grinned at him, blue eyes twinkling. "Caught me out, eh? Thought I'd see you settled in before going off north to beard the lion. Lions. Me da and both older brothers. Plus an uncle or two. I'm the black sheep o' the family, you know. Sent down from university. Shipped off to his majesty's army. Probably best forgot by now."

"Balderdash! You always had plenty of mail whenever it came in."

"My sister Mary. She always manages to keep me informed."

"So? What does she tell you now? Is all forgiven? I am not merely prying, Chet. After all these years, I am quite used to relying on your eyes and ears. I would hate to lose you, though I suppose the Sedwick steward is competent enough." Quint shuffled through some papers on the desk. "What is that fellow's name? Old Falmouth retired in '08."

"Stevens."

"See?" Quint held his friend's gaze inquiringly.

"I'll hang on here until I see you settled in firmly," Chet said. "I am in no hurry to set myself up for more rejection up north, though I'd not mind seeing my baby sister again. Been a long time." He sighed. "She's nineteen now."

"In any event," Quint said emphatically, "you are to stop hiding away in your room and in the servants' hall and take your place in this household as what you are: my friend and my guest. Is that clear?"

"Aye, aye, sir."

* * * *

Lady Margaret, Dowager Countess of Sedwick, had begun to talk of this afternoon tea within three days of her son's arrival home. Quint was not sure whether she was using the occasion to announce his return to the environs or her own emergence from deep mourning and return to the helm of this little frigate of society. It was, according to her ladyship, to be a deliciously elaborate informal gathering of as many as fifty of the "best people" of local society. Quint groaned inwardly, but steeled himself to perform his required role.

In the event, the weather gods smiled upon the affair and the afternoon turned out gloriously warm. Tables and chairs and colorful umbrellas were set up in the garden off the morning room and the library. The dowager and her son greeted their guests, who then mingled at their leisure, imbibing lemonade and tea and munching on cucumber sandwiches and other delicacies as well as Mrs. Hodges's famous ginger biscuits. Footmen had wheeled out a piano, which Harriet, Sylvia Hartley, and several other ladies traded off playing. Lady Margaret had finally shed her dismal black bombazine for a plainly styled gray linen gown, over which she had consented to wear the shawl her grandchildren had given her. Quint overheard her brag to another matron about the gift and he knew Harriet had persuaded her to show herself in the nursery wearing the shawl.

As a young man, he had endured more than one social event of his mother's engineering. Such had been his expectation of this one: something to be endured. Instead, he was pleasantly surprised. First off, he was genuinely interested in getting to know these people he knew would be his neighbors for the next several years or more. He began immediately to try to sort through the characteristics they exhibited and subjects they talked about so he could greet them intelligently at some future date.

Among the first people who came to his notice was the vicar. Mr. Justin Powers turned out to be a man his middle thirties, dark-haired, with a firm handshake and an athletic build. He was accompanied by his wife, Emma, a slim brown-haired beauty of an age with her husband. Ten minutes of conversation with the couple quickly disabused Quint of his previous ill-founded prejudice about the literacy of local vicars—at least of this one.

He turned away from the Powers couple to see Harriet Mayfield coming toward him. He drank in the sight of her. She had not gone so far as to offend the dowager by casting off all semblance of mourning, but she had donned a plainly styled dress of a deep jade green trimmed with metallic-looking bronze lace appliqués with the same lace repeated at the sleeves and square neckline. On her left shoulder she wore the flower brooch the children had given her. He smiled as she approached.

"I saw you talking with Justin and Emma Powers," she said.

"And you just could not wait to come and say 'I told you so,' could you?" he asked.

"I just wondered—that is, I hoped—"

He gave her a deep, mocking bow. "I bow to your judgment, oh woman of wisdom. They are very bright, very charming people. I shall enjoy getting to know them better."

She impulsively laid a hand on his arm and held his gaze. "Good. I am so glad you like them. They are among my very favorite people in the neighborhood. Emma and Anne were quite close—they came here the same year, both as new brides."

"Is that so?" he murmured, trying to cope with the intense physical reaction her touch and direct gaze were having on him. He welcomed the distraction of another guest.

Thus it was that this particular social event of his mother's brought another matter to the attention of Colonel Lord Quinton Frederick Burnes. He found himself surprised, intrigued, and—no! surely not jealous. Over a woman he hardly knew? Ridiculous. But there it was. No. It was just a sense of protectiveness and propriety toward a person temporarily under his care, so to speak. That was it.

Among his mother's guests were two men who immediately caught Quint's notice because of their attentions toward Harriet Mayfield. Sir Desmond Humphreys, a rather portly widower in his late forties with thinning blond hair, fawned over the dowager's hand, welcomed her son "home from the wars" in booming affability, then made his way ostentatiously to the side of Harriet, who was engaged in conversation a few feet away.

"Ah, Miss Mayfield," he called and hurried toward her. "My dear girl, I only this morning learned that you had returned to our midst. I have a new curricle. It is truly the jolliest of vehicles. You simply must allow me to take you out in it. Say tomorrow afternoon?"

She excused herself—reluctantly, it seemed to Quint—from the other folks with whom she had been talking and he was unable to hear her response to the man, but he did hear his mother's comment.

"I don't know why Harriet does not put him out of his misery and accept the man," the dowager said. "At her age, she is not likely to find a much better prospect."

"What? Are you telling me that fellow is hanging out to marry Miss Mayfield?" Quint was appalled.

His mother shrugged. "Did you not recognize his name? Humphreys. Owns those woolen mills that used to belong to the Leeds family. Your father wanted to buy them, but Humphreys beat him out. The man's a cit. His wife died four years ago and he wants to marry up this time. Thinks Harriet's connections will do it for him."

"That sounds rather crass to me," Quint said.

"My dear boy, the marriage mart *is* crass," his mother said, and turned to greet another guest.

The other man whose attentions to Harriet Mayfield caught Quint's notice caused him more concern, though he was perhaps not ready to admit to his own level of interest yet. This man was Captain Cameron Morris, late of His Majesty's Naval Service. Captain Morris was on an extended visit with his sister, Edith, wife of Squire William Douglas. The captain, with black hair and eyes so dark as to be almost black themselves, had the bearing and experience of a fellow military man. Quint immediately identified with the man and found much to like about him.

When he could finally get away from the duty of receiving his mother's guests, he was pleased to see that the navy captain, his sister, and her husband were part of a group that included Harriet and Chet, and Quint quickly joined that group.

He was not best pleased to discover an extraordinarily easy rapport between the navy man and Miss Mayfield. He wondered how deep that might go.

Chapter 9

That evening Harriet sat at her desk mulling over the events of the day. She had enjoyed the dowager's tea far more than she had expected to. She especially enjoyed seeing the Powers couple again as well as the Douglases and Captain Morris. These were people with whom she had spent many an evening in company with Win and Anne. For a while this afternoon they had recaptured some their old sense of camaraderie. She was genuinely pleased to see that Quint made an effort to acquaint himself with these members of the community, for she knew they would be helpful to him as he tried to slash his way through the jungle of local politics and local social alliances. *As the nominal head of Sedwick—until Phillip reaches his majority—Colonel Burnes will need people like these, perhaps more than he quite realizes yet,* she thought.

What she had not enjoyed so heartily was seeing Edmund Humphreys again. Harriet knew the man was keen on making her the second Mrs. Humphreys, but Harriet had no inclination in that direction whatsoever, and she rather resented Lady Margaret's trying to advance the man's interests. Even before Win and Anne's deaths, the dowager had often dropped comments about what a splendid match Humphreys would be for "a spinster such as Harriet" and how such a match would allow Harriet to remain near her beloved nieces and nephews "without unduly imposing on the family."

It was not that Harriet had an active dislike of the man. She merely found him a bit of a bore. His conversation centered mostly on his acquaintance with this or that person of social prominence or possessions he thought might impress others, like a matched team or this new curricle, for instance. And she was well aware that his chief interest in her lay with the facts that her father had been a titled member of the aristocracy and that her grandfather not only held a title, but was known to have connections with the royal family.

Captain Cameron Morris, on the other hand, was very interesting, indeed. She had first met him at one of the local assemblies and thought him one of the handsomest men she had ever met. He was charming as well. Even in London he was likely to appear on many of the most exclusive lists of guests for a ball or social soiree. She recalled seeing him at two such affairs during her recent sojourn in the city where they had happily greeted each other and chatted amiably of matters "at home." However, handsome as he was, charming as he was, Cameron did not loom large in Harriet's mind as a romantic figure, mainly, she supposed, because she had always regarded him as such a dear *friend*. She saw little reason to alter that status....

Her musings were interrupted by a knock at the door of her sitting room. She answered it to find Phillip and Maria there, dressed in their nightclothes and dressing gowns.

"I thought I had seen you both safely into the arms of Morpheus hours and hours ago," she said. Curiosity overriding her attempt to sound stern, she held the door open for them to come in.

Maria giggled and Phillip said, "A few minutes ago, perhaps, but hours and hours? That is surely an extreme exaggeration, Aunt Harriet."

"And Grandmother might see that reference to Morpheus as misleading the youth of England," Maria said primly.

"Perhaps, but I doubt she will be feeding me wormwood for breakfast," Harriet replied. "Now, what is that has you two darkening my doorstep at this late hour?" She gestured them to be seated on a settee upholstered in pale blue velvet and she took a matching chair nearby.

They both sighed and Phillip said, "We've been talking. It's about our having to go away to school—"

"Did you speak with your uncle again? I saw the two of you talking as we were riding this morning."

"I did speak with him. I suggested that we might hire a tutor such as Uncle Charles had done for Jeremy—just for a year or so—but Uncle Quint just seems to have his own idea in mind and won't even consider anything else at all." Phillip's reply ended on what was almost a wail of frustration.

"What did he actually say?" Harriet asked.

"He said that would not be the same as going to school and working with people who will be my peers—learning and solving problems in groups," Phillip said dully.

"He probably does have a point there," Harriet said.

"Yes," the boy agreed. "And I admitted as much. Aunt Harriet, it is not that I *never* want to go to Eton. Just not now. Not this year. I want to learn more of what it is to—to be Sedwick, you see." He bowed his head. "I—I don't w-want to b-be Sedwick, b-but I am. C-can I even do this?"

Harriet rose from her chair and went to his side. "Scoot over." She sat beside him and put her arm around his shoulders and quickly felt Maria's arm coming from the other side. "It is not a question of *can* you do it, Phillip. You are. You are Sedwick. And you are already doing it very well. Patterson, and Mrs. Ames, and Mrs. Hodges, Dolan—they all say you are assuming your duties better than anyone could have expected."

He squinted up at her. "Th-they do?"

"They do. They will be very proud to serve you just as they served your father."

"See? I told you so," Maria said softly, giving him a little shake. This earned her a brotherly scowl.

Harriet squeezed his shoulder gently. "You will make mistakes. Many of them. But you will learn from them. And everyone—everyone—from the lowliest scullery maid to your Uncle Quint will be trying to help you along the way."

"I think I can accept that, but I just do not see the need for me to leave—not now—not yet."

Maria looked around her brother. "I tried to talk with Uncle Quint, too."

"Did you?" Harriet asked. "What did he tell you?"

"He seemed less definite about a school for me. Perhaps more open to the idea of a governess for us girls—like maybe education matters less for girls."

"I do hope you misunderstood him," Harriet said.

Maria shrugged. "Perhaps I did."

Phillip balled his hands into fists on his knees. "Is there nothing we can do, Aunt Harriet? Nothing at all? I do not want to go away this year. I am not ready. May I not have some say in such matters?"

Harriet sat silent for some moments, letting her hand drift up and down the boy's back. Finally, she spoke slowly and softly. "Your Uncle Quint is your guardian, as you well know. He has the same legal powers as your father would have had, and I truly believe he means to fulfill that role in that spirit. I also believe that he has your best interests at heart."

"But he won't listen to me at all," Phillip moaned.

"Or me," Maria echoed.

Harriet rose and patted the boy on the shoulder. "In matters such as this, English law does not give women and children much room to maneuver. We are left mostly with the powers of persuasion. We still have some time before term starts. Perhaps we can persuade the colonel to change his mind." She gestured for them to rise. "But come now. Once and for all, off to bed with you both."

"Yes, ma'am," they murmured and kissed her on the cheek as they departed.

* * * *

Quint was just coming up the stairs when he happened to see Phillip and Maria scurrying from Harriet's room up the back stairs to the nursery rooms on the floor above. *Now what was that all about—at this hour?* he mused to himself as he turned toward his own chambers at the other end of the long hall. *Is Miss Mayfield trying to undermine my authority on this infernal school business?* Both Phillip and Maria had accosted him on the matter during the day, and, as he had fully determined earlier, he held his ground and made it clear that the current Earl of Sedwick would be going off for the same education his predecessors had had. As for Maria, he had been less adamant only because he was not as sure what their parents' wishes had been regarding their daughter. He supposed that was a subject about which Harriet Mayfield might be able to enlighten him, but for some reason it went against the grain to have to ask her. Nevertheless...

He settled into bed and turned up his lamp, prepared to lose himself in a novel by Sir Walter Scott that he had been delighted to discover he had not read before. Medieval knights and feats of derring-do were what he needed at the moment. But his mind kept drifting to those two youngsters and their aunt. Especially the aunt. And those laughing gray eyes—or were they blue?—as she teased little Elly about the pink crystal of the brooch. He smiled to himself at the image. Surely she was not encouraging the older ones' resistance to going to school. Was she?

Women!

And then there was that little bombshell his mother had let drop that evening. After a rather late light supper, the adults of the household had gathered in the drawing room to partake of tea or cognac. Harriet played the piano quietly, but idly; Quint and Chet were engaged in a card game at a side table; the dowager, at the main seating arrangement in the room, had been nattering on about the success of the afternoon's tea to her companion, when suddenly her discussion evolved to her upcoming house party and guest list and seemed not so idle after all.

"You remember Lady Barbara Riverton, do you not, my son?" his mother called to him.

"Yes, of course," he said in a neutral tone he was proud to have achieved.

"I thought you would." His mother looked at him archly. "She's a widow now, you know."

"I had heard that." Again, he was carefully noncommittal. He remembered very well reading that news in a well-worn newspaper in the Peninsula.

His mother babbled on, apparently unaware of, or intent on ignoring, his response. "Her period of mourning has been over for ages now and Lady Barbara is as popular as she ever was as a debutante. One of the 'Winsome Widows' as they are known. All three of them have accepted my invitation."

"How nice," Mrs. Hartley murmured over her teacup. "Your house party will surely be a success with such lively ladies in attendance."

"I hope so," Lady Margaret said. "Quinton, you should know that Lady Barbara added a postscript to her acceptance of my invitation. She said she is particularly looking forward to seeing you again."

"Did she now?" Quint had then pointedly set his cognac glass aside to concentrate on the cribbage game he and Chet were playing.

Now, he pushed the novel under his pillow, turned out the light, and allowed his mind to drift to a painful period of the past. Barbara Newhouse had been the leading debutante the year Quint had come home on his first leave. Honey-blonde hair, green eyes, a laughing disposition, and a figure that had men salivating combined to make her that season's "diamond of the first water." With her encouragement—or so he thought—he had fallen, and fallen hard. But then she had none-too-gently informed him that it was simply impossible that a lowly viscount's daughter with only a modest dowry could ever consider the suit of a second son with limited resources—regardless of how absolutely splendid that second son looked in his regimentals—especially as that second son's older brother was already married and was on the way to producing an heir. So, at nineteen, the beauteous Barbara had been practical and married the immensely rich Lord Riverton, who had at the time been in his late fifties.

And Lieutenant Burnes? That stalwart fellow had returned to the battlefield and made himself the best kind of military officer he knew how. The British Army with its vast and varied "tail" and the constant change of location in headquarters offered opportunities now and then for romantic liaisons, but for Quint, anything that might have turned out to be serious had been somehow quashed by circumstances. He had usually just shrugged and accepted such as the vicissitudes of war. It was true that he had harbored some resentment against Barbara, but he understood the realities of her life—were they not the realities of his own life as well?

That phase of his life had long been buried. He did not welcome the thought of having it resurrected. *Winsome widows, indeed! What the hell does that mean? And what did his mother mean, inviting them? Especially that one? Ah, well, this, too, will pass.* He punched his pillow into submission and deliberately turned his mind to the morrow. The very air had smelled of rain this evening.…

* * * *

Since the excursion to visit the cottagers was to take place in the afternoon, Harriet divided her morning between spending time with the younger children and reviewing the material she had gathered on cottage industries in general, but especially on local cottage weavers. Some of these families had been weavers for generations—and had served the Sedwick estate for just as long. She remembered visiting many of them from time to time with Anne in the past, but on those occasions her interest had not been so focused as it would be today.

Knowing that country folk could be even stricter about the proprieties than the dowager herself and that, moreover, these country folk had been quite fond of the previous Earl of Sedwick, she dressed for this outing in the most proper of half-mourning attire: a medium gray linen gown with a finely woven darker gray woolen shawl about her shoulders. Her only spot of color was the children's brooch, which she pinned at the throat of the high-neck dress. She appreciated what she took to be a nod of approval from Quint as he greeted her and Phillip in the entrance hall.

"I thought it best we not risk the open landau," Quint said, ushering them out to the closed carriage and handing her in. "Still too much chance of more rain."

"I suppose you are right," she agreed, deliberately trying yet again to ignore that delicious physical reaction his touch seemed always to engender. "Summer rains can be unpredictable." His fingers brushed hers as he handed her a basket, and for an instant, her gaze locked with his; she was sure he was as conscious of the current of…of…awareness between them as she was. Covering her own reaction, she concentrated on gathering her skirt to make room for Phillip and ask the boy, "Are you nervous, my dear?"

"About what?"

"Oh. We are taking the nonchalant mode, I see, for the new Lord Sedwick's first real outing in that role."

Phillip grimaced. "Aunt Harriet!"

She grinned at him. "All right. I'll behave."

Quint and Chet climbed in and sat opposite them and Quint signaled the driver to go ahead. They were also accompanied by two armed footmen, one on the bench with the driver, and one at the back of the carriage.

"You'll do just fine, my lad," Chet assured him. "An' if we come acrost anyone as say you don't, we'll come back an' dig us a dungeon under Sedwick Hall deeper 'n hell itself an' confine 'em to it for all eternity! That'll do 'em! Eh?"

Phillip giggled at Chet's exaggerated accent. "And feed them a diet of burnt bread and water."

"With maybe a spider for company," Harriet added.

"You are a cruel lot," Quint observed. "Good job our people are unlikely to need your ministrations."

The rain held off as the carriage stopped in front of the first of the weavers' cottages in a cluster of four cottages with surrounding outbuildings and farmland. Harriet knew that traditionally these families had survived as both artisans and farmers. The building at which they stopped was a two-storied structure of stone with a thatched roof. Approaching the covered stoop—Harriet, Phillip, then Quint and Chet—could hear the loud thwacks and thumps of the loom, and Harriet saw a young girl looking through a side window of what she took to be the living room on the right of the cottage door. Harriet lifted the knocker, but it had scarcely sounded once before the door was opened by a woman in her forties, wearing a kerchief on her head. Her husband stood at her side and behind them were several children ranging in age from adolescents to toddlers.

"Hello, Miss Harriet," the woman said. "What a nice surprise to see you! And Lord Phillip too. Oh! I mean, of course, it is Lord Sedwick now, is it not? I do apologize, my lord. It is just—"

"It is perfectly all right, Mrs. Enslow," Phillip said with a smile. "I am not at all used to the title yet myself, you see. So, please. Make nothing of it."

The woman dipped him a curtsy and said, "Thank you, my lord." She stepped back. "Do come in."

Harriet entered, followed by Phillip, then Quint and Chet. Harriet had been here before, but not at all sure that a weaver's cottage was familiar territory to Colonel Lord Quinton Burnes, she found herself trying to view their surroundings through his eyes. The building itself was rather large, for it was a farmhouse, accommodating multi-generations of a family, as well as housing a large working loom. The room they entered was actually two rooms—off to the left was the room that held the loom and cupboards for storing wool and cloth and other things needed for the business of the weaver's trade. On the right was the family living and dining area. It held a large dining table with chairs and benches such as would accommodate a family of perhaps a dozen people. The table was scrubbed to a fine shine and had a lace cloth in the middle with some small covered ceramic pots that Harriet assumed held often-used condiments. Other furniture in this half of the room included a horsehair sofa and two much worn upholstered chairs. In a place of honor was a bookstand that held a copy of the Bible.

A stone fireplace in the living room provided heat for the entire space and was situated so that it also provided much of the cooking facility for the kitchen in the room beyond. Outside the kitchen were sheds and barns for animals, tools, and so on. Family bedrooms were on the second floor. But the center of the dwelling—in every way—was the loom. The loom was the means by which the family survived.

As Harriet had suggested on the way, she made the introductions, then stepped aside. "Mr. and Mrs. Enslow, allow me to introduce his lordship's guardian, Colonel Lord Quinton Burnes and his friend Mr. Chester Gibbons."

Enslow bowed and his wife curtsied, but the man readily shook the hand Quint extended to him and said, "Welcome, sir. We heard as ye was to take over for the lad. Sad business, the loss o' your brother an' his pa that way."

"Yes, it was," Quint said. "We do not wish to take too much of your time, sir, but we are on an inspection tour as it were—trying to acquaint myself and young Sedwick here with what we are up against in trying to deal with matters of the estate. Anything you can tell us to help shed light on matters will help. I hope you won't mind that Mr. Gibbons will be taking notes for me—and Miss Mayfield will be asking questions and taking notes for a matter of her own interest."

Enslow's eyes were twinkling as he said, "Don't s'pose I'd mind at all—long as you don't think to toss me in that mill stream again."

Quint looked at him questioningly. "Wha—?" Then he hit his forehead with the heel of his hand. "Jason Enslow. Of course. Why did I not make that connection immediately?"

Enslow shrugged. "Bin more 'n twenty years now, ain't it? Ye and yer brother caught me and mine fishin' in yer favorite spot. Not a one o' us more 'n ten years old."

"That was quite a brawl as I remember it, but seems we had some good times after that," Quint reminisced.

"Aye. We did." Enslow's tone became more matter-of-fact as he added, "I'm not exactly sure what you want of us at the moment."

"Perhaps if you were just to go about your usual activities just though we were not here?" Harriet said brightly. "We will try not to intrude too much."

One of the older girls giggled at this suggestion, but a stern look from her mother quelled that, and the family quickly shuttled off to their usual positions: the mother hustled an older daughter into the kitchen; the giggler was soon at a spinning wheel in the living room; an older boy stood at the side of the loom; and the father was seated on the bench of the loom. Another girl of about ten was in charge of two toddlers on a rug in the living room.

Harriet could not help feeling somewhat embarrassed. How would she feel if someone came tromping into her life to examine it as though under a magnifying glass? She followed Mrs. Enslow into the kitchen, taking the basket she had brought into the house with her. In the kitchen she discovered an older woman and another child of about eight peeling potatoes.

"Hello, Mrs. Miller," Harriet greeted the woman, whom she knew to be Mrs. Enslow's mother. "And this must be—No!—It cannot be! Susan? All grown up so?"

The child giggled, curtsied prettily, and went back to peeling her potatoes. Her mother smiled gratefully to Harriet and Harriet went on in a more normal tone to the grown-ups. "I know this visit is probably an imposition, but we feel it is important that Lord Phillip get an idea of what it is really like to deal with estate business before he goes off to school, you see."

"We understand, Miss Harriet. Truly, we do. 'Tis hard times for ever'one. The loss of the lord, o' course. Folks out of work. The markets. Hard times."

"How hard for you and your family?" Harriet asked. "Be frank with me, please."

Mrs. Enslow gestured for Harriet to take a seat on a bench at the side of the long table at which the older woman and little girl worked, then sat across from her visitor. She leaned across and spoke sincerely. "Not as bad for Sedwick folks as for some—yet anyways. We—Enslows and a few others—we got a cow and a goat. We make our own cheese and the home farm shares the orchard with the cottagers and often shares when they butcher an animal."

Harriet picked up her basket and set it on the table. "Mrs. Hodges sent a jar of her lemon curd and some of her ginger biscuits. Also a special blend of mint tea she swears is just the thing for indigestion."

"How very kind of her."

"And here are a few other items I am sure you will find use for," Harriet said, quickly emptying the basket. "Now, I'd best get back in there and see that Phillip is not making a nuisance of himself. You know how young boys can be."

Returning to the other room, she found Chet taking notes on the price of raw wool and finished cloth and the amount of time it took to produce a given amount of yardage on the hand loom. They watched with interest as Enslow worked his loom, with his twelve-year-old son running the shuttle back to him after every pull of the great beater.

"Might I try that, sir?" Phillip ask of the weaver with some hesitation.

"You, sir? You wanta work me loom?" the weaver asked in surprise.

"With your permission, sir," Phillip said politely.

"O' course, my lord." The man looked at the boy's skinny legs. "Though I doubt your legs'll reach the pedals. But slide on here next to me—I'll work the pedals, you do the beater."

"All right!" Excitement sounded in the boy's voice as he slid onto the bench and reached for the heavy wooden lever.

The weaver worked the pedals, nodded at his son, who tossed the shuttle across the cocked threads, then ran around to catch the shuttle on the other side and return it to position when the threads were repositioned. Phillip grabbed the bar to pull it toward him and did manage—with an audible oomphf—to get the shuttle's thread pushed against the already woven fabric, but only just, and without the firm "thwack" that had accompanied each of weaver's pulls at the beater.

"I want to try again," Phillip said calmly.

The weaver nodded agreeably and they went through the motions twice more. Then Phillip slid off the bench and stood beside the weaver, looking in awe at the man and the machine. "You made it look so easy, sir," he said, touching the finished portion of the fabric. "And the work is so fine."

"Thank you, my lord. My Joey is about your age, an' he can't work the loom yet. But he'll be a fine weaver one day. An' I've no doubt ye could've been too if'n yer druthers had turned that way."

"Thank you, Mr. Enslow," Phillip murmured.

Harriet could have hugged the man for sparing the feelings of a young boy as he had. She wished there had been two sides of bacon in that basket of goodies she unloaded in the kitchen instead of only one! But there were still three other families to visit....

The men moved to the dining table to discuss details of the cottage weavers' business—how much raw material came from Sedwick sources, how much had to be obtained elsewhere and at what costs, market prices and factors that might affect them, and so on. While Chet took meticulous notes there, Harriet took notes of her own about the household that would be of interest to women readers of her articles, but that would probably not escape the notice of her male readers either.

Chapter 10

Visits to the other cottage weavers proceeded much as had that with the Enslow family. Quint was pleased to see the grace and maturity with which his nephew conducted himself. The Sedwick party had interrupted the last family at tea and, despite there being rather meager fare on the table, Lord Sedwick and his companions were readily invited to join the Smith family. His lordship, after consulting his aunt, refused ever so graciously with the excuse that he could not in good conscience keep his driver and other servants and cattle waiting any longer as it appeared to be threatening to rain again, but he thanked the Smiths very much for the kind invitation. Quint was sure that here, as at the earlier stops, Harriet's visit to the kitchen with her laden basket helped to assuage any sense of awkwardness or intrusion, and he sensed that people generally were favorably impressed with their new young lord.

However, he continued, albeit discreetly, to watch the boy and his aunt carefully throughout that day and now this to see if there existed any foundation to his persistent suspicion that she might be undermining his authority with their nephew. He had no idea what he might actually *do* should he find evidence of such. In fact, he was not at all sure whether anger or disappointment would motivate whatever response he might take.

He forced his attention back to his surroundings. Again he and Chet were ensconced in the closed carriage with young Lord Sedwick and his Aunt Harriet—this time on their way to inspect the Sedwick cotton mills in the town of Hendley, a drive of some of some forty-five minutes or so from Sedwick Hall.

He had observed something different about the intriguing Miss Mayfield as he handed her into the carriage. No, it was not the fresh lemony mint scent about her. Then it hit him. While she had not exactly put off mourning in a grand gesture, she had donned a well-fitted russet-colored gown trimmed with black grosgrain frogging and a matching pelisse. Fashioned with a sort of military look about it, he assumed it was probably a fine example of the best work of some London modiste. He reluctantly turned his mind from contemplating the delights of what the modiste's handiwork might be hiding to the conversation taking place on the opposite seat.

"Phillip, have you visited the mills before?" she was asking. "I do not remember your doing so."

"Um, not really, Aunt Harriet. I just waited in the carriage as Father had a word with the manager and retrieved some papers from the office. Have you?"

"No. Your mother invited me to do so once, but I had a conflict and needed to be in London. I do recall that afterward she was intent on persuading your father to visit Mr. Robert Owen and talk with him about innovations in his mill communities."

"Mr. Robert Owen?" The boy's voice showed only vague curiosity.

"Robert Owen?" Quint blurted. Caught off guard, he was unable to hide his surprise or modify a hint of disapproval, which, of course, she noticed immediately.

"Would you have objected, Colonel Burnes?" she asked in what seemed to be as much a challenge as a genuine question.

Glancing at Chet, who shrugged slightly and gave him a look of sympathy, he bumbled on. "I—uh—well—truth to tell, I am not precisely sure, but knowing my brother as I did, I am *quite sure* Win must have had serious reservations about some of the ideas Owen puts forth."

"What ideas? Why?" Phillip asked in what Quint was sure was genuine youthful curiosity.

There was a bit of silence, then Harriet answered, "It is somewhat complicated. As a mill owner like your father—and now you—Mr. Owen has broken with tradition in the way he deals with his workers."

Quint leaned back in his seat, one hand at his waist, and held her gaze for a long moment, then said, "Most of his fellow mill owners and a good many other leaders in the business world seem to take a rather dim view of his so-called 'breaking with tradition.'"

"I do not understand," Phillip said.

When neither of the boy's adult relatives leaped to respond, Chet did so. "Owen supports workers' rights to organize trade unions and agitate for higher wages and shorter hours."

"Needless to say, those things mean less profit for owners and they have a few objections," Quint said.

"'A few objections'!" Harriet's shocked tone was not entirely feigned, he thought, distracted for a moment by the way the intensity of blue in her eyes changed with the vehemence of her emotion. She continued, "Very rich, very powerful men wielding every weapon at their disposal to beat down poor people merely trying to exist amounts to more than 'a few objections.'"

Before Quint could formulate a response to this, Phillip asked, "Are the workers not paid adequately?"

"I suppose the answer to that depends on whether one is an owner or a worker," Quint answered honestly.

"It certainly does," Harriet asserted, but a little less vehemently. "However, Mr. Owen deals with far more than just worker's hours and wages."

Quint nodded. "Yes, he does. But he advocates for far too much far too soon."

"Is that not always the cry of those who have much to those who have so very little?" she replied.

He heaved a sigh. "Perhaps. But as you well know—surely you read those papers you write for—England faces unprecedented problems, and this trade unions business is fomenting serious unrest that the government will certainly have to handle—probably none too gently."

"That is a grim view," she said.

He smiled weakly. "Not today, mind you. Probably not until Phillip takes his seat in the House of Lords."

"Oh, fine," Phillip said lightly. "I and mine get to solve all the problems of the world."

"The eternal plight of youth," Chet said as they felt the coach slowing.

* * * *

Harriet had sensed the day before what she saw as an unusual watchfulness in the colonel's demeanor. She tried to assure herself that he was merely trying to see how well his ward might be taking to the responsibilities the boy would have to grow into—even as the colonel tried to get a better grip on the magnitude of his own responsibilities in the meantime—but she could not shake the idea that there was something more to the man's keen alertness. She was taken aback slightly by the conversation about Robert Owen and sorry now that she had brought it up.

Well at least you have some inkling of how he may view suggestions of reform along those lines, she told herself. At the same time, she reminded herself that, while she might hold legal title to the bulk of Sedwick debt, this man held the real command over how anything and everything was to be managed regarding the entire Sedwick earldom. She had absolutely no authority in that regard, power of the purse notwithstanding. *It is always some man who is allowed to make the real decisions in our world, is it not?* she groused silently, then gave herself a serious mental shake. *Good grief.* The actual, day-to-day business of running an estate, managing property, and so on had never been one of *her* ambitions.

By the time they had exited the carriage and made their way to the mill office, she had regained her composure and readily accepted the colonel's offer of his arm as they approached the mill office in a small cottage attached to one of the two large, five-storied mills. Quint simply opened the door and ushered Harriet in; Phillip and Chet followed right behind them.

"Good afternoon. Knowlin is it not?" He addressed one of two clerks behind a counter in the outer room.

The man scrambled to his feet from behind a desk. "Yes, sir."

"We are here to see Mr. Stevens. I believe he is expecting us."

"Yes, sir—my lord. He is. I'm to show you right in." He quickly opened the door to the room and announced, "Colonel Lord Burnes, Miss Harriet Mayfield, Lord Sedwick, and Mr. Gibbons."

Harriet saw John Stevens, a rather stocky man with gray hair, rise from behind a desk and come round to greet them. She judged him to be in his sixties. He was neatly dressed in gray trousers and a blue coat, but neither his person nor his surroundings were at all ostentatious. She liked that he singled Phillip out for greeting first.

"Ah, Lord Sedwick, I am most pleased to make your acquaintance, though I might have wished for a happier occasion for doing so." His pale blue eyes looked kindly at the boy over wire-rimmed glasses.

"Thank you, sir." Phillip offered his hand in a firm handshake. The man bowed to Harriet, "Miss Mayfield, welcome." She dipped him a brief curtsy. He nodded to the men. "Colonel Burnes. Mr. Gibbons. Nice to see you again."

"Thank you," Quint said. In an aside he explained to Harriet and Phillip, "Chet and I visited the mills very briefly before your return from London."

Inviting them to be seated on a worn brown leather couch and some equally worn leather-covered chairs, Stevens offered them tea, which Quint, with a corroborating glance at Harriet, politely declined for the four of them. He said to Stevens, "As I told you in my note, we are here today for a closer look. Lord Sedwick needs a better understanding of how this part of his holdings work—and, frankly, so do I. Miss Mayfield is not only

Lord Sedwick's aunt, she is a writer and wishes to do some independent research of her own, for which we have no objection. Mr. Gibbons will be taking notes for Sedwick and me."

Stevens nodded. "I see. Where would you like to start?"

Quint chuckled. "At the beginning? Why don't you just give us a quick overview of what we are about here and then we will have a look at both mills. I assume you have a copy of the account books in order as I requested?"

"Yes, sir. Knowlin will furnish them to you as we finish your tour of the mills."

"Fine. Carry on, then," Quint said with a polite gesture.

Stevens had seated himself so that the five of them formed a circle of sorts, with a small table at his elbow on which he had a pad with some notes he occasionally consulted as he rattled off what must have been a routine story for him.

"As you probably know, our two mills were built in the '80s under the direction of your great-grandfather, the fourth Earl of Sedwick," he began, with a direct look at Phillip. "I'm told he was something of a visionary and wanted to expand his interest in textiles beyond wool and decided to experiment with cotton as many others were doing at the time. Then, we obtained most of our raw cotton from India and Egypt, but Napoleon interrupted the trade from Egypt rather profoundly, so now it comes mostly from the former colonies, the southern states of the United States, if you will."

"Through ports in the east or west?" Phillip asked.

Harriet thought all three men were impressed with the young man's question.

"Both, my lord," Stevens replied. "But mostly our cotton still comes through Liverpool, then is transported by wagons or via the canal systems. If you are thinking cargo of raw material and machinery is expensive, you are quite right, my lord. So is transport of finished goods."

To continue his monologue, Stevens reached into a drawer of the table and pulled out a soft cloth-wrapped packet. He unfolded the covering to reveal small bundles of swatches of fabric, about six inches square, which he handed to Phillip and Harriet, who were seated on the couch nearest him. "These are samples of the fabrics we produce. Normally, we do not turn out all of these all the time, mind you. Depends on the market, you see."

"Quite nice," Harriet commented as, having removed her gloves to take notes, she felt the texture of the kinds of fabric, ranging from the heavy stuff one might use in upholstery work to the fine, almost sheer fabric used in the most delicate garments.

"Makes sense not to have all our eggs in one basket, so to speak," Quint observed when the swatches to passed to him.

Stevens nodded enthusiastically. "That is almost exactly the way our young earl's father and grandfather expressed it!"

"You mentioned transport as an expense," Quint said. "Would you say that is the major expenditure of the mills?"

Stevens raised a hand to rub along his chin before answering slowly. "It is certainly one of them, my lord. Obtaining the raw cotton is probably the major cost. In recent years the acquisition and maintenance of power looms has been hugely expensive. They are run by steam, of course, but still require the direct supervision of skilled weavers—and they are expensive in themselves." He looked at Phillip directly. "I mentioned earlier, Lord Sedwick, that your great-grandfather was something of a visionary in seeing the possibilities of cotton in our industry. Your grandfather was, too, in seeing the possibilities of the steam engine in the production of textiles. And your father was enthusiastic about continuing his work."

"Thank you, sir," Phillip said softly. "My father often talked to me about steam engines. He once introduced me to his friend Mr. Stephenson."

"Did my father, or my brother—or have you—or anyone else in this area—experienced any of the—uh—resentment—of the machines that has been reported elsewhere—say, around Manchester?" Quint asked.

"You refer to the Luddites and their breaking of machinery, I assume." Stevens's tone turned rather grim, and he went on when Quint nodded. "I think Mr. Humphreys had an incident or two. I do not know the details, though he did dismiss a number of his workers with no notice whatsoever! At the time there was some apprehension and grumbling among our people, but the old earl and his son managed to quell it well enough. And they managed to keep all our people on the rolls too—that made a huge difference in the way our Sedwick folks accepted the machines."

Both Harriet and Chet had been taking notes as Stevens talked, Harriet in more detail apparently than Chet, but she supposed he would be reviewing the books later with Colonel Burnes. She made a mental note to herself to compliment Phillip later on about how attentive and courteous he was being through a discussion that would not usually intrigue a boy in early adolescence.

Then Phillip surprised her as well as the rest of their company with yet another substantive question. "May I ask just how many people we employ in these mills?" Phillip colored slightly when all three men turned startled eyes upon him. He looked at Harriet and shrugged. She wanted to grin and hug him.

Stevens coughed. "Hmm. I'm not sure I can give you a precise number, my lord, but that information will certainly be in the books Knowlin has for you. However, there two mills, five floors each, plus the cellar. Twenty-five to thirty weavers on each floor with an overseer and handyman on each as well. Plus cleaning people and groundskeepers. I would suppose it comes to around two hundred people."

"That many," Phillip said, impressed.

"How many of those might be women and children?" Harriet asked, aware that Quint, especially, took note of her question.

"That, I am not sure," Stevens said. "I am merely conjecturing, but I think about a third of the weavers themselves are women. We had to take on more women what with the war on the Continent, you know. And children are often used for odd kinds of jobs—usually in conjunction with whatever their mothers are doing. It is fairly common practice in textile mills, as I am sure you must know."

"How young are the children who come to work in Sedwick Mills?" she asked.

Stevens began to look a little discomfited, but he answered forthrightly. "As long as they are working with one of the parents, we have a few as young as six, I believe. Our child workers are mostly between, say, eight and thirteen. However, most of our workers are adults—and most are men." His voice had taken on a slightly defensive note.

"I see," she said, turning just enough to catch Quint exchange a look with Chet that she found difficult to interpret, but she was fairly certain that, in a different environment, he might have been rolling his eyes.

Quint straightened in his chair, his hands on his knees. "Thank you, Mr. Stevens. I think you have provided us with a good overview of the workings of Sedwick Mills. Now, we would like to have a look around, if you would be so kind."

"Of course, my lord."

The five of them emerged from the small office building and climbed a few stone steps to the entrance of the nearest of the two mills, both of which sat on an incline that overlooked the Tayson river. Gazing upward at the brick building, Harriet could see each floor distinguished by a row of windows. Ivy crawled its way up much of the first and second story of each building, though it was cut away from the windows. Stevens led them up cleanly swept stone steps graced with a black wrought iron railing to the entrance, which was set off toward one end of the edifice. As they entered,

Harriet could see that bare wooden stairs ran up the inside of the building, with landings at each floor leading off to a huge room of looms. From the landing at the entrance, there were stairs going down to the cellar, which Stevens explained contained storage for bales of raw cotton and laundry facilities for washing finished cloth, as well as a tool room. These interior wooden stairs were not so neatly tended as the stone steps outside were.

Both these wooden stairs and the wooden floors of the loom rooms were dark and smelled of oil used in an attempt to keep the lint-laden dust at bay. This being a late summer day, several of the windows were opened slightly, but looked as though it been months since they had had a proper wash. In fact, they were so murky as to provide only filtered light—certainly too dirty to offer even a glimpse of a cloud or a patch of blue sky. There were a dozen large looms loudly at work as they entered, though Harriet could see that nearly everyone in the room was aware of the visitors in their midst.

The new young earl and his companions were introduced to the overseer on the first floor who had obviously been expecting them. Standing near the first of the looms, he explained its workings and they examined the quality of the cloth it was producing. The overseer was a stocky man in his forties with a shock of brown hair, a florid complexion, and bit of a bulging belly. He was dressed aa a laborer in heavy tan cotton trousers, a lighter cotton shirt, and wide black leather suspenders.

He explained, "This machine puts out one of our finer products. From here the cloth will be sent down to the cellar to be laundered, then up to the top floor to be printed. Probably end up in ladies' dresses."

Harriet tried to stay in the background for the most part as she observed the surroundings and quietly took notes. After all, it was not her place to put herself forward. She trailed behind as the men and Phillip went from loom to loom, sometimes stopping to comment or ask or a question, mostly merely looking, occasionally nodding affably. She noted that the work force was, indeed, very much as Stevens had described it. She did see several young children performing simple tasks such as sweeping up excess lint, and she thought she could readily identify which of the workers were their parents.

It was noisy. Besides the hum of the engines to run the looms, there were the loud thwacks and clunks and bangs of the process of making cloth. Occasionally a human voice called out a greeting or a warning, but for the most part Harriet found the workers rather a quiet lot.

At one point, Phillip sidled up to her and, speaking in a low voice, pointed at a machine near them. "Aunt Harriet, do look at those children."

"What about them?"

"That girl is no older than Sarah and that boy is no bigger than either of the twins."

"You are right, my dear. And there are at least two workers on this floor who are probably your age."

"I know." His voice was dull.

"Is something the matter?" It was the overseer who had noticed they were not trotting dutifully along in the "inspection tour" mode.

"Oh, no," Harriet dissembled. "I was just wondering what you use for light on truly dark days or late shifts."

"We have oil lanterns. Smelly, but they give off enough light to get the work done."

His reply brought to mind the smells of this environment. She quickly jotted notes about the oil on the floor, the dry smell of cotton lint floating in the air, and the occasional whiff of an unwashed body among the workers. It occurred to Harriet that her nephew was seeing a side of life he might never have imagined before. She *had* imagined it, but had rarely encountered it first-hand.

The tour continued with little variation except in the type of cloth being produced here and there. They visited each floor of both buildings, for Quint said—and Harriet agreed—that it was important that Phillip make his appearance to all the workers, not to slight any group.

On the fourth floor of the second mill, the tour was proceeding as it had elsewhere—the overseer this time a middle-aged man in black trousers and a black coat—when suddenly a woman working one of the looms near the door simply slumped to the floor. Harriet thought later it was a miracle that she had fallen away from the machine, for who knew what might have happened had she tumbled into the workings of the loom itself? She was a relatively young woman—probably about her own age, Harriet surmised. She was thin and dressed in a thin cotton dress that showed signs of wear, but seemed clean. She had smiled and greeted the visitors cheerfully as they had passed through earlier.

"Mama!" a girl child screamed.

They all turned abruptly, but Quint was the first to act. He squatted beside the woman and raised her to a sitting position. She was already coming around.

"I—wh-what happened?" she asked in a shaky voice.

The little girl, who could not have had more than seven years, now stood at her mother's side. The child was dressed in the same cotton print as her mother and had the same shade of reddish-brown hair. "You fainted again, Mama."

"No. I couldn't have," the woman insisted, already trying to loose herself from Quint's hold.

"I am quite sure you did, madam," Quint said, not allowing her to try to stand.

"Please. Let me up. I'll be all right." She sounded more embarrassed than hurt, Harriet thought.

"Just stay still a moment," Quint ordered, his arm still supporting her shoulders as others gathered around. "Get yourself together first. Take some deep breaths."

"Papa says it's 'cause she don't eat nothin'—gives me an' my brother her food when he's not lookin'," the little girl said.

"Oh, Betsy, please—do be quiet," her mother begged, clearly mortified.

Harriet knelt next to the woman and asked softly but sternly, "When did you last eat, Mrs.—?"

"Mrs. R-Reed," she stammered. "Y-yesterday morning. I think."

"Good heavens!" Harriet said. She looked up at those gathered around. "The poor thing just needs some food."

"Here. Give her this." Phillip held out something wrapped in paper. "It's a biscuit. Mrs. Hodges always thinks I am going to starve to death before she sees me again," he added sheepishly.

Quint took the packet, unwrapped it, and offered the biscuit to Mrs. Reed. She brushed his hand away. "Oh, no. I couldn't. Just help me up, please."

"You can and you will," he said. "I am not letting you up until you take the first bite."

She heaved a sigh, but did as he told her.

Quint glanced at the overseer for this floor. "Is there someplace she can sit for a while? And can you get her a drink of water?"

"There's a bench under the windows," the man mumbled. "I'll be right back with the water, my lord."

Hoping to spare the woman further embarrassment, Harriet helped support her as Quint stood and guided her to the bench, where she sat with the child standing at her knee. Harriet noted that she nibbled rather eagerly at the biscuit, but nevertheless broke off a bit to give to her daughter. The overseer returned with a ceramic mug of water, which he handed to Quint to give to Mrs. Reed.

Harriet sat next to Mrs. Reed on the bench and looked up at Quint. Seeing concern and confusion in his eyes, she said, "Why don't you and the others continue on and catch me up when you finish? I'll sit with Mrs. Reed to see that all is well with her before we leave."

"Th-that is not necessary," Mrs. Reed protested. "I am all right now. Truly I am."

Quint ignored her protest. "Thank you, Miss Mayfield."

Moments later, as her own party climbed the stairs to the floor above, Harriet sat with the mother and child listening to the clanks and thuds of the mechanical giants at work around the little threesome.

Chapter 11

Harriet sat quietly next to Mrs. Reed for a few minutes as the woman regained control of herself. She heard her say softly to her daughter, "Betsy, you go on back to your sweeping up. I'll rejoin you in a few minutes."

"All right, Mama." The little girl gave her mother a questioning look, but quietly obeyed.

Harriet searched for some way to introduce any of the dozens of questions she felt she should be seizing the opportunity to ask when the floor overseer approached and held out a square of cloth with a piece of bread and cheese on it. "Here, Miz Reed. It's a bit left over from me own lunch, but might tide ye over."

Mrs. Reed looked up and blushed. "Why, thank you, Mr. Pope. Th-that's not n-necessary—"

He shook the offering at her. "Yes, 'tis. Now you take it, woman. Don't be lettin' stubborn pride get in yer way."

"Yes, sir." She took the food and he quickly retreated.

"That was generous of him," Harriet said to make conversation.

"Yes. Mr. Pope is a nice enough fella. Not like some bosses, you know. Some are quick to use a whip or dock wages for the least little thing."

"Use a whip?" Harriet echoed, not bothering to hide her shock at the idea. She had seen no sign of overseers wielding whips this day.

Mrs. Reed swallowed hard around a bite of the cheese and bread. "Well, not so much in Sedwick mills, mind you. I heard his lordship—the young lord's da, ye ken—he didn't approve of such. But it happens often enough in other places—like where my husband works in Humphrey's mills."

"Good heavens," Harriet murmured. She could see that Mrs. Reed was regaining her strength and composure and she began to ask her general questions about the life of a mill worker. She explained that she planned to write about the lives of ordinary people but in no way wanted to intrude personally and Mrs. Reed should feel free to avoid answering any question that made her the least bit uncomfortable. In fact, Mrs. Reed seemed rather pleased to be thus singled out and readily responded to Harriet's queries. Afterward, Harriet was sure that when she finally wrote her articles, she would have much for which to thank one Mrs. Rosalee Reed.

* * * *

As Quint led the group back down the stairs, they paused at the fourth floor to pick up Harriet. She still sat on the bench where they had left her, though Mrs. Reed had returned to her duties. Quint searched Harriet's face and thought she looked sad. He gave her an inquiring look, but she merely smiled, brushed at a wisp of lint in front of her face, and asked, "Are we finished then?"

"Just need to pick up the books," he replied, offering her his arm.

When they were all settled in the coach, Quint could see that both Phillip and Harriet were unusually quiet. Thinking to break the conversational ice, he asked, "Did your day go well in terms of gathering information for your work, Miss Mayfield?"

"I think so. Yes. Thank you."

"And you, My Lord Sedwick," he said lightly to Phillip, who once again sat with his aunt directly across from Quint and Chet. "Were you pleased at what you have seen in some of your principal holdings?" Quint could see that something was troubling the lad, who now turned worry-filled eyes to his uncle.

"I-I am not sure. I do not feel that I know enough to be truly pleased or displeased. I feel so—so ignorant!" His last words were a hoarse whisper of despair.

"This *was* your first real visit to the mills, was it not?" Quint asked.

"Yes, but I did not expect to find so many really young workers—my age and much younger at the machines. I talked with one boy—he works twelve hours a day. Twelve hours. Works. I asked him if he ever had lessons and he just snorted at me. Then he looked scared." He turned in his seat to plead with his aunt. "I tried to reassure him, Aunt Harriet, but—" He sighed.

She patted his arm. "Never mind, Phillip. He will get over it."

"But he's only ten. And there were so many of them—some even younger, like Mrs. Reed's girl. Many of them—some adults, too, were dressed rather shabbily," he went on. "Like those people we saw in that one section of London we drove through. You remember?" He barely paused for her to nod. "And that poor woman without enough to eat. I had no idea people were so deprived right here in our part of England."

A heavy silence filled the coach and they heard clearly as the horses' hooves left the cobblestoned streets of the town and moved onto the hardened turf of the country road, and they continued to hear the jingling harness and turning wheels.

Finally, Chet said, "Try not to take it to heart so, lad. Believe me when I tell you the poor folk in this area have it much better than many I've seen. And not just in England. 'Tis the way of the world."

"I don't care! It is wrong!" Phillip said fiercely.

"Not now, Phillip," Harriet said gently, and the boy calmed, turning his attention to the window as the coach wound its way through magnificent autumn colors.

Nevertheless, Quint felt he should point out "Gibbons is right: it is the way of the world. But not all leaders of our part of it are satisfied with that. You heard what Stevens said of changes your grandfather and your father had made. When you are ready, you will continue their work."

The boy responded with a polite "Yes, sir," and turned back to the window. Quint exchanged a helpless gaze with Harriet, who merely shrugged and offered a comment about a fortuitous change in the weather.

The four of them rode for quite some time with the adults occasionally making innocuous comments now and then about the scenery or the activities they witnessed as they passed. It was, after all, autumn. Farmers were bringing in their last crops and many were obviously preparing for the final cattle market of the year to be held the next day. Quint had committed himself and Chet to accompanying Phillip to that event too. Moreover, in what he now considered to be a distinct moment of weakness, he had agreed to allow the twins to accompany them. That, of course, meant adding an extra footman to the entourage to keep track of those two imps while Quint and Chet and the new earl, along with Sedwick farmers, went about the business of buying and selling stock.

Because it was to be such a busy day with the market and all, everyone had agreed to forego the morning rides the next day, though Quint knew that Harriet had intended breaking her fast with the children in the nursery. When his mother and Mrs. Hartley did not appear for breakfast, he assumed they had taken trays in their rooms. He and Chet enjoyed dawdling over their coffee, and when they finally reported to the stable yard, Quint was shocked to see that not one, but two coaches had been outfitted with teams, drivers, and required attendants. Harriet stood near the open door of the second coach—the one without the Sedwick crest. She wore a traveling outfit of cobalt blue with a perky matching hat that sported silver ribbons. The thought flashed through his mind that she looked good enough to kiss, but what the devil was she doing here?

"Uncle Quint!" Sarah squealed and waved from within the coach. He could see Maria and Mrs. Hartley in the vehicle as well.

"What is going on here?" Quint demanded.

"We are going to the market too," Harriet said as Phillip came from around the rear of the vehicle.

"Isn't it exciting?" Sarah cried enthusiastically. "I ain't been afore, Maria's been lotsa times. So's Pip. But not me an' the twins."

Quint raised a mocking eyebrow at Harriet. "You actually think it within the realm of acceptability to cart young *ladies* off to a cattle market?" he asked in a silky voice. "Young ladies who just happen to be *my* wards—and thus *my* responsibility?" He watched with interest as her face paled and then colored markedly, first with embarrassment, then fury.

"I do most sincerely beg your pardon, my lord. It simply never occurred to me that you might object to something that is in the way of a family tradition."

"A family tradition!" He snorted. "I certainly do not recall Sedwick females buying and selling cattle—ever."

"No, of course not," she said sweetly. "But you may remember this market—like others of its kind—is more than just a cattle market, that, in fact, it is something of a *fair* with all sorts of peddlers displaying their wares, street entertainers, and the like. I am sure Phillip and the twins will be taking in some of those diversions too."

"Father and Mother always brought us once we had six years," Phillip said.

"They did?" Quint responded, recognizing defeat when it stared him in the face.

Just then his mother came bustling up. "Thank you, Harriet, for waiting for me. I see Sylvia is already here. I do hope that woman with the Belgian lace is here again this year. Oh, good morning, Quinton, dear."

"Mother." Without another word, he handed the ladies into their carriage and saw them off.

* * * *

Harriet took little part in the chitchat within the coach as it rolled out of the stable yard and through the village and then on to the market and mill town of Hendley. She was still seething over the colonel's outburst. *Good heavens! How was she to know his ever-so-noble lordship might object to the girls' going on that day's outing? Certainly his own mother had raised no objection in that regard. Quite the opposite. She had babbled on about it last night at supper.* Harriet concluded that only the presence of Maria and Sarah had surprised him and for that he blamed *her.*

"You are very quiet this morning, Miss Mayfield," Sylvia Hartley said from the seat she shared with the dowager.

"Aunt Harriet is sad because Uncle Quint yelled at her," said the precocious Sarah. "Uncle Quint makes people sad when he yells at them."

"Yelled at her? Whatever for?" the dowager asked.

"He did not know Sarah and I were coming today," Maria explained.

"Pish-tosh." The dowager waved a dismissive hand. "That boy takes everything too seriously. He will get over it."

"I daresay he already has," Harriet attempted to head off that line of discussion, but she noted Maria and Sarah shared a grin at hearing their austere uncle referred to as "that boy."

The cattle market was located outside the town some fifty yards off the main thoroughfare. Between the market and the town a wide expanse of field had been set aside to accommodate the vehicles of the men and boys attending the cattle market and the ladies and girls who would stroll about the nearby streets buying household items and trinkets from a variety of vendors and being entertained by street singers, puppet shows, and even a dancing monkey. As Harriet's little group exited their carriage, she was struck by the pungent smell emanating from the area of the animals, which she knew included horses, sheep, pigs, and even ducks and chickens, as well as both dairy and beef cows. A cacophony of animal sounds—lowing cows, bleating sheep, an occasional horse's neigh or triumphant screech of a rooster—assailed their ears.

Sarah jumped from the carriage and immediately started toward the fence surrounding the cattle market. "I want to see the pigs!" she yelled.

Her grandmother grabbed at her cloak to halt her in her tracks. "Oh, no, you do not."

Sarah stamped her foot and seemed on the verge of tears. "But, Grandmother, I only want to *see* them."

"You have seen pigs before," Maria said. "The Bensons always have them on the home farm."

"It's not the same," Sarah pouted.

"Nevertheless, you will come with us to the street fair," her grandmother said, taking a firm grip on Sarah's arm as the Sedwick females turned their backs on the cattle market and headed into the town.

In short order, the group divided as the dowager and Mrs. Hartley dawdled over a display of embroidery silks and Harriet accompanied Maria and Sarah, who were soon distracted by a Punch and Judy puppet show. Harriet was pleased to hear Sarah's giggles of delight at the classic slapstick fun. When the puppeteers took a break they walked on and soon joined a group watching a dancing monkey. The animal, dressed in a bright orange shirt and green shorts, wore a harness with a long leash that was attached to the wrist of a man who sat on a stool playing a concertina. When the music stopped, the monkey picked up a tin cup near the stool and held it out for members of the crowd toss in coins. Harriet reached into her reticule for a coin to give to Sarah. Those standing nearby readily allowed the little girl room to approach the animal. As Sarah gingerly put her coin in the cup, the monkey put a hand on his belly and bowed to her.

The crowd laughed at this, and Sarah emitted a little squeal of glee. "Oh, look. He likes me."

"'Course he does," the concertina man said with a chuckle. "My Dickie here likes all the pretty ladies."

Sarah beamed at this and extended a hand toward the monkey. "May I pet him?"

The man quickly took a firm grip on the leash. "Best not, my lady. Dickie's manners sometimes ain't the best."

"Oh." A disappointed Sarah drew her hand back.

To Harriet, the man said quietly, "He *is* an animal, you see—could be startled by somethin'—an' who knows?—" He shrugged.

"Of course," Harriet said. She took Sarah's hand and drew both girls along to the next distraction.

They happened upon a line of people waiting in front of a knife sharpener to avail themselves of his services. He was a man of some age—Harriet guessed at least sixty—and he was dressed plainly in leather pants and a heavy cotton shirt. He operated his sharpening stone with one foot as he guided his blades with his hands.

"Oh, look. There's Turkins!" Sarah pulled Harriet to stand before a tall blond young man standing in the line. He was dressed in the everyday brown and tan livery of the Sedwick servants. "Turkins! Why are you here?" Sarah demanded.

Wilma Counts

The young man lifted a bulky, long bag at his side and smiled at Sarah. "Mrs. Hodges sent me to get some o' her knives sharpened. Mostly we do 'em ourselves, but she likes 'em done real proper like when she can."

"Of course," Harriet murmured and gestured for Maria and Sarah to move along.

But Maria stepped closer and said, "Aunt Harriet, why is that woman staring at us?"

"What woman?" Harriet looked up and around, at once catching the gaze of Mrs. Rosalee Reed holding the hand of her young daughter Betsy as they walked in the edge of those moving along the street. Both mother and daughter were dressed in the same cotton print dresses they had worn on the job the day before.

"Mrs. Reed," Harriet called as she and her nieces walked toward the Reeds. "How nice to see you. My nieces and I are taking in the fair." Mrs. Reed curtsied and her daughter followed her lead.

Ever the impatient one, before Harriet could begin to make proper introductions, Sarah said to the other little girl, "I am Sarah. What is your name?"

"B-Betsy."

"Did you see the monkey?"

"M-monkey?"

"Yes! He dances! You must see him! Can I show her, Aunt Harriet? Can I?"

"'May I,'" Harriet corrected automatically.

"May I? Please?"

"If Mrs. Reed has no objection and Maria agrees, I suppose we can visit the monkey again," Harriet said with an inquiring look at her elder niece. Maria smiled, shrugged, and sighed indulgently.

"Ah, Harriet—Maria, dear! I was just saying to Sylvia that I hoped we might see you!" The voice of the Dowager Countess of Sedwick cut through the street noise and cries of nearby vendors as the woman herself and her companion appeared on the scene.

As she introduced Mrs. Reed and her daughter, Harriet cringed inwardly at the not-so-subtle coolness with which the dowager treated these strangers. Had the woman never before met Sedwick employees casually?

The dowager cleared her throat authoritatively. "Harriet, my dear. I can see that you and—Mrs. Reed, is it not?—have some sort of business to conduct, so I shall just take my granddaughters off your hands. Come, Maria and Sarah, you will spend the rest of the afternoon with me." With that pronouncement, she made a grab for Sarah's hand.

Bewildered, Maria looked to Harriet for direction.

Mrs. Reed made a point of stepping aside and taking her child with her. Before Harriet could decide quite how to respond, Sarah jerked away from her grandmother and ran to take Betsy's hand.

"I want to show Betsy the dancing monkey."

"You will come with me, child," her grandmother said decisively.

"No! I don't want to. Auntie Harry—please. Please, don't make me."

Sarah was in tears. Harriet knew—and she was sure that the dowager knew it as well—that Sarah was capable of throwing a full-fledged temper tantrum right here in front of God and everybody, but Harriet thought there was more going on here than just a spoiled child's show of temper. Outside of her family, Sarah did not have many friends, and none who were just hers alone. Moreover, Sarah was not close to her grandmother—but then, few of the children were.

Counting on the dowager herself wanting to avoid a scene, Harriet said, "Please let her stay, my lady. We shall just visit the monkey, then be along shortly. Maria may do as she wishes."

"I shall stay with you and Sarah, Aunt Harriet," Maria said.

"No surprise there," the dowager said tightly. With a swish of her skirt, she said, "Well, let us be off, Sylvia."

The man with the dancing monkey remembered Sarah and when the animal finished its act, it bowed particularly to Sarah, who clapped her hands and giggled.

"Isn't this fun?" she fairly squealed to her new friend Betsy as Harriet dug into her reticule to search for small coins to give each girl to drop into the monkey's cup.

"Thank you, my lady," Mrs. Reed said softly as she took her daughter's hand and departed. "I shall not forget your kindness this day—nor the other."

As Harriet and the girls made their way toward the field where their coach had been parked, they came upon a group of vendors selling drinks and foodstuffs. A number of wooden tables and benches were scattered about to accommodate customers and some patrons had laid out blankets on the ground. One of the tables Harriet saw had been commandeered by the Sedwick men, along with the dowager and her companion.

"Ah, here you are! Come join us, ladies," Quint invited. "I know my Lady Sarah will not refuse a sweet cake or a maybe a tart before undertaking that lon-n-ng journey home."

"Maybe just one," Sarah said with a coy giggle as she squeezed herself onto the bench between Quint and Chet and reached for a cake.

Harriet and Maria found places on the end of that bench, directly across from the twins, who had Phillip and then the dowager and Mrs. Hartley to their right.

"We saw a puppet show," Sarah announced to her brothers in a note of triumph.

"So did we," said Richard, deliberately taking the wind out of her sails.

"Well, did you see the dancing monkey?"

"Yes, we saw the dancing monkey." Robby mocked her tone and Sarah sat back, momentarily deflated.

"Never mind, Sarah," Maria leaned forward to look at her little sister around Mr. Gibbons, "the monkey bowed especially to *you*."

"Anyway, *we* saw a man sell his wife!" Robby topped his sister's story.

"You *what*?" Harriet asked, staring in shock, first at the boy, then leaning to stare down the table at the child's uncle.

"It's true, Aunt Harriet," Richard corroborated. "We were in the auction barn. This man leads a woman in with a rope around her neck—just like a cow—an' they started bidding on her!"

Robby picked up the story. "An' this other man bought her and she went away with him real quiet. Jus' like that! 'Tis true, isn't it, Phillip? Uncle Quint?"

"Yes." Phillip's tone was dull and he kept his head down.

"Yes," Quint said. "That is the way it happened, but, as I told you before, the less said about that incident, the better."

"Oh. I forgot." Robby sounded chagrinned and directed his attention back to his food.

The general conversation turned to other sights of the market: a bull that had broken free of its hobbles, an impromptu horse race, friends not seen in a long time, but Harriet found it difficult to let go of that terrible scene of wife selling the little boys had witnessed.

She had, of course, heard of such. Facetiously known as "the poor people's method of divorce," it allowed a *man* to dispose of unwanted "property" without going through the enormous expense required by first the secular and then the ecclesiastical courts in a proper legal dissolution of a marriage. *Poor* women, *of course, had no such recourse*, Harriet thought bitterly.

In the coach on the return journey, Harriet sat between Sarah and Maria, across from the dowager and Mrs. Hartley. The older ladies and Maria leafed through fashion magazines and Sarah played with a small figure of a monkey.

"Auntie Harry," Sarah said in a serious tone.

"Yes, dear?"

"Do you think I will be able to see Betsy again? I really like her."

"I do not know, love. Betsy must work with her mama, you know."

"I should not think so," the dowager said firmly.

"But I *like* Betsy," Sarah protested.

"I meant to speak to you later on this matter, Harriet, but I suppose now is as good a time as any." Harriet braced herself. "I cannot believe that you think the Reed woman and her child of a class to be suitable associations for my grandchildren."

"They are Sedwick people, my lady. We happened to meet them on the street. Not to acknowledge them would have been rude."

"It appeared to me that you went far beyond mere acknowledgment," the dowager said. "I gave you sufficient opportunity to support me in that little scene and perhaps teach both Maria and Sarah a valuable social lesson, but you chose to ignore me—perhaps to pursue some agenda of your own. Frankly, I see no need to encourage familiarity in the lower orders. I will not have my grandchildren unnecessarily exposed to riffraff."

Harriet was nearly speechless with anger. "Lower orders? Agenda—" She hardly knew where to begin and found herself grateful when young Maria, ever the peacemaker, interceded.

"But, Grandmother, Mother and Father, and Grandfather, too, insisted we should respect the people whose labors make our lives possible."

"Yes, my darling child. Respect. There is a fine line between respect and familiarity and one must learn to maintain it, my dear. I am sure that your Uncle Quinton will see to that as one of the requisites of the education of his wards."

Harriet stared out the coach window fuming inwardly. *So: It was an abomination to have the dowager's granddaughters exposed to hard-working people like the Reeds, but the grandsons being exposed to an obscenity like wife-selling was a matter not even worthy of one's notice?*

Chapter 12

In the next two days Quint had hoped to get a moment alone with Harriet. He knew how shocked she had been at the eight-year-old twins having witnessed that wife-selling incident and he wanted her to know that, indeed, he himself would never have willingly subjected innocent children to such a scene, but the whole business had been over and done with by time he was scarcely aware of what was happening. Quint had allowed the younger boys to accompany the Sedwick farmer, Benson, and his young sons into the auction barn as Quint, Chet, and Phillip inspected a couple of mares another neighbor was considering selling; they would then meet Benson and the boys in the barn. Quint had had no qualms about entrusting the twins to Benson's care—Benson, and his father before him, had run the home farm of Sedwick for as long as Quint could remember. But by the time they had finished inspecting the mares and made their way to the auction arena, the scene there was nothing short of chaotic. Quint had breathed a sigh of relief and extended a hand in gratitude to Benson when he was able to retrieve his nephews.

Since Saturday's market, Quint had found little opportunity to explain to Harriet and he feared she still thought the worst of the whole affair. She had joined the men and Phillip for the usual morning rides, but so had Maria, and soon enough Harriet and her niece, along with a groom, were off on jaunts of their own. On Sunday afternoon Phillip had sought a private word with his uncle. Quint cringed inwardly, for he thought he knew what was coming.

"I want to discuss my going to school," Phillip blurted even as he came through the library door.

Quint turned from where he had been standing staring out the window, wondering if those clouds heralded rain. He sighed and reached deeply for at least a shred of patience. "There is simply nothing to discuss. I will not shirk my responsibility in this matter, nor will I allow you to shirk yours." He gestured for the boy to take a tan leather-covered wing chair on one side of the fireplace, and he took the matching chair on the other side.

"Uncle Quint—sir." Phillip was apparently striving for a "man-to-man" tone. He sat forward on the edge of the chair, his hands clasped between his knees. "Please understand that I have no wish to shirk my responsibilities. Indeed, I feel I need to know them far more thoroughly than I do in order to prepare myself adequately."

"You will get that preparation at Eton, just as your father did. And your grandfather before him. And then university. You will be prepared. Believe me. You will be."

"Yes. I understand that. I do not reject the idea of school."

"Well, then—"

"Just not yet." Phillip held his uncle's gaze for a moment, but did not hold the eye contact. Apparently seeing no encouragement there, he looked at the floor and went on. "It-it seems to me that I could have a tutor for this next year and *then* go away the following year. Meanwhile, I could go about estate matters with you as I have done these last few days. I have learned a great deal doing that!"

Quint grunted noncommittally.

"Cousin Jeremy had a tutor all last year. Aunt Harriet said he—that tutor—might still be available."

"Oh, she did, did she?"

"And a tutor could work with the twins too."

"Was that also your Aunt Harriet's idea?"

Phillip looked up. "I—I am not sure, sir. She may have mentioned that. Or perhaps Maria did."

Quint decided to change direction slightly. "Phillip, how old are you?"

"Sir?"

"How old are you?"

"Th-thirteen. My birthday was in July."

"Thirteen. You should have been in school already—for at least a year. Actually, two, or even three." He paused and softened his tone. "You do make some good points, Phillip, but I am sorry—we simply cannot put this off any longer."

"I-I am not ready, Uncle Quint. Truly, I-I am not ready." Phillip stood, a stricken look on his face.

Quint leaned back in his chair to look up at him. "Not ready? To be a schoolboy? Seems to me you are *beyond* ready, my lad."

"I am not ready to be Sedwick." This came as an outburst and Quint thought there might have been something like a sob at the end of it, but Phillip hurried from the room before Quint could reply.

As the door closed behind the boy, Quint who had risen too, sat back down and ran a hand through his hair. *Good God. What now? I swear, Win, you dealt me a hand I cannot play. God knew what He was doing when He made you the father, not me. But you had to go and second guess God Himself. I suppose this is giving the two of you quite a laugh....*

He shook his head and returned to his desk and those infernal books he had dragged back from the mill visit, trying to correlate those with the books kept by his father and brother.

Sometime later, Chet came in. Seeing Quint immersed in the two sets of books, he quipped, "Ah, I see you at your favorite pastime, oh, noble lord of the manor."

"Keep that up, Chet, and I shall be inclined to invite you to join me in grass for breakfast."

Chet shook an admonishing finger at him. "Ah. Ah. Ah. You *know* dueling has been illegal in England for lo! these many years." Chet came around to look over Quint's shoulder. "Problems?"

"Not Really. That is, not in the books themselves. Both sets of books show the same sad state of affairs. There is a tremendous load of debt here—two, maybe three generations of it. And it has changed hands more than once! Sedwick is, as you and I thought earlier, in troubled water. But it is hard to determine the level of the flood when it is not clear—at this point—how much or to whom all the debt is owed. Make that debts. Plural."

"No help from Stevens's books?"

"None that I can see. Boskins, the Sedwick solicitor in London, has not responded to my letter." Quint ran a hand through his hair again and heaved a sigh. "I suppose I shall have to make a trip to London. How do you feel about going to London, Chet?"

Chet threw up his hands in mock defense. "Not me, my lord. Please. Not me."

"Maybe we could just run away to sea together. Get away from all this. Is that not what happens in story books?"

"Alas, alack." Chet's sympathy was not entirely lacking in sincerity.

Quint grimaced. "Exactly." He motioned Chet to draw up a chair beside the desk and shoved a set of the books at him. "Now. Let us see where and how we might squeeze a few more shekels out of these farms and mills."

* * * *

"He would not listen to me—not really. Just said I should already be in school," Phillip moaned to Harriet and Maria in the evening of the following day when the children initiated yet another of their bedtime conferences in Harriet's sitting room.

"Well, that is that," Maria said. "There is nothing more to do, is there, Aunt Harriet?"

"Not that I can think of. But truly, Phillip—Maria—try not to be so glum about this turn of events. I thoroughly enjoyed my years at school. I met my best friends there. And, Phillip, your father always spoke well of *his* school days. I think you will get on well there."

"No doubt I will," Phillip agreed. "It is just that things seem so uncertain here at the moment. Frankly, I do not think Uncle Quint is as confident about the state of matters at Sedwick as he would have us believe he is. Aunt Harriet, did you listen to the questions he was asking the overseers and Mr. Stevens?"

"Yes, I did, and you may be right, but those are matters your uncle must work out. He is in charge, you know."

"I do know. I just wish he would include me more fully. There is so *much* I must learn."

"And you will surely do so—all in good time, Phillip." She stood to hurry them on their way. "For now, it seems we must take things as they come. At the moment, that means off to bed with both of you."

"No. Wait." Maria put a hand on her brother's arm. "Did Uncle Quint say anything about me—about my going to school?"

Phillip shook his head. "Not a word. But neither did I ask."

"Men!" Maria muttered and Harriet had to agree with that sentiment.

"Sorry, Maria," Phillip apologized.

"We shall know soon enough," Harriet assured her as she walked them to the door and kissed each of them good night.

She returned to her desk and the article she had been writing. Having put aside the plight of England's poor—that of mill workers in particular for the moment—the Lady Senator was taking up the issue of wife-selling, pointing out the injustice of such a practice to half the population of a nation that had outlawed buying and selling black slaves several years before. She went on to attack the sordid circumstances of such events, insisting that they were demeaning for all parties concerned. Harriet had spent much of her time since that Saturday sale talking with others about the subject; she spoke at length with her friends the vicar and his wife, and she had called on the local magistrate, a man in his sixties who had come across a few such cases in his tenure as a jurist. He pointed out that the law frowned on it, but was rather ineffectual and, after all, it was rather rare. Still, she wrote, it happened, and it was wrong!

The children had not mentioned the incident again, though she supposed the subject might come up with the Prince Regent's recurring attempts to shed himself of his troublesome wife. Harriet diplomatically avoided touching on that at all in her article. Nor did she broach the topic with either the children's uncle or their grandmother. In fact, she had not talked much with either of them in the last two days. They had all been polite enough, exchanging idle chitchat at breakfast, but nothing of substance. She knew Quint had spent much of this time sequestered in the library with Chet and she had a strong suspicion as to the subject of their discussions, but did not feel she should barge in with her probably unwelcome views.

As for the dowager, that exchange at the market still weighed heavily with Harriet. Lady Margaret's snobbery had been tempered in the past by the fact that she did not actually live in the Hall, and by the innate grace and generosity of spirit of a daughter-in-law she had been unable to bend to her will—also by her son's support of his wife. Harriet had hoped the younger son would show the same temperament his brother had, but she was still unsure of him.

However, she was sure of one thing: the Dowager Countess of Sedwick would like nothing better than to see the last of one Harriet Mayfield at Sedwick Hall. And were it not for Anne's seven adorable children, Harriet would like nothing better than to oblige her.

The next morning at breakfast, to the delight of Phillip and Maria, Quint announced that, weather permitting, tomorrow would be a great day for their picnic unless their grandmother or their Aunt Harriet saw reason to object. Neither lady did, and the youngsters were eager to share the news with the nursery set.

Quint rose and said, "When you have finished your breakfast, Miss Mayfield, might I have a word with you in the library?"

"Of course, Colonel." *Now what?* she wondered, but deliberately took her time with her second cup of tea.

"You wished to see me?" She closed the library door softly behind her as Quint came from behind the desk to stand directly in front of her.

"Let us sit, if you will." He directed her to a long couch. She took one end of it; he, the other. "I have a couple of questions regarding this business of school for Phillip, and for Maria."

"I should have thought you had quite all your answers on such matters by now."

"I would have thought so too," he said, giving her a direct look. "Allow me to cut to the heart of the matter. Are you deliberately trying to undermine my authority with my wards?"

"Am I *what*?" she demanded indignantly.

"You heard me. Twice Phillip has come to me suggesting he should have a tutor instead of going to Eton. I gather the idea came from you."

"No. It did not. That is, not precisely."

"Not precisely. What does that mean?"

"My Uncle Charles—Charles Montieth, that is—had a tutor for his son Jeremy until this summer. Jeremy is Phillip's cousin, you know, and the two boys spent time together when we were in London. They got on quite well."

"And the thought that a tutor would conveniently be on hand to work with the twins as well—where did that come from?"

"Now *that* may have come from me. I am not sure. It is not unreasonable."

"I agree," he said, surprising her. "A tutor for the younger boys is not unreasonable at all. Nor is a governess for the girls. I have discussed this at length with my mother, who tells me we have imposed on you far too long."

"Imposed on me? Imposed—?" She tried to digest where this was coming from, but decided she would consider it later and face the other issue first. "To set the record straight," she said in an emphatic tone, "*No, Colonel Burnes, sir,* I most assuredly have *not*, in any way whatsoever, sought to undermine your authority with any of the nieces and nephews we share. If anything, I hope I have tried to reinforce your position in their lives. They need you as a stabilizing force, now more than anything. All of them. But especially Phillip, I think. He was very close to his father and still feels the loss profoundly."

Quint sat very still for a moment, but his tone was sincere when he said, "Thank you for that." He paused, then added, "My other question concerns Maria. Apparently Win and Anne intended sending her to a certain Miss Pringle's school. I think you have some familiarity with it?"

Harriet smiled. "Some. I spent several of the happiest years of my life there."

"Then you would recommend it?"

"Emphatically. It has maintained its reputation for the very highest standards."

"From the few notes they left, Win and Anne seem to have had their minds made up regarding Miss Pringle's school," Quint said.

Harriet nodded. "I tried to remain neutral, but I think they were leaning that way." She paused, and then plunged ahead. "However, I do think Maria's going away to school this year would have been dependent on Phillip's doing so, and, frankly, I am not at all certain Win had made up his mind on that issue yet when the accident occurred."

"Their grandmother feels both children should be in school."

"Oh, I am sure she does."

"What does that mean?" He gave her a quizzical look.

"Nothing. Nothing at all." Harriet bit her tongue, but she shrugged and stumbled on as he continued to hold her gaze. "Merely that members of Lady Margaret's generation do not always welcome the presence of children at various activities."

"That is rather a harsh view."

"I do not mean to suggest that Lady Margaret does not love her grandchildren. I am quite sure she wants the best for them." *And only* she *knows what is best,* Harriet added to herself.

"I am sure you are right," Quint said.

"Was there anything else, Colonel Burnes?"

"No." He stood and extended a hand, which she took to rise and stand next to him. There was a long moment in which his dark hazel eyes held her gaze in what seemed a mesmerized eternity. She felt the heat of his body and smelled the spiciness of his cologne. For an instant, she thought he might be about to kiss her. For an instant, she wanted him to. Then he stepped back and she hurried out.

She stood outside the closed door for a full minute or more, her hands clenched at her side. *You weak, stupid, fickle female!* she railed at herself. *You would have allowed that man to kiss you. Worse: you would have kissed him back!*

She continued up the stairs, doing her best to ignore that full-length portrait of him on the landing, but continuing to chastise herself. The colonel had all but outright accused her of colluding with a child against what might be in the child's best interest! And she had considered kissing him? And, God help her, she still wondered what that would have been like!

* * * *

The weather the next day, Quint was thankful to see, was most cooperative. It was one of those glorious days of September that remind one that summer still has a hand on the reins of power. Late in the morning, two open carriages set out to convey much of the Sedwick household—and a sufficient contingent of servants—up the river from the Hall to the ruins of an ancient abbey.

"The abbey was established by one of the followers of William the Conqueror," Quint explained to Chet, "but thoroughly destroyed during Henry VIII's rampages against the Church. Then—as so often happened all over England—church buildings became quarries for new structures."

Quint and Chet had chosen to ride and did so at a slow walk beside the carriage transporting the dowager and her companion, along with Maria and the twins. Phillip sat beside the coachman, who had mostly turned the reins over to the young earl for the short journey. Sarah sat like a princess in front of Quint.

"Faster, Uncle Quint. I want to go faster." Sarah began kicking her feet, but the horse chose to respond to the man in the saddle.

Quint put a hand on her foot. "This is fast enough. Now behave."

"She can ride in the carriage with us," her grandmother said.

"No-o-o." Sarah snuggled against Quint, but quickly turned her attention to Tippy, one of the two stable dogs trotting along with the entourage.

Quint glanced back at the other carriage, which held Harriet Mayfield and the two youngest children, as well as one of the children's nurses and two other servants as well as numerous baskets and bundles, plus the cat Muffin and the dog Sir Gawain. He knew she had chosen to ride in the second carriage, and for a brief moment, he had wondered why. Maria could have easily ridden with her little sisters for such a short distance. It was only seven miles!

When they arrived at the ruins, riders dismounted and carriages quickly disgorged their passengers. Children, dogs, and the cat scattered in glee as the servants set about laying out blankets and covered dishes. Having tied up their horses, Quint and Chet stood next to the knee-high ruins of a wall looking out over the terrain.

"This is beautiful," Chet said.

Quint surveyed it, trying to take in the scene through his friend's eyes. "Yes. I think I'd forgot just how splendid this view is." The abbey had been built on a rocky cliff overlooking a bend in the river. The opposite bank, considerably lower, displayed a panorama of farmland and woodland with here and there gray stone buildings jutting out of fields or a wisp of smoke floating up from among the trees. Overall, a plethora of shades of green land with the blue sky, feathery clouds, and silvery river added contrast to please the eye.

Harriet had come up beside them in time to hear their comments. She held the two-year-old Matilda astraddle one hip. "It truly does bring to life the work of a poet, does it not?" she asked.

"I assume you refer to the work of Mr. Wordsworth," Quint said.

She glanced at him, one eyebrow raised. "Why, yes, I do."

He grinned at her apparent surprise, but whatever reply he might have made was lost as his mother approached.

"Harriet, dear," the dowager admonished, "there is really no need for you to cart that child about like some peasant woman. We do have servants for that sort of thing, you know."

"Tilly and I are quite comfortable," Harriet replied, brushing a curl off the little girl's face. "She just woke up."

The child snuggled her face against her aunt's breast. *Lucky Tilly*, Quint thought. He turned to call to Phillip to help map a court for a game of pall-mall. There followed a good deal of cheerful squabbling as they decided upon teams for the game, finally settling on a team of "men" versus "women," though certain of the "men" complained that they were outnumbered and that Elly and Tilly would need help hitting the colorful balls through the wickets. Eventually it was sorted out and the game proceeded—boisterous, noisy, and great fun for all.

Quint kept a sharp eye especially on Phillip and Maria throughout, for they were to leave late the following week for their respective schools. Both seemed content with that decision now, and today both seemed happy to engage in a purely family outing. Phillip, especially, was being amiable and cheerful, even kind and helpful to each of his siblings. Quint surmised that Phillip was recognizing the transition in his life for what it was, and his heart went out to the lad.

Soon enough, the raucous game came to an end, and they all repaired to the lunch laid out on the blankets in what had been the center of the cloister of the abbey chapel. In a corner where two walls met, a servant had built a fire to boil water for tea. They feasted on roasted chicken and beef, cheeses, bread, vegetable and fruit salads, and an assortment of condiments, as well as biscuits, tasty cakes, and tarts.

They still sat on or near the edges of the blankets when Quint observed, "Mrs. Hodges outdid herself."

"That she did," Harriet agreed. "Maria's favorite lemon cake and Phillip's favorite tart!"

"Not to mention lemonade for tender palates and wine for those not so tender." Quint lifted the bottle to refill glasses as needed.

The meal reduced to bits and crumbs, the two youngest seemed about to succumb to the arms of Morpheus at the knee of Nurse Tavenner. The other children were engaged in an impromptu game of hide-and-go-seek loosely supervised by Phillip and Maria. Chet lay stretched out at the edge of one of the blankets. The dowager sat in a folding chair that had been brought especially for her and set so as to give her a commanding view of the scenery and of the party. Mrs. Hartley sat on the blanket at her feet. Quint noted that Miss Mayfield had chosen a place that allowed her mostly to avoid direct interaction with his mother. Not that he could blame her overmuch...

His mother's snide comment about peasant women brought to mind other instances of seemingly chance comments from his mother alluding directly or indirectly to Miss Mayfield. He sighed inwardly. Sooner or later his mother would probably precipitate some sort of confrontation in that quarter. *But not today, God willing. Not today.*

He stood, and looking down into Harriet's beguiling eyes, said, "Miss Mayfield, have you seen the view of the river from the remains of the bell tower?"

She looked up at him questioningly, but readily took his hand and rose. "I am not sure that I have."

"Oh, surely you must have done so," Lady Margaret interposed.

"A spectacular bit of scenery. It quite reminds me of a walking tour I once took with my first husband," Mrs. Hartley began.

The dowager cut her off. "Yes, Sylvia. Would you mind handing me another of those ginger biscuits?"

Chet raised the arm he had slung over his forehead, winked at Quint, and gave him a lazy grin.

There had once been two large buildings between the cloister and the bell tower. Harriet walked beside him and, when they were out of earshot of the others, asked, "Have you something on your mind, oh lord and master of all that is Sedwick Hall and beyond?"

"Perhaps consigning saucy women to a dungeon? But—alas—in years of searching, Win and I never found a dungeon here." She stumbled over a large stone; he gripped her upper arm to steady her, catching a trace of her perfume, an airy blend of spring flowers. Reluctantly, he released his hold, and his voice was more serious, "However, I am wondering if I am imagining things—or perhaps seeing them as I *want* to see them. Has our Phillip now fully accepted the idea of going to Eton next week?"

She stopped, facing him. "I noticed it too—the change, I mean. I do not know. He certainly *seems* more positive, more optimistic. One can hope...."

They had reached the ruins of the bell tower and stood on what was left of part of the wall. The tower itself had once been a circular structure some twenty-five feet in diameter, situated so that it seemed to hang over the river and provided a clear view in both directions of the waterway.

"It probably had a wooden base at the top for the bells," Quint explained, "and from its position, it must surely have served as a major defense position, for it affords such a clear view of possible approaching enemies."

Harriet smiled. "Ever the soldier, eh?"

He shrugged. "I suppose we should be getting back. I just wanted to affirm that you and I are on the same page regarding our mutual nephew."

"We seem to be."

He did not like the hesitancy he sensed, but he would not make an issue of it now. He stepped down from the wall and turned to offer a hand. As she reached for his hand, her foot caught on a protruding brick and, with a small yelp, she fell against him, tumbling both of them to the ground. Instinctively, he grabbed her to him and managed it so that she landed more or less on top of him, her face close to his. Out of breath, they stared intently at each other.

"Are you all right?" he asked.

"I-I think so." She pushed against his shoulder to rise.

He put a hand behind her head to bring her lips to his—gently at first, but in an instant, she was clearly, urgently sharing the enthusiasm of the kiss, welcoming his eagerness to probe deeper. Then, they parted and she rolled to the side.

Looking at him rather sheepishly she whispered, "Oh, my."

They scrambled to their feet and she began brushing at her skirt.

"I—uh—do I owe you an apology, Miss Mayfield?"

She looked up at him, her eyes quite blue, and full of laughter—as was her voice. "Oh, I hardly think I could cry blame for that—do you? And considering the circumstances, do you not think it should be 'Quint' and 'Harriet' now?"

He grinned at her. "As you please."

"However, I hardly think this was wise of either of us," she said primly. "And you are right. We really should be getting back."

He grinned again. "If you insist."

Chapter 13

During the rest of the afternoon Harriet managed to maintain an outward demeanor that belied the inner turmoil wrought by that kiss. She teased and cuddled the youngest and played games with the older children and adults. Yet always in forefront of thought and emotion was the sensation of Quint's lips against hers. Whenever their eyes chanced to meet, there was a glint of knowledge, a twinkle of warmth that told her he also remembered.

She admonished herself repeatedly for such foolishness. After all, she was no green girl fresh from the schoolroom. She had had her share of kisses and caresses. But, Lord, none like this. Nor had her response ever, ever been so immediate and so intense....

The sun was beginning to set by the time the picnic was truly over. Back in the stable yard when both carriages had been emptied of passengers, Harriet pulled Phillip aside for a quiet word, whereupon the boy quickly gathered Maria, Sarah, and the twins, and approached their uncle and grandmother.

"Uncle Quint, Grandmother, we should like to thank you for a most enjoyable day," he said with a very correct bow.

"How sweet," the dowager said.

"You are most welcome," Quint said with a meaningful glance at Harriet. "I'm sure I enjoyed this day quite as much as *any* in recent memory."

She smothered a full-blown smile in response, but did not turn away from his gaze.

Later she did smile fondly to see that even the usually exuberant twins had been so "played out" this day that they did not object to the early supper and only one chapter of the current story being shared at bedtime. Having seen the children tucked into their respective beds, Harriet gathered up a bit of needlework and, joining the other adults in the drawing room below, waved Quint and Chet back to their seats at a chess table, and took a chair nearby.

"So—" The dowager was obviously continuing an interrupted line of discussion. "I was right: a picnic will be a perfect form of entertainment for my houseguests. We shall have it early on, though, while the weather is most likely to hold. My goodness! It is less than three weeks away! Are you sure we are prepared, Quinton dear?"

"Yes, Mother." He sounded more resigned than enthusiastic, Harriet thought. "The guns have been cleaned and the gamekeeper assures me there are sufficient grouse in the woods."

The dowager, occupying her favorite gold plush upholstered chair, clasped her hands in approval. "And next week all the guest rooms will be aired and the ballroom will be dusted and shined to a fare-thee-well— such as Sedwick has not seen in years! Oh, how I do love a house party."

"Yours were always such a delight, Lady Margaret," Sylvia Hartley said, as if on cue. "You gave one attended by the Prince Regent himself, did you not?"

"Why, yes, I did," Lady Margaret replied, "though he was not yet the Regent in those days."

"Nevertheless, he managed to put a serious dent in Grandfather's supply of port," Quint offered in an aside to Chet.

"Quinton Burnes." The dowager addressed her son in the mock tone of a mother admonishing a child. "You will not speak so of a member of the royal family."

"Just repeating what was said, ma'am."

"Even so—"

"The prince is said to have a taste for fine wine," Mrs. Hartley said.

"Well, you may rest easy, Quinton dear," his mother said, "Prince George is not on my guest list this year."

"Good." He stood and went to the sideboard, where he replenished his own and Chet's brandy drinks and poured one for Harriet after lifting the decanter with a silent question in her direction. The older ladies were drinking tea. "We shall drink to George's absence. And," he added with a quick wink at Harriet, "to the especially fine day we've just had."

She nearly choked on the first sip of brandy, covered nicely, and rolled her eyes at him—which brought forth a grin.

"Did I miss something?" Chet asked.

"Nothing important," Harriet said. Quint raised an eyebrow.

Feeling that she had interrupted the men at their game and the ladies at their conversation, Harriet finished her drink and excused herself with the plea that she was working on the final copy of an article and wished to get it to her editor in the next mail. She slept fitfully that night and later than usual the next morning.

She stood near the long work table in the middle of the kitchen stuffing the pockets of her riding habit with carrots for Miss Priss when a young groom from the stable came rushing in through the outer door.

"Beggin' pardon, Miss Mayfield, Mrs. Hodges," he said excitedly. "Dolan sent me for his lordship—for the colonel. He's needed—real quick like."

"Why? Is something wrong?" Harriet asked, alarmed.

"It's the young lord. Lord Sedwick." The young man's voice rose an octave in a stage of panic.

At that moment Quint, with Chet right behind him, entered the kitchen, apparently on the same mission that had originally drawn Harriet here.

"Sedwick?" Quint's alarm reflected Harriet's. "What is going on with Sedwick?"

The young groom turned wide eyes on Quint. "D-Dolan sent me for you, sir! Lord Phillip—he come out and ordered mounts for you an' him an' Mr. Gibbons, jus' like usual. We brung 'em out an' got 'em ready, an'—an' afore we could stop 'im, the young lord, he—he jumped onto *your* horse—right onto Lucifer's saddle and kicked him into a furious run. Man! Can that horse go! Caught us all by surprise, sir. We jus' didn't know *what* to do for a minute or so. Then Dolan yelled at me to come get you and he jumped on Etna and went after Lucifer an' his lordship. Others is gettin' more mounts ready."

"Let's go," Quint said.

"I am coming too," Harriet said.

"That won't be necessary," Quint said.

She ignored him and rushed out the door behind him and Chet. By the time she reached the stable, the men were already off on the mounts that had been previously saddled. By the time hers was prepared, and she and a groom were on their way in pursuit, she was considerably behind—and very worried. *What in the world would have possessed Phillip to take out that devil-driven horse of his father's?*

She could see the men a dismaying distance in front of her, and that they were frighteningly close to the cliff over the river! She just hoped they knew what they were about. This was a favorite riding trail, but was one leading directly to the cliffs. And that is exactly where they were when she saw Quint and Chet jump from their mounts to join the groom Dolan bent over an inert form on the ground. The black stallion, its reins hanging loose, stamped around quietly at the edge of the scene.

"No. No. No-o-o," she cried, urging her mare to an even faster pace. Cursing at the awkwardness of unhooking her leg from the tree of the side-saddle, she hastily slid to the ground and rushed over to peer down at the still form of her nephew. She knelt beside him, her gaze immediately locking with Quint's. "Is he—?"

"He's alive. Unconscious, but alive." Quint squatted at the boy's waist on the same side of the prone figure as she; he pointed at Phillip's left leg, which lay at an odd angle. "It looks as though he may have broken that leg."

"His head is bleeding!" she cried in alarm, and began fishing for her handkerchief to press against the wound.

"Dolan thinks he hit that stone when he fell." Quint jerked his head toward a boulder about the size of a small keg. He reached to raise Phillip's head gently to allow her more efficient access to the wound, then handed her his own larger handkerchief.

"Hold this, please," she said, covering her own panic at seeing so much of Phillip's blood soak into the white cloth. She took Phillip's own neckcloth to tie the pad in place.

"Well done, Madam Doctor Mayfield. I sent Hankins—he came out here with Dolan—back for a wagon and to go for the doctor."

"Shouldn't we move Phillip to that grassy plot? H-he looks so vulnerable just lying there." Her voice caught.

Quint shifted in his crouching position to slip an arm around her waist. "Shh. Try not to think the worst." She felt his lips moving against her temple, but it was his baritone voice more than the reassuring words that brought her comfort. "Chet has been looking him over head to toe. Chet was as good as any of McGrigor's men at spotting how badly a man might be wounded. What say you, Mr. Gibbons?"

Chet, who had been kneeling at Phillip's feet on his other side, stood and came to stand near Quint and Harriet, his blue eyes full of worry and sympathy.

"The lad's suffered a broken leg, as you can clearly see. Probably a concussion from that blow to the head. Best see if we can bring him 'round. Head wounds can be tricky."

"Oh, poor Phillip." Harriet felt her shoulders slump, but she appreciated the unspoken support of these two men. Three. For Dolan, who had dutifully seen to the immediate care of the animals, was also deeply concerned about the fate of this man-child on whose fate all of the Sedwick earldom ultimately depended.

"Far as I can see," Chet announced, "that blow to his head and the broken leg are the worst of it, though he winced some when I touched that right ankle. It might be sprained."

"Dear God. Both legs injured," Harriet said.

"It might not be so very bad," Quint said. "But what in the world possessed him to take out Lucifer? Dolan? What happened?"

Dolan shook a head of reddish-brown hair in confusion and gave Quint a bleak look. "I really don't know, sir. The young earl—he come out earlier than usual, said you and Mr. Gibbons was comin' right soon, an' we should saddle the usual mounts—which we did. The horses to be rode was all tied at the rail proper like an' Tucker an' me stepped into the tack room. 'Twasn't more 'n a few seconds, I swear. The lad knows them horses well enough! The next thing we know Lord Sedwick, he jumped onto Lucifer's saddle and jus' took off! Shouting and kicking to make him go faster—as though Lucifer ever needed much encouragement to go faster. The other horses were straining at their tethers and bellering their objections. It were right chaotic here. I sent Tommy up to the Hall to notify you an' Tucker an' me went after these two."

"Quite right," Quint reassured him, even as they heard a wagon and another vehicle as well as a couple of riders approaching. The other vehicle turned out to be a gig driven by Herbert Babcock, a man of middle years who had served as the local doctor for as long as Harriet could remember. Spry for a man of his years, he quickly brought his horse to a halt and jumped down, bag in hand, ready to render service to his patient. "What have we here?"

Quint and Chet filled him in as the doctor made his own hurried assessment that mostly concurred with theirs. Phillip began to regain consciousness and to thrash around a bit, but any movement of his leg brought a cry of pain.

Harriet still knelt at his head and placed a comforting hand on his brow. "Shh, Phillip. Try to be quiet, dear. We know it hurts. Dr. Babcock is here."

"Mmmm."

As the doctor directed, a heavy blanket was spread on top of a crude patchwork quilt of course fabrics and mismatched colors. With Dolan's help, Quint and Chet slowly and gently transferred the injured youth to the blanket. Harriet fought against tears of her own at seeing Phillip wage a battle against weeping in front of his uncle and the other men. The tight clench of his jaw said volumes about his pain. As soon as they had Phillip arranged in the wagon, Harriet, having already turned over care of her mare to one of the grooms, was handed in to sit next to Phillip, managing to fashion a pillow of sorts for his head by turning under the corner of the blanket-quilt. Quint and the doctor also climbed onto the bed of the wagon, both taking care to joggle the vehicle as little as possible as they did so. Quint sat at the boy's waist on the same side as Harriet, opposite the doctor. When she could spare a glance for the two men, she tried not to be further worried by the solemn looks on their faces.

The wagon began to move. Harriet cast a startled glance from Phillip to Quint and the doctor, then raised her gaze to see that Chet, Dolan, and other grooms were in place to accompany them. She was also slightly startled when she felt Quint's reassuring grip on her hand.

"He will be all right. He has to be."

"Yes," she whispered, holding his gaze.

The wagon jerked across a large stone and Phillip screamed in pain.

"There, there, son," Doctor Babcock said. "Hold on now. I am not about to lose you—or any part of you—thirteen years after helping your dear mama introduce you to what the poets call 'this veil of tears.'"

"Especially when we have the ever-cheerful bedside manner of one Herbert Babcock to see us through it, eh?" Quint asked.

Babcock merely shrugged and fussed with the lighter blanket covering the patient.

The distance back to the Hall was only a matter of about four miles, but Harriet thought it would never end. She thought they felt every single pebble the iron wheels touched. Anything larger earned superlatives in description and brought forth cries from others besides injured boy.

"Any idea why the boy was out on that wild beast hardly anybody ever dared ride but his father?" Babcock asked. Harriet thought Phillip cringed at the question; he closed his eyes tightly and seemed to be trying to shrink his whole body into itself.

She felt Quint glance at her before responding to the doctor. "No. Not really. He mentioned maybe riding Lucifer someday, but it was always *someday*—in the future. The distant future. Who knew the future was now?"

Just then they all felt the wagon hit a particularly hard bump and the patient let out a cry. Harriet bent over him, patting his shoulder. "We are almost there, Phillip. Hold on, sweetheart. You can do this."

"We Englishmen have to keep that 'stiff upper lip' in front of this Scot, you know," Quint said with a gesture at Chet, who rode beside the wagon directly within Phillip's line of vision. Harriet saw the boy give the two men a weak grin as the entourage made its way into the stable yard.

Four of the biggest, tallest footmen gently carried their young lord up to his room, which, by his own request, remained his old room in the nursery suite. For a fleeting moment and with a touch of amusement, Harriet also recalled *why* this room in the nursery room was still his lordship's bed chamber of choice. Some two months after the accident that had robbed the earldom of the sixth holder of the Sedwick title—and while the man who *should* have been in charge of the entire estate still lay in France recovering from wounds—the dowager countess had simply taken it upon herself to have herself and her companion moved into the main Hall. In essence, she took over as the countess she had once been....

At the time, Harriet had wondered at the woman's audacity, but in truth it was simply none of her business, was it? And then had come that business of Phillip's room. Harriet had joined the children that day. They were all having lunch together in the nursery. The dowager, who rarely visited the nursery rooms, chose to appear just as the maids were clearing the table. Phillip stood at his grandmother's entrance, and, at his urging, so did the twins. Harriet motioned for a maid to draw up a chair for Lady Margaret next to Phillip at the large round table.

"Phillip, dear," the dowager said in that voice adults use when trying to convince young people they are on the same level, "now that you are the earl and have the order of everything, do you not think it time you took your proper position and moved into the earl's chambers?"

Phillip stared at her, shocked. "Wha-at? You are saying I sh-should move into F-Father's room? But that room is Father's!"

"Phillip—dear boy." His grandmother was talking down to him now. "It is the *earl's* room. And you are the earl now."

Phillip gave his grandmother a speculative look. "Did you not say I now have the ordering of everything?"

"Within reason—until your Uncle Quinton arrives to take over his duties as your guardian," she said, almost agreeably.

"Good. I order that I shall stay where I am. My present accommodations suit me very well." He stood. "Now, was there anything else, Grandmother?"

"Why—uh—no, dear."

* * * *

Quint admired Phillip's fortitude. The boy had allowed himself few outcries of pain, only a moan or a grunt now and then. Nurse Tavenner quickly produced a nightshirt, then she disappeared along with one of the footmen. Presently, the footman returned with two large buckets of hot water and Tavenner came back with wooden slats for a brace, towels, and cloths for bandages.

"Just ring us if you need anything else," she said.

Quint had not remembered Babcock as being quite such a chatty fellow, but he was grateful to the man for a running monologue, explaining to the patient and bystanders what he was doing and why. "Ready, lad? With your uncle's help, we shall put that bone back in place, then strap some wooden slats next to it to hold it in place. Now, I'm not going to stand here and lie to you and tell you it won't hurt. It will. Something terrible. So—do as the Bard says, lad, and 'screw your courage to the sticking place.'"

Phillip grimaced. "H-he—I mean she—was talking about *murder*."

"Eh? Why, so she was." Babcock look up at Quint. "Smart lad."

"Doc?" Phillip asked.

"Yes, my lord?"

"Would you mind allowing my Aunt Harriet to be here?"

The doctor raised his eyebrows in surprise. "Miss Mayfield? Well—'tis not common—usually we try to protect our ladies from such, don't you know?" Babcock shot Quint an inquiring glance.

"Well—whatever Aunt Harriet wishes," Phillip said weakly.

Quint turned toward the door. "I will ask her. I am sure she is hovering right outside."

And so she was. Not "hovering" exactly, but anxiously awaiting word, pacing from one window to the next. It was still fairly early in the afternoon. Mid-September sunshine appeared warmer than it was, but the golden light outside Sedwick Hall belied the atmosphere of concern and apprehension that now pervaded within. Chet sat on a chair nearby. Catching a snatch of their conversation, Quint gathered that they, too, were preoccupied by the overwhelming question of *why?*

"Just hard to tell what gets into a lad's head at that age," Chet was saying. "Trying to prove oneself a man. Not quite knowing how."

"That is one explanation at least," Quint said, stepping closer to Harriet. He laid a hand on her arm, wishing he could enfold her in his arms and offer the comfort her gaze told him they both needed. "Phillip has asked for you."

"Of course." She turned immediately toward Phillip's door.

"Just a moment. We have not set the leg yet, nor tended the head injury. Are you quite sure about this? I've seen grown men faint at the sight of a little blood."

"You did not see me do so, did you?"

"No, but—"

"I promise to maintain proper decorum, Colonel," she said primly.

"As you wish. Chet, you come along too. I suspect you and I have had far more experience in this line than any of Sedwick's footmen."

"Aye, aye, Colonel, sir."

In Phillip's room, Quint dismissed the footmen, drew up a chair for Harriet near Phillip's head, and placed himself and Chet at the doctor's disposal. Babcock took up his running monologue as he laid out the tools he would use to set the leg. Quint could see that the doctor's calm tone and straightforward explanation were effective in calming the patient. That—and the fact that the patient had a tight grip on his aunt's hand.

Reclining against three large pillows, Phillip endured the setting of the leg with a kind of quiet stoicism that Quint would have found remarkable in a soldier on a field of battle. There was something—well—*weird*—about seeing it in one so very young. He gave himself a mental shake. After all, many soldiers—of all ranks—were but youngsters Phillip's age. Some younger even.

"I am very proud of you, Phillip," Harriet said softly, brushing the boy's hair off his forehead as the doctor tied the last piece of the brace into place. "Your parents would have been pleased too. You handled this well."

Phillip gave her a bleak look and, with the hand she was not holding, he pointed at his bandaged leg. "Aunt Harriet! This was my fault. Nothing I try to do turns out right."

"It will, my dear." She caressed the hand she still held. "It will. You must simply give it time. Trust me."

He jerked away from her, then yelped at the sudden pain this brought to his leg.

"Here, here, my lord," the doctor protested. "Do not be about undoing my work now, will you, Lord Sedwick?"

"Not good form, my lad," Quint admonished.

"Sorry," Phillip muttered.

"Let us see to that head wound," the doctor said. Once again, he kept up a running commentary as he worked. "Hmm. Not bad. Not so very bad," he murmured when he was in position for a thorough examination. "I shall not lie to you, my lord. When I clean this wound, it is going to sting like the very devil. Feel free to scream at me or curse me if you wish. I've had men three times your size faint dead away on me when they were getting bits of their flesh sewn back together. Again—feel free to send me to Hades 'til this is over."

Phillip gave him a weak grin. "Th-thank you, Doc."

In the event, Phillip screamed, Quint and Chet winced, and Harriet silently wept. But soon enough it was over. The doctor was putting the finishing touches on the bandage, and then Quint and Chet restored the room to some semblance of its previous appearance, taking care not to joggle the patient around in his bed.

"I will leave you something for the pain, but unfortunately, you cannot use it for several hours yet," the doctor said, handing Quint a vial. "We must be careful about allowing patients with head injuries to sleep too soon."

"We shall take good care of him, Doc," Quint assured the medical man. "Can't let your good work come to naught." He shot a penetrating glance at his nephew. "Are you all right, Phillip?"

"Yes, sir. I mean, I-I think so. My leg hurts. So does my head. But I have no doubt I will l-live."

"That is good news indeed," Harriet said. "For I have no doubt that four of your six siblings are waiting none too patiently to see for themselves the truth of that statement."

He grinned feebly. "Maria, Sarah, and the twins."

She nodded.

"And the other two?"

"They too, but not 'til after their naps."

Phillip was quiet and seemed to be staring unseeing out the open window. Quint exchanged a brief, quizzical look with Harriet, but, finding her expression hard to read, shifted his attention back to Phillip. For a moment, Quint thought the boy might be about to cry.

"I'm sorry, Aunt Harriet. It was not supposed to end this way, was it?"

"Phillip?" she asked.

Chapter 14

"Phillip?" Harriet repeated, but receiving only a dull "umm?" by way of response, decided she had misunderstood the ramblings of one in pain. She glanced at the others. The doctor shook his head and shrugged. Chet murmured something sounding like "poor lad." Quint gave her a hard, inquiring look and appeared about to say something, but the doctor was gathering his instruments and tossing them into his bag.

"I shall be going now," he said. "Just keep him quiet, but don't let him sleep for a while—not 'til, say, after supper. One must take care with head wounds. Let those others in—they will help distract him, I'm thinking."

"Yes, Doctor," Harriet said.

"I shall see you out, Doctor," Quint said to Babcock. "I have a couple of questions, if you don't mind."

"Not at all. Not at all."

"And I shall see if I can sneak us some of Hodgie's lemon drop biscuits and a spot of tea or lemonade, if you think you can prevent our patient jumping out of bed and escaping from us," Chet said with a wink to the others, eliciting a smile from Harriet and a weak grin from Phillip.

"I shall try," she said.

When Chet was gone, she looked at Phillip, who now sat upright, with pillows behind and on either side of him, but her beloved nephew refused to hold her gaze.

"Phillip," she said gently, "you will have to explain yourself, you know. To your uncle, your grandmother. All of us. I should think the earlier, the better, my dear."

His gaze, full of confusion, locked with hers, but only for the briefest moment, then went to the window where a breeze fluttered the white lace curtains.

Her gaze followed his. "Would you like me to close the window?"

"No. I like the breeze."

She allowed a long moment of heavy silence, then pressed, "Phillip?"

He turned his face toward her, his expression distraught. For an instant, she thought he might burst into tears. But he did not. "Phillip?" she pressed again, more gently this time. "Would you care to explain to me what happened out there this morning?"

He brought a fist down on a pillow. "I-I'm not sure I can."

"Please try." She reached to clasp his hand—the one he had balled into a fist in the pillow—but he jerked away from her.

They both sat in stunned silence for a moment, then Phillip said, "I am sorry, Aunt Harriet. Truly I am. I do not mean to be rude. Certainly not to you."

"Of course you do not."

"It—it is just that the last few days—visits with the cottage weavers, the mills, the mines—not to mention a good many other things—" He heaved a long, shuddering sigh. "I tried to explain to Uncle Quint. You know I did. H-he just would not listen to me."

"You thought taking Lucifer out would somehow catch your uncle's attention?"

"Oh, Aunt Harriet, I don't know what I thought!" He swiped at a telltale tear at one eye. "I just knew something like this—or worse—would happen if I did, and it was all I could think to do. He is sending Maria and me away next week!"

The last phrase ended on something like a sob, but it was punctuated by a knock on the door, which had been left slightly ajar.

"Just a moment," Harriet called. She grabbed a clean cloth left lying near the basin, quickly dampened it, and handed it to Phillip. "Can't let the urchins see you distraught."

"Thanks," he said, wiping furiously at both eyes.

She was not surprised to see that the "urchins" were not alone.

"Found these lurking in the hallway," Quint said, ushering in Maria, Sarah, Robby, and Ricky; he carried Elly on one hip and Nurse Tavenner carried in Tilly.

Harriet exchanged an inquiring look with Quint, but it told her nothing of what she wanted to know: how much of Phillip's conversation he might have overheard.

"So—is it true?" Robby ask eagerly, dashing into the room and plopping his elbows on the bed near Phillip's arm. "Did you really an' truly take ole Luc'fer out?"

"Ow-ow!" Phillip yelped. "Get him off. Off!"

Quint grabbed the errant twin, pulled him away from the bed, and planted his little backside on a straight-backed chair against the wall. "Here, now. What were you told about behavior in a sickroom?"

"I forgotted. 'Sides, 'tis only Pip."

Quint gripped his shoulder. "Who happens to be His Noble Lordship, Seventh Earl of Sedwick, and it would behoove the lot of you to remember that bit of family history."

"Y-yes, sir."

Elly stood by the bed and tentatively touched Phillip's hand. "Does your leg hurt real bad, Phillip?"

"Not too bad, unless it gets shaken up." He cast an accusing glance at Robby, who pretended to hide his face in shame. "Actually, my head hurts worse right now."

"Some willow bark tea would help with that," four-year-old Elly said in an authoritative tone that had all the adults in the room smiling.

Phillip grinned at her. "On your recommendation, oh, learned one, I shall give it try."

At this point, the dowager sailed into the room like a royal vessel making its way to port. To everyone's relief, she had given up her deep mourning, but she still arrayed herself in subdued outfits. Today it was a mauve linen day dress trimmed in purple ribbons that flowed behind her.

"Phillip, dear, you have had us all worried sick. I do hope you have learned to mind the word of your elders."

"Yes, Grandmother." He seemed to struggle for a "dutiful" tone.

"And let this be a lesson to the rest of you too," she added, taking the chair a servant set for her near the foot of Phillip's bed.

Robby, still on the chair where Quint had put him, was behind their grandmother; he ostentatiously rolled his eyes at this. Ricky shook his head and looked at the floor; Phillip bit his lip; Maria looked away, but her eyes twinkled.

Sarah, however, took a position at center stage, put her hands on her hips, and said, "Does this mean Phillip need not go off to school next week? Surely, if he cannot even walk—"

Quint, who had taken a position near Harriet's chair, leaned forward to say quietly, "That child is too precocious by half!"

Harriet smiled up at him. "Yes. She does have a tendency to cut to the point with little preamble." She saw Phillip and Maria exchange significant glances and wondered if Quint had caught that too as all eyes were directed to him for a response to Sarah's observation.

He hesitated, then said, "Well, as to that, much will depend upon what Dr. Babcock has to say when he comes to visit again."

"In any event," the dowager said, "I should think that over the years, there have been dozens of boys at that school with crutches or braces—or even Bath chairs, should it come to that."

"No-o-o!" Phillip moaned in something close to an animal howl. He turned stricken eyes to Harriet. "Please, Aunt Harriet. You won't let them send me off like some—some c-cripple, will you? Please?"

Harriet caressed his arm that lay on the pillow near her. "Do calm yourself, Phillip," she said in a soft murmur. "It will be all right. You will see."

An unusual stillness settled on the room with the children glancing from one person to another. The dowager sat forward on the edge of her chair and addressed her grandson sternly.

"Phillip, you need to understand that the matter of your education is quite simply none of Miss Mayfield's business. Your going to school is entirely a Burnes family affair and I am sure that even she will agree that her opinion counts for very little regarding such a *family* matter."

Harriet held the other woman's gaze and lifted one eyebrow. "Ah, you put it so succinctly—and graciously, my lady." She started to rise from her chair, but felt Quint's hand pressing on her shoulder.

"It matters to me," Phillip said.

"This is not a matter to be discussed just now," Quint said just as the hall door was being shoved open.

"You see, laddie," Chet was explaining to a footman who helped him push in a laden tea cart, "it's just as I said: a right proper tea party we shall be having here."

"Ah, that's better," Quint said, instantly lessening the tension in the room. "Maria, since this is largely a party of the nursery lot, will you do us the honors and pour?"

"Of course, Uncle Quint," Maria said with a smile and a curtsy.

Harriet looked up at him and nodded her appreciation of his singling Maria out so. She was pleased to see the children immediately lapse into their usual ease and fun with one another even as they were solicitous of Phillip's possible pain. She was also pleased when their grandmother chose not prolong her presence with the group.

* * * *

Quint was glad when he could at last leave the nursery set to themselves and to such adults as he deemed better able to deal with them for the nonce. He escaped to the library for what he intended to be a short respite, but was dismayed to find his mother right on his heels.

"A word with you, Quinton, dear."

"Of course, Mother." He sighed inwardly and held the door for her.

She swept into the room, took a seat on a leather couch, and patted the space next to her. He ignored the gesture and sat on a round chair nearby, crossing his knees.

"Something on your mind, Mother?"

"I am wondering what you intend to do about Miss Mayfield once my house party is over."

"Do about—? Good heavens! What need—?"

"Try not to be so obtuse, my son. It cannot look good for her—a single female—to remain here as some sort of permanent guest. Even she must recognize that it is not quite proper."

"Is this something that must be resolved this instant?" he asked, standing.

"Perhaps not, but I should like to see it settled sooner rather than later. You must hire a proper governess for the younger children once the elder two are off to school, and then Harriet can return to London. Your bachelor household will hardly be a suitable place for her." She stood too and snapped her fingers. "I have it! The Montieths accepted the invitation to my house party—they always used to do so—she can return to London with them!"

Quint turned away from his mother, not wanting her to try to read his expression. The thought of Harriet's not being a part of life at Sedwick Hall came as a shock. A distinctly unpleasant shock. "Later, Mother. There will be plenty of time to deal with this. Now, if you will excuse me, I have a huge stack of paperwork to muddle through."

She pressed her lips together and left the room in a huff. Quint had been hard at the "huge stack of paperwork" for over twenty minutes when the butler entered to announce visitors: Edward Boskins, the Sedwick family solicitor, and his clerk. Quint rose in surprise to greet them.

"Mr. Boskins! I must admit my surprise at seeing *you*, for I was on the verge of seeking your help in trying to get a firm hold on that." Quint gestured to the desk, laden with ledgers he had brought from the steward Stevens, and those he had dug out from the desk and cupboards in this very room.

Boskins, a stocky, middle-aged man with graying brown hair, lifted a hefty attaché case and chuckled. He had warm brown eyes that bespoke sympathy. "I am afraid, my lord, that I may be adding to that lot—changing perspective, at least. But first, allow me to introduce Clarence Davis, my chief clerk. I have brought him along to take notes for us, my lord."

"Colonel will do," Quint said, guiding them to comfortable chairs and sending the butler for refreshments and for Chet before reacting to the man's words. "Hmm. That could bode either good or ill, I suppose.

Having found advice from Chet Gibbons to be invaluable for over seven years now, it simply did not occur to Quint to leave him out of something that might prove crucial in dealing with Sedwick now. When the refreshments—and Chet—arrived, that was how Quint introduced Chet to Boskins, who nodded his understanding. The conversation was casual— news of the changes in leadership in Vienna with Wellington replacing Castlereagh, the latest on-dit of the Prince Regent's ongoing wrangles with his wife—then Boskins sat back and reached for his attaché case. "Your letter arrived in our office in a most timely manner, Colonel Burnes."

"How so?" Quint asked.

"Only a few days prior to that we received this from the Seton-Trevors Bank. I think you will find it most interesting." He handed Quint a thick sheaf of papers. "The first ten pages are a summary-overview," he said, reaching for another biscuit.

Quint read the pages with increasing consternation, handing Chet each sheet as he finished. With about the third page, Quint exchanged a quizzical look with Chet, ran his hand through his hair, shook his head, and returned in wonder to his reading.

"I am simply not believing this," he muttered.

Chet returned the last sheet. "You know that adage about not looking a gift horse in the mouth."

Quint, already rearranging the pages to peruse them again, mumbled, "I also know enough to beware of something for nothing and so on." He read them again, more carefully. Then he laid them on the low table in front of the couch he shared with Chet and gave the solicitor in a chair opposite them a hard stare.

"All right, Mr. Boskins, what is going on here?"

"Frankly, Colonel Burnes, I am not sure. I put my own people to investigating immediately, and I have taken the liberty of hiring a Bow Street Runner who handles such criminal matters, but none of us feels there is anything criminal involved here."

Quint pointed a shaking finger at the papers. "So what in all God's green earth is going on? If someone is trying to take advantage of my nephew, I swear I will call the bastard out."

Boskins shifted in his chair. "I came here today hoping to find some answers myself, sir." He glanced from Quint to Chet. "Are you sure you wish me to be absolutely frank about Sedwick family business?"

Quint chuckled and waved a hand at his desk and its stacks of papers and ledgers. "Mr. Boskins, you may find it interesting to know that Mr. Gibbons has spent the best part of the last what?—three weeks?"—he glanced at Chet who nodded—"working on this with me. Chet has a better mind for such matters than I do and he is as bewildered by the state of Sedwick affairs as I am."

"That I can understand," Boskins said. His brow wrinkled in thought and he stared off at the window, then back at Chet. "Gibbons. Chester Gibbons. You would not by any chance be one of the sons of the Laird of Aberdeen?"

Chet heaved an exaggerated sigh. "Told you folks would figure it out."

Quint grinned.

"Just too big a secret to keep."

"And we tried so hard."

Boskins smiled rather sheepishly and shuffled his papers in a businesslike manner. "Yes. Yes. Well. As I was about to say: this"—he pointed at the papers Quint had laid on the table—"came as something of a shock to my brother and me." He glanced at Chet. "Our firm has handled Sedwick affairs since—" he paused.

"The great flood," Quint said.

"My brother Bruce and I have been concerned for some time—ever since we came into control of the firm when our father died. Your grandfather was still alive and—well—let us just say the fifth earl was not very amenable to listening to a couple of young whippersnappers as he called us tell him how to handle estate matters."

"Grandfather could be contrary."

The visitor nodded. "To make a long, far too familiar, and far too painful a story short—he saw little relationship between the income and outgo columns of a ledger book. Your father was, as they say, 'a chip off the old block.' His efforts to keep up with Prince George and that crowd wrought near havoc. As Sixth Earl, your brother was desperately trying to get hold of the problem, but..."

"Time just ran out for Win," Quint said.

All four men were silent for a moment, then Boskins said, almost hesitantly, "My brother and I have had serious misgivings about Sedwick affairs for some time. We discussed them at length with your brother. Now, with this new development, we thought it prudent to have a thorough discussion with you."

Quint sat back, exchanged a knowing look with Chet, and gave the visitor a sort of "go ahead" gesture.

"At first," the solicitor went on, "the gaming debts seemed innocuous enough. Heavy, mind you, but given Prinny's lot, not unusual." Boskins coughed and looked a bit embarrassed. "Even your mother's vouchers were not outlandish given her friendship with the late Duchess of Devonshire. But then our conjectures were that someone—or more than one someone— might be deliberately using gaming debts and other obligations as a means to undermine the very foundation of Sedwick holdings.

"Very interesting," Quint said. "Very interesting indeed, for Gibbons and I have just recently come to the same conclusion. Have your investigations turned up a name—or names?"

"We thought we had until recently." He pointed at the papers.

"And that was—?"

"Sir Desmond Humphreys. The man seems determined to create a monopoly on the local weaving industry. Or at least he may have had such an intention."

"But no longer does?"

"It would seem to be impractical if the Sedwick mills are out of the picture."

"Do he—and several others as well—not hold mortgages on both our mills? And sundry other unentailed properties spread over three counties?" Quint fought unsuccessfully to keep the bitterness out of his voice. *How could his own parents have done this to their children and grandchildren?*

Boskins smiled and pointed at the papers again. "Held. Past tense."

Quint sat up straight. "I do not understand this at all."

"And I was rather hoping you would be able to enlighten me," Boskins said. "Seton-Trevors assure me their transactions are perfectly legal and backed by perfectly honorable business people. Seton-Trevors is one of the City's most respected financial institutions."

"But what the devil does all this mean?" Quint asked. "How am I supposed to deal with this—this unknown entity?"

"So far as we can see, that is the situation: someone has managed to buy up all the outstanding debt against Sedwick," the solicitor explained.

"And can collect at any time," Quint said.

"Theoretically, perhaps. But what these documents actually boil down is that so long as current management—that is largely you, Colonel—continues to see things run efficiently, that will not happen."

Quint snorted. "'Efficiently.' What does that mean?"

Boskins shook his head. "The question is a good one. So far as we can determine, the person holding this bond merely wants to ensure the young earl's interests are handled with integrity until he himself can take over."

"If you read closely," Chet said, nodding in the direction of the papers, "it looks like this fella maybe doesn't know you, Quint. Or, not well at least. Just look at the safe guards he puts in place—a bank *committee* to approve inordinate expenses, for instance."

"I've no objection to the fellow's seeking to protect Phillip, but I must say I deeply resent his insisting on remaining anonymous," Quint said. "I find that insulting."

"Can't say as I blame you," Chet said.

"On the other hand," Boskins said, "this anonymous benefactor may have saved you a monumental scramble for funds. In our inquiries, we turned up a good deal of talk that this Humphreys fellow was planning a major move in the textile industry late this summer, but it seems something put him off."

"Saved you having to sell the London townhouse, eh, laddie?" Chet said to Quint.

"Perhaps," Quint conceded. "Still, we do not know who this Seton-Trevors connection is or what he hopes to get out of what he is doing."

"At this point, perhaps a cautious 'wait and see' is the most prudent approach," Boskins said. "It did occur to me that the Montieth family have strong financial ties in the City and the young earl has family ties there, has he not?"

"Yes." Quint was delighted to have found a logical solution to the dilemma. "The Earl of Hawthorne is Phillip's great-grandfather! That must be it. The old man wouldn't know me from Adam."

Boskins put up a hand in the universal "halt" sign. "Hold on, son. I had that very idea myself. It was a demmed good one too. In fact, I put it to Hawthorne and his son Charles when I happened on them in White's one evening. Well, truth to tell, I was not the only one. That Seton-Trevors Bank deal was the big news that day—that and Princess Caroline and her Italian cavalryman. Anyway, both Montieth men denied having anything to do with it—insisted they had financial matters enough of their own to keep them occupied."

Quint had always prided himself on being a good judge of men on short acquaintance and he readily accepted Boskins's assessment of the situation he faced. He closed the matter by saying, "As you say, sir, wait and see. At least until something requires a different approach."

Quint felt this business was by no means finished, but it could certainly be postponed in view of more pressing issues, could it not? To this end, he invited Boskins and the clerk to remain as guests at Sedwick Hall for a day or two. He explained about the accident only this morning but Lord Phillip would surely be better able to meet with his solicitor the following morning. The prolonged visit would also give him, as the earl's guardian, an opportunity to work out long-term financial goals and so on with the solicitor.

But for at least a part of this day, one Quinton Burnes had quite another matter on his mind.

Chapter 15

Harriet was not surprised when a footman brought word that Colonel Burnes would like to meet with her in the morning room at her convenience. While it was more or less expected, the summons nevertheless produced a disproportionate share of butterflies. After all, what did *she* have to answer for? And to one Quinton Burnes at that?

In truth, though, she was worried. Deeply worried. That little caper this morning was not just the act of an adolescent boy trying to prove himself a man. To what extent should she have seen it coming? Those mood swings she had attributed to ordinary uncertainties of life obviously went much deeper. *Some mother you'd make, Harriet Mayfield! And thanks ever so much, my dear Anne,* she muttered to herself as she rushed to respond to the royal command.

He was just coming through the French doors from the patio outside as she entered the room from the hall. He dropped a gardening tool in the edge of a flower pot, removed his gloves, and reached for his coat.

"Ah, Harriet, very prompt, I see."

"You needn't bother with the coat for my sake, Quint." She could have added, but did not, that she rather liked seeing the way the muscles rippled across his back and arm under his cotton shirt.

"Thank you." He gestured to two white wicker chairs at a small table with a round glass top set in a bay window. "This is my favorite room in the Hall since your sister's remodeling," he added, holding her chair for her.

"Really? Mine too."

"Well, at least we start on an amicable note." He settled into the opposite chair. "I want to know what you think about that incident this morning."

"What I think about...?"

"Ah, Harriet, do not do that with me, please."

"Do what?"

"That. Repeat what I said just to give yourself more time to formulate a clever response."

She raised her eyebrows, then grinned sheepishly, and looked away.

"Coward," he teased softly, then in a more normal, far more urgent tone, said, "Please tell me what you know about what was going on in Phillip's mind for him to pull such a stunt as that."

"I—I am not sure."

"Oh, come now. You know all my brother's children better than I do. Better than anyone, I daresay. And I know about your nightly tête-à-têtes with Phillip and Maria too!"

"What? You have been spying on us? Them? Me?"

"Do come down out of the boughs, my lady. At least so long as to remember that my bed chamber is on the same floor as yours. I have seen you bid them goodnight—rather late, I might add—on at least two occasions as I came up to bed. This afternoon I heard Phillip say to you something like 'nothing he planned went right.' Now I am asking you: do you know what was behind his mad dash with Lucifer? What he 'planned'?"

"I—I am not quite sure—" she started.

He reached to move a bowl of flowers in the center of the table to maintain better eye contact with her. It occurred to her that she had answered his summons wanting to put him off, to deflect, to defer, but what she faced in those hazel eyes was sincere concern—for Phillip, but for her as well.

"Please understand me, Harriet. I would not ask you to break a confidence, but I cannot work well in the dark, so to speak. Contrary to an impression you may have formed of me heretofore, I deeply respect and value the care you have given my wards." He grinned. "I even condone your spiriting them off to London."

She smiled, glad to have the atmosphere lightened. "Thank you, sir. I know we both want what is best for the children. If only that 'best' were so easily known."

"Aye, there's the rub," he said.

"But I do not have the answers you seek," she went on, "confidential or otherwise. Phillip has been deeply unhappy of late—but you knew that already."

"I thought it might be largely a clash of wills—his and mine. I remember such a furious resentment of my father! Of course, even then, Win and I had some idea of what devastation Father and Grandfather had already wrought upon Sedwick." He paused, ran a hand through his hair, and looked up at her, embarrassed. "Sorry. I just assumed you knew."

"I did—do. Win was not one to suffer in silence. Neither was Anne." He sat more erect in his chair. "So. Please. Tell me what you can about my—our—nephew."

She leaned forward, shoulders hunched, hands clasped on the table. "Despite longer, closer proximity, I am not sure my understanding is any better than yours. Whatever is going on with that young man, it is not merely a clash of wills. Do put your mind at rest on that. Phillip is very much at war with Phillip. Win saw that, I think, and worked at giving his son opportunity to prove himself."

"Did Win ever allow him to ride Lucifer?"

"Never. Nor would Phillip ever have thought to ask—let alone just take off on his own as he did today. He was *afraid* of that horse!"

"Do you think he did so this morning deliberately?"

"Wh-what do you mean?"

"Did he plan it ahead time? Harriet, that whole scene did not just happen. Phillip went out there, told the stable hands this bird-witted story about Chet and me being right behind him, and, as soon as their backs were turned, off he went! And on a trail he and the horse knew well. Then, later, he laments to you about how nothing he plans turns out right—at least that is what I thought I heard."

Harriet swallowed hard and raised one hand to her mouth and pressed hard. She could feel tears threatening and desperately wanted to hold them back. "You heard correctly."

"What did it mean?"

"I am not s-sure." It came out almost a wail and she could no longer hold back the tears. She heard his chair scrape as he got up; then he was pulling her out of her chair and into his arms.

"Sh. Don't cry, Harriet. Please, don't cry," he murmured into her hair above her ear. "We'll get through this. Phillip will get through this. So will that damned horse Win was so in love with."

"You think so?" She gazed up into his eyes, the question coming out between a sob and a giggle as his lips claimed hers. Tenderly, at first, then more and more hungrily. It did not escape her notice that she responded just as eagerly, her arms tightening about his neck, her hands digging into his hair. Then he showered small kisses over her face, kissing away her tears.

"Yes, I think so," he said, maneuvering her toward a white wicker couch with three large colorful floral cushions on it. She sat at one end and he sat next to her, one arm about her shoulders. "Now. Out with it, please. Help me understand what is going on with that boy." He sighed. "Then maybe you can help me understand what is going on with *this* boy." He jerked a thumb at his own chest.

She smiled. "I shall try with the boy upstairs. You are on your own with the other one. I've a rather confused girl to deal with myself."

"Point taken." He clasped her hand to give it a gentle squeeze.

"To be completely honest, Quint, I do not know fully how to answer about Phillip. I think he is a very troubled young man—has been for some time. Did he intend to harm himself this morning? I have no idea. I am inclined to think it may have been a combination of vague plan and opportunity presenting itself."

Quint pulled back to look at her more directly. "You mean he has considered this before? Planned it earlier?"

"No. No. At least not that I know of. But young people sometimes get peculiar ideas in their bids for attention. Maybe they read too much *Romeo and Juliet* or the like."

"Oh, sure. Blame the bard," Quint said. He pulled away farther and sat forward on the couch, his elbows on his knees. "In any event, I am sure that both you and Phillip—and probably Maria as well—will be pleased to know that you win. I give up."

"What? I have no idea what you are talking about."

"I have decided to let you all have it your way—we shall hire a tutor for Phillip and the boys and a governess for Maria and the girls. Unless, of course, you have developed some major objection at this late date."

"I have no objection at all," Harriet said, "and I am quite sure both Phillip and Maria will find this welcome news indeed. But may I ask *why*—especially now?"

"That saucy little know-all, Lady Sarah Burnes, put her finger on it—the boy would arrive at school—already two years late, if you ask me—and now unable to navigate his new world on his own. A year with a tutor will do him just as well academically. Do you not agree?"

Harriet grasped his hand, which had returned to the cushion between them. "Of course I do." She closed her eyes and raised their joined hands to her cheek. "Of course I do. And Maria?"

"I thought I would leave it up to Maria," he said, turning Harriet's hand in his to caress the palm. She could hardly marshal her thoughts for the way those tiny caresses were flooding her body with feeling, but she leaned closer to him and managed to say, "Have you discussed this with your mother?"

"My mother is not their guardian. I am." They were both quiet for a moment, then he shook the hand he still held. "Is there some quarrel—antipathy—between you and my mother?"

Harriet slowly withdrew her hand and sat a bit more rigidly. "Um—not exactly—not overtly. I think—" Harriet spoke slowly, reluctant to speak ill of the woman who was, after all, his mother. She braced her shoulders. "I think she may have found it somewhat difficult to accept Win's choice of a bride."

Quint grinned. "'Somewhat' would be a glorious understatement, according to letters I had from him. I was in India at the time. Probably not so much his choice, but that he chose for himself, regardless of how eligible his choice might prove to be, thus ignoring *her* choice."

Harriet nodded. "Lady Barbara Newhouse."

"Who?" he asked sharply.

"Lady Barbara Newhouse—she is Lady Barbara Riverton now. She and Anne came out the same year, but Lady Barbara was clearly the leading debutante of that season. However, Anne just snapped Win up from under the noses of all the *ton* who had expected Lady Margaret to pull off that match for her son." Harriet smiled at the memory of her sister's happiness that year, but suddenly she became aware of a strange stillness in her companion.

He stood abruptly and looked down at her. "Are you sure of that? My mother was actively promoting a match between Barbara and Win?"

Something in his tone as he said the woman's given name gave her pause, but she looked up and answered openly. "Well, no. To be perfectly honest I was not privy to such delicate information at the time—I was still in school. But I was allowed to attend the wedding and that was the common talk—especially among Anne and her friends. I am remiss in repeating it at all—particularly after all these years."

"Never mind." He reached a hand to draw her to her feet. "Mother is one of those people who simply likes to have things go her way. Unfortunately, that cannot always be so."

Harriet thought there was more to it than this, but she had no clear explanation for the change in his demeanor. They parted, agreeing that they would go together after the evening meal to give Phillip and Maria news of the change in plans for school.

* * * *

Quint spent much of the remainder of the afternoon distracted by Harriet's revelation that his mother had once actively promoted a match between his brother Win and Barbara Newhouse. How was it that he had heard nothing of that possibility when, home on leave three years later, he was himself buzzing about Barbara like a bee about honeysuckle? He *had* known that his mother—by then the dowager countess—and the younger woman were close friends and he remembered thinking at the time how nice that was, as Barbara had lost her mother some years before. He also knew that his mother then, as now, wielded a good deal of influence in social circles. Truth be told, he had been far too preoccupied in his pursuit of the beautiful Barbara to pay it much attention. But now—only a few days ago—his mother had been explicit in informing him that Lady Barbara would attend the house party. What was *that* about?

He was also feeling conflicted about those kisses he had shared with Harriet. Both times he had been seized by impulse and circumstance, and in each instance the embrace been just—well—*right*—somehow. And comfortable. She responded with simple honesty. No coyness or brazen teasing. He wondered how those changeable gray eyes would appear in the full throes of passion.

He gave himself a mental shake and set about his duties as host to the evening's guests through pre-supper drinks in drawing room and the meal itself. Recalling his mother's caustic comments about Harriet earlier, Quint suggested the gentlemen have their after-supper drinks along with the ladies and their tea in the drawing room.

He could tell his mother was a little put off by this shift in the social norm, but she managed to continue the polite chitchat that had been the table conversation. She had, after all, had an ongoing though distant acquaintance with the solicitor, Mr. Boskins, for several years. Quint noted, however, that she had effectively relegated Harriet to the sidelines as soon as drinks were served.

"Harriet, dear, would you play for us please? Something soft, perhaps?"

"Of course, my lady."

Quint thought Harriet preferred such a role this evening as she took to the pianoforte, but he quickly offered to turn her pages for her, thus eliciting a small moue of displeasure from his mother.

"Miss Mayfield plays exceptionally well," the dowager said to her guests. "I doubt she needs such help, my son."

"Nevertheless…" Quint said brightly, carrying his and Harriet's drinks over to the instrument.

He allowed the music and conversation to flow for some time, but eventually he extended a hand to Harriet to rise and he announced to the others, "If you will excuse us, Miss Mayfield and I wish to inform Phillip and Maria of the decision regarding their schooling and it is almost their bedtime."

The dowager looked perplexed. "Surely that was quite clear this morning."

"I think not, Mother."

"Oh, do not, I pray you, tell me you have changed your mind about sending those youngsters off to school." This came as something of a surprised wail from Lady Margaret as she suddenly sat more erect on the settee she shared with Mrs. Hartley.

"As a matter of fact, I have, Mother."

"Or had it changed for you." The dowager shot a scathing look at Harriet.

"Do not blame Harriet." Quint immediately gave himself a mental kick on seeing his mother's brows fly skyward at his use of Harriet's given name in company. He shared a glance with Chet, who nodded sympathetically, and with Boskins and the clerk, both of whom seemed rather confused. He hurried on, "I happened to recall just how schoolboys were likely to welcome a newcomer who was the least bit 'different'—shall we say."

"Well," she said in a great show of concession, "it is not the done thing, but you *are* their guardian."

"Yes, I am." His hand at her back, he nudged Harriet toward the door. "Miss Mayfield."

In the hallway, Harriet, conscious of the slight touch of his hand at her back and the faint scent of sandalwood soap, said, "I doubt you have heard the last of that."

He merely shrugged.

They found Phillip and Maria playing cribbage at a small table pushed up to Phillip's bed. Phillip wore a maroon bed jacket over his nightshirt and Maria had on a blue robe over a frilly cotton nightgown. Her hair hung in a single plait over her shoulder and down to her elbow. Both youngsters looked up with eager smiles when Harriet and Quint entered the room.

"I was hoping you would come by before that foul-tasting potion worked its magic," Phillip said, directing his gaze to his aunt. Then he added in an exultant tone, "I beat Maria at cribbage—twice!"

"Hah!" Maria said. "Only because I felt compelled to humor an invalid, don't you know?"

"Not true!" Phillip protested.

Quint pulled chairs up for him and Harriet near Maria. "No bickering," he said. "Your aunt and I have come to share some important news with you."

Phillip and Maria went very still and immediately looked to Harriet. She, though, looked to Quint, who gestured for her to go ahead.

She gave a slight negative shake of her head. "This was *your* doing, sir."

He sat back in his chair and crossed his legs, his hands interlaced on his knee. "So-o-o. The long and short of it is that after careful consideration, I have decided to agree to your request, Phillip, and allow you to be tutored here at home for at least the next year."

Phillip's smile—a mix of surprise, delight, and hero worship—brightened the whole room. Quint thought, *Parents must live for moments such as this.*

"Thank you. Thank you, Uncle Quint. I promise that, when the time comes, I shall not quibble about going to school at all."

"Fine." Quint leaned forward and extended his hand, which Phillip took in his most grown-up manner. "I shall hold you to that, Phillip. For now I expect you to take some part in the process of our finding a tutor for you, so best you get yourself out of this bed soonest."

"Yes, sir." The smile became even broader if possible. Phillip exchanged a look with his aunt, then added, "As to that, sir—"

He was interrupted by Maria. "But what about me? If Phillip is allowed to delay a year, might I do so as well?"

Quint glanced at Harriet before answering. "That depends."

"Depends? On what?" Maria sounded worried.

"Don't tease her, Colonel Burnes," Harriet said.

"As you wish, my lady." He turned to face Maria directly. "It depends on what your wishes are after you have thought about it carefully. We are to have a proper tutor for the boys of the family and a proper governess for the girls. You, my dear, may choose for yourself whether to spend this coming year learning at home—or away at school."

"I am allowed to choose?" she asked in surprise.

"Yes. I happen to trust your judgment."

"Oh, Uncle Quint!" Maria jumped from her chair, took the step or two to his, threw her arms around his neck, and kissed him resoundingly on the cheek. "That is the nicest thing anyone has ever said to me!"

"I take it she likes the idea," Quint said, disentangling himself.

"It would appear so," Harriet said.

"I *love* it!" Maria said, returning to her own seat. After a moment, she said, "I think I should prefer to be at home too. And if I could be permitted to have some lessons with Phillip—say, in history and mathematics—I will love it even more."

"I should think that would pose no problem," Quint said, noting even as he said the words Harriet's raised eyebrows. "But for now, it seems to me that a good dose of sleep is finally in order for our patient. We can discuss this all in further detail tomorrow."

"Aunt Harriet, you will tell him about Mr. Knightly, won't you?" Phillip asked.

"Yes, dear."

Quint and Harriet saw Maria down the hall to her own room, at the door of which the girl hugged them both and said, "Thank you. Thank you for—for trusting us."

As they proceeded down the narrow back stairs, Quint behind Harriet asked, "What *was* that little trick of the raised eyebrows when Maria mentioned occasional lessons with Phillip?"

She stopped on a step below him and turned to look up at him. God! She was beautiful! And that flowery scent she wore had been tantalizing him for hours, it seemed. "That will have to be handled with a degree of finesse, I should think."

"Now what?"

"I hardly think her grandmother would approve such unladylike conduct."

"But her Aunt Harriet does?" He nudged her along.

"Of course. But then her Aunt Harriet is a notorious bluestocking, or hadn't you noticed?"

Succumbing to temptation, he moved down to her step, put an arm about her shoulder, and kissed her. It was a quick kiss with a satisfying response. "Hmm," he mused, "I suppose I *had* noticed, there are all those other delicious qualities to behold as well."

She merely smiled, shook her head, and moved along down the stairs. Soon enough they arrived at her door.

He leaned close. "You *could* invite me in to behold those other qualities all the better."

She gave him a quick kiss. "Not tonight, sir. Not tonight." She was through the door and closed it before he remembered he had wanted to ask her about that Mr. Knightly Phillip had mentioned. Ah, well...

Still—that "no" had not been absolute, had it?

Chapter 16

Life at Sedwick Hall the next two weeks continued at a furious pace. Lady Margaret had the staff at sixes and sevens preparing for the influx of guests for her house party, which was to commence during the last week of September and would go on until end of October. Harriet became an unwilling witness to the dowager's plans late one morning as she sat outside the open patio door of the morning room, reading. Or that had been her intent: find some alone time and revel in a novel. But she must have dozed off, for suddenly she was nudged alert by voices in the room beyond. By then it would have been awkward to announce her presence, so she huddled into her book, hoping to escape notice.

The dowager was saying, "Be sure every guest room is properly aired and that we have hired sufficient local folk to supplement our domestic staff."

"Yes, ma'am," Mrs. Ames, the housekeeper answered.

"'Tis already done, milady." This voice was that of Patterson, the butler. "And we've accommodations for your guests' personal servants."

"I have three footmen and as many maids cleaning in the ballroom even as we speak," Mrs. Ames said. "The chandeliers will sparkle like jewels! We shall move in the potted shrubbery you ordered next week. I must say it will look quite spectacular for your ball."

"I do hope so. Besides some thirty or more houseguests, I've invited anyone of note in the entire local neighborhood." Lady Margaret sounded self-satisfied. There was a pause and a faint sound of movement before she continued, "Now. I want you to examine this list of accommodations for our guests. The Earl of Hawthorne and his wife are, as they always do when they visit Sedwick, to have the lake view chamber near Miss Mayfield's rooms. His son Charles Montieth and his wife are in the one next to that one. That way, poor dear Phillip will have ready access to that side of his family and they to him."

"That is very thoughtful of you, milady," Mrs. Ames said, and Harriet silently agreed.

"Hawthorne likes being near his grandchildren," the dowager said, then hurried on. "While you are seeing to the preparation of those rooms, Ames, please do a quick inventory of the furnishings. I am thinking of renovating that entire suite of rooms when Miss Mayfield removes to London with her family after the party. For now, though, I shall simply remove to the countess's chambers for the duration of the party. After all, those rooms *were* once mine. They may as well serve again."

"Miss Mayfield is leaving Sedwick permanently?" Mrs. Ames asked in what sounded like awed surprise to Harriet.

"Well, now that we are hiring a proper governess, there is little need to impose on her further," Lady Margaret explained.

"Do the children know this yet?" the butler asked.

"No."

"Ah, I thought not."

"No," her ladyship repeated, "nor is there any reason for them—or any of the other staff—to know just yet. Is that understood?"

"Yes, ma'am." The two servants spoke at once.

Harriet was stunned. She had always known she was not one of Lady Margaret's favorite people, but this seemed to show a level of antipathy she had not suspected before. *Oh, come now,* she chastised herself, *you just blithely ignored her hints about "a bachelor household" and so on.* The dowager's voice caught Harriet's attention again.

"Lady Barbara Riverton is to be assigned the rose room just around the corner from my son Quinton's chambers. That is clearly an accommodation for a lady, but you must make sure *she* is the lady assigned that particular room. Is that clear?"

"Yes, ma'am," Mrs. Ames replied, "but, my lady, if she is a *special* guest, may I suggest that the blue room three doors down is somewhat more elegant?"

"It is, but it will not do," the dowager said dismissively. "'Tis a matter of location," she added airily.

"As you wish, milady," Mrs. Ames said.

Harriet rolled her eyes.

She wondered if Quint would welcome his mother's machinations on his behalf. *And damn his eyes if he would!* Relishing the memory of his kisses, she recognized this thought for its sheer jealousy.

But she could not let go of what she had heard. *So. Lady Margaret, having failed to procure the beautiful Barbara for one son, would try for the other?* Did that even make sense? She gave herself a shake. Who was she to try to follow the entangled thinking of the dowager countess?

Besides, she had other worries. Like how to tell the children she would be leaving them…

* * * *

The very day after the accident, Quint knew Harriet had sent word to her grandparents, who had intended to arrive at Sedwick Hall for the dowager's party early enough to see their great-grandson off to school. His accident added urgency to their trip and they, along with their son Charles and his wife, Elizabeth, would arrive at the Hall a week to the day following the mishap.

As it would happen, though, these two couples would arrive with an entourage larger than usual even for upper-crust Englishmen. They would be traveling with not only their own personal servants, but they would also be conveying Sedwick's new tutor and governess to their positions. For Quint, the way this turn of events had come about had been something of a revelation.

That day following the accident had been an eventful one. First, the doctor had arrived midmorning and marveled at the resilience of youth. He also produced a pair of sturdy wooden crutches that he, Quint, Chet, and a footman or two managed to whittle into size and shape for this patient. Each instrument was a rough T-shaped bit of wood, the broad bar of the T to fit under the arm, with the long shaft having a handle lower down. The crossbars and handles were heavily padded with toweling.

"Now, it is going to take time to get used to these," Dr. Babcock warned his patient. "Do not—I repeat: do not—try to run any races with them. At least not this week."

"Yes, sir." Phillip grinned at him and stood awkwardly on his own after being helped to that position by Quint and the doctor.

"Best let these fellows haul you about for the most part until the leg heals some, then use the crutches." The doctor gestured toward a footman.

Phillip nodded, reluctantly, it seemed to Quint, then gave up the crutches and sat on a chair.

When the doctor had left, Phillip asked Quint, "Did Aunt Harriet tell you about Mr. Knightly?"

"No. She did not."

"Oh." Phillip looked embarrassed. "I'd best let her tell you. I'm ready to meet Mr. Boskins now."

Because Phillip, at thirteen, was of rather a slight build yet, the large footman simply lifted him in his arms and transported him down to the library, where the Seventh Earl was properly introduced to his solicitor and given a cursory overview of his affairs before his guardian determined that enough was enough. Later, as he was taking his leave, the solicitor commented to the guardian that he had been most impressed by the young man's grasp of the intricacies of his affairs.

After the midday meal, which Harriet had taken with Phillip and Maria and the other children in the nursery, she presented herself in the library, where Quint was once again toiling through the dilemma Boskins had left in his wake.

"I do hope I am not disturbing you," she said.

"I welcome any distraction from this," he said, rising and waving a hand at the desk.

"I should like to discuss this business of a tutor and a governess, if you do not mind."

He grinned. "Now why am I not surprised?" He led her to the wing chairs flanking the fireplace, and she sat after rearranging the small pillow on the seat of hers. "Has this something to do with a Mr. Knightly?" he asked.

"How did you know?"

"Call it a lucky guess."

She gave him an impatient glare. "Mr. Knightly was—until about a month ago—tutor to Jeremy, Phillip's—and my—cousin. He has not yet taken another position, but my Uncle Charles considers him a very capable educator, and I, too, have been quite favorably impressed by him."

"I see." His tone was noncommittal.

She sighed and went on as though she were reading from a resume. Mr. William Knightly is thirty-six or thirty-seven years old, the son of a London barrister, and grandson of a judge of the assize courts. He was educated at Harrow and Cambridge. Injured in a hunting accident, he walks with a cane and a limp, but he nevertheless manages young boys quite well enough."

"But you *have* met him?"

"Yes. I found him very knowledgeable and amiable. Jeremy quite liked him."

"I believe I told you once before, Miss Mayfield, that I respect your judgment. Therefore, if this man is still available, I am willing to give him a chance."

"Thank you." She flashed him that always devastating smile that seemed to awaken certain portions of his anatomy.

"Have you a similar candidate for the position of governess?"

"As a matter of fact, I do."

"I meant that as a facetious question," he said impatiently.

"I know. But truly, Quint, I do have the perfect candidate for you."

"And you know she is perfect because—?"

"Because she was *my* governess!"

He snorted. "We do not need some female in her dotage that that saucy Sarah will run rings around."

"I beg your pardon," she said in mock umbrage. "I had but seven years when Miss Clarkson came into my life. Anne and I were her first charges. I think she was—perhaps—nineteen at the time."

"Which, as I said, puts her quite in her dotage now, eh?" He looked very serious for a long moment, then slowly grinned.

She stared at him for that moment, then snatched the pillow from behind her and tossed it at him. "Hmmphf! I think she is not yet forty, though she had talked once of retiring. Her mother left her a small legacy."

"And she is willing to come out of retirement now?"

"For me, according to my grandmother. And for these children—whom she *has* met—when we visited London in the spring. I do believe you would find her most satisfactory."

He sat in silent contemplation for a few moments. Finally, he sat straighter, his hands on his knees, and held her gaze. "Fine. At the risk of repeating myself, I shall accept your recommendation on Miss Clarkson as well as Mr. Knightly on a trial basis at least. While I readily admit that this saves me a good deal of botheration in advertising these positions and interviewing God knows how many candidates, I cannot ignore a nagging suspicion that I have been had."

"Sir?"

"Do not go all formal on me at this point, Harriet. I have a distinct feeling that you and those two lovable brats upstairs have put one over on me...."

"Certainly that was no one's intent," she said.

"Nevertheless, I have to wonder what other surprises you may have lurking in my future."

Harriet looked away, but did not respond to this sally. When she had left and he returned to the mess on his desk, he paused and wiped his forehead, as it occurred to him to anticipate just how his mother was going to take this bit of news.

The very next morning his mother pounced on the issue of a tutor and governess. Quint had known he would have to discuss it with her sooner or later, but he had been hoping for later. This was one of those overcast mornings when, foregoing her customary ride, Harriet took breakfast from a tray in her room or with the children later. Thus she was absent from the dining room this morning, and Quint half suspected that she deliberately sought to avoid excessive contact with his mother. So, at the breakfast table that morning, there were just Quint and his mother, along with Sylvia Hartley and Chet Gibbons, both of whom the dowager occasionally seemed to regard as merely pieces of furniture.

She greeted them all collectively as she entered the room, filled her plate at the sideboard, signaled the footman for coffee, seated herself next to Quint, and opened fire. "Well, Quinton, if we are to have a tutor and a governess on hand in time for my house party, we really must act quickly!" She paused to sip her coffee and perhaps let her general distaste sink in before going on. "Very few of *my* friends will prove of much help. Those who still employ such persons would not relinquish good ones." She heaved a dramatic sigh. "We shall have to deal with one of those horrid agencies that take in just anybody. Oh, good heavens! Shall we have to go all the way to London to find decent help? I do not know whether such is available in Derby. Certainly not in Hendley!"

"Derby may have such an agency, Lady Margaret," Mrs. Hartley said soothingly. "I do believe the squire's wife obtained her new housekeeper from an agency in Derby."

"Still, we've very little time," her ladyship said impatiently. "This is just one more worry before my party—one we did not need at all, I might add."

Quint reached to pat her briefly on the shoulder. "Not to worry, Mother. It is being handled."

"Being—? What? Already? But how can that be?"

"Harriet—Miss Mayfield—knows of two eligible parties that may be exactly what we need."

"Harriet? Harriet? What does *she* know of rearing children? I should think you would have at least had the courtesy to consult your own mother on such an important matter."

Quint glanced at Chet and rolled his eyes slightly. Striving for a patient tone, he said, "As you pointed out, Mother, time is a factor here. It occurred to me that you would have little objection to persons who come with recommendations from the Earl and Countess of Hawthorne and thus we might well employ them at least on a trial basis. Do you, indeed, have such objections at this point?"

She was flustered. "Well—uh—that is—no, I suppose not. It is just that I do not like having some—some stranger making decisions regarding persons to be employed in my household."

"Mother," he said gently, "first of all there are no 'strangers' involved here. And, secondly, Sedwick is Phillip's household. At best, you and I are but caretakers."

"Yes, of course," she said hastily, but Quint wondered if she had listened to what he had said, especially as he heard her go on to Mrs. Hartley, "It is just that no woman should have to tolerate another—an outsider—having intimate knowledge of her household affairs."

"I understand perfectly, dear lady," Mrs. Hartley sympathized.

Quint was sure this was not the last of it, but he let the matter drop for now.

* * * *

Ever since the visit to the mills and her acquaintance with Mrs. Reed, Harriet had been working furiously on a series of articles on the working conditions of England's laboring folk. She had talked at length with many Sedwick workers who told her of their experiences elsewhere. While both she and they saw much room for improvement at Sedwick Mills, they also agreed that matters were often worse elsewhere. A twelve-hour work day was the norm, but it was often exceeded by as much as two hours or more; accidents were generally deemed the fault and responsibility of the workers regardless of maintenance of equipment; and standards of cleanliness varied radically from questionable to deplorably unhealthy. Writing as the Lady Senator, she ended one article by asking how many owners—many of whom were respected members of the House of Lords—would invite members of their own families even to visit some of these facilities they themselves owned.

This brought a rash of angry letters to the editor, whose private note to Harriet was "At least we know they are reading!" But he printed only the mildest of such missives.

The Lady Senator then turned her attention to living conditions and daily life of mill workers initially, but soon found her concern broadening as she became more and more aware of the plight of other types of workers as well. One whole article was devoted to the shame of the nation's forgotten veterans—soldiers left to wander the highways and byways seeking work now that their usefulness to England had been used up on foreign battlefields.

Another was a blistering expose of the use of child labor, children as young as four or five set to sorting coal, for instance. Besides deploring the sheer waste of talent and ability of the nation's youth, she leveled a scathing attack on those who would knowingly and willfully enrich themselves on the backbreaking labor of innocent children.

Finally, she aimed her pen at the run-down, overcrowded living conditions of mill workers, miners, and other factory workers. Apartment buildings, often owned by the owners of the mills or mines, not only housed twice as many human bodies as they should, but saw little or no upkeep. Garbage and sewage were often strewn about the streets and alleys awaiting a good rainstorm to take some of it away. Communal toilets behind the buildings were as overflowing as the dwellings themselves. Basement apartments sometimes had only bare earth as flooring and became tracts of mud during storms. Was it any wonder so many perished of consumption?

While the series of articles were actually written over a period of weeks that extended from even before the visit to the mills, their publication was to be spread over the early weeks of autumn and beyond. In fact, Harriet feared one or two of them might appear in print during the weeks of Lady Margaret's house party. This might be unfortunate, but there was nothing she could do about it now. In any event, the Lady Senator's identity, though not a secret, was not widely known, was it?

* * * *

Still not entirely sure of Phillip's state of mind, Harriet kept rather a close watch on him, though she tried to do so unobtrusively. In those first days, he was largely confined to his room and the nursery wing. She made a point of visiting him after her morning ride, sometimes then having breakfast with him and his siblings. She encouraged Maria and the other children to spend time with him, and saw to it that he was taken outdoors and allowed ample exercise. The young man relished showing off his expertise on his crutches.

Phillip and Maria's nocturnal visits to Harriet's chambers were replaced by Maria and Harriet's visiting him. These get-togethers often started now with the twins and Sarah joining as well after the two youngest were put to bed and included guessing games and the usual pleas for "just one more chapter" of the current bedtime reading. Harriet detected in Phillip no sign of the depression or melancholy she had observed earlier. *Had it really been all about school?* she wondered.

On the evening of the fifth day after the accident, the story time finished, Harriet had just sent the twins and Sarah off to their beds when there was a knock at the door. Maria, being nearest the door, answered it.

"Good evening," Quint said. "I hope I am not intruding?"

"No, not at all," Maria and Harriet replied in unison.

"Good evening, sir," Phillip said.

Quint drew up a straight-backed chair, turned it back toward the bed, and straddled it, resting his arms on the back of it and his chin on his arms. He gazed at Phillip. "So? How fares the invalid? The crutches working out all right?"

"Yes, sir. I've fallen only once, but luckily Heller was there to catch me."

"What are footmen for, eh?"

"Uncle Quint, do you think I might go riding soon—perhaps tomorrow? On Etna, not Lucifer!" he added hastily with a laugh. "Aunt Harriet said I should ask you as you had had experience with leg injuries and would know."

Quint smiled at Harriet. "Oh, she did, eh? We should probably ask the doctor when he comes tomorrow, but I am sure we can find some way to get you mounted again sooner rather than later."

"Thank you, sir."

There was a moment of quiet, then Quint addressed Maria and Phillip. "We have missed you two in the dining room at meal times these last few days. Do you think the two of you might quit lurking about the nursery and rejoin us there?"

They looked at each other, then at Harriet, who smiled and nodded at them.

"Yes, sir," Phillip said. "I am managing quite well on my crutches now."

"Of course we will," Maria said.

Later, when she and Quint had seen Maria to her room and they were in the hall outside her own rooms, Harriet paused and asked, "Had you an ulterior motive in your visit to Phillip's room this evening?"

He leaned close. "A couple of them. Invite me in, and I will explain."

"*You* are a devil," she said softly, but she stepped into the room and motioned for him to follow. He closed the door firmly and immediately took her in his arms and kissed her quite thoroughly. He had one hand behind her head as the other caressed her back from her shoulders to the round of her buttocks. Nor was her response any less thorough as she slipped her arms around his neck and pressed her body ever closer to his.

Finally, in a husky whisper he said, "Yes. That was, indeed, one of my motives." He kissed her again. "And if I am a devil, you, my love, are a most alluring temptress."

"Neither of us is behaving properly." She and moved toward her favorite chair, pointing him toward the blue settee.

"Oh, no." He grabbed her hand and pulled her down next to him, pinning her there with his arm about her shoulders. Even when he buried his face against her neck, she refused to pretend to protest; just being close to him, feeling his warmth, smelling him—it was all so comfortable, so perfect somehow.

"You said that was *one* motive," she prodded.

"Hmm?" His breath on her bare skin was doing wild things elsewhere in her body.

She spoke more firmly. "What did you have in mind with that business of Phillip and Maria being more of a presence in the dining room?"

He pulled away slightly and turned to face her more directly. "Just that: 'more of a presence.' I know that Phillip is quite young—Maria too—but he *is* the Earl of Sedwick. With this infernal house party coming up, I want it very clear to all and sundry that, young as he is, *Phillip* is head of all that is Sedwick. We may as well set the pattern early on."

"But it is your mother's party, is it not?"

"Essentially. But before the first guests have arrived, I intend that she understand that while she is the hostess of this grand affair, *Phillip* is the host, broken leg or no. Maria and I will assist. It should work, should it not? Especially as the first guests to arrive will likely be his grandparents?"

Harriet felt tears in her eyes. She moved closer to him, slipped her arms around his neck again, and kissed him. "Oh, Quint, I think it is wonderful." She paused. "But your mother will not like it."

"I know," he said glumly. "But it must be done. I think." He brightened and tightened his hold on her, his hands caressing wherever they managed to touch, his mouth and tongue doing marvelous things to hers. After a bit of this bliss, he whispered, "Does this mean you will invite me into your bed to discover those other qualities of the wondrous Miss Mayfield?"

She drew back, but only slightly, feeling a little dazed. Her gaze locked with his, her eyes searching, seeking. Finally, she said, "You know, I think I will. Yes! I will."

She stood, extended her hand, and led him into her bedroom.

Chapter 17

Harriet had thought about this moment for days—ever since that kiss in the abbey ruins. Well, all right. At first it had been in the vague nature of idle musing: what would it be like to make love with a man like Quinton Burnes? Not that she had first-hand knowledge of the act with any man as yet. However, at twenty-seven she was ready for such, was she not? Lately, whenever he had been near—merely in the same room—her mind would drift to a kiss or a touch and her body would respond. Then it was no longer "a man like…" Instead her desire focused on *him* and tonight she could not, would not deny it any longer.

Was she in love with him?

This thought had crossed her mind often enough in the last few weeks, but she invariably tried to put it aside as irrelevant. It was simply out of the question for Harriet Mayfield to lose her heart to Quinton Burnes. That was not in the plan at all.

"Are you having second thoughts?" Quint asked softly as he closed door between her sitting room and the bedroom. "It is all right if you wish to," he said, pausing in the act of shrugging out of his coat.

"No. Are you?" She had turned up the lamp on her bedside stand and it spread a soft glow over the entire room.

He tossed the coat on a bench at the foot of the bed and, closing the distance between them, slipped his arms inside her robe to fondle her breasts through the thin fabric of her nightgown as he kissed his way from the hollow of her throat to her lips. Her hands tugged at his neckcloth and shirt buttons.

"Your maid?" he asked.

"Dismissed before I went up to Phillip's room."

As she often did, she had prepared for bed before joining the children to bid them good night with their bedtime stories, prayers, and good night hugs and kisses. She relished these evening rituals with the children more than ever now. So she had appeared in Phillip's room with her hair already in its long, loose night-time plait, held in place by a single blue ribbon. She wore a lacy cotton nightgown, over which she had donned a blue silk robe, tied at the waist. She had been surprised and embarrassed at having Quint see her in such dishabille, but what could she do—other than brazen it through? Now it had come to this.

"I would not have you the object of gossip, Harriet."

"I thank you for that, kind sir," she whispered, sincerely moved by his consideration. "I think we are safe this night."

"May I?" he asked, lifting her braid off her shoulder and loosening the ribbon that bound it. He ran his hands gently through her hair and bent his head to drink in the smell and feel of it. He slipped the robe off her shoulders and it pooled at her feet. She heard his sharp intake of breath and saw sheer hunger in his eyes as he gazed at the way her breasts mounded under the fabric of her gown, the nipples clearly outlined. He reached to cup them in his hands, his thumbs tweaking the nipples and sending bursts of feeling flooding through her.

She struggled to pull his shirt free of his trousers, desperate to feel, to touch the warm bare skin beneath. "You have me at a disadvantage, sir," she muttered.

"One moment." He quickly ripped the shirt tails loose and then tossed the shirt over his head and on top of his coat.

Marveling at the expanse of golden muscle and a dark V of hair in the lamplight, she could not resist repeated caresses from his waist to his shoulders.

"And now who has whom at a disadvantage, my dear?" he breathed against her ear as he shimmied the hem of her gown over her rump, pulling her closer, so that she felt the full evidence of his need pressing into her belly. She fumbled ineptly with the buttons on the fall of his buckskins.

"Allow me, love," he said. Having effectively rid her of the nightgown, he deftly stepped out of his shoes and pulled off the buckskins.

They stood simply staring at each other for a moment.

"My God, but you are beautiful," he whispered.

"You are not so bad yourself, my lord," she said with a soft laugh. "I am thinking a Greek hero comes to mind."

"Come, my little bluestocking—into the bed." He tossed back the covers and nudged her onto the bed, but before joining her, he stepped across the room to the washbasin, where he grabbed up a towel. Returning, he pulled her close and effectively demonstrated that previous kisses were but a sampling of what this man was capable of.

With his hand, magic fingers, tantalizing lips and tongue, and words of encouragement, he not only played her body like a finely tuned musical instrument, but he led her into triumphs of ecstasy in playing his. Somewhat to her chagrin when she thought about it afterward, in the end she had been reduced to a begging mass of incoherence.

"Please, Quint. Yes! I want— I want...I need—"

And when he entered her, she welcomed him eagerly, lifting her pelvis to give him better leverage, losing herself to everything but this act and this man. Then, suddenly, he stilled. He just stopped.

"No." She wanted to scream, but it came out a whimper. "No, Quint. Don't stop. Please."

Slowly, he pushed into her again, watching her face closely as he did so, kissing her tenderly as he picked up the pace again. Then it was she who stilled as she felt a short burst of pain.

"Sh. Hang on, my love," he murmured, moving gently until she was writhing beneath him and demanding more from both of them. Suddenly she felt an explosion of bliss within herself. A few moments later, she felt him go rigid, and, to her surprise and regret, she felt him withdrawing from her. A split second later she realized he was spilling his seed into the towel.

He rolled to her side and they lay entwined, both spent, for several moments.

Finally, he said, "*That* was amazing."

"Yes. It was. I had no idea it would be so wonderful."

He rose on one elbow and glared at her. "Good God, Harriet, you might have told me!"

"Told you what?"

"That you were a virgin."

"Why on earth would I tell you such a thing as that?"

"A man likes to know these things when he beds a woman."

"Well, now you know," she said, gazing at him open-eyed.

He sighed. "Now I—Ahah! I knew it!" he exulted.

"Knew what?" she asked, bewildered.

"Your eyes. They are blue. Really, really blue. Not gray. I knew they would change color when you made love."

"That is ridiculous."

"Harriet, my sweet, are you not aware that your eyes change color with your emotions? Rather like the weather, really. The grayer, the more foreboding; the bluer, well—"

"Ridiculous," she said again, but not so forcefully this time.

"I'm sure the children know this—probably instinctively. I've seen them studying your face for how they should react to something you've said."

"Well, of course. That is how real human beings interact," she said, "not like soldiers who behave like automatons—all that 'yes, sir, no, sir' stiffness."

"And you know this from your vast experience of army life, I take it?" He tickled her ribs, thus bringing her fully and reluctantly out of the afterglow of their lovemaking. He flicked off the covers, saying, "I'd best not be discovered in your rooms in the morning, let alone in your bed."

"Goodness, no," she agreed.

He then totally surprised her. She watched as he went, stark naked, across the room to the washbasin, where he proceeded to dampen a cloth and unashamedly clean himself. He then dampened another cloth and returned to her, where he gently and thoroughly cleaned away from her body any perceivable residue of their night's activity. She lay in silent wonder as he performed these ablutions, but he did them with such tenderness and care that later, when she thought about it, she knew that it was at that moment that she *knew*—yes! she was in love with him.

"Move over," he said, nudging her. "Remove your ever-so-loveable self from the middle of this bed. Let us see the damage."

"Wha-a—?" she cried, but she moved.

"Harriet, I told you I would not have you the object of gossip. Not in this house. What happens when the maid sees blood on your sheet?"

"Blood on my sheet?" she asked blankly. But there it was: two bloody smudges against the whiteness of the bedsheet. "Oh."

"Oh, indeed. That is what happens when one deflowers a virgin. If I'd known—"

She sighed and grabbed the damp cloth from him. "Do save the lecture. Get another wet cloth and a dry towel too. I doubt any male of the species knows how to clean properly."

He rolled his eyes at her and did as she instructed as she began scrubbing furiously at the small bloody spots on the sheet.

When he came back, he leaned over and kissed her soundly. "I did not do such a bad job on you, did I?"

Embarrassed, she squeaked out a "No," and kissed him back, equally soundly.

"Here now. *That* could keep us here 'til noon—and caught for sure."
He set about helping her scrub.

"I think it will dry completely by morning," she finally said, pulling
on her nightgown. "Thank you for helping me."

"The pleasure was all mine," he said, pulling on his buckskins. "In my
next life, I shall be a washerwoman."

"What a waste that would be," she said, admiring the way the muscles
of his upper torso worked as he donned his shirt.

"Good night, Harriet." He lifted her chin with a finger to kiss her softly.
"Or is it morning?"

"Morning."

"I hope you will not be harboring regrets about this." He sounded unsure
of himself as he stood at the door.

"No, I will not," she said firmly. "However, it would never do for this
to become a habit, would it?"

"Oh, I don't know," he said, grinning, but when she cuffed his shoulder,
he added, "No, no. You are right, of course. Still—"

"Incorrigible," she muttered and closed the door, then stood leaning
her head against it for several moments. "What *have* you done, Harriet
Augusta?" she whispered aloud. "It was all right—sinful, perhaps, but
inconsequential—for an unmarried woman to *dream* of such, but you
broke the rules."

As she turned back to her bed, she spotted his neckcloth lying on the
bench. She grabbed it up and pressed it to her face, savoring the smell.
Careful to avoid the damp spot in the middle of the bed, she lay cradling
the piece of cloth that still held a bit of the essence of him, the smell
helping her recall—happily—nuances of what had just transpired. She
fell asleep smiling.

* * * *

Quint too went to sleep with a smile on his face, but the next morning
he awoke thinking, *How stupid was that, Burnes? And here at Sedwick
too, where it had always been not just a rule, but almost a sacred law: no
taking advantage of female employees. Well, Harriet was not an employee,
was she?* But he knew that was splitting hairs.

He was a little wary about seeing her later. In his experience, women
were funny about sex. They could be extremely shy and coy—and Harriet
had been a virgin, for God's sake!—or they could become rather triumphant

and possessive, sending little secret smiles and manufacturing surreptitious touches. All of which he had found annoying or vastly amusing on previous occasions. But here—at Sedwick?

He needn't have worried.

Harriet was among the last to arrive for breakfast that morning because she and Maria had waited for and assisted Phillip, who, under protest, had been carried down to the dining room door by the footman Heller. Then Maria handed him his crutches and Heller held the door for the three of them to enter. Others at the table applauded as Phillip took his seat; greetings were exchanged; and Harriet and Maria filled plates at the sideboard for themselves and Phillip.

Suddenly everything seemed very normal, even routine. Except for the fact that Quint found it hard to keep his eyes off Harriet. That she sat directly opposite him, on Phillip's right, made it no easier. She wore a cheery yellow cotton day dress with a print of orange flowers and green leaves. It had a deep square neckline trimmed in white lace that allowed a hint of that luscious cleavage and elbow-length sleeves ending in white lace. She wore simple gold earrings and a gold locket on a chain. Her hair was swirled in tight braids atop her head, but he kept seeing its near-black mass spread across a pillow in lamplight.

He forcibly turned his attention to the other females at the table and was glad to see that Maria too no longer opted for the dark colors of half-mourning. She was dressed in a pink cotton print with small purple and white flowers and a large purple sash about the waist. A purple ribbon held her brown hair in place. His mother still usually appeared in more subdued colors, and she did so this morning. Sylvia Hartley, as always, followed the dowager's lead.

Oh, yes, Harriet was by far the more delectable feast for the eyes.

However, his attention to the women's attire had triggered something in the recesses of Quint's mind. He looked at Phillip in a gray jacket over darker trousers and shook his head in thought.

"Phillip, do you by any chance own proper evening wear?"

"'Proper evening wear'?" the boy repeated blankly.

"Whatever for?" the dowager asked.

"Mother," Quint began patiently, "If I am not mistaken, in your schedule for the house party, there are two formal dinners and, of course, the culminating ball."

With a clatter, the dowager dropped a forkful of egg onto her plate. "Good heavens, Quinton! Surely you are not suggesting a child—a mere schoolboy—be a presence at this party. Why I would be the laughingstock of the *ton*. I will not have it!"

Quint drew in a deep breath and looked toward the ceiling. "I suppose we *could* send out notes that the hostess—the Dowager Countess of Sedwick—is suddenly indisposed." His mother looked stricken at this.

Others at the table seemed suddenly fascinated by whatever was left on their plates, not quite knowing where else to look during this colloquy between Quint and his mother. Phillip, as Quint had established earlier, sat at the head of the table, which when there were so few in attendance was shortened. The dowager sat at the opposite end, and others were spread about as suited them.

Quint went on in a calm tone. "It has always been my understanding that the tradition of the Sedwick house party in the autumn was established by the third earl to ingratiate himself with King George the Second."

"Yes, that is so," his mother agreed, "and it continued every year until four years ago when—when her sister put a stop to it!" She pointed a trembling finger at Harriet.

Harriet half rose in her seat, but Quint raised a hand to stay her. "I am sorry, Mother," he said. "That is simply not so. It was your son, the noble Winston, who decided that Sedwick could no longer afford that extravagance. Decided wisely, I might add."

"B-but we *are* having it now?" She seemed on the verge of tears.

He sighed. "Yes, Mother."

"But, truly, you are not serious about including a child at such a gathering, are you, my dear? It is simply not done."

"Not only is he to be included, he is to host this event," Quint told her.

"He is *what*? Now that is beyond enough!" She stood, rigid with anger.

"Just hear me out before you fly too high into the boughs," he said patiently.

She sat back down, her hands clasped before her on the table.

He went on. "This tradition began as a hunting party sponsored by the Earl of Sedwick. If we are going to pick up the tradition again, I see no reason to substitute a surrogate for the real thing."

"Surrogate, indeed," she snorted. "You know very well that you as the minor earl's legal guardian and I as Dowager Countess of Sedwick are perfectly acceptable as host and hostess."

"Probably," he conceded. "And it will be equally or more acceptable if the host is the earl himself and the hostess is his grandmother, the Dowager Countess."

She slumped in defeat. "Why are you doing this?"

"I want it known immediately and emphatically that the Seventh Earl of Sedwick is one Phillip Burnes and that, young as he may be, he has considerable backing that he could call upon should the need arise. Although many of the most powerful men of the realm are in Vienna trying to divide up Europe, there are a sufficient number of them left in England—and on your guest list—to fulfill my purpose."

"This just seems so extraordinary," she said in a resigned tone, but perhaps she was coming around. Quint saw Harriet and Maria exchange brief little smiles.

"It will be all right, Mother. Trust me," Quint said. "You may start a new trend. Besides, Maria and I will be there to support you and Phillip."

"Maria?" Lady Margaret squeaked and looked up in shock. "But she is only a child too. You really are determined to have the whole of society laughing at me." She buried her face in her hands.

"She's of an age with Phillip," Quint said. "I'm guessing he will appreciate the support of at least one person his own age, eh, Phillip?"

Phillip, clearly overwhelmed, nodded and mumbled his assent.

"Surely you do not mean to foist such young persons into all of the activities I have planned for my adult guests," the dowager said.

"No, that would not be fair to Phillip and Maria," Quint said. "I would ask them to attend the two formal dinners and serve in the receiving line before the ball. They will excuse themselves when you give the signal for the ladies to withdraw at dinner and after the first dance at the ball. If he wishes to do so, and his leg permits him to do so, Phillip may accompany me during the hunting."

"Oh, jolly good," Phillip said.

"I see that you have planned this out in quite some detail," his mother said, "and I must wonder that you never once thought to consult *me*."

Having discussed most of this with Chet before, Quint glanced at him now, but got only a rueful shrug and a look of sympathy in response. Quint reached for his coffee cup and took a drink before answering his mother. "As I said, Mother, I want it known that Sedwick will not be taken advantage of with impunity—and several of your invited guests are just the people to ensure that the word gets out."

His mother grimaced. "Politics! You are just like your father—using a party to play some political game or another!" Her tone was resigned, and Quint knew he had won the day.

* * * *

Harriet was perplexed by that scene at breakfast between Quint and his mother. He seemed genuinely concerned about a threat to Phillip, but he was not being forthcoming about it. She noted, though, that before they had all departed the breakfast table he had charmed his mother into sending for the dressmaker and tailor this very day to see to formal attire for the two youngsters.

Maria, of course, was thrilled at the turn her and Phillip's lives had taken. The two of them joined Harriet in the music room after breakfast.

"My first ball! And I am but fourteen!" Maria exulted as she twirled around the middle of the room.

Phillip, who shared the piano bench with Harriet, said petulantly, "I do not want to host any dinners or stand in a silly receiving line either."

"The penalties of being the first-born male," Maria taunted. "One feels so-o sorry for the duties you must fulfill."

"My leg probably won't be mended."

Harriet patted his arm. "It should be. Or well on its way. You will do well. Both of you. Come now. Let's do that duet—the one with all the trills."

"All right."

Maria took a seat nearby and pretended to be an appreciative audience.

Later in the day, Harriet made a point of tracking down Quint and finally found him in his usual haunt, the library, though not behind the desk as usual. He was stretched out on a couch, an open book face down on his chest, his eyes closed. She immediately started to retreat.

"Don't leave," he said. "I'm not asleep, though Mr. Wordsworth and Coleridge have been doing their best." He sat up on one corner of the couch and patted the cushion next to him.

She took a nearby chair.

"Like that, eh?" he asked.

"I prefer not to be tempted just yet."

"'Just yet,'" he mused. "All right. I can live with that. Maybe." He paused. "I assume you have something on your mind."

"I do. I am wondering about what you said at breakfast. Have you some reason to believe Phillip may be in some sort of danger?"

He did not answer immediately and when he did, he seemed rather unsure of his response. "Not directly, so far as I can determine. I am sorry if I worried you. There has been a recent financial development relating to the estate, but, frankly, it is not something one need trouble a woman with."

She thought she might have been able give him some information about that "recent development" until he raised her hackles with that comment about not troubling a woman. "You might be surprised," she said and abruptly stood. "But if you think Phillip faces no harm—?"

He stood too and took a step toward her. "He will be fine. I shall see to it." She looked up at him. "And Sedwick?"

"I am working on that. Do not worry that pretty little head of yours about it." He bent his head to kiss her, but she quickly sidestepped out of the way.

"I have something I must see to," she said hastily, and left.

She was fuming. *How dare he? How dare he turn into one of those arrogant men who treat women as brainless toys?* Truth to tell, though, she was as furious with herself as she was with him.

She could not hold onto that fury for long, though.

Two hours later it had to be put aside, for Sedwick Hall welcomed the arrival of the young earl's great-grandparents and their full entourage.

Chapter 18

Always happy to enjoy the company of her grandparents, Harriet welcomed their arrival with even more enthusiasm than usual. She needed this diversion to take her mind off what was transpiring in her life and at Sedwick these days. She also welcomed the presence of her grandfather and her Uncle Charles, for she wanted to discuss with them further the actions she had taken with regard to Sedwick debt. Her original motive for keeping her role secret had been valid: then, she did not know this man Quinton Burnes. His father and grandfather had plunged the earldom into the sad state that Phillip was inheriting. What might he do? Now that she *did* know him, how much was her own opinion of him skewed by the fact that he was simply the most attractive man she had ever met? Was her judgment trustworthy?

Harriet had met the entourage at the door as they arrived and sent word to Quint and the dowager that, since it was so late in the afternoon, she would see to these guests until they would all gather in the drawing room before supper. After the newcomers were all shown to their rooms, the Hawthorne couple's first consideration was to see all seven of their great-grandchildren. They spent over an hour oohing and aahing over achievements and discoveries since the children had departed Hawthorne House in London. Harriet saw to getting the tutor and the governess settled, then spent a half hour bringing Charles and Elizabeth up to date on life at Sedwick—careful, of course to omit the most recent, most momentous event of her own existence.

Resigned to her son's alterations in her house party plans, it had been the dowager's idea that tonight's supper might be a sort of rehearsal for those that Phillip would host later. Convinced that the woman wanted to see Phillip or Maria commit some faux pas that would justify banishing them from the upcoming festivities, Harriet did her best to bolster their confidence with little hints and reminders as she and they followed the others at some distance down to the drawing room.

Finally, Maria whispered impatiently, "Aunt Harriet, we get it. Phillip and I are not country bumpkins, you know."

"I do know. I'm sorry. I am already proud of you both. You look so grown up and fine."

Phillip was attired in the conventional dark evening costume for men; Maria had on a pale blue silk with a fashionable high waist, capped sleeves, and long, white kid gloves. "I feel so much the lady!" she said to Harriet as the maid placed the finishing touch of a blue ribbon to hold her long hair, for all had agreed that it might be stretching the point to allow a girl of such tender years to put her hair up yet.

Not only was Harriet alert as to how Phillip and Maria would bear up under the strain of being so suddenly thrust into an adult milieu, she was also very keen to see how her grandfather and her Uncle Charles interacted with Quint, whom they were undoubtedly meeting for the first time. Neither of them remembered him from a few social affairs they all might have attended during a single season years ago. So, she watched carefully as they greeted each other cordially in the drawing room before the butler announced that the meal was being served. She saw no overt signs of antipathy, but who knew what that might mean?

The dowager had tasked Harriet with the duty of introducing William Knightly, the tutor, and Sophia Clarkson, the governess, to the rest of the assemblage; "after all, you know these people," the dowager had said dismissively. Since this was, ostensibly, but a family supper, the tutor and the governess had been invited to take the meal with the family, as they customarily would, unless the master or mistress of the Hall were entertaining. Determined that Mr. Knightly and Miss Clarkson have as pleasant a beginning to their tenure at Sedwick as possible, Harriet initially stuck by them rather nervously. Soon enough, she saw Miss Clarkson in conversation with Sylvia Hartley—she learned later that two had distant cousins of some sort in common—and that Mr. Knightly was deep in conversation with Chet Gibbons and Charles and Elizabeth Montieth.

Her grandmother and the dowager, of course—both highly respected members of the *ton*—had an acquaintance that went back not just years, but decades. Both of them—along with the patronesses of Almack's—had long been looked to as arbiters of what was acceptable in *ton* behavior. Harriet nodded to herself approvingly at seeing the two women in conversation and then seeing them both smile indulgently as Maria and Phillip, with a proper curtsy and bow, joined them.

"You see." It was Quint's voice low in her ear. "You need not have worried so. They are doing fine. So are Knightly and Miss Clarkson."

She turned toward him. "How did you know—?"

"I knew. You feel responsible. But it is out of your hands now. Completely." He leaned slightly closer, but not so much as to draw attention. "I've missed you," he whispered.

Her gaze locked with his for only a moment, and she was sure her eyes reflected the same hunger shining in his. She lowered her lashes. "For heaven's sake, Quint, not here. Not now."

"Later, then," he said.

"Later, what?" asked Charles as he and Elizabeth approached them.

"Ah, I was asking Miss Mayfield if she would play the piano for us later," Quint said in a quick recovery.

"I shall be pleased to do so," she said. "And perhaps Phillip will consent to play a duet with me."

"He plays that well, does he?" Charles asked.

Just then the butler came in to announce that the meal was being served and the company made their way to the dining room, where Phillip graced the head of the table, with his great-grandmother, the honored female guest, on his right, and his Aunt Elizbeth on his left. His grandmother served as hostess at the other end, with the Earl of Hawthorne on her right, Charles Montieth on her left. Others had been designated seats along the side as befitted their ranks insomuch as possible in such an informal setting. This was, after all, something of a tutorial, was it not?

The evening continued as smoothly as anyone could have hoped for—or perhaps as smoothly as she and Quint had separately hoped for, Harriet thought later. The new tutor and governess had both shown themselves to be persons of intelligence and good breeding, and neither of the young people had in any way brought their grandmother even the slightest hint of disgrace. Phillip gracefully, if somewhat reluctantly, agreeing to that duet had been the icing on the cake, as far as Harriet was concerned.

* * * *

Because the next day had dawned overcast and kept up a persistent drizzle, folks at Sedwick Hall mostly opted to stay indoors. In the afternoon Quint was playing billiards with Chet and the Montieth men in the game room, when the butler brought word that he had an unexpected visitor and showed him the card of Sir Desmond Humphreys.

Puzzled, for he had arranged no meeting with the other local mill owner, Quint said, "Show him to the library." He excused himself from the game in progress and took himself off to the library, though he had been quite enjoying furthering his acquaintance with the Earl of Hawthorne and Sir Charles.

He found Humphreys standing gazing at a small tapestry hanging on one side of the fireplace, depicting a unicorn in an idealized forest scene. Humphreys was dressed in a bottle green coat over a silver embroidered waistcoat and black trousers—all of which stretched slightly at the seams. His neckcloth was tied in an intricate pattern such as a man of perhaps a third of his middle years would sport.

"Sorry to keep you waiting," Quint apologized, indicating they should sit in the wing chairs flanking the fireplace.

"Quite all right." Humphreys jerked a thumb at the tapestry. "Just trying to recall all that symbolism."

"I never got beyond the purity of the unicorn myself," Quint admitted. "My brother was the medievalist." He offered the man a drink, which Humphreys politely declined, so Quint merely waited for the other man to state his business.

Humphreys cleared his throat. "I think you know that your father and I were quite good friends."

"Yes, sir."

"And, of course, you know that we enjoyed gambling quite a bit." Humphreys chuckled self-consciously.

"Yes, sir. I knew that too."

"Then I am quite sure you know that, when he died, I held substantial notes on the Sedwick Mills."

"If you are here today to collect on those—"

Humphreys put up a hand. "No. No. Hear me out. I later used those notes as collateral on a bank loan. Recently, I learned another party had bought them from the bank. I assume that party was not you."

"No, it was not, though I am not sure at this point why that should matter to you, sir."

"To tell you the truth, I was on the verge of buying back those notes when this other bloke beat me to it. I have people trying to identify him now so that I might buy them back from *that* person."

"Why? If I may be so bold as to ask," Quint said.

"It has long been a dream of mine to combine my mills with those of Sedwick to create an enterprise that might truly be competitive with Manchester mills. That is why I loaned your father that blunt to start with. I was negotiating with your brother when that unfortunate accident occurred, but he was reluctant to sell."

"So—you want me to sell you Sedwick Mills?"

"Yes. It is my understanding that, as the young earl's guardian, you have full authorization to do so. I should like to buy out your remaining interest in the two Sedwick Mills—that will give me sufficient leverage, I believe, to deal with this person who now holds those notes." He sat forward in his chair and splayed his pudgy hands on his knees. "I am prepared to pay enough that you may find it helpful in dealing with other aspects of Sedwick affairs."

He named a sum that, had Quint not been on guard, would have taken his breath away. As it was, he merely raised an eyebrow and said, "You seem to know—or think you know—a prodigious amount about the affairs of this estate."

"I make it a point of staying aware where my business interests are concerned." Humphreys stood. "I shall give you time to consider my offer. I know you have a great deal going on here in the next few weeks."

"Yes, we have," Quint said. "However, I can tell you right now that I am no more inclined to diminish my nephew's inheritance by any substantive degree than his father was."

"I understand your 'inclination,' sir, but sometimes necessity dictates otherwise, eh? My offer is good, should you wish to think it over some more." He offered his hand, which Quint shook perfunctorily.

He was eager to discuss this development with Chet, but it also crossed Quint's mind to bring it up with Hawthorne and his son too. After all, the two were reputed to be very astute businessmen, were they not? But not just yet perhaps...

He turned his thoughts to a much more pleasant, though equally perplexing subject—Harriet. Clearly, she had been avoiding him. Well, to be fair, she had not so much *avoided* him as merely sidestepped his subtle and not-so-subtle attempts to be alone with her. She was friendly and amiable enough with him in company. And with the arrival of her relatives, there had been plenty of company. Not to mention the usual intermittent presence of seven children. Why had he not noticed their excessive demands on Aunt Harriet for this or Aunt Harriet for that before? *Good job we did hire a governess,* he groused to himself.

It was in this frame of mind that he started to return to the game room for perhaps another round of billiards. Passing by the slightly opened door of the music room, he heard a soft melancholy tune on the piano. He peeked in. Harriet! And she was alone! He entered the room silently, closed the door firmly, and hurried over to kiss her on the nape of her neck before she could miss a note.

"Wha—?" she called out as he slid onto the bench beside her. "You rascal."

"Perhaps." He slipped an arm around her waist, noting happily that she did not object or move away. "You have been avoiding me," he challenged.

"No, I haven't." She reached for the sheet of music from which she had been playing.

He stayed her hand. "Look me in the eye and say that again."

She gazed at him directly and smiled sheepishly. "All right. I have. A little. I do not trust myself around you, Colonel Burnes, sir."

"Ahah!" He lowered his mouth to hers, his lips and tongue eliciting precisely the response his body desired. He lifted his head to murmur, "My God, Harriet, I want you so much!"

Allowing only another moment of such promising bliss, she gently pushed him away. "Obviously, I have reason to distrust myself with you, Quint. Enough, my darling."

"Never," he insisted, going for another kiss.

She pushed at him harder. "Quint! Do behave."

"Oh, all right." He knew he sounded like one of the twins denied a treat. "I shall come to your rooms tonight."

"No!" she said in alarm. "You know my family are in the very next rooms in that hall! You could be caught. You said 'no gossip'—remember?"

"You do not *want* me to come to you?"

She closed her eyes and sighed. "I do not want you to be caught, embarrassed."

He gave her a quick kiss. "I won't be. I shall come well after the witching hour—say, two o'clock? Surely, the whole house will be sleep by then. Just be sure to leave your doors unlocked."

"You are impossible," she said with a laugh, but she kissed him back. And she had not said "No," had she?

He whistled a merry tune all the way to the game room.

* * * *

Two o'clock. Two o'clock. Two o'clock. The time danced through Harriet's mind frequently during the rest of the afternoon and evening. When Quint's gaze occasionally met hers during the gatherings in the drawing room before and after supper, "two o'clock" seemed an almost palpable message. Surely others were aware? But apparently not. Conversations flowed at their usual pace and, surprisingly enough, she was able to take a lively part in them. Well, why not? Harriet Mayfield was rarely at a loss for words. Unfortunately, at the dining table she sat across the table from Quint; it was hard not to feast her eyes on him. At one point, she was sure the dowager had darted a piercing look from Quint to her. Thereafter, Harriet concentrated on her food.

With the London relatives visiting, the good nights to the children had taken on something of a festive atmosphere. Through choruses of "I'm not sleepy yet" and "Just one more story," Harriet led the way from the youngest to the eldest two, for as usual, Maria was sitting at Phillip's bedside. Tonight, Quint was there too.

"Uncle Quint says I can go riding tomorrow if the weather allows us," Phillip said eagerly. "He says Dolan has fixed a stirrup to accommodate my leg and I can actually ride!"

"That is wonderful news," his great-grandmother said.

"But remember: absolutely no jumping!" Quint warned. "A really hard jolt would not only hurt like the very devil, but it could do real damage."

"Yes, sir."

After some discussion of the proposed morning ride, Quint excused himself and the others too made their good nights. As Harriet and her relatives reached her door, her grandmother and Aunt Elizabeth shooed their husbands on ahead—they intended to stop for a few minutes for some "girl talk" with Harriet.

"Well, Father," Charles said, "that puts us in our place. I suppose they are cooking up some scheme that we will be expected to pay for eventually."

"Count on it," his father replied.

Harriet was puzzled, but welcomed the two women into her sitting room. They shared the blue settee and seemed slightly uneasy, then her grandmother spoke.

"We are wondering, Harriet, if you feel as comfortable here at Sedwick as you have always seemed to be in the past?"

Caught off guard by the question, Harriet fidgeted in her favorite chair and hesitated in her response. "I-I am not sure how to answer that, Nana. I love the children—now more than ever, perhaps."

Elizabeth explained. "It is just that this evening your grandmother and I remarked to Lady Margaret about how lovely our rooms were with that splendid view of the lake and all. She replied, 'Oh, yes, is it not? That view is one reason I am having that entire wing remodeled when Harriet removes to London permanently after the party.' We had no idea you were planning to remove to London permanently, so we hardly knew how to respond to her."

Harriet drew in a deep breath. "I cannot say that I 'had no idea'—I have had some broad hints that perhaps my welcome of late was less than wholly warm in that quarter—but I had made no definite plans as yet. Perhaps I should have. Telling the children will be so difficult."

"Lady Margaret also made a point of mentioning that what with her son in residence here, this is essentially a bachelor establishment," Harriet's grandmother added.

"But, Nana," Harriet protested, "she herself moved in here within three weeks of Anne's passing! Locked up the dower house completely and moved her belongings and her companion into the Hall. It is hardly the conventional 'bachelor household'—not with such a formidable chaperone."

"I know," her grandmother replied placatingly. "It is a bit of hairsplitting on her part. Lady Margaret has always been one to use the rules of social propriety to suit whatever purposes she has in mind. I do not know what it is, but I am sure she has *something* in mind, and that it will in the end, redound to her favor."

"Gran!" Elizabeth said. "I do not ever remember hearing you so—so suspicious of another person."

"Just remember that I have known Lady Margaret for nearly fifty years. Society and family obligations have often thrown us together, but we have never been what one might remotely term bosom friends."

"I would not think you would be," Harriet said. "The two of you have very little in common."

"Except those children upstairs," the older lady said sadly, pointing at the ceiling.

"Yes, there is that," Harriet said and Elizabeth nodded.

The other two rose to take their leave. Harriet stood as well and said, "Thank you for sharing that tidbit with me. I must confess that I have been vacillating, but I will set my maid to packing my things and be ready to accompany you when you return to London. It will be easier for me to leave now that Miss Clarkson is in residence."

"Selfishly, I look forward to having you in London," Elizabeth said.

"I, too," Harriet's grandmother said.

Harriet hugged them both tightly, and said good night with tears in her eyes. She rang for her maid to prepare for bed. She informed Collins of the plan to remove to London, but asked her to do the packing quietly and not to make mention of the plan below stairs. Harriet did not want the children to know of her leaving until she could explain it to them herself.

When Collins left, Harriet recalled Quint's undoing her nighttime braid and running his fingers through her hair. She loosened the braid herself, brushed out her hair and checked that both the hall door and one between her sitting room and bedroom were unlocked before crawling into bed. She lay awake staring at the round glow of the lamp on the ceiling, but she must have slept, for the next things she knew were a warm hand on her shoulder and soft lips against her cheek.

"What time is it?" she asked with a yawn.

"Not yet two. I could wait no longer." He quickly kicked off his slippers and shed his shirt and trousers to slip in beside her. He pulled her close to kiss her hungrily and run a hand the length of her body. "What is this, milady?" he said with a bunch of cloth in his fist.

"My nightgown, I would guess."

"That will not do. I want to touch you, feel you." He demonstrated by reaching beneath the gown to perform slow, seductive caresses. "Your body and mine. Skin to skin." His voice was a husky whisper.

"Picky, picky." She sat up and pulled the garment over her head.

He gathered her close, burying his face in her hair against her neck, one hand roaming freely. "That's more like it," he said. "I've dreamed of this for two full days."

Her own hands by no means idle, she said, "Is it terribly wanton of me to admit that I have too?"

"Probably, but I love it that you are." He proceeded to show her just much he did love her wantonness as he urged her to more and more of it.

Afterward, they lay together, bodies intertwined, just talking. Harriet could not remember such a sense of pure sharing with another human being—not even with her beloved friends did she feel so utterly peaceful. They talked of many things: their shared nieces and nephews, of course; their own childhoods; her article on abandoned soldiers that had just been published; his initial positive impressions of the tutor and governess; along with little murmurs of appreciation of this or that aspect of the other's anatomy. Ultimately, they made slow, wonderful love again and Quint took his reluctant leave of her.

"What would you say if you got caught?" she teased as he was dressing.

"That I was taking the servants' stairs down to the kitchen for a snack because I was hungry," he said. "The servants' stairs *is* just outside your door, you know."

"Clever," she said.

He bent over the bed and kissed her. "Get some sleep. Remember we are riding in about four hours."

But before she slept, she put her nightgown back on and rebraided her hair. Then she reveled in reliving much of the last couple of hours and realized that that they had made love twice this night and both times Quint had taken precautions as he had that first time to ensure she not end up with child. She wondered how many other men under such circumstances would be so considerate.

Chapter 19

The next day all of Sedwick Hall seemed to hold its collective breath as the young earl went riding for the first time since his accident. In fact, it was a large party of riders—a dozen or so what with a couple grooms along "just in case." Harriet was pleased to see that William Knightly, despite a crippled leg, welcomed the opportunity to join in the ride. Phillip would not want for a riding companion when she left. She thought this day signified some sort of milestone for Phillip. He was more cheerful and optimistic than she had seen him in a long time—maybe since before the loss of his parents.

Because there were so many riders, they were scattered over a great deal of Sedwick real estate, not always within sight of one another. At one point Maria had ridden off with Elizabeth to show her a favorite view, leaving Harriet alone except for a groom. But not for long. Quint appeared at her side on the always overactive Lucifer, but Quint seemed to have the stallion well in hand. The groom moved off.

"Well, what do you think?" Quint asked her. "Were we wise to allow Phillip to ride so soon?"

She smiled, liking that he said "we" just as though she had had any say in the matter. "It has been a long while since I have seen him so happy."

"He should be happy," Quint said bluntly. "He has his little corner of the world arranged exactly as he wants it. Not all of us can do that so easily."

"I know." She allowed her worry to show as she held his gaze. "I should hate for any of Anne's children to be as crassly manipulative as that sounds."

"That broken leg should temper any self-satisfaction at merely getting his own way. That was a high price to pay."

"There is that," she conceded.

"In any event, I am sure you and I will be able to remind the noble Seventh Earl from time to time that he has feet of clay."

"You," she said. "You will remind him. I shall not be here."

"Not be—what are you saying?"

"I am returning to London with my grandparents after the party. Did your mother not tell you?"

"No. No, she did not." He sounded annoyed and would have pursued the subject, but just then Phillip and Charles approached them.

"I think our boy has about had the course for his first day out," Charles said.

"Is that so, Phillip?" Quint asked.

"Afraid so, sir. The leg aches something fierce all of a sudden."

"Still, you did very well to stay out so long," Harriet assured him. "I shall go back with Phillip," she said to Quint and Charles. "You two continue the outing." She signaled the groom to accompany her and Phillip back to the stable.

That afternoon the rest of Lady Margaret's guests began to arrive and within the next few days the hallways and public rooms of Sedwick Hall were abuzz with such of England's finest as her ladyship had been able to collect in this rather peculiar year. During a gathering in the drawing room before the evening meal, she pronounced herself—in a small conversational group—as quite satisfied that no one had sent his or her regrets this year.

Sylvia Hartley, ever ready to stroke her benefactress's vanity, said, "I daresay, my lady, you have pulled off the social coup of the year—especially in view of the fact that so many of Europe's most powerful men are still in Vienna dividing up that horrid Boney's empire."

"What is more," said Judith, Viscountess Pearson, one of the so-called "Winsome Widows" and a popular *ton* hostess herself, "they have drained London of acceptable society. One could scarcely make up a suitable guest list even during height of the season!"

"Well, now," drawled Lord Beaconfield. "I would not say drained entirely—there's still thee and me."

While the other women all laughed at this sally, Harriet merely grinned at him and raised an eyebrow. She had been surprised at first to see him among the guests. *Ton* house parties had never held much interest for Gavin Castlemere, Lord Beaconfield, so far as she knew, and she did know that his sporting interests lay more with his sailboat than in hunting grouse. It turned out that he was escorting his mother, a sometime friend of Lady Margaret, and his younger sister, who had just made her debut this year. Apparently, his sister had developed a *tendre* for a certain Lord Avron, who was another of the guests, and whom Gavin's mother was convinced was a rake. Hence, Beaconfield was here in the role of knight-protector. And he was ever so delighted to find Harriet in residence.

"Too bad that nephew of yours is not at least five years older. We might divert her interest in that direction," Gavin said. Then, more softly, he said, "By the by, my friend, you are ruffling some rather significant feathers in the halls of Westminster."

"I—?"

"That piece on child labor. Apparently, it hit home in certain quarters of Parliament."

"Good."

He put a hand on her forearm and held her gaze for a long moment. "Take care, my dear. I would not see you hurt."

She gave his hand a brief pat. "Thank you."

As she moved away from Gavin, she nearly stumbled into Quint, who had clearly seen that little by-play. With Lady Riverton tugging at his arm on his other side, he merely smiled and nodded in passing. She felt a distinct urge to stick her foot out and trip him, but restrained herself. She had had no time alone with him since that blissful two o'clock assignation—and that had been ages ago. Well, over a week at least. And yes, she had longed for him. Desperately. She could not deny that, but she repeatedly told herself how utterly foolish that was. Here she was: spinning daydreams about a man she had known for—what?—all of perhaps three months. And she had no idea how he felt about her. How stupid was that?

She consciously turned her attention to the persons assembled in this room. Yes, the Dowager Countess of Sedwick had done herself proud. Besides Lord Beaconfield, and, of course, Lord Hawthorne, she had snagged two other members of the House of Lords in Lord Hastings and Lord Ridgway, both of whom were here with their wives. Harriet knew that for Lady Margaret having all three of the "Winsome Widows" accept her invitation had been a real feather in her cap.

The three had arrived on the same day, Lady Barbara Riverton traveling with her young cousin, Lord Avron, as her escort. Less than an hour later, Lady Angelina Bachmann and Lady Judith Pearson arrived together— along with a retinue befitting princesses. Harriet had been thankful she had been out when they arrived, and it was not until supper that evening that she greeted the day's arrivals, most of whom she had had at least a passing acquaintance with over the last few years.

Apparently, Quint had been out all that day too. He put in his appearance in the drawing room that evening after Harriet's.

"Quinton, you naughty boy," his mother trilled. "Where have you been all day? You were not here to greet our new arrivals—and such lovely additions they have brought us." She proceeded to announce all who had arrived that day, including the Ridgeway couple as well as the three young widows.

"Sorry, Mother. I was tied up with the gamekeeper." He bowed to the guests she had pointed out. "I do apologize for not being on hand for your arrival."

"Oh, la! Such formality for such old friends." Lady Barbara quickly stepped toward him and extended both her hands, which he had no choice but to take and bow over most particularly as she went on. "It is wonderful— simply wonderful to see you again at last, Quinton. I had hoped to see you in London before now."

"Thank you, Lady Barbara." His response seemed somewhat stiff to Harriet.

Harriet thought Lady Barbara Riverton came by her reputation as the most beautiful of the Winsome Widows quite honestly. She had honey-blonde hair that just missed being the proverbial "spun gold." She also had striking green eyes, dark brows, a short, straight nose, a rosebud mouth, and a complexion that other women envied. She was taller than average, but seemed even taller because of her willowy build, which tonight was emphasized by a pale green, fashionably high-waisted silk gown.

In gold taffeta with a bronze net overskirt, Harriet felt like a positive frump next to this paragon. Nor did she feel any better when she learned that Lady Margaret had designated Lady Barbara as Quint's dinner partner. Only later did she notice that the woman had paired Gavin with Lady Angelina Bachmann. As for herself, she had no cause for complaint: her dinner partner was Chet Gibbons, whose sardonic observations about the human species Harriet invariably found amusing, but Harriet doubted her ladyship had had that in mind when she determined who would partner whom at the dining table.

* * * *

Quint had been apprehensive about seeing Barbara again. After all, she was the only woman he had ever seriously considered marrying, and, in retrospect, he had seriously misjudged both her and himself. Yet in seeing her again, actually touching her, all he could think was "why?" He wanted to laugh. But he did not. He was a good boy. Played his role properly.

Thinking about that whole "reunion" scene later, he had to admit that yes, Lady Barbara Riverton was certainly a beauty. Still. But it was a pair of changeable gray eyes that kept catching him unaware, not the practiced witchery of those green orbs. *That is what it is,* he told himself, *practiced witchery. Why did I not see that years ago?* He finally settled on callow youth and vulnerability as answers to that question. And he was damned well not traveling down that route again, despite the apparent lures she seemed on the verge of offering.

Pronouncing the heavens themselves on her side, Lady Margaret welcomed the ensuing days of gloriously warm weather as she set in motion details for her grand picnic to include not only her houseguests, but certain local notables as well. Besides turning out three meals plus sundry snacks each day for well over a hundred people, what with guests and their servants, Mrs. Hodges and her kitchen crew were tasked with coming up with picnic baskets fit for royalty. Folding chairs and tables, colorful awnings, blankets, utensils for brewing tea on the spot, and serving dishes—all of which had to be taken by wagon out to the abbey ruins. Guests would arrive by carriage or horseback. Quint knew that his mother, working with the housekeeper and the butler, had planned everything down to the minutest detail. Only when he found himself driving his curricle out to the ruins with her and Lady Barbara as his passengers did he begin to wonder just how far her attention to detail had really gone.

Later, in strolling about the abbey ruins, he kept recalling that other picnic, the family picnic weeks earlier. The one where he had kissed Harriet for the first time. He wondered if she was remembering that too. But when he glanced over her way, she was laughing up at Beaconfield. Again.

"They make a fine couple, do they not?" said a female voice at his side.

"What?" he said, startled, then realized the speaker was Lady Suzanne, Beaconfield's younger sister, a pretty little thing with a heart-shaped face, brown hair, and big, innocent blue eyes. She reminded Quint of Maria.

"They make a fine couple," she repeated. "At least Mama thinks so. And they are such good friends as well."

"Is that so?" Quint asked.

"Oh, yes. Both writers. Both belong to that literary club and all. Dull stuff, if you ask me, but—" She shrugged.

"Not everyone's cup of tea, eh?"

"Ay, Lady Suzanne, it's your turn," Lord Avron called from the pall-mall game.

"Oops. Pardon me," she said to Quint and dashed back to the game.

He shook his head.

Beaconfield and Harriet?

* * * *

Knowing English weather for its usual capriciousness, Harriet had earlier conjectured that, unless the dowager allowed children to attend this affair, there would be little opportunity for such an outing for them again this year. Knowing, too, that she might never have another chance at such a frolic with them, she argued vigorously for their inclusion. She first broached the topic at breakfast one morning before any of the guests but her own family members had yet arrived at the Hall. Harriet was pleased to see that only she, the dowager, and Quint had come down as yet. Servants had not yet set up the sideboard fare, they were so early.

At first, the dowager had dismissed Harriet's suggestion out of hand with the condescending comment, "Harriet, dear, I am sure you must know house parties such as mine are designed as *adult* affairs."

"I thought with Phillip and Maria already there—"

"And you know my thoughts on *that,*" the older woman snapped.

"I would be most willing to help with the children, keep them from interfering in any way," Harriet said. She looked at Quint, hoping to enlist his support.

"No." Lady Margaret's face had a closed look to it. "No. I would have to allow others as well, and I will not have a pack of brats running around, screaming, ruining my party."

Two footmen brought in heavily laden trays and set up covered dishes on the sideboard, then placed coffeepots and teapots and racks of toast strategically along the table.

Quint reached for a coffeepot. "Come now, Mother. You know a picnic is the sort of thing that brings out the child in all of us. That is why you thought of it in the first place."

"That is not the point and you know it," she replied, but before she could expound upon just what the point was, Phillip and Maria came in, followed by their visiting great-grandparents and Charles and Elizabeth. Right behind them were the tutor and governess, and, finally, Chet and Mrs. Hartley. Harriet knew very well that Lady Margaret would like to consider the subject closed, but even knowing she would chastise herself for pettiness later, she refused to let that happen.

After all the "good mornings" were exchanged and the newcomers supplied with food and drink, Harriet said, "We were just discussing having all the children at the picnic, not just Phillip and Maria."

Elizabeth paused, her cup halfway to her mouth, glanced at Harriet, and set her cup back in its saucer. "Oh, Lady Margaret! What a brilliant idea! A picnic always wants the frivolity of children, does it not?"

"Makes us remember where we came from," her husband said.

"I like it, Lady Margaret," Lady Hawthorne said, but Harriet had counted on her grandmother's "liking" it.

The dowager glared at Harriet, but accepted the inevitable and pretended it was all her own idea.

Now, in the event, Harriet tried to be true to her word in helping the nursery maids keep the children entertained. Nor was there such a "pack" as the dowager had feared. Besides her own seven grandchildren and three additional children of houseguests, local people had brought to the picnic only another seven youngsters, and none of these was under five.

Harriet was sitting on the edge of a broken wall retying the ribbon on one of Sarah's braids, when she became truly aware of other picnickers not far away. She and Sarah were about twenty feet from three or four small groups lounging on blankets spread near the food tables. A very substantial lunch had been served, but folks still lazed about, imbibing champagne and lemonade and nibbling biscuits. The nearest group, she noticed, included the Ridgeways, Lady Margaret, and Lady Barbara. Close by, on another blanket, was Lord Beaconfield and Angelina Bachmann. Seeing Gavin glance her way, Harriet lifted an eyebrow. He smiled and shrugged. Angelina, apparently aware of this byplay, stared at Harriet and smirked. She leaned close to Gavin to whisper something.

Suddenly Quint was sitting on the wall next to Harriet. He leaned around her to grin at Sarah. "We could get one of those knives used to slice the ham we had for lunch and just cut that braid off. Then you would not have that problem."

"Uncle Quint!"

"It was just a thought," he said.

"*Not* a good one," his little niece quickly retorted.

"Saucy little wench, is she not?" he said to Harriet.

"Auntie Harriet! Did he just call me a 'wench'?" Sarah asked, indignant.

Harriet laughed and hugged her close. "I think he did. But he meant it kindly. He loves you very much."

"Oh." Sarah jumped down to stand in front of Quint, her hands on her hips. "Is that true?"

"Quinton, darling," the dowager called from her blanket.

Quint waved his mother off to answer Sarah with a wide grin. "Yes, Poppet, it is true. All of it." He picked her up and kissed her on the cheek. She threw her little arms around his neck and kissed him back vigorously.

"I love you too, Uncle Quint. But I don't think gentlemen is apposed to kiss ladies in public." She wriggled free and scampered off.

He laughed and let her go. His gaze meeting Harriet's was full of emotion.

"Quinton!" his mother called again, her tone more imperious. "I have just been telling Lady Barbara of the view from the old bell tower and she has expressed a desire to see it. Do be so good as to show it to her."

"Of course, Mother," he said, but he whispered "Later" to Harriet before he shoved himself off the wall.

Not caring to join those still lingering around the picnic tables, Harriet started to circle around the corner of what had once been the west end of the abbey chapel. There, amongst a mishmash of broken and toppled statuary, young trees, and full bushes already showing autumn foliage, she found Sarah and the twins with several other children of like ages playing a rollicking game of hide and go seek. Nothing would do but that Aunt Harriet should join them. They were having such carefree fun, Harriet could not resist joining their laughter and squeals of delight. Until she noticed they had an audience approaching.

That the group included her friends the vicar, Justin Powers, and his wife would not have disconcerted Harriet at all. But here were Angelina—on Lord Beaconfield's arm—and Lady Barbara clinging to Quint like—like she owned him. And Harriet: disheveled, out of breath, and feeling sweaty! She stood still and the children gathered around her.

"You see?" Angelina was saying in her cute little girl voice, and looking cool and elegant in a plum-colored frock, "did I not tell you aright?" She made a sweeping gesture with one hand and arm, making sure not to lose her hold on Lord Beaconfield. "I present to you a fairy tale come to life: Snow White and her dwarfs!" She pretended to be counting. "Oh, dear, there were only seven originally."

Lady Barbara laughed and tugged at Quint's arm. "Oh, my, that is so funny. Quinton, darling, is that not hilarious? Angelina, you are so very clever."

Angelina preened.

Then Sarah stepped in front of Angelina, put her hands on her hips in a characteristic pose, and said very precisely, "I am *not* a dwarf, my lady. Nor are my brothers or our friends."

Harriet put a hand on the little girl's shoulder. "It is all right, Sarah. Lady Angelina meant no offense."

"Goodness, no," Angelina said. "I do not go around seeking to insult babies."

At this, Sarah stamped her foot. "I am not a babe, either."

"Of course you are not," the Bachmann woman said, but then added not quite under her breath, "You are merely a very spoiled little girl." Aloud, she said to Gavin, "Perhaps we should leave."

He looked helplessly at Harriet and led Angelina away even as she continued muttering about the proper deportment of children.

Sarah looked up at Quint near tears. "Was I bad, Uncle Quint?"

He freed himself from the Riverton woman and knelt to put an arm around Sarah. "Not so very bad, Poppet, but you must learn to let people's casual comments just pass you by. 'Tis hard sometimes, though, even for grown-ups."

"Even if they are not true?" she asked.

He nodded very seriously. "Even so."

She was quiet for a moment, then said, "I do not think I will like being a grown-up."

This brought a chuckle from the remaining grown-ups in the group, and then Emma Powers said to Harriet that she and Justin had come looking for their three children to take their leave. Quint declared that the approach of sunset was a signal for all to be leaving. Servants had already packed up most of the things they had needed this day. Harriet rode back to the Hall in a carriage bearing Phillip and Maria, along with Mr. Knightly and Miss Clarkson. Theirs was one of the last vehicles to leave.

As she looked her last at the ruins, Harriet felt a wave of nostalgia wash over her. Today had been fun, but how on earth was she to tell the children there would be no more such days?

Chapter 20

Quint had found little opportunity to confront his mother about Harriet's leaving. Always she seemed occupied with this or that female guest. Finally, late one evening, as the entire party was splitting up, saying their good nights preparatory to seeking their bedchambers, he simply put a hand on her arm to detain her and said quietly, "Mother, I should like a word with you, please."

"At this hour?" she protested, but when everyone else had left, she sat back down on the corner of a couch and looked at him expectantly.

He took the nearest chair and asked bluntly, "Did you tell Harriet she must leave Sedwick?"

She immediately took umbrage. "No, I did *not*. Did she say I did?"

He shook his head, but she went on before he could say anything.

"Miss Mayfield," she said, emphasizing the formal term of address, "*may* have heard of my plans for renovation of that wing where her rooms are located. I do remember mentioning that casually to Lady Hawthorne and her daughter-in-law, Elizabeth."

Quint sat back and ran a hand through his hair. "I fail to see why your nebulous plan for some possible future renovation would necessitate her leaving with her grandparents after your party."

The dowager shrugged and shifted in her seat as though to rise. "Well, she cannot stay here forever—we have been over this before, Quinton."

"Yes. We have. And your reasoning makes little sense so long as you reside at Sedwick Hall, surely you provide adequate chaperonage."

"But, my darling boy," she said sweetly as she stood, "then she would have to be *my* guest—which she assuredly is not. Now, if you will excuse me—" She started for the door.

"It makes no sense," Quint repeated. He rose politely and stopped her in her tracks with his next words: "And there will be no renovations to the Hall. Anywhere. The estate cannot afford them. Should you wish to make improvements to the dower house, those, of course, would be your business—and funded by your widow's endowment."

"Good night, son." She nearly slammed the door.

"Good night, Mother." He sat back down in resignation, but became alert when he heard the door open again. But it was not his mother returning. He stood.

"Lady Barbara."

She came close and he smelled the heavy scent of gardenias. "Good heavens, Quinton, I was once always *Barbara* to you—even *Barbara darling* or some other endearment—may I not at least be *Barbara* to you again?" she begged.

"Of course," he said in a rather neutral tone.

"I left my reticule in here," she said. "Oh, there it is." She walked over to a small table on which lay a small silver bag on a silver chain. Quint had no doubt the bag had been "forgot" by design, but he merely waited for her make the next move.

Which she did.

"I have so longed for a moment alone with you Quinton."

"We had had several such moments at the picnic," he said.

"Oh, but we might have been interrupted at any moment by—by someone else—or" she shuddered "or by some child demanding your attention." She emitted a false little titter of a laugh and moved closer to him. He could feel her body heat and while his anatomy was not immune to overtures from a beautiful woman, the rest of him seemed disinclined to follow through.

She slipped her arms around his neck and pressed her body close to his. "Kiss me, Quinton. Kiss me as you did all those years ago."

And, God help him, he did.

But as her lips moved and opened seductively to him, he felt little in the way of response. He gently pulled away.

"I-I'm sorry, La—uh—Barbara. This is just neither the time nor the place."

"What do you mean? We once meant something—a great deal—to each other."

"A long time ago. And—if you recall—it was *you* who decided we would not suit—I think that was how you put it."

"But things have changed. We can—"

"Not here. Not now. Not at my mother's house party."

"Quinton, darling," she cooed, moving an arm's length away, but not releasing her hold on him, and openly laughing at him. "Even you know that the rules simply do not apply at house parties. Your mother certainly knows that! Why else did she give me a chamber so very convenient to yours, my dear?" She gazed at him a long moment, then said, "At my request, I might add, based on fond memories."

He stepped back. "You must be joking."

"Well, no." She picked up her bag and let it dangle from her wrist, "But you *do* know which chamber is mine should you care to avail yourself of that knowledge. Oh—and do be sure to call me *Barbara*."

"Yes, ma'am." He smiled as she let herself out.

Earlier Quint had thought of perhaps knocking at Harriet's door this evening, despite having heard Sir Charles tease her about "those late-night hen sessions you women get up to." However, these encounters—first with his mother, and then with Barbara—had somehow tainted any time he might now have with Harriet.

* * * *

In the first few days following the picnic, Harriet had two encounters that helped reinforce her decision to return to London with her grandparents. Perhaps there was something providential about the way matters seemed to be stacking up against her continued presence at Sedwick Hall. One day after the midday meal Quint and Chet had taken the gentlemen off to the game room for billiards, checkers, and card games—as well as a good deal of ale and such other drink as pleased the guests. The ladies would be similarly entertained in the drawing room with card games or stitchery or whatever they wished to occupy themselves with. Tea, lemonade, or ratafia were offered to slake their thirst. In general guests, male and female, were encouraged to relax and regenerate however they pleased.

Having ridden hard that morning and for longer than usual, Harriet was content to work on a piece of embroidery she had neglected for lo! these many months. She knew of writers who *could* write what later became polished pieces on little snippets of paper in the midst of rooms full of people such this one, but that was not one Harriet Mayfield—or the Lady Senator, either. Even as this thought ran through Harriet's mind with a mental sigh, Lady Pearson bustled over to take a seat next to her on the rose-colored sofa, her own embroidery hoop in hand.

"May I join you, Miss Mayfield?"

"By all means, milady."

"Do let us be *Judith* and *Harriet*. After all, we have known each other for years. We came out the same year, did we not?"

"I believe we did," Harriet agreed. "As you wish, Judith."

"Good." Judith seemed to be searching for a topic as she bent her soft brown hair over Harriet's piece of embroidery. "What is it that you are working on?"

"A small tapestry—meant to depict Cassandra sounding the alarm to the people of Troy."

"My. You truly are a bluestocking, are you not?" Judith said, but it was not said unkindly.

Harriet laughed, leaned close, and whispered, facetiously, "That's what they say."

"Nevertheless, it is very nice work," Judith said graciously.

Harriet thanked her, wondering a bit at this particular overture from one of the Winsome three. She had never garnered such attention from any of them before—well, except for Angelina's ridicule, which perhaps had *some* explanation in its being some sort of holdover from schoolgirl rivalry. Tiresome and petty at this late date, and best ignored.

For a moment Harriet concentrated on rethreading her needle and Judith busied herself with her own work, then Judith quietly cleared her throat. She gave Harriet what could only be described as a look of sympathy.

Sympathy?

But before Harriet had time to ponder that, the other woman spoke. "I am wondering, Harriet, whether you are—uh—aware of a—uh—'history'— between Lady Barbara and Lord Quinton."

Harriet was nonplused. "Whether I am—?" She settled on the ploy of ignorance to buy time. "I have no idea what you are talking about. And he prefers the title *colonel*."

Judith immediately took an apologetic tone. "Oh, my, I do hope I have not offended you in any way."

Harriet waved a hand dismissively. "Not at all. Why on earth should I be offended?"

"Well—uh—I—that is—some of us—have seen the way you and— Lord—uh—Colonel Burnes look at each other, and I just thought you should know that there *is* this history, you see—"

"And you thought to warn me away so your friend could have a clear field—is that it?" Harriet ask in a carefully neutral tone.

Judith drew in a sharp breath. "I would not have said it so crassly. I merely hoped to spare another woman being hurt if possible."

Harriet held her gaze for a long moment before deciding that yes, she seemed sincere. "Thank you, Judith. I appreciate your concern, but, truly, neither you nor Lady Barbara need worry yourselves."

"I—I just thought you should know," Judith said weakly.

"And now I do," Harriet said, setting aside her needlework and preparing to escape.

Judith leaned closer as though to share a secret; her voice lowered as she said, "Oh, but did you also know that Lady Margaret is actively promoting a match between her son and Lady Barbara?"

"Really? Again?" Harriet feigned mild interest.

Judith nodded. "It's true. Again. I think she hopes it will work this time for Barbara would make such a biddable daughter-in-law—not like your sister at all."

"No, I doubt Anne was very 'biddable.'"

"But that is rarely the case between those members of a family," Judith said, gathering her embroidery work and rising. "If you will excuse me, I must speak with Lady Charlotte Ridgeway."

Harriet wanted to ask whom she was going to warn *her* against, but was too glad to see her leave to detain her.

Two days later the second encounter took place and it started at least in the very same room.

Lady Margaret and her houseguests were receiving a number of local callers in the afternoon. The drawing room was abuzz with conversation in several groups, the norms for such calls being more relaxed in the country than in London. Among the local people paying calls was Sir Desmond Humphreys. Harriet had been mildly surprised to see him, having heard he was away from the area—and he had missed the dowager's picnic. It was unlike Sir Desmond to miss any local social affair of note. He apologized loudly and profusely to Lady Margaret on his arrival for having missed her picnic.

"I was in London these last weeks on business that just would not wait, my lady. Please believe me, I would not miss a fete of yours for any but the most dire of reasons."

"How flattering," she gushed.

Later, as he seemed on the verge of leaving, he specifically sought out Harriet, who was just turning away from a group standing near the French doors leading out to a balcony overlooking the gardens two floors below. The day was warm and the room was full; the doors had been opened to allow in fresh air. Humphreys touched her elbow and said, "Might I have a private word with you, Miss Mayfield?"

She gave him an inquiring look, but found no reason to refuse him. She gestured toward the open doors. "There is no one on the balcony. That should provide sufficient privacy, I think," she said, ignoring a slight look of disappointment on his face.

As usual, he was dressed in the latest of male fashion, in this instance a maroon coat, a gold embroidered waistcoat, black satin pantaloons, and a neckcloth tied in a complicated knot that defied the imagination almost as much as his garments seemed to defy certain laws of elasticity in their materials.

He guided her to a far corner of the balcony and looked back over his shoulder cautiously.

"Is something wrong?" Harriet asked.

"Oh, no," he answered, with what seemed a condescending chuckle to her. "It is just that a man wishes for a good deal more privacy for what I am about to ask you."

Harriet felt a tremor of dread, but before she could forestall him, he rushed on. He took both of her hands in his. "Miss Mayfield, we have known each other quite some time—several years in fact. I have long admired you and have of late grown quite fond of you. You would make me the happiest of men if you would consent to marry me."

"Oh, my goodness." She tried to break the connection, but he retained his grip on her hands. Her first thought was that his speech sounded practiced. She wondered if he did it before a looking glass. Then she wanted to laugh at the incongruity of that thought, and she knew this man's sense of self-importance was far too fragile for any but the utmost solemnity. She gave the hands gripping hers a vigorous shake and he loosened his grasp. "I am aware, Sir Desmond, of the immense honor you do me, but I simply cannot accept your offer."

He dropped his hands to his sides and said bluntly, "I cannot believe at this late date you are holding out for a better offer."

"No, that is not it." She wanted to slap him, but merely added the trite "I simply feel we would not suit."

"Well, my dear Miss Mayfield, I happen to think we would suit very well indeed," he growled as he grabbed her by her shoulders and pushed her against the wall, outside direct line of vision from the French doors of the room. His face was close to hers; his breath smelled of fish and onions; his voice grated. "You may have heard me say I just returned from London."

Angry now, she was ready to spit in his face. "Why should I care where you have been?"

His smile was really just a baring of his teeth and he still had hold of her shoulders. "Because, dear girl, I went there to buy back my notes on Sedwick Mills—only to find someone had beat me to it."

Harriet felt a frisson of fear travel the length of her spine, but bravado won out. "So?"

"It just happens that I have a family connection who sits on the boards of a number of the City's financial institutions—including the Seton-Trevors Bank."

Harriet put a hand to her forehead.

Now his smile was more real, though just as repulsive. He seemed to wait for her to say something, but when she did not, he said smugly, "Exactly, my love." He lowered his hands and went on in a more persuasive tone now. "As I see it, were you to marry me, we could leverage Sedwick's guardian into selling us the remaining interest in those mills and we would thus have a very substantial hold on the textile industry in this county, what with my mills too."

"Yes, I can see that," she said.

"And, if it will make you any more amenable to marrying me, I will have it written into the marriage settlements that I will change my will so that you will have complete and absolute control of that enterprise on the occasion of my death. Given the rather considerable difference in our ages, that should be of some interest to you."

She drew in a deep breath and said very quietly, but very firmly, "Sir Desmond, *nothing* would make me more amenable to marrying you. It is simply out of the question."

He stared at her balefully for a long moment, then rubbed one hand across his face and stepped back slightly, though his body still blocked her way. "Well, then," he said, "I am willing to buy your interest in those mills for twice what you paid for those notes. That gives you a handsome profit on that transaction. I am sure if you discuss it with whoever has authority over your financial affairs, you will find he will take the offer when I present it to him." He stepped away, allowing her to flee.

"Don't hold your breath for that," she said over her shoulder.

She thought she heard him mutter "You'll be sorry," but she ignored it.

And of course the first persons she encountered as she came through those French doors were Quint, his mother, and Lady Barbara. Quint looked at her and at Humphreys right behind her.

"Harriet?" Quint put out a hand, but she mumbled "Sorry" and brushed past him. She heard the dowager make an inane comment about a lovers' quarrel.

* * * *

Although he had followed through on his decree that Phillip be acknowledged the official host of this house party, Quint found that often he had to step in and take the lead, especially in organizing matters of traditional all-male activities, such as an expedition to a local pugilistic exhibition that was to be held in the market arena in Hendley. Having polled the guests as to who wished to ride to the affair, who wished to drive their own vehicles, and who wished to avail themselves of Sedwick carriages and drivers, Quint made sure all were adequately provided for in the way of transportation and that they were all supplied with food and drink once they reached their destination.

So long as he stayed close to his uncle or Mr. Gibbons, Phillip was allowed to accompany the gentlemen, but none of the younger boys were, for Quint remembered all too well that such "exhibitions" often got out of hand, erupting into brawls. Grown men could fend for themselves, but Quint was taking no chances with eight-year-olds!

He knew his mother had planned an elaborate tea party for the female guests and that she had invited a considerable number of local ladies to join them. She had even hired a local group of actors to provide entertainment: they would turn one area of the ballroom into a theatre of sorts and perform scenes from Shakespeare and popular plays of the day. Harriet and Mrs. Hartley had been prevailed upon to provide soft music while the dowager's guests imbibed tea and lemonade. Quint privately thought those two had the patience of saints, but Harriet had told him that playing the piano spared her having to engage in unending meaningless chitchat—or pretend to do so.

The big outings for the men were, of course, the grouse hunts. They had been lucky in having good weather for both, especially the last one, which involved not just the houseguests, but also several local men that Quint felt he wanted to know better. On that basis alone he might not have included Sir Desmond Humphreys, but, he reminded himself, he had no business deliberately giving offense in the name of Sedwick. Once again Phillip was the nominal host of this event, and the invitations had been issued in his name.

Lying in his bed late one night, sleepless, wanting Harriet, and trying to force his mind in other directions, he had to smile at the idea of Phillip as host. His mother still chafed at the idea, but she did not hesitate to claim it as all her own when the Marchioness of Hastings lavishly praised her for such an original idea after that first formal dinner.

"I vow, Lady Margaret, you will have set a new a trend. Every London hostess will be seeking ways to project young people into the center of things. Though few are as suited to the role as your young Phillip. He looks so well in his evening wear, and his manners are impeccable," the woman gushed.

"Yes, he does well, does he not?" the dowager had agreed proudly, and looked toward her son, thus directing attention at Quint, "but Phillip had the best of role models in all his family members."

Quint had nearly snorted at this, recalling the straits into which the boy's grandfather and great-grandfather had thrust the earldom, but he allowed his mother to have her day.

The Marchioness of Hastings was not the only guest to praise this unusual elevation of a young person, though. Quint found the approval of Lord Hawthorne far more gratifying. His lordship had pulled his mount even with Quint's one morning as the group of riders were returning to the stable.

"I must tell you, Colonel Burnes, that his great-grandmother and I have been not a little worried about that lad." The old gentleman pointed with his riding crop at Phillip, riding ahead and laughing up at Chet. "He took his father's death so very hard," the old man continued after a long pause. "Phillip talks with me a good deal. Told me about your visits with the weavers and the mills. I think your easing him into what it is to be the Earl of Sedwick is an excellent notion."

"Thank you, sir." Quint was carefully noncommittal.

"Don't know if that was your full intent," the old man went on. "Oftentimes when a person inherits as young as our Phillip has, there are those around him that get delusions as to their own level of authority or power. I think perhaps you have sufficiently squelched any such pretensions."

"I hope so, sir." Again, Quint kept his tone neutral, but he was amazed at the insight the man had. It was almost as though the Earl of Hawthorne had seen the Dowager Countess of Sedwick's handwriting in some of those ledgers within days after her eldest son's accident—and before her other son had arrived on the scene—or that significant dates and amounts seemed to have been altered and on certain documents, also in her distinctive script. Ah, well, he reminded himself, the Hawthorne couple had known his mother far longer than he had. The solicitor Boskins had laid some of that incredible debt squarely in her lap too.

As a young man he had seen his mother play that role of the guileless female even as she cleverly schemed and manipulated those around her— mostly her husband, who, Quint had thought, invariably underestimated her. As he looked back on it, what he had learned from his parents' marriage was mostly what he never wanted in that institution for himself. Perhaps that was why he had never been truly sorry it had eluded him. And if this party had done nothing else, it had managed to show him what might have been, for he saw much of a younger Lady Margaret in Lady Barbara.

A great deal of this—along with the ever-present worry about the state of Sedwick finances—was on his mind as the large party headed out for the last great grouse hunt. Quint was disappointed, but later not overly surprised to find that Sir Desmond Humphreys had finagled a position in the same blind from which Quint would be shooting with Chet and Phillip. Humphreys wasted no time in chitchat about the hunt.

"Colonel Burnes, have you considered my offer to buy Sedwick's remaining interest in those mills?"

Quint replied promptly. "I have. Although there was no need to do so. My nephew and I have no interest in selling."

"May I ask if you are in negotiation with the party owning the other shares?"

Quint glanced at Phillip and Chet, glad Phillip had sense enough not to say anything, then said, "You may ask, but I feel no obligation to respond at this time."

He saw a flash of fury pass over Humphreys's face before he turned away. "Have it your way." Soon enough, Humphreys left, saying, "I think I'll pop over and see how Squire Douglas and Captain Morris are faring."

Quint was glad to see him go.

Immediately Phillip asked, "What did he mean about buying Sedwick Mills? We are not selling them, are we?" He sounded worried.

Quint explained very briefly, and in broad terms, trying not to load down those young shoulders with the entire burden of Sedwick debt—or the cupidity of certain of the boy's predecessors. "I have told him no on your behalf, Phillip, but I will explain in far greater detail if you wish to see the books and all."

Phillip stared at him. "Good God, no. I trust you, Uncle Quint. Father trusted you. I trust you." He grinned. "Besides, I probably will not understand them much. Maybe when Mr. Knightly finishes with me..."

Chet punched him affectionately on the shoulder. "Good lad, this!"

Chapter 21

On the day of the ball, Harriet skipped the midday meal with the gaggle of adults in the dining room in favor of spending time with the children. She had put off for too long the painful duty of telling them she would be leaving. Sitting around the large round table in the main room of the nursery, they were having trifle for dessert.

"Ooh, my fav'ritest," Tilly cooed.

"Just see you eat as much as you wear," Robby said.

"Master Robert, that was unkind," Nurse Tavenner admonished, wiping at Tilly's cheek.

The boy made a face. "I'm sorry, but look at her bib!"

Harriet knew Robby was showing off for the three children of guests who were sitting with them, but she said, "Tilly has enjoyed her luncheon. When she is as grown up as you are, she will have learned to use her serviette."

"Oh," he said sheepishly, for his still lay near his place.

Their laughter broke off when Harriet said, "Now, children, I have something important to tell you." They sensed something serious and the room grew very still. She hoped her voice would not break. "When Nana and Poppy go home to London, I am going with them." The children had, since their own sojourn in the city, adopted Harriet's pet names for their shared ancient relatives.

Everyone was quiet for a moment, then Elly asked in an excited voice, "Are we going too? I want to see the efflemunt again."

"She'll never get that right," Robby said in disgust.

"No, darling," Harriet answered the little girl. "You will stay here and have lessons with Miss Clarkson just as you have been doing the last few weeks." She tried to keep her tone bright.

"But you're coming back, aren't you?" Sarah asked. "This is only for a week or two, isn't it—like before?"

"No, Sarah. I do not know how long it will be, but certainly I *will* come to visit you just as soon as I can and perhaps you will be able to persuade Uncle Quint to bring *you* to visit *me.*"

Elly jumped down from her place at the table and came to stand at Harriet's elbow. "No! I don't want you to go."

Harriet put her arm around her. "I am sorry, sweetheart, but I must go." She raised her head to smile brightly at all of them. "And I want you to write me often—each one of you—and tell all the things you are learning and doing."

Elly looked up at her with tear-filled eyes and asked plaintively, "Auntie Harry, don't you love us anymore?"

Harriet came undone. She twisted in her chair, gathered Elly onto her lap, and buried her face in the little girl's blonde curls. "Of course I do! I love you more than anything in the whole wide world!"

Maria came to Harriet's rescue. She gathered Elly into her own arms and spoke ostensibly to Elly, but Harriet knew for the benefit of all her siblings. "Come on, Elly. Do not make this so hard for Aunt Harriet. Can you not see she is as sad about leaving as we are to have her go?"

"But—" Robby started.

"No *buts,* Robby! Leave it!" Maria ordered.

And he did.

Harriet merely mouthed a "Thank you" to Maria and hastily left the room.

Right outside the door she stumbled into Quint's open arms and broke into sobs. He pressed her head against his shoulder, murmured soft words of comfort, and simply held her, caressing her back for several moments. At the time, she was scarcely aware of anything but the terrible sense of impending loss at leaving those young people she loved so dearly. Later she recalled just how Quint's arms had been an immediate safe haven for her.

Within moments, she regained control of herself and stepped back, flustered. "I—uh—thank you. Why are you here—in the nursery wing—at this hour?"

"Looking for you. When you did not appear for lunch, I had an inkling of where you were and what you were doing—"

She saw such a deal of sympathy in his gaze that she nearly burst into tears again. "Oh, Quint, I just did not think it would be so *hard,*" she said. "I have always known this day would come, but it was always *someday*—you know?"

Without quite realizing it, they had taken the back stairs from the nursery down to the door of Harriet's suite. He opened it, stepped inside with her, and embraced her again. "Do stop talking about it as though you will never see them again. This is by no means permanent."

"I know."

"God, how I've missed you!" He settled his mouth on hers.

"Mm. Me too."

"And what I would *like* to do now is march your sweet body right into that other room and—"

She pulled away and pretended shock. "Colonel Burnes! Sir! My dear old grandmother could come in here at any moment!" In a more normal voice, she added, "Besides, there's your mother's grand ball tonight."

"Oh, yes. That." He held her gaze for a long moment. "Are you truly all right now?"

She nodded. "I will be. Thank you." She stretched up to give him a quick kiss. "But I needed that."

His hand on the door handle, he smiled down at her. "That, and much, much more, my sweet."

Not wanting to dwell on the pain of that scene in the nursery, or even the sheer pleasure of Quint's comforting as an antidote, Harriet sought her usual method of escape from life's troubles: sleep. She took off her outer clothes, crawled into bed, and had a long nap.

She awoke wishing she could skip the ball, that somehow she could be whisked away—like some character in an Eastern fantasy—into some new time and place. Just get through this and be back in her old life in London and then—

And then?

"Aye, there's the rub, eh, Hamlet?" she muttered to herself.

She dressed in her newest ball gown, one she had purchased in London in the midst of her rebellion against wearing all those dreary colors of mourning and dreaming about the shades of nature. The dress itself was a deep cerulean blue silk with a wide, deep V neckline extending from the shoulders. The brooch the children gave her hung on velvet ribbon matching the gown just at the top of her cleavage. Collins had woven a matching ribbon through her hair. The gown had a sheer, gossamer-like silver overskirt. She wore silver kid slippers and long silver-colored gloves.

"Don't forget these," Collins said, holding out aquamarine earrings.

She dashed upstairs to fetch Maria and Phillip and say good night as she had promised to the others.

"Ooh! Look! Auntie Harry is wearing our pin," Elly pointed out and immediately demanded that Harriet prove she remembered which stones stood for whom. Luckily, she did.

Maria, in the customary white for a young girl not yet "out," came in for her share praise. Her gown was silk and heavily embroidered with pink rosebuds and draped with a long pink sash across one shoulder. Phillip stood tall and straight in his black evening dress, leaning on only one crutch now, it too painted black with the padding covered in black silk.

"You two are looking just too smart for words!" Harriet said.

With Nurse Tavenner carefully protective of Harriet's and Maria's finery, the good night kisses and hugs were achieved to everyone's satisfaction and the three were on their way down to collect Lord and Lady Hawthorne and Sir Charles and Elizabeth before going on to the ballroom.

Harriet, with Phillip and Maria, was several steps behind the grandparents and Charles and Elizabeth, when she heard Phillip whisper, "Ask her."

Maria touched Harriet's arm, and spoke softly, tentatively. "Aunt Harriet. Phillip and I want to know—is Grandmother—or—or Uncle Quint—forcing you to leave Sedwick?"

Harriet stopped abruptly, and so did they.

"If they are, I swear I will *never* forgive them," Phillip said, his jaw clenched.

"Nor will I," Maria said.

Harriet stood so she faced them squarely. She could not lie to them. Not now. She settled on an evasion. "You must not think that. It—it is truly quite complicated, you see, what with the change in plans for your education and for the younger ones and—well—I need to be in London to do some research there—and everything just seemed to come down at once—don't you see?"

They nodded—reluctantly, it seemed to her.

She gathered them into a group hug, wary of Phillip's crutch, and said, "Come now. Big smiles. Balls are supposed to be full of gaiety."

Maria clapped her hands in delight as they entered the ballroom, which had been transformed into a fairy-tale forest with potted trees and flowering shrubbery here and there. The dowager, in a maroon gown and headdress with tall maroon ostrich feathers, fussed at them as they arrived and immediately settled Phillip into place at the head of the receiving line, then herself, Quint, and Maria. Harriet knew Lady Margaret had wanted only herself and her dear "Quinton" in that line, but, she thought bitterly, *We do not always get what we want, do we, milady?* She took a seat on the sidelines, along with her Nana, Poppy, Charles, and Elizabeth, watching and visiting as the room filled up and the orchestra tuned their instruments. It would be some time before all the guests arrived, for besides her houseguests, the dowager had invited literally anybody who might have a claim to be somebody for miles around. Her grand ball was to be *the* social affair for—well, for this miserable year at least, as she had put it to Elizabeth. Looking out on the room as it filled up, Harriet and Elizabeth agreed that Lady Margaret had achieved her goal: a veritable squeeze.

When the dancing began, Phillip and Maria, as planned, joined Harriet, and Quint led his mother out for the first dance.

"I still wish I could dance," Maria said wistfully.

"I know, love," Harriet said. "But think what a shocker that would be. You are already the talk of the tabbies, just being here. Now go along, both of you. Mrs. Hodges is sending a special tray of goodies up to the nursery rooms just to celebrate your first ball."

"I'll wager that was *your* idea," Maria said, kissing her aunt on the cheek.

"Never mind whose idea. It is there. Save me a piece of lemon cake."

"All right."

When Harriet looked up from seeing Phillip and Maria off, Quint was no longer dancing with his mother, but with Lady Barbara. She gave Elizabeth an inquiring look.

Elizabeth grinned. "You missed it! Right in the middle of the set, Lady Margaret grabbed Lady Barbara's hand—she was standing on the edge of the dance floor—and put it on Quint's arm—said something about dancing being for young people and sat down!"

"Is Lady Margaret ill?" Harriet asked in alarm.

"Does not seem to be. She was fanning herself, but not especially vigorously."

"Hmm." Harriet had no more comment than this.

However, Elizabeth did. "If you ask me, she is a bit too obvious in pushing that match."

Harriet shrugged. "What will be will be."

"You are in a strange mood, my girl. Come on. Cheer up. This is a ball. I shall have Charles dance with you."

"No. Don't," Harriet said, then wished otherwise as she saw Sir Desmond Humphreys approach her as the orchestra was beginning the notes of the next dance. *Botheration! It was a waltz!* The man's formal evening wear was as tight-fitting as his other clothing, and he seemed to be having some difficulty navigating his way through the crowd. As he got closer and started to speak, Harriet realized he was already quite gone for drink. *Good heavens. He must have arrived here half drunk.*

"M-may I have thish dance, Miss Mayfield?" he asked, his voice surprisingly clear, but for that one little stumble.

But carrying, Harriet noted with a cringe, as she also noted that others standing nearby were Quint, his mother, Lady Barbara, and Lord Beaconfield. "I am sorry, Sir Desmond, I am not feeling well at the moment. Perhaps a country dance later?" The thought of this man's arms about her in a waltz was slightly nauseating.

"What? Think you're too good to dance wit' me? I'm not askin' you to marry me—now." He laughed the raucous laugh of a drunk delighted with his own joke, totally unaware that his audience did not share it.

Charles rose from where he had been sitting next to Elizabeth and took Humphreys by the elbow. "See here, my good man. The lady said no. A gentleman must simply accept that."

Humphreys shook free and looked at Charles bleary-eyed. "Just who are you to be saying I'm no g-genulmun?"

At that moment Quint and his mother came closer, apparently to try to defuse the situation. Their movement caught Humphreys's attention. He pointed a trembling finger accusingly at Lady Margaret.

"You," he said. "Y-your la-ship—you told me—tol' me—she'd accept my suit. But—but she didn't." He swallowed visibly and gave Harriet a hang-dog look. "Turned me down flat."

The dowager looked stricken. "I never—! Oh, good heavens! Get him out of here before he creates any more of a scene!"

Quint signaled two servants to do just that, but Humphreys was not going easily by any means. He was not a big man, but his silk clothing was slippery and held together well under stress. He slid out of their grasp, and, breathing hard, turned his attention on Quint.

"And you, Burnes. What a fool you are! Have no idea you've a cuckoo in your nest, do you?"

Harriet held her breath. She knew exactly what was coming. She glanced at her grandfather, who stepped close to put a hand on her shoulder.

Quint said, "Humphreys, you are drunk. Now, let these fellows get you some food and some coffee and a place to lie down."

By now this part of the ballroom commanded the attention of every living being in the room. Nevertheless, with a strong footman holding to either of his arms, Humphreys raised his voice even more. "You still do not know, do you, Burnes, that *she* owns those shares of Sedwick Mills—*and* all that other Sedwick debt as well?" His drunken laugh ended in a cough.

Harriet closed her eyes, but she was sure he made a dramatic picture in his black evening wear pointing his accusing finger at her. She sank her head against her grandfather's chest. The old man's arms tightened protectively about her as Quint moved closer to them.

"Is what he says true?" he asked quietly, holding her gaze steadily.

Harriet nodded, her cheek rubbing painfully against the metallic silver thread of her grandfather's waistcoat.

"I see." Quint's voice was calm, detached. He turned and walked away.

The dowager stared at Harriet in utter surprise, then followed her son. Soon the orchestra picked up the melody of a popular dance and the floor was once again full of color and the sounds of a grand ball as Harriet and her family members quietly left the ballroom.

The next morning she broke her fast with the children in the nursery and she was determinedly cheerful in telling them goodbye and admonishing them to write her faithfully. She made a point of charging Miss Clarkson and Mr. Knightly with the extra duty of seeing to it that the twins and Sarah and even Elly supplied the teachers a missive for Aunt Harriet once a week—or else.

"Or else what?" Robby demanded. "You won't be here."

"Ah, but I have my secret agents willing to help me," Harriet warned. "If I do not get my letters, Mrs. Hodges just might end up being too tired or too busy to make those ginger biscuits or lemon tarts you like so well."

"No fair," Robby wailed.

Harriet gave him a hug. "Just write to me, Robert. I want to know all about the latest adventures of Sir Gawain."

"And Muffin?" Elly asked.

"And Muffin." Harriet gave the eldest of the siblings direct looks. "Phillip, Maria, I will look forward especially to hearing from you. I know you will not let me down."

"No, ma'am," they said in unison.

Three hours later, the coaches had been loaded and she had said her goodbyes to servants with whom she had been in almost daily contact for months now, and intermittently for years before. But of the leading adults of Sedwick Hall, she had seen nothing this day. She told herself she regretted there had been no opportunity to clear the air with Quint before she left, but so be it. The man was angry. Perhaps he was hurt as well as angry. She was the last to go out to the waiting coach and as she started out the door, Chet detained her.

"Couldn't let you get away without saying goodbye," he said, offering his arm to walk her to the vehicle.

"Thank you," she said. "It is nice to know there is at least one adult in this household who does not hate me."

"Few as hates ye, lass. Quite the contrary, I'd say. Quite."

"I did not mean this to happen, Chet. Not this way."

"I know, lass. Unlike some I could name, I have read those bank documents—all of them. Eventually, this will all come out. You'll see."

"It will for Phillip—and for his earldom and what he can, in turn, do for the others. That was always the end that justified the means."

He not only held her hand as she mounted the step into the coach, but held her gaze very directly. "I'm thinking there is much more of concern here than just young Phillip and his inheritance."

"Chet—" she started to admonish.

He released her hand. "Just don't do anything rash, lass. Don't do anything rash. Give it time. It is not only the mills of the gods that grind exceeding slow."

She smiled. "Goodbye, Chet." Impulsively, she kissed him on the cheek before taking her seat next to her grandmother, who patted her hand and said, "Goodbyes are always so hard."

* * * *

From an upstairs window overlooking the stable yard, Quint had observed that farewell kiss. "Damn and blast!" he muttered to himself. Why should he care that she so freely showed simple affection to another man? He found himself—hours later—still consumed by cold fury. Why had she not told him? Good God! She had sat in that mill office, heard Stevens recite those problems in detail—and she knew all along! Was it some kind of game? Was that it? A joke?

No, that did not make sense. The sort of cold, cynical calculation it would take to enjoy such a joke was simply not in the makeup of a woman who could be so protective of children's feelings over such thing as, say, a gift to their grandmother. Or one so innocently generous in sharing her body. And she had been—both innocent and generous in the act, had she not? A virgin, for God's sake! That was it, wasn't it? She had shared her body with him. And all the while—he realized now—he had thought they were sharing something more. *Was that it?* He asked himself again, and came up with same answer and more. *That was it.* He knew for a certainty it was. There was more. He had fallen in love with Harriet Mayfield. Deeply, irrevocably, eternally in love. With Harriet. And she did not even trust him.

And beyond that, what did he have to offer a woman like Harriet Mayfield? As an ex-soldier, he had whatever his commission was worth when he sold out. That was it—and the distinction of being the Sedwick heir's guardian for a few more years. After that scene with Humphreys at the ball, a few discreet questions among other guests had been highly revealing. Apparently even his mother had been ignorant as to the extent of Harriet's wealth.

"Good heavens! Had I known—" But Lady Margaret left the rest unsaid, and Quint thought that was probably just as well.

"And what is more," one of the lady guests said enviously, "as a woman, *she* has total control of that vast fortune. What woman gets that kind of power?"

He suddenly realized that his brother's wife must have come to her marriage with at least a comfortable dowry. But not enough to keep Sedwick afloat. He needed to go over those books again—and those infernal bank documents. Chet had been at him about those. Which brought him back to thinking about Harriet again. God! How he wanted her. Yes, that luscious body, but beyond that the woman who laughed with him and at him, the woman who could kiss away a child's tears and take Parliament to task because soldiers were sleeping in the rain in Spain. He wanted her. But she was forever out of his reach now. And that was that. Life was life. Get on with it.

He watched until the small group of coaches was out of sight.

Over the next three days the remaining houseguests left Sedwick Hall to move onto another such affair in another part of the kingdom, or to return to their own estates.

All but one.

"I have asked dear Barbara to stay on for a while and she has agreed until St. Nicholas Day in early December. Is that not wonderful news?" Lady Margaret announced at breakfast the second morning after the ball.

Quint smiled and murmured an appropriate welcome to Lady Barbara, who returned his smile and said brightly how very much she had enjoyed her stay so far. Quint glanced at Chet, who had the cheek to grin at him and wink.

Phillip and Maria, along with their respective teachers, had already left the breakfast table for the library or music room when the dowager made her momentous announcement. Quint wondered idly how they would react to it. Not that it mattered, but he had not seen Barbara around the nursery set at all, though he knew her to be the mother of a five-year-old son, heir to an earl. He remembered asking her at the picnic if she missed him.

She had looked at him, surprised. "Heavens, no. I know he is well cared for. That is all that matters. I prefer children beyond the 'puling' age," she said with a laugh, "out of the schoolroom—or even university!" She had then assumed an ultra-shy demeanor. "Oh, dear. Now you will think me a terrible mother."

He had shrugged. "Not necessarily." He had drawn her attention to a peculiar cloud formation, and shortly afterward, he and Barbara had been on the fringes of that Snow White scene at his mother's picnic.

Sometime after the other guests had left, Quint lay stretched out on the wicker couch in the morning room one afternoon, actually recalling how much both he and Harriet enjoyed this room, when his mother popped in on him.

"*There* you are," she said. "No, don't get up. You look too comfortable."

"You were looking for me?"

"Earlier. Sylvia and Barbara and I went into Hendley shopping. We thought it would be nice to have you drive us." She sat down in a chair that gave her face-to-face communication with her son. Quint silently thanked whatever gods had spared him that drive.

"Quinton, dear," she began with a phrase that always put him instantly on alert. "You really should be a little more attentive to Barbara."

He twisted his head on a large green and yellow pillow to look at her more directly. "Why? She is *your* guest, is she not?"

She leaned forward in her chair. "She is *our* guest, and I invited her for *you*. Well, to be honest, for you and for her."

"Mother—" The word came out as a bit of a moan.

"It is time you married, and dear Barbara would be perfect for you. You would be perfect for each other."

"You mean she would be perfect for *you*," he said sourly. "Yes, Lady Margaret. No, Lady Margaret. I quite agree, Lady Margaret."

"Don't be mean-spirited. I admit that we get on quite well, but I should think it would be a definite plus if a prospective bride got on well with one's mother."

He yawned. "It might—if said 'one' were looking for a bride. I am not."

"Don't be obtuse, my dear. She is yours for the asking—surely you know that. Moreover, she is *very rich*. And you are not."

"You mean her late husband, the Earl of Riverton, was very rich."

"No, I mean *she* has a huge fortune."

Quint snorted. "There was certainly no sign of such ten years ago when she insisted she had to hang out for a rich husband."

His mother looked smug. "Ten years ago, that was true. But then she inherited from a bachelor uncle who doted on her and a rich husband who settled a huge amount on her when she gave birth to his son—not to mention an outrageously generous widow's portion."

"Well, good for her," Quint said disinterestedly.

"Quinton! Can you not see: if you marry Barbara, we can buy back those notes!"

"We?"

She ignored him and rushed on. "We shall be free of those horrid Mayfield connections. Things will be as they were when life was good and beautiful."

Chapter 22

The weeks following the dowager's house party, and through to the end of the year and beyond, were the most miserable of Harriet's life. When she had lost her parents, she had had Anne as a constant in her life. In losing Anne, she had drawn ever closer to Anne's children. Now, not seeing them daily, not hearing of their little or great troubles and triumphs as they occurred was—well—heartbreaking, no matter how much she chastised herself for dwelling on her misery.

Nor was it only the children who occupied her thoughts morning, noon, and night. Looming beyond, over, and always was Quint. Especially the nights—there he would be. Quint: his face—that faint growth of whisker still visible during an early morning ride, his quick teasing grin, his voice in telling Sarah he loved her, his kiss—Ah, God! his lovemaking. How was she supposed to put these out of mind—out of heart? No doubt she would—one day—see the children again. But would she ever see Quint again? Be allowed to explain why she did what she did? Daily she went through the routine of "brace the shoulders and carry on"—that is what Miss Pringle's girls were taught to do. But, dear God! It was hard.

She lived for letters from Sedwick. Miss Clarkson and Mr. Knightly kept her updated—briefly, and merely as a courtesy, for the children's guardian was their employer. Harriet was glad that both of them seemed to have settled happily into their positions, for that was what Ricky, Robby, Sarah, and Elly needed: *settled*. So did Phillip, Maria, and Tilly, but not to the same extent, perhaps. The children were good about writing their weekly letters, though Harriet sensed they had sometimes been prodded into writing—especially Robby, who occasionally mentioned his continuing to deserve his ginger biscuits and lemon tarts. Phillip and Maria were as faithful as they had promised, and it was from their letters that Harriet gleaned her real news of Sedwick.

Phillip reported that besides his regular lessons with Mr. Knightly (whom he liked very much, by the way), he was continuing to enjoy studying piano with the vicar's wife once a week. Harriet wrote back to encourage him in that endeavor, for both she and Emma Powers thought Phillip quite talented. Harriet thought his music also provided the young man a sorely needed emotional outlet. She was best pleased, though, by Phillip's report that his Uncle Quint had insisted the young earl be present for a twice-monthly meeting with Mr. Stevens and floor leaders at the mills. Phillip reported that he himself had little to say in these meetings, but he was learning a good deal. She could tell he was thrilled to be included, to be treated like an adult. She had thought of writing Quint a note to thank him for including the boy, then thought better of that. He might think her presumptuous, or condescending, or...

From Maria she received newsy bits over all those weeks that were amusing or insightful, often making Harriet homesick—for that was what Sedwick had become: home. It was Maria who told her Lady Barbara had left Sedwick sooner than she intended and in something of a pet—and why.

According to Hodgie—I overheard her talking with Mrs. Ames—and you must never tell them I eavesdropped!! Anyway, Aunt Harriet, you will find this hard to believe, but apparently Lady B thought Grandmother was going to persuade Uncle Q to marry her! Mrs. A said there had been "something there years ago, but the colonel wasn't no green boy any more" and it did not work....So, Lady B left, and Gran was that angry with Uncle Q. They are still not talking much. I thought she might move back to the dower house, but I think she liked Mama's rooms too well—and running things here—or trying to! Uncle Q says she is to make no more changes—and to undo some she has made—including moving out of Mama's rooms! So—Guess what? She moved into yours! He was angry about that, but he let it go....Uncle Q. spends most of his time sequestered (are you impressed with that word?) in the library. Or, weather permitting, riding the very devil out of Papa's devil horse. Especially now that Mr. Gibbons is gone—at least for a while. I did tell you, did I not, about his sister coming down here from the Highlands to "drag him back to see his family" she said. She was a fierce one—I wish you had met her! He promised to come back soon....We missed you sooo much at Christmas! We had the Yule log and carols and wassail and the smells of spices and greenery—even a kissing ball! But it just was not the same without you—and Mama and Papa, of course. Maybe next year—

Harriet refolded the letters and tucked them away. "Maybe. Maybe next year, Maria." But she hadn't much faith in that. Before restoring the box of letters to its place in a bureau drawer, she withdrew Maria's last letter, which carried a troubling postscript:

P.S. The two youngest of the Powers brood have contracted chicken pox! Do you suppose its progress to the Hall is inevitable? Sigh. (But do note that big word, oh favorite aunt of mine: If nothing else, writing you is improving my vocabulary!)

Harriet had not found it difficult in London to fill her days with activities and people she enjoyed. She rode Miss Priss in the park nearly every morning, sometimes with her friend Lord Beaconfield, more often with just a groom, though occasionally her longtime school friend Lady Henrietta Parker—Retta—joined her. She chose always to ride early, before the nursemaids arrived in the park with their little charges. She made and received social calls, often accompanied by her grandmother or Elizabeth. She renewed her association with Retta's favorite charity, which helped abused women and children. And she picked up where she had left off with the literary group, all of whom told her how much they had missed her.

Gavin, Lord Beaconfield, had called for her and accompanied her to that first meeting. As they settled into his coach on leaving, he said, "They were all sincere, you know, Harriet. They have missed you."

"I know, and I am appreciative," she said.

"I know you miss the country life," he said with a smile, "but surely the last few weeks have reassured you that London still has much to offer."

"Yes, Dr. Johnson, 'He who is tired of London—'"

"'—is tired of life,'" he finished with a chuckle. "But Johnson aside, I doubt you are tired of life."

"Gavin, what are you trying to say?"

"Two things, actually. First, you have not written anything since your return. Why?"

"I cannot give a reason other than it all seems so pointless, does it not? You walk in those oh-so-sacred halls of power. What do you see being accomplished—really?"

"I will admit it is slow, but even the gods grind slowly, you know."

Feeling herself go very still at those words, she said after an instant of pause, "You are not the first to tell me that in recent months. What was your second thing?"

He shifted on the seat to face her—they were sharing the forward-facing bench of the coach—and he wore a serious expression. "The second thing is in the nature of a confession."

"A confession?" She stared at him.

He held up a hand. "Hear me out. I went to that house party at Sedwick because my mother nagged me into looking out for my sister. She has also been after me—for years—that it is time I married. I finally agree with her. I went there primarily to propose to you."

"Oh, Gavin." She lowered her gaze. "But you did not."

"No," he said bluntly. "I saw that there was something in the air between you and Burnes, so I backed off."

She was quiet, searching for a response.

He went on. "I am not the only one who noticed, by the way. Lady Pearson mentioned it to me." He paused for a long moment, and still her thoughts were so tangled she could not speak. "So, now that you are back here, back in the old groove, so to speak," he continued, "the question is—"

"No, Gavin, do not. Please. I beg you," she said hastily.

He laughed softly. "No, my dear. I was not going to pop *that* question— not for a while at least. I was about to ask just how much of the real Harriet is London getting these days? You often seem to be decidedly distracted."

"You, sir, know me too well." Incongruously, she recalled Miss Pringle's "brace the shoulders" line; so she did. "I suppose I have been, but I am glad you did not ask me *that* question, my friend. For that *is* what you are to me: a most valued friend."

"As you wish." He moved closer to put his arm about her shoulders and gave her a very friendly hug.

As they parted, he promised to meet her in the park in the morning.

* * * *

"You shouldna' ha' let her go. You should ha' gone after her."

Chet's words the morning Harriet left and repeated only once—when Chet himself left—had rung like faraway cathedral bells in the caverns of Quint's mind for weeks. At night they rang louder and more persistently. Chet had first uttered those words as he encountered Quint just entering the library after seeing Harriet leave.

"You do not understand, Chet. It is more complicated than that."

"Only to you stiff-necked English," Chet said. "That girl loves you—I'm sure of it. And I am damned sure you love her."

"Leave it, Chet."

"As you will, Colonel, sir."

Quint had just sat down at his desk, still unsettled by that conversation, when his mother bustled into the room.

"Thank goodness, *that* lot are on their way. May we be spared their company in the future."

He looked up and raised an eyebrow. "You are overlooking the rather significant fact that they are blood relatives of Sedwick's Seventh Earl, are you not?"

She heaved an exaggerated sigh and sat down heavily in one of the wing chairs. "That scene last night at my ball was beyond enough! I intend to make that Mayfield chit pay dearly for embarrassing me so. By the time I am through, the whole *ton* is going to know how she is trying to cheat her own nephew out of valuable property. Taking advantage of an innocent child! How could she? She will not be received in any reputable house in all of London!"

Quint sat still for only an instant. Then he dug into an inside pocket of the coat he was wearing, retrieved a small key, and unlocked a desk drawer. He took out a small bundle of mismatched pieces of paper and a ledger book. He walked over to stand towering over his mother.

"You will do no such thing, Mother. And you had damned well better see to it that none of your minions take on such a nefarious task, either." He might have been dressing down one of his subalterns on the Peninsula.

She looked up at him, her face white with rage, but something in his demeanor tempered the rage with apprehension, if not downright fear. "Do not swear at me," she said weakly. "I am your mother. 'Nefarious.' Indeed."

"How about 'malicious,' then? Or one of your favorites: 'bad *ton*'?" He refused to tone down his sarcasm, but his voice became cold and iron-hard as he went on. "If I hear even the faintest whisper of what you have just outlined—from you or anyone else—the tabloids will have a holiday with this information."

He tossed the small bundle of papers in her lap. He could tell by the way her face went even whiter as she fingered through them that she recognized gambling vouchers she herself had written at London gaming tables. He opened the ledger to a given page and pushed it under her nose.

"You will, of course, recognize the handwriting on many of these entries. Interesting that so many of the vouchers and entries here seem to have materialized *after* Win's death and *before* I returned to England. *Now* tell me who was taking advantage of a situation." He snapped the book shut, snatched the papers from her hand, and sat in the opposite chair.

"You do not understand, Quinton, darling." She was begging. "I was trying to mend matters."

"And when you got in even deeper, how did you hope to escape?"

"Sir Desmond offered to help if—"

He felt a cold chill of disgust slither through him. "Oh, good God. A London procuress has more honor."

She started to rise.

"Sit down," he ordered. "I meant what I said. If there is the faintest whisper of scandal pertaining to Harriet, I will release the truth to the tabloids."

"You cannot hold me responsible for what others might say." Her self-righteous tone indicated she had regained some of her bravado.

He stared at her until she looked down at her hands. "You pride yourself on being such a social queen of the *ton*. Here is your chance to prove just how influential you might, in truth, be. Surely, you have enough presence in your set to squash patently silly rumors before they take hold."

"You have no sense of family loyalty," she said petulantly.

"Perhaps. But somehow, I did manage to acquire the basic concept of the meaning of honor, Mother." He stood and held up the bundle of vouchers. "These were neither mine nor my brother's." He locked them and the ledger back in the desk.

"You might begin, Mother, to control some of the damage that has been done as the rest of your guests leave," he said and walked out of the room.

The following morning she had made her announcement of Lady Barbara's extended stay, and Quint conjectured that she had devised yet another scheme, but he felt sure he had shielded Harriet from one of them at least. The Dowager Countess of Sedwick feared scandal involving herself every bit as much as she relished spreading it at the expense of others. Far more, in fact.

* * * *

"Harriet! You will never believe whom I encountered at the Betworths' just now!" Elizabeth was so anxious to tell her news, she seemed positively flustered as she entered the Hawthorne drawing room. Harriet and her "Nana" had been receiving morning callers, but the last ones had departed just before Elizabeth arrived. Only that morning Harriet had received in the mail Maria's letter with the worrisome postscript about chicken pox in Sedwick village.

"No, I suppose I won't unless you tell me, Elizabeth."

"Lady Margaret!"

"She is here—in London?" Harriet asked.

"For the moment. But only just. She did not even open Sedwick House. She is staying with the Goughs—you may remember Colonel Gough was on Wellington's staff in Spain." Harriet and her grandmother exchanged amused glances, for the usually restrained Elizabeth was talking so fast her words were nearly tumbling over each other.

"Mrs. Gough is Lady Margaret's cousin," the older lady informed them.

"Yes. Well," Elizabeth rushed on, "it seems the colonel is to join Wellington again in Vienna and his wife invited Lady Margaret to go with them 'so she will have some company.' They are leaving immediately for the continent!"

"Lady Margaret will be in her element in Vienna, what with half London's elite already there," Nana observed mildly.

"So she is not at Sedwick Hall," Harriet mused aloud.

"Are you thinking of visiting there?" her grandmother asked. "It has been some time, my dear. I am sure that unpleasantness will have blown over by now."

"N-no. Not really," Harriet said slowly, but she refused to share what she *was* thinking: *Quint will be in that great house with sick children on his hands.* Immediately, she braced her shoulders. *Do try not to be such a ninny—the Hall employs a staff of over fifty!*

A few troubling hours later, telling herself she had not yet made a decision, she nevertheless set Collins to packing and sent a servant to inquire about post chaise transportation to the north. Meanwhile, she would await further word from Sedwick, grabbing up the mail eagerly each morning. So far there had been no word that any of *her* lot were ill—but, after all, it usually took at least a week for that childhood disease to manifest itself. What to do? If she just appeared at the Hall, would she be allowed to stay?

Five days later, fully packed, but still hesitating, she sat at the piano in the drawing room idly playing whatever tune came to mind. She was interrupted by the Hawthorne butler.

"Miss Harriet, there is a gentleman to see you."

"Who is it, Thompkins?" she asked, expecting to be handed a visiting card.

Thompkins cleared his throat. "Said he'd rather present himself. Shall I send him away with a flea in his ear?"

"A gentleman?"

"Dressed like one."

Thinking the visitor might be someone with information about workers' "corresponding societies"—clubs being formed surreptitiously to fight for workers' rights about which Harriet was interested in writing—she said, "Show him in, but Thompkins, stay close by."

"Yes, ma'am."

She stood near the piano, waiting, and a few minutes later, the door opened and Quint walked in.

She gasped.

Then she quickly collected herself, curtsied slightly, and said calmly, "Colonel Burnes. This is a surprise."

What an inadequate word, she thought, as she drank in the sight of him, absolutely unable to tear her eyes away from him. He was dressed fashionably in a dark green coat, a dove-colored waistcoat, dark trousers, and Hessian boots. His neckcloth was tied simply. The green of the coat reflected the almost green of his hazel eyes, which gazed at her steadfastly.

"I was afraid you would refuse me if gave him my name," he said, nodding toward the door.

"I would never do that," she said stiffly, visualizing what it would be like to have him hold her again—and quickly hating herself for the vision. She raised her voice slightly. "It is all right, Thompkins." The door clicked shut.

"Why are you here?" she asked, unable to hide her anxiety. "Are the children all right?"

He smiled faintly. "Yes—and no. Our young people are mostly all right. When I left the Hall, only Elinor, Matilda, and Robert had so far succumbed to a bout of chicken pox that is running rampant in the village. But Sarah and Richard were not feeling at all well."

"Oh, dear. Maria wrote me about the Powers children."

"It started with their family," he said, no longer looking at her directly.

"I'm sorry," she said. "Won't you sit down?" She gestured to a grouping of an overstuffed couch and two chairs. He waited for her to take one of the chairs, then took the other one.

"Half the village children are sick with it—and many adults as well," he said.

"And the Hall?" she asked.

"As I say, when I left, only three of the children, but that was three days ago. They could *all* have it by now." He sounded truly worried. "Moreover, because so many of our servants are relatively young, half of *them* are already down with it. Those of us who had it as children ourselves are pressed to keep tending them."

"Oh, my goodness," she murmured sympathetically.

He twisted in his chair to face her directly, his expression anguished. "Harriet, I am here on a mission of sorts. I have come to ask you— please—to come back to Sedwick Hall with me. Those lovable brats Win and Anne left us have driven me crazy since you've gone. Not a day goes by but one or two or more of them ask me, 'When is Aunt Harriet coming back?' Elly breaks my heart crying for 'Auntie Harry' as we try to get her to stop scratching her poxes. They need you to come back, if only to prove that you will."

"Of course I will go back with you," she said. "In fact, I am already packed. We can leave tomorrow morning, if you wish."

"You will? You are? We can?" He was clearly dumbfounded.

She explained about Maria's letter and her premonition of just those events that had transpired. "I-I just was not sure of my reception if I showed up unannounced," she ended lamely.

"Oh, my God. Harriet." He stood, pulled her to her feet, and buried his face against her neck. She drank in the scent of him. His voice was muffled against her skin. "It is not only the children. I am here for me too. I have missed you every hour of every day since you left."

She did not answer him; she merely moved her face for a better angle to kiss him. Their arms tightened around each other and it was long, deep, utterly satisfying kiss of homecoming.

He raised his head to say, "I do love you, you know."

"I do now," she said with a laugh. "And I love you too. So now what? Seems to me we've already taken the next step."

"Now we marry and live happily ever after—is that not what Snow White and her prince did?"

"Such things occur much easier in fairy tales, I think. In fact, as I consider it, my returning to the Hall with you is fraught with difficulties." She nudged him toward the couch where they sat very close, arms entwined.

"My mother is off to the Continent," he said.

"I know, but *ton* gossips are still right here in England too. I cannot bring down a sordid scandal for Phillip and Maria and the others to live with. You must go back to them. I shall come when my grandparents or Charles and Elizabeth can join me."

"No. We shall leave tomorrow as you suggested." He withdrew from an inner pocket of his coat a piece of paper and handed it to her. "I stopped at Doctors Commons before coming here."

"A special license? My heavens! You were sure of me, were you not?"

"No, my love," he said, nuzzling her neck. "Just very, very hopeful— and trying desperately to anticipate any difficulties in the way of what I wanted—and what I want most is you. Forever."

"Did no one ever teach you to be careful what you wish for, my dearest?" she asked between a series of kisses and caresses that were growing more and more heated.

"May I ask just what is going on here?"

The voice of her grandmother from the open doorway abruptly interrupted. However, Harriet detected laughter beneath the show of shock. Quint jumped up. "I can explain, Lady Hawthorne. Truly I can."

"I should hope so, young man," the old lady said, continuing her pretense of shock. "Would you not agree, dear?" She stepped aside to allow her husband entrance.

"Must I call him out, my dear?" the old man asked his wife very seriously.

"I wanted only this," Quint said, embarrassed.

Harriet was embarrassed too, but she could not help laughing. "Nana. Poppy. Do stop. Quint and I are going to be married."

"After that display, I should hope so," her grandfather said.

"About time," her grandmother said. "Took you long enough to come to your senses."

They were married the next morning in that same drawing room. Three days and two blissful nights later, they arrived at Sedwick Hall and began to deal with the happily short-lived chaos of a great manor house turned into a temporary hospital.

Epilogue

"Did I not tell ye, lass, it would come out all right?"

Chet Gibbons had finally managed to return to Sedwick Hall as he had promised nearly a year after his sister dragged him off to the Highlands to make amends with his family. He had stopped by earlier in the year, but only briefly, as he was on his way then to join Wellington's forces gathering in Belgium to deal finally with one Napoleon Bonaparte. That task accomplished, Chet was back again. He and Harriet were riding together on a beautiful autumn morning as Quint rode ahead, forcing his stallion to keep to the pace of ponies ridden by the twins and Sarah.

"That you did," she said, "but, believe me, it was not easy."

"He's a proud man," Chet said. "Has all these English ideas about money and all."

"That was not much of an issue with us. Although English law gives a husband control of all a wife's money and property, Quint would have readily allowed me control of mine. In fact, he told me he wanted nothing to do with it."

"Would have? But did not?"

She smiled. "We worked it out. I continue to harangue the government about its abuse of children working in mines and the sordid conditions in workhouses while he uses my fortune to rescue Sedwick—which he is well on the way to doing. He loves all that numbers stuff and nonsense. I hate it. Eventually, Sedwick will be profitable enough to pay us back."

"So—young Phillip comes out all right in the end."

"And so will we."

"And you got Lady Margaret to return to the dower house. Good girl! That must have taken some doing."

Harriet laughed heartily. "I did not touch that one! Quint moved her back while she was in Vienna, then wrote to tell her what he had done—oh, and, incidentally, that he and I were married. What I would not have given to have been a fly on the wall when she read that letter!"

"So many changes here in just a few months' time," Chet said. "Phillip told me—before he and Maria left for school—what a time he had persuading you and Quint to take over the chambers of the earl and countess."

"Both Quint and I felt that would be presumptuous, but Phillip just insisted—said as long as we were doing the jobs, why not? He all but threw a tantrum over it! Said he would take over later when he comes home with a countess and needs that much room."

"Then what—for you and Quint?"

"By then, the dower house—maybe? That is a joke. Who knows? It will not be a problem—there is all that property my father left me."

"Both Phillip and Maria seemed happier this year about going off to school than before."

"They were ready. And their first letters are positive."

"Their absence is leaving empty space in the nursery wing, is it not?"

Harriet laughed and touched her waist. "Not for long. Quint and I are working on the first replacement, though we have not made that public yet."

"Ah, well—congratulations to both of you." Chet laughed with her.

"Now stop grilling me about the Hall and its inhabitants, Chet Gibbons, and tell me: are you going to take Quint's offer? Will you be taking over as Sedwick's steward when Mr. Stevens retires in a month or so?"

"Yes, I think I will. The colonel and I work well together."

"Hmm. Then Emma Powers and I must see what we can do about finding you a wife...."

Printed in the United States
by Baker & Taylor Publisher Services